Beaufighter Blitz

Also By Russell Sullman

To So Few

BEAUFIGHTER BLITZ

RUSSELL SULLMAN

LUME BOOKS

LUME BOOKS

Published in 2022 by Lume Books

ISBN 978-1-83901-494-9

Typeset using Atomik ePublisher from Easypress Technologies

www.lumebooks.co.uk

For two exceptional British women:

'The Missus' – Zakia; wife, mother, best friend, muse and award-wining clinician

'Madeleine'- Assistant Section Officer Princess Noor-un-Nisa Inayat Khan, GC, MBE, MiD, CdeG

Prologue

Set deep within the murky cloak of night, lying heavy and sullen before the aircraft's rushing pace, *Leutnant* Bruno von Ritter's anxiously probing eyes, tingling and tender and aching with strain, at long last saw the shadowed enemy coastline of Britain materialise faintly before them, gradually gaining in substance.

Wraith-like, the darker irregular strip of land merged with the gloom began to take on a more discernible shape and form before them with each passing second, as he and his crew drew ever closer to it in their destructively potent low flying Ju88C night fighter.

Despite the sudden urgent compulsion he felt prickling in his muscles to pull back hard on the control column and take the heavy fighter up higher, where it was safer from the obstacles that remained hidden by the darkness until it was far too late, Bruno held the aeroplane steadily on course, resisting the brisk and lively ground effect caused by keeping them at such a low altitude, low enough (hopefully) that the detection systems of their adversary would not see them, yet uncomfortably aware of the icy nearness of the churning and ravenous flecked black waves below.

"There...," words barely whispered, his voice was hushed, as if the unseen foe might yet hear him were he to speak out aloud, staring eyes still trying to penetrate the dismal murk.

Bruno blinked his eyes rapidly to moisten and soothe them, but they continued to sting him painfully.

Damn the British.

Why didn't the stupid, obstinate idiots just surrender? They had no chance, isolated and alone as they were now that the *Reich* owned most of Europe. The continent belonged to Germany, won with blood and courage, and the British were like scrawny rats helplessly trapped in a corner, doomed and without hope.

They *must* know it. The only realistic hope for them was to sue for peace. Why continue such a hopeless fight? It made no sense whatsoever.

They must be mad.

Idiots.

The coast was a lot closer now, looming large, and a spike of fear pierced sharp through his chest.

If there were enemy flak batteries sited where that drunken fool from *Luftwaffe* intelligence said they weren't, it could be all over for them very, very soon.

Bruno rolled a sticky tongue around his mouth, desperate to moisten his lips, swallowed and then coughed in an attempt to clear his knotted throat, and spoke out, the quiet words harsh with tension and effort, far harsher than he would have liked.

"Enemy coast ahead."

As ever before combat, waves of terror and excitement ebbed and flowed hot and cold through him in equal measure.

"Where are we, Rudi?" He asked, one gloved hand needlessly adjusted the flying goggles already placed comfortably in position.

His *Bordmechaniker/Beobachter* (the crew flight mechanic), an aircrew NCO whose role was the aircraft's observer and ammunition loader, *Feldwebel* Rudolf (Rudi) Weiss, replied in a voice that was as quiet as his own had been moments earlier.

"On course, *Herr Leutnant*. You can see the coastline of Norfolk dead ahead, port and town of Cromer ten kilometres to port."

Bruno scratched his neck nervously and licked his painfully dry lips once more. "ETA to target?"

"Ten minutes, sir. On schedule." Over the intercom Bruno fancied he heard the faintest of tremors in Rudi's voice.

The latent tension was heavy within the glass house of the Junker's cockpit, draped uncomfortably over the three of them.

He cleared his throat yet again, eyes fixed on the landscape looming ahead and zipping past in a dim blur. "Good, Thank you Rudi. Mouse?"

The crew's *Bordfunker/Bordschutz*, acting as the crew radio operator and rear gunner, *Feldwebel* Gustav ('Mouse') Maustein, was seated facing the other way, his eyes keenly searching the black night sky behind and around the racing Junkers, and now he shook his head slowly, "Nothing behind, *Herr Leutnant*, all clear."

Bruno pulled back gently on the control column, and the Ju88C began to climb upwards.

The powerful vibration coursed vigorously from the control column up through his arms, and to Bruno the fighter seemed to strain eagerly at the leash, as if she could smell her prey, the two powerful Junkers Jumo 211J engines throbbing forcefully on either side of the glasshouse canopy beneath which they sat, the massed 2,802 horsepower generated driving them swiftly and powerfully onwards into the dangerous heartland of their enemy.

The Ju88 cleared the cliff edge easily, eagerly bounding upwards smoothly, like the thoroughbred she was, the increased ground effect

3

of land pushing them upwards, smoothly corrected by his pilot, and Rudi quietly breathed a surreptitious sigh of relief as Bruno settled the fighter back into level flight.

The *Herr Leutnant* was awfully fond of low flying; Rudi thought sourly, far lower than either of the fighter's crewmen liked or were comfortable with.

There were always too many hidden things that they could collide with scattered all around when flying this low at night time. It was terrifying how quickly objects emerged from the night, leaving little time for reaction.

It would be an awful waste to come all this way and then wrap themselves around some unseen electricity cables or a factory chimney stack seen too late.

Rudi lifted his flying goggles, and unobtrusively wiped the greasy sheen of cold sweat from his face with his flying scarf, looking nervously out through the Perspex.

Bruno noticed his observer's reaction, and smiled to himself.

Best to keep the boys focused on the task in hand. Wouldn't do for them to fall asleep on the job, so to speak.

He checked the switches on the console once again, and ensured his pilot-operated forward firing weapons were ready to use, safeties off, the engines safely within acceptable limits, droning contentedly.

There could be no test bursts of the guns, though, for the thunder and flash from their firing guns might give them away to the random roving eyes of their enemy, whilst the sound might betray them to the enemy's sophisticated listening devices.

The drone of the engines ought not to be that easy to pinpoint by the British from the ground.

But, with a bit of luck, over enemy territory tonight, he'd get the

4

chance to fire the potent Three 7.92mm and the 20mm MG FF cannon housed in the nose in front of his aircraft very soon.

The thought of it made his blood rush with excitement, his muscles tingling at the thought of unleashing the deadly firepower.

Those arrogant bloody day fighter hotshots may well scoff, but he'd not exchange places with any of them, not even for the controls of a nippy little Bf109E.

Let them tough it out in the bright, dangerous skies with the damnable Spitfires and Hurricanes.

More fool them.

Bruno had duelled with RAF Hurricanes once before, during the *Blitzkrieg* in a Me110 over the fields of France.

Those few intensely strained moments had been the most gut-wrenching experience of his entire life (worse even than being chased by Ilse's father, immediately after that outraged worthy discovered Bruno with his daughter *in flagrante* in his old barn).

He smiled fondly at the lovely memory of the smiling, flushed girl, tanned legs spread wide and reclining comfortably on their cosy bed of straw, and then of his naked, terror-filled flight through the dark fields afterwards, the sporadic shouts and booming of the shotgun in the darkness far behind hastening him on his way.

But the single-seater RAF day fighters of which he was so terrified were as good as blind in the dark, completely unsuited for night fighting, incapable of tracking raiders through cloaked skies, and so Goering's airmen were now conducting a full-scale night bombing campaign.

No more tiered ranks and layers of heavily-laden bombers shimmering and glinting in the blinding daylight for swarming squadrons of RAF fighters to intercept and harass and destroy mercilessly.

No more smoke-filled daylight skies and the falling, burning, shattered remnants of friend and foe alike.

Not after the pointless slaughter of the previous year, the lines of close friends, their half-remembered faces now mere faded recollections.

Rather than with a series of devastating punches by waves of massed bombers, now the *Luftwaffe* would attack in an unrelenting and constant succession of deadly throughout the night, every night.

The few enemy defences that there were would be swamped and the British helpless, rapidly succumbing beneath the massive onslaught of the mighty *Luftwaffe*.

Soon, the enemy would sue for peace, and the war would be over.

Deutschland Uber Alles. Für immer.

Forever. What a glorious and heady thought!

And he would play his part in making it so. The thought thrilled him and he smiled to himself at the prospect of what lay ahead.

Glorious years of peace and prosperity lay ahead for the *Reich*.

Europe would know a golden time of greatness as a part of the Greater Germany under *Der Fuhrer*.

Those who once sneered, who had punished a weakened Germany after the end of the last war, would know what it was to be amongst those fallen from grace.

But not, hopefully, before he had earned for himself his *Ritterkreuz*, the highly desired Knight's Cross of the Iron Cross which Bruno craved so very much.

The *Herr Oberst* had received his Knight's Cross after twelve aerial victories, and Bruno was not that far behind, for he himself had already accounted for eight enemy aircraft (and save for a Belgian Hurricane, all of his kills had been RAF bombers).

With just a little luck, and a few more kills, the Knight's Cross would be as good as his!

6

Bruno was already well respected for his combat record in *Nachtjagdgeschwader 2* at their *Gilze en Rijen* airbase in the Netherlands, and for his earlier *Blitzkreig* experiences in the Low Countries campaign as a Me110 *Zerstorer* pilot.

Those earlier experiences had already earned for him the Iron Cross, his uniform proudly bearing both First and Second classes of the medal, but now he desperately craved the Knight's Cross around his neck as well, for that would place him above the others, a man apart, one amongst a very select few, a seasoned champion not only of the air but of the very *Reich* itself.

It would make him a man to be reckoned with, a heroic Teuton, recognised by all, and one to be trusted with authority and great responsibility.

Bruno fancied with pleasure that he could already feel the weight of it sitting at his throat as he continued to scan the enveloping darkness before them, and imagined the effect it would have on those around him, admiration in the eyes of women and envy in those of the men.

With the Knight's Cross hanging from around his neck, he could demand whatever he desired, for he would be a hero amongst heroes, one of the pioneers of a glorious Thousand Year Empire.

"*Herr Leutnant?*" it was his rear gunner, Maustein.

Immediately he was alert, heart banging like a gong within his suddenly tightening chest, the delightful secret fantasies of true golden glory, serried accolades and hordes of adoring women banished, at least for the moment.

"Yes? What is it, Mouse?"

The gunner's deep voice was tentative. "*Herr Leutnant*, I thought I saw something…high and to starboard, on a parallel course, just for a moment."

Involuntarily, Bruno stole a glance upwards. "What was it?"

"I'm not sure, sir, it *was* there, but I can't see it now…"

Bruno twisted his head.

"How high was it, Mouse? What did you see? Was it one of their fighters? Rudi? Can you see anything?"

"About a thousand meters, I'd guess, sir…um, wait…"

Bruno concentrated on maintaining his course, holding the big fighter on a steady heading, anxious eyes straining forward, resisting the temptation to search the skies above and to starboard himself.

Rudi shook his head, face pressed against the side of the canopy, as if it might make it clearer. "Can't see a fucking thing, sir, and it's blacker out there than Mouse's hairy arsehole."

The good *Feldwebel* had such a colourful turn of phrase…

Mouse exclaimed suddenly, triumphant, "Yes, there! I see it! Herr Leutnant, I can see it quite clearly now, twin-engine type, a medium or light bomber I'd say, Blenheim, but I'm not certain. Definitely RAF, I'm sure of it."

Bruno's heart leapt in excitement and anticipation, "Tell me. Heading?"

"Similar heading, flying parallel to us, about two hundred sixty, sir."

"I can see it now, sir," added Rudi, with hushed excitement, but then he added, "But what about the target?" His eyes were large in the darkness, "Shouldn't we continue on to Oulton?"

"Forget the target, Rudi, Oulton can wait. Let's get this one." He thought for a moment, "Besides, if he's a Blenheim fighter I don't want him above and behind me in the darkness. He's our target now. Rudi, direct me."

"Yes, *Herr Leutnant.*"

Over the next minute or two, his crew guided Bruno carefully into an optimal position behind and below the enemy bomber.

Despite the darkness, Mouse's keen eyes had correctly identified the mysterious aircraft.

It was indeed a Bristol Blenheim, a British light bomber that was a great deal slower and somewhat less manoeuvrable than Bruno's own Ju88C.

More importantly, it had a rear facing gun turret, and so Bruno crept carefully into position behind and below the bomber, into the turret's blind spot.

In the far reaching darkness, he hoped not to be visible to anyone who might be lying down in the observation blister beneath the Blenheim's nose.

No time to waste, then, for they might be discovered at any moment by roving enemy night fighters, or noticed by their prey. Let the others look out for him, his duty and concentration lay ahead.

Quickly lining up the British bomber in his *Revi* reflector gun sight, Bruno took one last look at the Blenheim, complete and untouched, carrying a crew relieved to be above their homeland once more after an operation deep inside occupied Europe, perhaps already planning their next day's activities, an afternoon picnic, or a trip to the cinema in the evening with a loved one?

"*Achtung,* firing guns."

He pressed the push button switch for a long three second burst, and his guns roared their song of hatred, buffeting the Junker's airframe with their recoil, roughly raking the Blenheim mercilessly in a destructive arc of battering death.

As cannon shells tore into the fuel tanks, an intense sheet of flame slashed back from the devastated bomber, searing light slicing through the darkness.

Bruno felt the airframe begin to vibrate and bounce uncomfortably

9

in the troubled air of the enemy's slipstream, and he eased the power down, opening the distance between them.

A piece of the enemy bomber's port wing broke off, whirling away pitifully as if to escape the destruction, followed by a burning cinder trail of smaller fragments.

Night vision impaired by the sudden brightness, Bruno watched the enemy plane's nose drop as the Blenheim began its final dive.

His crew kept a careful watch, but their night vision had been impaired by the flaring explosion of light.

The Blenheim was breaking apart as it fell, a streamer of flame dripping fragments, and there were no parachutes, his gunfire had caught them all, instantly killing the three men aboard with that unforgiving burst, on the final part of their journey home.

With a sudden flash, the flaming lump of molten metal that the Blenheim had become splashed brutally across the night shrouded countryside, scattering burning fragments over a wide area, the torn pieces landing so very close to where the bomber had set out earlier that night.

"Victory, *Herr Leutnant*! Superb shooting! That fucking *schwein* will never bomb us again! *Congratulations!*" Rudi crowed gleefully over the intercom. "He never even knew we were behind him, the dozy bastard!"

"Well done, sir." Mouse rumbled, subdued, alert eyes never leaving the huge expanse of sky behind and around their fighter.

Have to maintain one's image as a stern Teutonic warrior, thought Bruno, even as a wave of relief sluiced through him, speak calmly; don't let them see your pleasure, or the strain.

"Thank you, boys. We did it. That's one more for us, one less of theirs."

"Nine victories! *Nine!* Sounds good, *Herr Leutnant*. Really good." Rudi cackled, "Almost into double figures, sir! Well done! Continue on for RAF Oulton? Want to make it two for tonight? Get number ten?"

Bruno considered. The defences would be aware they were here now, and the element of surprise had been lost.

Their target airfield would be blacked out now, alerted to their presence, its returning aircraft urgently redirected to airfields outside the danger area.

There might even now be enemy fighters heading their way.

It was unlikely they would get any more luck tonight at Oulton. To risk themselves might be madness, courting disaster on the heels of their victory.

But might the enemy actually expect him to flee for safety after this triumph?

And if so, should they continue on to their target?

Or might the target think this attack was one of a series, and be even now be on a heightened awareness for attack?

So.

What now? An important decision had to be made.

And quickly, if not sooner!

To continue, or to return? Was the risk worth it? Which was it to be? He drummed his fingers on the control column's handlebar absently as he considered the decision.

In the far distance, flaring pinpricks of light danced and sparkled prettily, reflected dimly by the brooding clouds above them, marking the death and destruction of the enemy.

The bomber boys were out in force, still hitting the British hard, showing the fools that they were beaten.

He made up his mind. "We've been lucky, no reason to test our luck tonight, boys." He looked at his gauges, "We've still got enough fuel for a short patrol south west of the Frisian Islands. If we're lucky, we might pick up one of their mine-laying bombers."

"But I hate water, *Herr Leutnant*, whales and U-boats drop shit in it." the gunner protested.

Good, stolid Mouse.

"Mouse, why didn't you join the army? The Luftwaffe doesn't just fly over land."

The gunner continued to single-mindedly scrutinise the night sky with distrustful eyes.

"Both of my cousins are married to soldiers, sir." He sucked on a tooth, "Can't stand either of them."

Rudi's interest was piqued. Mouse rarely spoke of home. "You can't stand them? Why? Because they're soldiers?"

"No you thick bastard. I can't stand my cousins. Their husbands are OK."

The gunner thought for a moment, and then added, "For soldiers, that is."

Bruno grinned tightly, but his restless eyes were still busily searching the darkness for a hidden enemy, and his fingers and nerves still quivered from the adrenaline.

"I could have a quiet word with the *Herr Oberst*, my dear Mouse. Get you a nice comfy posting at headquarters perhaps, a nice big desk, a comfortable chair for your bum to shine, and all those pretty little auxiliaries to look after? Think it's something you could manage, old fellow?"

"With your permission I'll stay, *Herr Leutnant*. I'm better with a gun than a pencil. And where would you be without me protecting your arse? Rudi's as useless as a beer mug with a hole in its base."

Rudi grunted, "Fuck off, thick man."

Bruno nodded. "Good. Then it's settled, you can stay. I feel safer having you there behind me, anyway."

Rudi was rummaging around busily in his flying satchel. "Fuck

12

me," he muttered, "You speak such crap, Mouse. I can't tell where your mouth ends and your arsehole begins, with all that shit flowing out of you. Damn dumb gunner. Shut your trap."

The words were said without rancour, just move and countermove in an endless game of banter.

Rudi found what he was looking for and he pulled it from the satchel. "All this fighting has given me a bit of a thirst, would you care for a cup of coffee, sir?" He brandished the thermos flask questioningly.

"Ersatz?" Bruno shook his head. "No, that shit gives me wind, but give one to Mouse, his mouth must be bone dry after all that bloody chattering."

Rudi barked a laugh at that, sharp and stiff with strain.

Behind them, Mouse just grunted, although Bruno was sure he could *feel* the gunner grinning.

Bruno pulled the heavy Junkers fighter into a smooth sweeping turn, ignoring a complaining Rudi as hot black coffee slopped over his gloves and onto his flying overalls.

"Put down that cup Rudi, you hound, and give me a course for the West Frisians. We'll patrol for a quarter of an hour or so, then back for *schnapps,* a creamy coffee and bed. For you two at least. Me, I'm going for a nice long bath and then a good fuck in town to celebrate."

Rudi laughed, "Yes sir, *Herr Leutnant.*"

Mouse just grunted again.

The sound of the *Jumo 211J* engines faded to a whisper, and then was gone, leaving behind it the blistering pyre, already guttering and dying, the twisted and glowing remnants all that remained of an RAF bomber and its three man crew just moments earlier.

Three plucky RAF flyers, veterans of many missions over occupied

13

Europe, dead this night in an instant of awful fire and destruction, their memorial to be one more victory bar added onto the end of the painted score line steadily growing on the rudder of Bruno's Ju88C.

Chapter 1

Pilot Officer Harry 'Flash' Rose DFC, AFC, MiD, RAF, drew back his fist and punched the Group Captain squarely on the nose, spreading it across the senior officer's face in a satisfying splatter of gloriously vibrant red ruin, and knocking the Groupie violently back into his chair.

"I say, my dear boy, are you quite alright?"

Rose sighed and opened his eyes, dragging himself away from the delightful fantasy of thumping the droning old windbag square on the chops.

The aforementioned old windbag was leaning across the large desk, nose whole and unharmed, and Rose was surprised to see genuine concern in those watery eyes.

"Oh dear. My dear fellow. Are you feeling quite well, young man? Would you like a glass of water or something? A nice hot cup of sweet tea, perhaps? Yes?"

Rose forced a smile onto his face, "No, thank you, sir. That's quite alright." He pushed the gratifying vision of the blood-spattered face regretfully from his mind.

It wouldn't do at all to bash a senior officer in the chops, no matter how boring, particularly here, in the heart of the Air Ministry itself.

The Group Captain settled back onto his chair with a deep sigh, like a large blue-grey balloon deflating sluggishly, the straining chair complaining sharply.

"Thank goodness for small mercies. When you closed your eyes, I thought you were having a funny turn. Are you sure you're quite alright, old man?"

Rose figuratively kicked himself at his obvious lack of attention, and for drifting into that rather satisfying but shameful daydream.

"Yes, sorry sir, just felt a bit tired, long day, and all that." He looked out of the taped-up window, the view of the cold clouded sky outside partially obscured by the dirty grey barrage balloon sullenly floating low overhead. It had been given a name by the locals (what was it, *Maggie? Aggie?*), but Rose had already forgotten it.

It was late January 1941, some months since he had been shot down the previous year, and he was eager to get back up where the action was.

Yet there was a stir of fear that eddied unsettlingly within the inner recesses of his soul.

"It's as I said, Rose, you may not be ready to go back to it yet, why don't you wait a little longer, hmm? What if you had one of those funny turns in the middle of a dogfight? Hm? Wouldn't do, would it? Old Johnny Hun would have you on a platter."

Dear God. "Send me back, sir, please?"

"The MO said that you may not be ready for it, yet, Rose. To be honest, he had some strong reservations, and so do I. I know that you've been passed fit for flying, but your eyes took a while to recover. And that injury to your leg was quite bad, too. I'm not convinced that you should be up there in a Hurricane or a Spitfire quite yet."

Under his breath, Rose cursed. *I should have left the damned stick at home with Molly.*

Molly. The thought of his beautiful bride made him relax a little, and he smiled involuntarily with pleasure.

The Group Captain smiled back at him with relief. "There, I knew you'd understand. Why don't you come back and see me in a fortnight, old man?"

Blast it! "Please, sir. I'm going crazy here on the ground. You know how desperate the demand for pilots is. Send me to Wick. I've a friend who's the CO of a Spitfire outfit there."

The senior officer looked unconvinced, so Rose added defiantly, "He could look after me."

It would be wonderful to see dear Granny again. His friend had written again, still bemoaning the fact that he was so far from his extended network of girlfriends and his favourite drinking places.

Behind his desk, the Group Captain positively bristled, "Good Lord, no! I can't have you flying around over the North Sea. You're not ready for that sort of thing!"

He scowled mildly at Rose. "No, no, no! What if your engine conks out, and you come down in the sea? What then, hey?"

Oh God, what's the old fart wittering on about now?

Rose tried not to sound defensive, and kept his voice carefully level, "I'm not quite sure what your point is, sir?"

"Good grief, Rose. With dodgy eyeballs you might get lost, report your position wrongly or something. And with a gammy leg, how could you swim? And that's assuming you can swim. No, Wick is out of the question, I'm afraid."

The Group Captain waved vaguely at Rose with one careless hand. "You've already done a lot; some would say you've done more than enough. Why don't you try ground duties for a few months? How does that sound? Eh? We've got a couple of positions available here at the Ministry? I could do with a good assistant, myself. I could find

17

something useful for you to do? You could do some really helpful work here at the Ministry."

God forbid! It was grey and miserable here, he thought, like a damned mausoleum.

Rose tried not to let his dismay show, keeping his face carefully expressionless, fingers gripping his knees tight.

The Group Captain beamed proudly at Rose. "You should be very proud of your record, young man. Twenty years of age, an experienced fighter pilot with seven confirmed kills to your name already and goodness only knows how many damaged and probables."

He nodded approvingly, and tapped the desk with a gnarled finger.

"You were certainly in the thick of it, Rose. Damn good show. I can see you're no slouch."

Rose cleared his throat and leaned forward slightly. "Actually, sir, with respect, it's actually eight confirmed victories."

Although, if truth be told, it really ought to be nine. But who's counting?

The Bf109 which Rose inadvertently collided with in that last, explosive combat, unofficially his ninth 'kill', had not been confirmed as definitely destroyed, instead being classified as a probable.

Sergeant Morton, his (very) young wingman in that fearful final dogfight (and now a recently promoted Pilot-Officer with a very well-deserved DFM, flying together with dear 'Granny' Smith from an airfield in the north of Scotland), was incensed by the rejection, as it was he who had seen the smoking enemy fighter crash after the collision, and confirmed the victory.

But the powers-that-be in their wisdom would not permit it, and Rose's official score remained as eight confirmed kills.

He hardly mattered, for he was alive and well (sort of) and happily married to his incredible and lovely Molly.

And in reality, the only thing that really, truly, mattered was that the German onslaught had failed, *Der Fuhrer's Sealion* invasion plans in tatters, and Britain remained unconquered and free.

They'd repelled the invaders, albeit at a bitter cost, and the Germans had tasted the choking ashes of failure for the first time in this whole bloody awful war.

The Group Captain's shaggy eyebrows climbed in astonishment. "Good God! Eight, you say? Even better! I'm sorry, dear boy. I was never all that good at arithmetic, bit of a duffer with sums, unforgivable, ought to have checked, please do forgive me."

He pointed to Rose's chest. "However, there's no question of your extraordinary accomplishments, Rose. My, you've a goodly collection of ribbons and things beautifully arranged there beneath your wings to show for it already. The Distinguished Flying Cross, an Air Force Cross, a Mention in Dispatches, and, um, what's that other ribbon? I don't recognise it?"

At the end of Rose's colourful row of medal ribbons, arranged neatly beneath his silken RAF wings flying badge, was one with vertical blue and black stripes.

Rose thought affectionately of the courageous, outrageous and appallingly fragrant big Pole who meant so very much to him.

"It's a Polish medal, sir, the Silver Cross of Virtuti Militari. Means Military Virtue, apparently. I flew alongside the CO of one of the Polish Squadrons at Duxford last year. He served as a Sergeant and then a Pilot Officer with Excalibur squadron. He's an incredible chap. He recommended all of the pilots on Excalibur for the medal, insisted we receive it. A very fine officer and airman, sir, very fine indeed, and I'm very proud to say that I also consider him a very dear friend."

The Group Captain nodded sagely. "Ah yes, Squadron Leader Cynk. I've heard of him. I'm rather glad he's on our side, I must say. A bit of a lunatic, but a real lion in the air, by all accounts."

Rose smiled fondly to himself.

Cynk had been an Usher at their wedding, kissed everyone and anyone, cried copiously during the ceremony, drank like a trooper and disappeared halfway through the reception with one of Molly's WAAF bridesmaids, both reappearing some time later looking more than a little dishevelled but blissfully satisfied.

At the time, an outraged Molly pursed her lips in censure and glowered menacingly at Cynk, receiving in return a cheeky wink and a kiss blown her way from the unabashed Pole, although the already glowing bridesmaid flushed an even brighter pink and looked away in embarrassment.

An incredibly courageous and unflinching warrior in the air, certainly, but a legend with the ladies as well, a reputation well known and earned. Astonishing, really, considering the gallons of scent the big Pole doused himself with and the odious smell of his cigars and cheroots.

"Well, I can't offer you a flying position on an operational fighter squadron, I'm afraid, Rose. I'm not convinced that you are quite ready to dogfight against Goering's finest yet. I'm sorry."

Rose's heart sank with despair. It felt as if the floor had given way beneath him, but a treacherous part of him felt a disloyal prickle of gladness.

But how could he sit in some safe, cushy job when others were fighting and dying? What kind of man would that make him? And how could he look Molly in the eye? Harry Rose, scared of losing her, and terrified that he might be less than she deserved.

She deserved a hero, not some craven coward, hiding in the shadows whilst others faced the danger.

The older officer snuffled, "And no, I'm not questioning your ability; your record speaks for itself. Your courage and ability are in no doubt. The thing is, we're conducting fighter strikes into Nazi-held

20

territory, and I think that if you were shot down, escape and evasion would be a bit of a problem for you. And old Johnny Boche might torture you for secrets by concentrating his dastardly efforts on your poor old leg."

He sniffed again and withdrew a creased handkerchief from his sleeve. "No, I'll not do that to you. You deserve better. You've suffered enough for you country, dear boy." He blew hard into the hanky.

Molly would be so glad if he remained on the ground, but the dispirited Rose felt tearful, "I need to do something, sir. Please, is there nothing?"

Even to his own ears he sounded desperate, and Rose cringed inwardly in embarrassment and shame, and his eyes and face grew hot as he fought to control his emotions.

The Group Captain carefully tucked away the hanky and looked hard at him for a moment. Then he gave a long low sigh through his nose, and nodded slightly to himself, as if in satisfaction.

"Yes, she said you'd be like that. You wouldn't take a cushy posting, whatever I offered. Oh Lord. Alright then, if you're so dashed keen to get back up there and give Jerry a punch on the nose, then I suppose there is something that I can offer you."

Hurrah! War, here I come! A frisson of hope danced straight up his spine, and a bolt of fear flared just as quickly back down it.

She'll hate me going back, but what can I do? She's such an incredible woman, amazing in every way. She deserves someone special. How can I sit back when others are fighting? I must be worthy of her…

And then there came the artful voice of caution.

Be careful what you ask for. Wait until you know what it is before you start celebrating…

The Group Captain scratched his chin and peered at the sheets of paperwork chaotically cluttering his desk.

"Now where did I put it...?"

Rose shifted in anticipation, and found himself leaning forward expectantly, his stick falling to the floor unheeded.

He gazed at the jumble of papers. Good grief, he thought in astonishment, how did the man make sense of the bedlam of his desk?

"Um, can I help, at all, sir?" *We're going to be here all ruddy day*, he despaired.

The Group Captain snatched up a crumpled sheet of paper from the horrendous display of disarray with an exclamation of triumph. "Hah! Got you! I knew you were there!"

Rose sat back, trying not to fidget, heart thumping.

Come on then, what have you got for me?

The old man scrutinised the paper carefully, "Mm. Yes. Have you nay experience flying aircraft with more than one engine, Rose?"

Oh no. Oh my God. Blenheim fighters. Oh God...

Rose's thumping heart sank again. The thought of flying the poorly performing Blenheim fighter horrified him. Against the aircraft of the Luftwaffe's fighter arm, it would be like flying something with the dogfighting capability of a lump of lard.

Fuck me...

He realised that the senior officer was still looking at him expectantly, awaiting a response. Right then, "Oh, er, no experience at all, sir, I'm afraid."

Give me something else, please...

The Group Captain's eyes and mouth crinkled when he smiled. "Not to worry, my dear boy, we can soon sort that out. I'm going to arrange a quick conversion course for you at 17 OTU, should have a veteran like you up to speed in about a month or so."

Conversion course? Oh no! Bloody hell!

"Um, I'm not sure about this, sir…"

The Group Captain shook his head in surprise. "Good Lord, man, I thought you were keen to go and fight! You were set on giving Hun a bloody nose a moment ago."

"I've experience in flying Hurricanes, sir, as you know. I know and understand single-engine fighters. I'm not sure that I'm suitable for Blenheims."

"Blenheims? Blenheims? Who said anything about Blenheims?" His voice rose quaveringly, "What're you gibbering about, Rose? I want you to fly night fighters, man! Beaufighters, not bally Blenheims!" He looked around furtively, as if Goebbels himself might be concealed in the dusty shadows of the cold and empty grate, lowering his voice and leaning forward conspiratorially.

"Well, you'll begin by flying Blenheims for a wee while, of course, but only for training, but do keep it under your hat, old man, all a bit hush hush, y'know. You'll find out why soon enough."

Yippee! A thrill of anticipation and excitement streaked through Rose, and his fingertips tingled as he tried to control himself.

Nightfighters! Beaufighters! He felt like bouncing up and down on the chair. Like many of his contemporaries, Rose had heard stories of the rugged new heavily armed twin-engine fighter.

And he would get the chance to fly one! Rose smiled at the thought.

"Ah, I see that's perked you up a bit, hasn't it?" the Group Captain settled back onto his chair, reached for his teacup, shook it then looked into it, and then sadly placed it back onto its saucer. "No tea!" he reached for his telephone and spoke to his secretary, "Morag, be a love and please bring us some more tea, right?" he nodded at the telephone receiver, "Oh, and some of those very lovely biscuits? Hm? Oh yes, please. Thank you, my dear."

He gently replaced the receiver, and looked back up at Rose, "Your experience as a fighter pilot will hold you in good stead, Rose. You're invaluable. No, don't be bashful, man. It's true, we both know it. We need experienced men like you flying our night fighters. The beastly Hun is doing the majority of his bombing at night now, thanks to you boys, so we need skilled men to intercept and destroy him in the darkness."

The Group Captain beamed. "We've got some clever ideas in the pipeline, but hunting at night is going to be the very devil of a job. It won't be the same as a bounce in daylight. You won't be able to see very much." He raised grey eyebrows and sucked in his lips.

"D'you think you're up to the job? There's no shame if this isn't for you. You've earned a rest."

Rose squared his shoulders manfully, "I can do it, sir. Let me have a crack at it, please."

"Good man, your experience will be very useful. I'll issue the orders for the twin-engine conversion course; you should hear something within forty-eight hours."

The Group Captain smiled and nodded gently, "She speaks very highly of you. Said you're a good man. I think you'll do well, young man."

She? Who might the Group Captain mean, wondered Rose. It was the second time that he had mentioned that a mystery woman had spoken well of him. "Sir, may I ask who it is that has spoken of me to you?"

The gentle smile warmed, "Forgive me, Rose." He winked, "Or perhaps I should call you Flash? You served with my niece at Foxton last year. She's married to Squadron-Leader Denis. I believe he was your flight commander on Excalibur squadron last year?"

For the first time, Rose noticed the name plate on the desk, and it read: *'Group Captain Derek Edward Atkins OBE MC MiD CdeG RAF.'*

Oh! *Oh! Of course!*

Dingo Denis and the lovely Dolly! Memories of a smiling Australian newly promoted to Squadron Leader, eyes crinkling with pleasure and strong white teeth bright in a tanned face, with his lovely blushing bride, both blissfully happy despite all they had seen and suffered.

So Group Captain Atkins was Dolly's Uncle! Good Lord! He must have known all the time that Rose would jump at the chance of going back into battle! The old duffer had been sounding him out.

"I must say, sir, that it was a mite unfair of you. You knew who I was all the time." Rose remarked reproachfully.

"Not really, I needed to see that it was the right thing for you, and now that we've met, I know that it is. You went through a rather a lot in a very short time, and you might not have been as ready as you think you are."

True enough, Rose pondered silently. *Am I ready? I suppose I'll find out soon enough.*

"So, tell me about the Beaufighters, sir?"

"They pack a fearsome punch, and you'll be part of a two man team. That's all you need to know for now. You'll need to complete the conversion course first, old man, and you'll crew up there, too. You might get to fly Blenheims, but as I said, it'll only be for training purposes. Got to bring you up to speed on twin-engines kites. Slowly, slowly, catchee monkee, eh, what? Don't run before you can walk, eh?"

"Two-man team, sir?" *Oh, Lor'! I'm not sure I like the sound of that.*

There was a knock on the door and a young Wren poked her head through. "Tea's ready, sir, may I bring it in?"

Dark shoulder length hair, grey eyes and a soft lilting Scottish burr that awoke memories of Skye.

"Ah, Morag, thank you, thank you. Please do bring it in, my dear, there's a good girl."

Morag carefully brought in a tray loaded with tea and biscuits, and laid it gingerly on the horrendously cluttered desk, "Please sir, let me clean up in here? It'll be a lot easier to find things, then." The tray began to slowly slide to one side and she grabbed it hurriedly.

"Good gracious, my dear girl, if I let you at my papers I won't know where anything is, so I daren't. Don't worry your sweet little head, it's all under control."

Morag *tsked-tsked* and shook her head reprovingly, but said nothing more, balancing the tray carefully.

Rose contemplated her pert bottom with interest as she laid down the tray in front of the Group Captain, who nodded approvingly after surveying the contents.

Very nice, very nice indeed, thought Rose, completing his own detailed survey of Morag's delightfully curved buttocks.

But his palms had cupped and caressed smooth buttocks even lovelier than Morag's this very morning, and *that* lovely bottom continued to feel simply magnificent beneath his fingers and his lips, even after two whole months of decidedly wonderful married bliss.

She still tasted absolutely amazing, too. Every part of her, like a sweet and juicy fruit, fragrant and wonderful.

That was one gorgeous bum that he'd never tire of fondling or caressing or kissing.

But then, the same was true of course for the rest of his slender dark-haired beauty for that matter. Every time they touched, he tingled with joy.

And then he felt ashamed, there was so much more to the girl than just her magnificent body. So much more.

I love her for all that she is.

Harry Rose, happily married man, sitting in the Air Ministry and lusting like a schoolboy after a pretty girl.

Morag turned to go, caught his eyes lingering on her bottom and smiled warmly at him.

She stopped at the door and looked back, her pale cheeks pink and those clear grey eyes on Rose, "If you need anything else, sir, just ask."

The eyes momentarily flicked fondly for a moment to Atkins as he fussed over his papers, before returning to meet Rose's, "Anything at all. Please do ask."

Atkins, reaching for the prize of the teapot and thinking she was speaking to him, looked up and shook his head, "Awfully kind, Morag, but this'll do very nicely, ta very much."

The girl disappeared, closing the door quietly behind her. His eyes remained on the closed door for a moment.

Oops. Mustn't look, you're a wedded man now, best behave like one, mate. Besides, you're married to the bravest, sweetest, most beautiful girl in the world.

Nothing else compares.

But a secret part of him was pleased by the girl's interest. And her eyes had dared him. And that bum looked rather delectable...

Stop it.

Atkins brandished the teapot triumphantly like a trophy. "Can I offer you a cuppa, Rose?"

"Oh, thank you very much, sir, that's very tempting, but I've arranged to meet someone."

"Of course. You're sure? Digestive? No? Well then. It's been a great pleasure to meet you, old chap. Good luck on the conversion course. I'm sure you'll do well. You'll get your posting at the end of the course. In the meantime, I'll get Morag to start things off."

Oo-er, daren't start anything with Morag! There's a rather delectable WAAF Flight Officer who might boil my balls in bleach if I dared to!

"Thank you very much, sir," Rose said earnestly, "I'm very grateful for the opportunity. I'll wait for the orders to come through. If that's all?" He got to his feet, retrieved his cap and stick, and turned to go.

"I'm glad to be of help, dear boy. By the way, Dolly and Dingo send their best." He picked up the sugar and plopped two heaped teaspoons of sugar into his tea, pondered, then added a third.

"Please do thank them for me, sir, and pass on my very warmest regards to them."

Rose reached for the door knob.

"Oh, and Rose?"

He stopped, his hand still on the doorknob, and turned to Atkins, eyebrows raised questioningly. "Sir?"

The Group Captain raised his teacup in salute, and a brown wave slopped dangerously up against the edge. "Do me a favour? Get one of the buggers for me, will you? Two of the swine would be even better!"

Rose nodded grimly, "It would be my pleasure, sir. Very much so. I promise I'll do my best for you."

The slim WAAF was sitting with her back to him, an open book in her hands and a cup of tea growing cold next to the powder blue cap on the table before her.

He stood for a moment behind her, admiring the way her lustrous hair was pinned up, the beautifully smooth pale perfection of the exposed skin of the nape of her slender neck, and the way in which the blue uniform hugged her trim figure.

She sensed him standing behind her, and she turned, smiling warmly, her eyes bright. On her tunic she proudly wore the medal ribbons of the George Cross and the Polish Bronze Cross of Merit with Swords.

Rose uncertainly removed his cap, "I say, is this chair taken, miss?"

The sweet voice was a little petulant, "It is, but he was supposed to be here about half an hour ago, he's late, so you might as well sit with me instead. I think he's forgotten about me already."

Molly tucked a napkin into her book as a bookmark, and put it down carefully beside her cold tea.

He leaned close, inhaling her fragrance, admiring the graceful curve of her full lips, "He must be a fool, then, if I may be so bold. An absolute idiot, even. A girl like you should never be kept waiting. I reckon you must have married beneath yourself. He's obviously a moron, and he clearly doesn't deserve you. Would you care to have dinner tonight with me, instead?"

Her beautiful dark eyes were troubled. "I'd love to, and you do seem rather nice, but I'm not sure that I should. I've only been married for two months, you see, and he swears that he loves me." She tilted her head slightly, eyes cool, "I'll bet that he's been eyeing up the dolly birds at the Air Ministry."

Remembering the sight of Morag's buttocks, and the piece of paper she had secretively passed to him after his meeting, since crumpled into a ball and tossed (with just a touch of regret) into the Thames, he shook his head piously.

"Not at all. Wouldn't dream of it."

He lowered his voice and touched her hair. "You're the most beautiful girl I've ever seen, absolutely exquisite, so I'm sorry, but I won't take no for an answer." Her tresses were like silk beneath his fingers and he sighed, "Exquisite."

She glowered dangerously at him, "What do I always say?"

And in harmony together they quietly chorused, "*Flattery will get you nowhere!*"

They laughed, and she leaned towards him, grabbing his tie and pulling him even closer, to kiss him lingeringly, warm soft lips opening

29

against his, her tongue fleetingly probing his mouth, tasting of gloriously sweet love and Elizabeth Arden lipstick.

Every time she kissed him, his legs turned to jelly, but he'd never tell her. Caesar would not have behaved like that when he kissed Cleopatra, surely? Real men didn't feel like that, did they? 'Course not.

But it felt wonderful, nevertheless. He closed his eyes in enjoyment, and when she pulled back from him, he sighed sadly. "I missed you so much, my love."

She laughed softly and let go of his tie. At an adjacent table, a heavily bearded and stocky Royal Navy officer shook his head in outrage.

What was the world coming too? Young people nowadays had no sense of decorum, canoodling like that.

Disgraceful! He picked up his tea cup sharply and hot tea slopped back onto his gold-ringed sleeve. Skin smarting, he smacked it back down onto the saucer with a harsh clatter.

But Molly only had eyes for Rose. "Missed me, did you? Missed me? You rotten fibber! It's only been two hours since you left for your meeting at the Ministry, you awful rogue."

"Exactly! It's been far too long!" he sighed again, licked his lips as he drank her in hungrily with his eyes, "I love you, Molly."

"Not half as much as I love you, you awful, naughty boy! So, what news? Are they taking you away from me?" *Oh, I so wish you would take a cushy posting where I knew you would be safe…but then you wouldn't be the man that I adore. Oh God, Let it be near…*

He lowered his voice, "I'm not being posted overseas. I met Dolly's uncle, and he's putting me on a twin-engine conversion course –"

An icy dread stabbed her heart. "Heavens! Blenheim fighters?" *Oh God, not those old wrecks!*

He could see the sudden trepidation in her eyes, even though she tried hard to hide it, her smile turning stiff and fixed.

"Oh gosh, no, my sweetest, no, not Blenheim fighters!" Rose wrinkled his nose and grimaced, "although I may have to train on them to begin with."

If not Blenheims, then what…? Molly clutched his hand tightly, loosening her grip almost immediately, "Oh Harry, what then?"

He looked around, unconsciously mimicking the Group Captain, and leaned closer, lowering his voice to a whisper, "Night fighters, more specifically, Bristol Beaufighters!" he sat down opposite her and leaned back with a pleased grin, the thrill of anticipation still fresh within him.

"Beaufighters?" she looked back at him doubtfully.

"Honestly," he chided, "for a stunning popsie with a George Cross, and there aren't many of those y'know, you're awfully edgy!"

She looked down self-consciously at the blue ribbon with the little silver cross on her left breast. "Don't call me a popsie, you horrid, obnoxious child, and the only thing I'm concerned about is that they might send you so far away that I couldn't nag you day and night."

He leered at her, "I'd not let them part me from you, my little sugared honey."

She shook her head sadly, wiped dry eyes, "How did I get lumbered with a lecher like you? What went wrong?" a long sigh escaped her, "I had such hopes and dreams…"

"Don't feel bad, sweetest trinket. It's just that I'm me and you're you, a helpless woman, and because you're only a woman, you just can't help the way you feel."

He smirked at her, "Don't feel too bad about it, gorgeous, there's nothing you can do about the desperate attraction you feel for me."

He eyed her pompously. "Why, you're only behaving like every other woman in the world would behave, y'know, my little sticky sweet. You're simply helpless against my charms. My allure makes a mindless puppet of you. A moth to a flame."

Molly snorted in a rather unladylike manner, and half-raised one slim hand.

"Oh really? Is that so? The only irresistible attraction here is the one that the palm of my hand is feeling for the side of your fat head!"

Rose covered his mouth, eyes wide in feigned shock, "Oh my goodness! How can you speak so about the one you adore? What kind of woman are you?"

"I'm a woman who is completely and helplessly in love with you, I must be crazy, God help me, but that's the kind of woman I am." She leaned forward and placed both hands onto his lap, dangerously close to his groin.

"Oh, that's nice to know," he squeaked, thrilled and horrified all at the same time, shifting in position and looking around uncomfortably.

The palms of her hands were warm on his upper thighs.

Fortunately, the senior naval officer had already left, thereby saving himself from a coronary.

Molly's right hand slid higher, and her thumb began to slowly stroke the shaft of his penis.

"You've gone very quiet all of a sudden, Pilot Officer, cat got your tongue?" She arched an eyebrow elegantly, and smiled sweetly at him.

He inhaled her scent and felt himself jerk involuntarily beneath her gentle caress. Uh-oh, it was getting a bit tight down there. He was both horrified and thrilled by his predicament.

What a girl! And all mine! Cripes!

"I was just deciding whether to stay here and let you continue to do that really rather nice thing that you're doing to my very best bits, or to jump up and run for the hills as fast as my little legs will carry me before the police arrive to arrest us both for lewd conduct."

Her smile became positively feral, "Oh, you haven't seen anything yet, young man."

Rose found his throat had become unbelievably dry, and he swallowed jerkily.

She licked her lips and her forefinger ran lightly along the length of his dangerously burgeoning tumescence.

"Crikey! Um, shall we go back to the flat, Ma'am?" he croaked, and in his mind he wondered forlornly if it were possible for him to walk without drawing attention to the terribly inconvenient bulge in his trousers produced by the girl's gentle ministrations.

Molly's eyebrows arched seductively again, her lips glistening in anticipation and those dark, liquid eyes were full of warm promise.

She gripped him through the fabric, her fingers firm and delightfully warm against his hardening penis.

"What a lovely idea, young man. I thought you'd never ask!"

Chapter 2

A thin trickle of fine dust spilled lightly from the roof above, sprinkling delicately onto his sweat-sheened face once again, and ineffectually Rose tried to blow it away.

The dust and sweat were rapidly congealing, creating a mask-like thin layer akin to a coat of plaster, and he would have preferred to wipe it off his face, but Molly was tucked comfortably against his right arm, snug against the wall, snoring softly.

A trail of saliva trailed elegantly from the corner of her beautiful mouth to nestle onto the silk wings and ribbons on his chest.

The very nice elderly lady whose corned beef sandwiches and chipped flask of strong hot sweet tea they had shared earlier was lying on his left hand, dead to the world, mouth gaping to reveal pink gums and a flopping denture, rather nattily draped in a filthy looking blanket that smelled of cats and cabbage.

His hand was tingling atrociously but he daren't move it, lest he wake her.

After all, she was also very kindly sharing her (rather limited) space on the platform with them, and if it were not for her thoughtfulness, Rose and Molly would have only had the space on the bottom steely step of the escalator.

In fact, they were very fortunate indeed to be there at all, because the first of the night's inhabitants usually arrived to stake their family's place on the London Underground's platforms just after 4pm, whilst the trains were still running busily and crowds of commuters thronged the stations.

The low thump and trembling aftershock of yet another explosion above ground (was it near or far?) was just discernible, felt rather more than heard, and for the umpteenth time he hoped desperately that a water pipe had not been breached by this latest bomb.

It would be ironic to escape the fires in the streets above to drown below them. No use worrying about it, he tried telling himself for about the thousandth time. If it happened it happened. But the thought didn't make him feel any better.

At least it would wash away the putrid stench, he thought. Somehow, the choking, disgusting reek of sweating, unwashed crowded bodies, cigarette smoke, food and human waste did not seem as bad as when they'd first found their way onto the platform.

The station's public lavatories, initially only meant for use by a small number of commuters in peacetime, now proved unable to meet the demand of hundreds of people, and there had been more than a few open chamber pots on show, adding to the poisonous atmosphere.

Amidst the snoring and quiet conversation an outraged voice shouted out at the other end of the platform, *"Oi, you dozy cunt! That's my sodding leg you're pissin' on! Go on, fuck off out of it, you daft tosser!"*

Rose sighed and transferred his gaze from the curving wall with its posters of Max Miller, Jack White and Syd Dean, from which the dust lazily drizzled down onto him, and looked along the platform to where the Inspector, John Humphreys, was walking precariously along the platform edge, checking that all was well, and sharing a reassuring smile or a quick chat with those still awake.

He caught Rose's eye for a moment, and touched the peak of his cap briefly with one forefinger in quiet salute.

Unable to move, Rose nodded cordially in response.

Humphreys stopped for a moment, squatting down to talk for a moment with an elderly couple.

Thank God for people like him, thought Rose with admiration, idly watching the high, thin haze of sluggishly coiling cigarette smoke lurking sullenly beneath the platform's roof, veiling the sodium lights..

Humphreys and those others like him are the ones, no matter how hopeless things seemed, who hold the whole thing together, he thought.

It's so easy to forget those who quietly and without fanfare manage the routine business of keeping our country running smoothly despite the added complexities and dangers of wartime. They take on these appalling trials every night, and just get on with it.

I'm lucky. At least I get the chance to shoot back. These poor buggers just have to carry on in the midst of all of Jerry's hate.

He turned his head marginally, licked dusty lips and glanced at the darkly foreboding mouth of the tunnel close by, thinking with dread of the roving feral monkeys, and he shuddered involuntarily.

Molly stopped snoring for a moment, but her breathing remained calm and measured and she did not awaken, instead snuggling deeper against him.

Earlier, when they first made their way onto the platform (with Rose keeping as far from the edge as possible even though no trains were now running), they passed beside the Inspector talking to a large group of children, and stopped to listen.

"So kids, would you like to hear about the wild London Underground monkeys?"

The little faces gleamed with anticipation, and one little girl shouted out, "Ooh, yes please, mister!"

The Inspector smiled warmly, squatted down onto the platform, and balanced himself forward on straight arms and the knuckles of his hands, playfully feigning the posture of an affable gorilla.

"Well, a few years ago, when you lot weren't even a gleam in someone's eye, we had a cage of monkeys waiting for a train."

"What's a gleam, mister?"

Sweat shone on his forehead but the smile didn't slip. "Doesn't matter, little 'un. And you can all call me Johnny, OK?"

"Why were they waiting for a train, mister?" asked a little boy with scabby knees and something unpleasantly green dangling from one nostril. He couldn't have been more than eight years old.

"I was getting' to that, pal." The warm smile still glowed, "Well, they were sitting comfortably in a cage near Notting Hill waiting to go back to their circus tent, because the circus was going on a tour of the northern cities."

Scabby knees piped up, "My Dad says that Northerners are all…"

"Yes, alright, chum," the Inspector interjected hurriedly, "Anyway, someone very naughty let the monkeys out. 'Course they scarpered, but the police managed to catch some of them straight away, some were found asleep in the market, and one got stuck in a coal locker and gave himself up."

"I fell asleep in my sister's pram once," volunteered the little girl shyly.

"Did you, sugar?" the smile had slipped ever so slightly, and was there the hint of a twitch in those calm eyes? "Must have been awfully comfy. A very nice place to sleep. Well, anyway, although some of the monkeys were caught, they didn't get them all!" the Inspector looked around him expectantly.

"I couldn't get out by myself," continued the little girl, "and I was proper busting, so I did a wee-wee in it."

Nonplussed by this latest awful revelation Humphreys scratched his short beard and searched for an appropriate response, "Ah. Uh…"

"How'd they catch the monkeys, mister? My Nan says the Rozzers couldn't catch a cold," offered scabby knees brightly.

The Inspector's eyes glittered under the murky sodium lights, and he rallied bravely. "Does she? Does she indeed. Hm. OK. Right then. Well, the Rozzers, er, I mean the Police, are still looking. Some people say that the monkeys are still out there, hiding in the tunnels, waiting for children travelling without their parents."

The children stared at him, and even Scabby Knees seemed impressed.

The Inspector looked towards one of the dark, open mouths of the tunnel, then back at his audience, and his voice dropped to a loud whisper, "and I've heard tales of children DISAPPEARING!"

His eyes opened wide as the last word boomed out of his mouth, echoing hollowly along the chamber, and he bounded upright, hands outstretched and clutching for them.

Rose and Molly both jumped, and the children scattered as far as the space allowed them to with screams and howls of laughter that reverberated up and down the chamber.

Rose watched the children spread out as they rushed back to their respective families.

The Inspector thumped his chest in a suitable bit of apish posturing, then cupped his hands and called out after them, "Don't let the monkeys eat you, children, and stay close to your parents! Sleep well! Nighty-night!"

Rose navigated past a collection of steel pots and pans wrapped in a table cloth and an ornate and chipped chamber pot half-filled with some evil-looking dark ochre fluid, within which a half-submerged something unmentionable floated.

There were beads of the vile fluid liberally scattered around the pot, and he kept as much distance as he could away from them. *Uck.*

He held out his hand, "How d'you do, Inspector. That was some tall tale!"

The Inspector took his hand, "Why thank you, but no need for the Inspector thing, the name's John Humphreys, and believe or not, but that was no tale." He sniffed and, removing his cap, pulling a hanky out of the crown and wiping his face. "Phew, it's warming up nicely tonight."

Despite the frozen iciness of the weather outside, the huddled mass of bodies generated enough heat to make the temperature of the platform almost unbearable, and Rose could feel sweat running down into the small of his back.

The foetid odour just made it worse.

Humphreys popped his handkerchief back into his cap and replaced it smartly on his head.

"Back in 1926 a troupe of monkeys, trained as a Jazz Band apparently, believe it or not, not circus performers like I said to the kids, was let out of their cage by thieves, and although most of them did get recaptured, there're still three or four unaccounted for to this day."

"Oi! John, come'n 'ave a cuppa and a sarnie wiv us!" shouted a woman's voice stridently.

"Thanks, Hev, just give us a minute, and I'll be along directly. Keep it warm for me, yeah?" Humphreys gave the woman a thumbs-up for the offer, and shrugged apologetically to Molly and Rose for the interruption.

"So, they say the monkeys lived under the platform at Latimer Road station for a while, they might even be there still, for all we know. There've been efforts to capture them loads of times, but no joy. Even after all these years, we still get reports of sightings, and food often goes missing."

"Good Lord!" Rose was surprised. He had been certain the story was a fairytale. "Oh, gosh, where are my manners? I'm Harry Rose and this is my wife, Flight Officer Molly Rose." *Molly Rose, how fine that sounds!*

"Really Inspector, do you think it was appropriate to scare the children so much? Aren't they scared enough? Don't you thinks telling them stories like that is a terrible idea?" Molly's contralto was cool and distant, her eyes stony.

Uh-oh, thought Rose, and mentally braced himself. He'd seen Molly before when she was angry. It wasn't pretty.

Better run for cover while there's still time, chum.

But Humphreys just smiled affably and nodded. "Ah. Yes, Ma'am, I can see why you'd think that, and it might seem cruel, but kids can be dreadfully inquisitive, and we've already had more than one of the pluckier ones exploring the mysteries of our tunnels at night."

The corners of Humphreys' lips turned down. "On at least one occasion that I know of, we had a pair of little 'uns who must have wandered off, and then gone to sleep on the tracks. They were still there when the electrics was turned back on. A work crew found the bodies."

He shivered involuntarily and looked away, "What are we supposed to do when it's time for the trains to start again? London can't afford to stand still."

Humphrey's eyes were serious now, faraway, glistening with some memory.

The smile had gone.

"I can't bear the thought of someone's youngster down the tunnels when the rails are switched on again in the morning. Every one of these kids're too precious. Putting the fear of wild and dangerous

40

animals into the little tyke's heads is one way of keeping the little monkeys, if you'll pardon the expression, safe and sound and close to their families."

Molly's cheeks flushed pink in mortification, but her lips quirked upwards. "Oh, I see. I understand. I'm sorry, John. I didn't realise. Should've known better, spoke too soon. Silly of me."

Dearest Molly, thought Rose warmly, if ever she was wrong, was never reluctant in admitting it.

She touched Humphreys' arm briefly, "On behalf of the children and their parents, thank you for keeping them safe, and please do excuse my words. I spoke out of turn."

After the events of the previous year, Rose and Molly both appreciated how precious children were. The *Luftwaffe* had seen to that.

Pleased by her compliment, Humphreys waved away the apology shyly, not seeing the sudden glistening of Molly's eyes.

But Rose *felt* her pain, knew the tears were there, and his hand slipped surreptitiously into hers and squeezed her fingers gently, and in response she gratefully took his hand as if it were a lifeline and squeezed him back.

"No problem at all, Ma'am. I can see that you care, it's written all over your face. Just wish I could do more for them. When this is all over, and we've properly spanked old Adolf's arse," he smiled shyly, "if you'll pardon me for saying so Ma'am, these kids'll be the future for us. Our future. We all have to do our very best in making sure they make it."

An example of that hoped-for shining future now sidled up beside him. Scabby knees had returned, this time clutching the hand of a little girl with dirty cheeks and golden curls.

"Mister, me Ma says our Lil's a cheeky monkey. Is she one of them's yer lookin' for? Is there a reward?" he smiled expectantly.

41

The little one beamed angelically at them and picked her nose.

Humphreys laughed and shook his head ruefully, "No, mate, I'm sorry, she isn't one of them. Nice try. You'd best keep her. Take your Lil back to your Mum and Dad, and look after her well. Keep an eye on her, yeah? Don't let her wander, and don't you go wandering about now, either. You settle yourself down for a nice bit of kip, pal, OK?""

Scabby knees looked crestfallen, and turned to go, "Fuckin' 'ell," he muttered crossly, "C'mon, Lil."

Another jagged tremor pulsated through the chamber, its echo resonating back through his nerves, there was a muffled drawn-out thump like a wet sackful of sand and books falling to the floor somewhere overhead, and more dust sprinkled liberally across his face.

Molly began to snore gently again (*Good grief, how does she do that?*) whilst the nice lady next to him muttered something incomprehensible in her sleep and shifted in position, moving partly over onto her back, her right buttock warmly enveloping Rose's trapped hand like a large hot sponge.

She mumbled something incomprehensible, broke wind gently, and sighed happily in her sleep.

An errant strand of Molly's hair tickled his nose and he blew it away carefully with a soft breath, careful not to disturb her.

He felt the plaster-like masking layer of oily sweat and dust on his face crack uncomfortably as he blew out, and he grimaced uncomfortably.

His gammy leg was aching on the hard floor now, and he shifted his own buttocks stealthily, careful not to disturb his pair of sleeping beauties, and crossed his legs to take the pressure off it.

Bloody hell, what a fucking awful war. I've got Molly slobbering all over my ribbons, and some nice old girl whose name I don't even know farting onto my hand.

Rose sighed and closed his eyes, trying to blink away the dust and grit as he did so.

He was totally exhausted.

Despite the appalling noxiousness of the environment he found himself in, and the uncomfortable position he was squashed into, Molly's closeness and warmth was so very comforting that he felt blissfully content.

Thank you, Lord, for giving me such good fortune.

So long as no water pipes were breached by the bombing, and the feral monkeys of the London Underground didn't come a-calling, they were reasonably safe, and Rose would try and get some sleep.

Chapter 3

The shiny little red sports car screeched to a stop at the barrier, skidding a little as it did so, at RAF Dimple Heath's main gate with inches to spare, the smell of burning rubber, oil and hot metal filling the flaring nostrils of the white faced and staring sentry.

Incredibly, despite the speed of its approach, the wet road and the icy conditions, the little car didn't hit him.

Bloody hell, fuck me... thought the stunned sentry with relief, glad his bladder hadn't involuntarily emptied.

For a moment there, it looked as if the bloody thing would smear him across the barrier like strawberry jam on toast.

He noticed that the girl behind the windscreen was smiling expectantly at him, and that there was an RAF officer sitting next to her in the passenger seat.

If he hadn't been holding his breath in fear, he'd have been amused by the expression of frozen terror on the pale face of the young officer.

Hmm. It seemed that the Flight Officer was able to terrify others as well as himself with her ridiculous driving.

It was irritating that the Flight Officer had managed to elicit a less than professional reaction from him, denting a professional manner that he, Corporal Suggs, veteran of the North-West Frontier, prided himself greatly with. However, the strained look on the face of the man sitting next to her eased his sense of mortified outrage somewhat.

The officer was rubbing one red and watery eye vigorously with one trembling hand, face still pale, and not just from the bitter cold.

"Are you quite alright, sir?" Suggs asked deferentially, trying not to smile at the young officer's expression.

The Flying Officer shook his head jerkily. "I had my eyes open just now and I think I caught a fly with one. My fault, really, corporal, usually I have the sense to keep them closed when the Flight Officer is driving. I used to scream occasionally, but I found that the larger insects used to get lodged in my throat, and besides, bird poo has such an awful, sour taste."

He dabbed his moist eye with a handkerchief, "Besides, I think the Flight Officer thought my cries were ones of enjoyment and encouragement. The louder my screams, the faster she went. Better to just suffer in silence."

Molly smiled brightly at Suggs, and the Corporal walked to the passenger side of the car, but he spoke to the girl.

"Ma'am, it really is important that you slow down before you get to the final approach for the main gate. Of course, I do actually know you," *and you've scared the shit out of me before,* but he didn't say it (couldn't say it), "but if we've got a new sentry on, he might think you're some loony fifth columnist trying to blow up some aeroplanes."

She laughed aloud, "Oh, Corporal Suggs, you do say the funniest of things, do I really look like a fifth columnist to you?"

Molly's eyes were bright with merriment and her response was depressingly cheerful, despite the bitter cold.

No, he thought dourly, carefully keeping his expression neutral; *you just look like a very dangerous and crazy woman in that bloody 'orrible little red car.*

"With the greatest of respect, Flight Officer Rose, Ma'am, I'm not quite sure what a fifth columnist looks like? Could look like you or me for all I know."

Suggs sighed sorrowfully to himself at her chirpy response, and turned his attention to the officer sitting beside her, stretching out his hand.

"May I see your papers, please, sir?"

The young officer held them out, "Corporal, I could not agree with you more. I have spoken to the Flight Officer about this on occasion, but she and I have yet to reach a mutual agreement on the issue."

He paused as the sentry took his papers and cursorily examined them. "Unfortunately, neither Corporals nor Flying Officers can give orders to Flight Officers, so I'm afraid we will continue to only be able to advise her robustly in the strongest of terms."

The Corporal smiled stiffly with bloodless lips in response, trying to stop his hands from trembling in reaction as he tried to read the documents.

Hm, Flying Officer Rose, eh? Was this the Flight Officer's mystery bloke? Interesting…

"Thank you, sir. Would you report to the Adjutant, please? Perhaps the Flight Officer could take you?" Suggs looked questioningly at the girl. "Ma'am?"

"I'll take him straight there, Corporal, thank you. Headquarters building?"

The Corporal nodded, handed Rose's papers back to him, and smiled in sympathy at the young officer.

Good luck to you mate, you're a brave bugger. Flight Officer Rose might be beautiful, intelligent, sophisticated and a hundred other delightful things, but I'd not let her drive me for all the tea in China. You're welcome to her.

"Please keep your speed down, Ma'am?" Suggs request was plaintive.

"Of course, Corporal, I'd be more than happy to." The eyes danced with gaiety, and she smiled winningly, "Don't I always?"

The sentry, bad-temperedly trying not to return her smile, saluted them both dourly and gestured to his grinning colleague sheltering in the guard's post to raise the barrier.

I know that you always hide inside the guard house whenever that little red sports car shows up, Nobby, you cheeky little fucker.

Next time she turns up in that flamin' red thing you can risk your own life and limbs, he thought sourly, as he watched the sports car and its occupants enter the airfield at a far more sedate pace.

For fuck's sake! I know there's a war on, but this is bloody ridiculous. I'd rather be shot by a Nazi paratrooper than be squashed by a barmy WAAF racing her bloody sports car like she was at Monte fucking Carlo...

As they drew up to the station headquarters building, Molly pointed at a metal T2 type hanger some distance away. She had been posted to the station as head of the WAAF detachment whilst Rose had been on his twin-engine conversion course, and had already given him inside information about life at RAF Dimple Heath.

"The squadron's Beaufighters are mainly looked after in that one. There's another adjacent to the hard standings east of the main runway, but there's a Turbinlite unit using that one."

Rose stared at the hanger she indicated with interest. He thought the idea of trying to light up an enemy aircraft with one aircraft mounting a searchlight and shooting it down with a second was untenable in the true realities of air combat.

Meanwhile, Molly was still chatting animatedly, obligingly offering him more helpful information about his new posting.

"The CO's a Wing-Commander called James; he started on

Blenheims, nice man but a bit of a martinet, I think. Quite different from dear old Donald, likes a chat. All the paperwork has to be in order, otherwise he gets really annoyed, and he loves war correspondents, apparently. James makes sure we have lots of visiting acts, though."

She chuckled, "Rob Wilton was here last week, went down a storm, although some of his jokes were a bit blue."

Curious, Rose asked, "Were there any WAAFs there?"

"Most of my girls were, but none of them so much as batted an eyelid, whilst I was blushing as bright as you like! Me! An old married woman!" She shook her head sadly, "I don't know what the world's coming to!"

Molly slowed the car for a WAAF crossing in front of them, "James is the acting station commander, has been for absolutely ages, and I think he's hoping it'll become permanent."

A frown creased her smooth forehead as she watched the girl cross, and she half-stood in her seat, "Elsie? *Elsie!* Are those stockings regulation?" She shook her head severely at the agitated girl, "Good God, girl! How many times? My office in half an hour! And make sure you're properly dressed. Dismissed!"

Molly turned to smile apologetically at her husband as the flustered girl fled.

"But I ought to be very grateful, really," she continued as if nothing had happened, tucking a loose strand of hair under her cap, "He's the one who had me officially assigned to Oulton, technically I'm only here on secondment, and I'm formally on strength here under my maiden name, otherwise there's no way we could both be serving on the same station. The Air Ministry would see to that."

Because of the potential consequences and complexities of service people being in a domestic relationship and living on the same station during wartime, the King's Regulations directed that married couples would not be allowed to serve together.

Molly eased the car carefully into a free space in front of the HQ building, "There's a squadron of Wellington bombers here, too, but it's really only a glorified flight, under a Squadron Leader. I think the rest of the unit are serving somewhere a bit warmer. Not sure quite where. Careless talk and all that."

RAF Dimple Heath began life as a satellite airfield to RAF Oulton, but in an airfield expansion plan of late 1940, completed by W & C French Ltd, it became a fully operational one.

The airfield's main concrete runway was 1,375 yards long, concrete with an asphalt covering, and had two ancillary runways. The enclosing boundary track included 30 pan type dispersal areas, with access tracks mainly on the northern flank of the airfield.

There were one type E and one type J aircraft sheds at the northern end of the field, whilst the personnel accommodation and other airfield buildings were located at the north-western part of the airfield.

Molly pulled the handbrake with a jerk and undid her seatbelt. "Well, my darling, here we are!"

"Well, I have to say that the arrival was both nicer and scarier than the last time I arrived at an operational posting, although the driver was definitely very much prettier last time," she punched him lightly on the arm, "Ow!" And then, tempting fate, "And of course the speed he drove at was a bit more sensible."

She punched him again.

"Ow! Stop that!" he rubbed his smarting arm.

"I drove you all the way here because I'm a nice, kind girl, I could have let you walk, you know."

They were renting a beautiful little cottage on the outskirts of the picturesque little village of Dimple situated a mile away from the airfield.

"Yes, I suppose I should thank you for the kindness, although I'm told the journey ordinarily takes more than ten seconds. And I must say, the three little flying beasties I swallowed on the way here made an interesting addition to that delicious breakfast you made for us," he replied mournfully, adding, " I must say that I'm glad you missed the pigeon, though. I don't think I could have managed a whole one at this time of the morning."

Molly giggled. "Moan, moan, *moan*. Your breakfast's still in your tummy, isn't it? You haven't brought it up, have you? Honestly, Harry, you're such a drama queen."

"I suppose I really ought to keep my trap shut," he grumbled.

"Don't worry, my silly darling man, I just don't listen to you anymore, I ignore everything you say, after all, it is only nonsense that you spout," she soothed him kindly.

"At least I fly reasonably well; I'm not a total waste of space."

"Yes, dear," she agreed softly, "I suppose there is that," she giggled suddenly, "and I must say, there are some things you really are actually rather good at."

Rose thought happily back to the night they'd blissfully shared together. "Mmm. Yes, it was a pretty good night, wasn't it?"

She put her gloved hand over his, and he felt the warmth of her through it. "The very best."

"Thank you for sharing it with me, gorgeous."

"My pleasure, my darling," Molly replied softly, and licked her lips, "very much so."

They smiled at each other conspiratorially, and she leaned forward to kiss him gently on the lips, a fleeting kiss, but one that still made his heart race.

"Oh, hullo there, Molly, this your young man?"

Rose looked around to see a Flight Lieutenant walking purposefully towards the car.

He was small, even shorter than Rose, with a solid, compact frame. He had a walking stick and a very pronounced limp.

"How d'you do, old man? I'm Kelly, the Adjutant. It's a pleasure to meet you. Your good lady wife has done us proud, before she came we didn't know our elbows from our, erm, well, you know!"

"Hush, Adj, we need to keep it all a little low-key," Molly reproved.

"Oops, sorry Molly! Loose talk and all that." Kelly tapped the side of his nose conspiratorially.

Rose stood carefully and stepped out of the car, leaving his walking stick in the car. He had exercised his injured leg mercilessly over the past few weeks, and now he mostly tried not to use his stick. They shook hands, sizing each other up with interest. Kelly wore a Navigator's flying badge and the ribbon of a DFC.

"Hello, Adj, yes, I'm Harry Rose, it's a pleasure."

"Delighted, I'm sure. Heard you were a Hurricane bod, eh?"

"Yes, sir. Up until September last year when I got shot down, but I've just completed the twins conversion and Beaufighter familiarisation, and now I'm all yours."

Kelly lowered his voice, "Did you pick up an AI operator at the Beaufighter unit, chum?"

"I'm afraid not, sir. Or at least I did, but he was posted onto some hush-hush outfit." He still missed Morrow. "Damned inconvenient, to say the least."

"Not to worry, old chap, we'll sort you out with someone, at least until we find a suitable candidate."

"Thank you, sir that would be very helpful."

"Well, come along, come along. We'll go and see the CO, he's also

51

acting as the station commander, so he has rather a lot on his plate. He doesn't get the chance to fly often, but he does try. He's not the easiest of chaps, but he'll always be there for you if you need him. And, I must warn you, he does like to talk a bit."

Rose made a noncommittal noise.

Molly touched his arm, "Harry, I'm off to conduct my section head's meeting, see what the girls have been up to whilst I've been off the station. Shall we have some lunch together? The Assistant Section Officer in charge has a really lovely recipe for Lamb Hot Pot. You should definitely try it when you get the chance."

"That would be lovely, erm, Ma'am. I look forward to it." He held her hand for a second longer than a junior officer should, and he saw the love glow in her eyes.

There was nothing else that needed to be said, but she whispered, "So now it starts again, my love. Good luck!"

Kelly led him past a pair of diligently typing WAAFs to an inner office. On the door was engraved the legend 'Station Commander,' whilst beneath it, the card name slider read 'Wing Commander Reginald James DSO RAF.'

"Please, Harry, may I call you Harry? Do hang up your greatcoat and cap, Harry. Still damn cold. Eh? What? Would you like a cup of tea?"

"Thank you, no, sir. I just had some breakfast." Rose hung his cap and greatcoat on the coat stand, turned to face Kelly again.

The adjutant examined Rose's row of medals approvingly. "Nice to have someone with combat experience, it isn't the easiest thing flying around up there in the dark. I should know, did almost a whole tour on Wellingtons before this." He rapped on his left foot with his walking stick, the action producing a metallic clang.

"I'm sorry, Adj."

"I'm not, still got a splinter-free bum and my precious head is still on my shoulders, for which I'm extremely grateful. I'll leave the heroics for you young bucks." He looked at the door, "So, ready to enter the lion's den?"

Rose gulped. *Oh Lord, here we go.* "Yes, sir."

James was seated behind his desk, looked up quizzically from the papers and put down his pen.

"Flying Officer Rose, sir." Kelly limped over to the radiator and held out his hands to warm them.

The Wing Commander stood and walked around the desk to shake Rose's hand. His smile seemed sincere, "Good to meet you, Rose. I hear you're known as Flash, so that's what I'm going to call you, OK?"

He didn't stop to allow Rose to respond, "I'm pleased to welcome you onto the Squadron, combat experience is always welcome. Pity it's day combat, you'll find night combat a whole different kettle of fish, but it's going to give you a head start. No wonder the old Hun scuttles in under darkness. You and all the others gave 'em a damn good bloody nose in daylight, so they'll not try it again, I think. Now the fight is a nocturnal one. We're the ones the nation's depending on now. You're a lucky boy, you know. You're going to be writing history again. I was up with the squadron last night and we got a probable and a damaged."

Goodness me, the man doesn't even stop to breathe! Can't even get a word in!

Rose wasn't sure if he should be amused, bemused or astounded.

James was still talking, "I hear you caught a bullet in one paw, and of course the lovely Flight Officer Rose is your good lady? Mm? This could be a good story for the papers; we'll have to discuss it some time." He slapped his forehead lightly, "Oh Lord, no, we can't! We need to down play it, don't want our Molly shipped back to Oulton."

The Wing Commander perched on the edge of the desk, whilst behind him Kelly caught Rose's eye and shrugged with a sheepish smile.

James continued talking. "So, you've been credited with eight kills, damned fine record by the way, so you know how to lead, aim and shoot, which is a lot more than I can say for a lot of these dumplings we're receiving as replacements. It's a lot harder to judge distance and deflection in the darkness, and the only way to be sure is to climb up their arses before you shoot. You'll have to aim carefully, because you often get only the one shot, without tracer to judge your aim, although the DeWilde rounds tell you when you hit, if you choose 'em, I would if I were you, and if you don't hit ol' Johnny Hun first time, there's a better than even chance he'll get away in the darkness, because he might be faster. In fact, the bugger often is."

He stopped suddenly, "Damn it! I'm doing it again! Listen to me blathering on and on, sorry Flash, but when you get me started you'd need to fire at least one 20mm cannon shell up my backside to stop me; you'll get all the gen you need from the boys, and I want you to do some air tests and practice intercepts as soon as possible, perhaps later, maybe for a couple of days to get your hand in, get familiarised with a kite. Oh, I didn't mention that, did I? We prefer to get the crews to adopt a particular kite, so that you can get used to its little foibles. That way you don't have to get used to a kite every time you get up there, you know what it is going to do each time when you're carrying out an intercept. I'm sure you did the same when you were on Hurricanes. Oh goodness! We need to sort out an operator for you as well, didn't you have one during familiarisation?"

He tapped his nose, "Oh yes, he developed some sort of sinus complications, or something, didn't he? All rather interesting."

The Operator Rose had originally been crewed with was an ex-Cambridge physics tutor, before the man had been mysteriously transferred to important 'Hush-hush' duties just as they completed the training and familiarisation course. Morrow had been an agreeable, considerate man, albeit a little pompous and absent-minded. The sinus complication thing a useful fabrication.

Nonetheless Rose was very sorry to lose him.

They'd got on well, and had worked quite efficiently together. In their free time during training, it had been quite fascinating to hear some of the philosophies that had existed in that interesting man's head.

James was still happily chattering away, "Where was I? Of course! I shall have to get someone for you for a couple of trips to get you settled in before we get you ready for your first op..." he stopped again, brow furrowing.

"Sod it! I'm still doing it. I only wanted to welcome you to the squadron. You'll fit in well, I can see that you will. Look, I'll leave you in the Adj's capable hands, he'll sort you out, won't you, Adj?"

Kelly nodded solemnly, "I'll do my best, sir. Come on, Flash." He opened the door.

A bemused Rose shook hands with the beaming James and then let Kelly quickly lead him back out.

The adjutant stopped outside and smirked at Rose in the ante room.

"Well, old chap, you came back out alive, though a mite deaf, I suspect."

He thought for a moment, rubbing his chin, "First things first. We need to sort out an operator for you; I need to have a little think. I think I have a likely candidate. Nip over to the Mess, would you, Rose old chap, whilst I try to sort something out. I'll meet you there."

"Gotcha, Adj." Rose reached for his cap and coat. "Um, could you just point me in the right direction?"

The Officer's Mess was empty when Rose arrived, but for a base primarily concerned with night-flying, this was quite normal. It was still a bit early for those who weren't flying tonight.

He picked up a book that had been left on an armchair; it was a dog-eared and rather tatty-looking copy of Tolkien's, *'The Hobbit.'*

But he wasn't in the mood to read, and he put it to one side and sat down. At least it was warm and snug in here.

The poor old ground crews out there were working in the freezing cold, in draughty hangars if they were lucky, most without mittens. Endless hours spent tinkering with cold metal, with little if any appreciation and no medals.

They were the real heroes, keeping the kites flying whatever the conditions.

He closed his eyes, pleased to be back at an operational RAF station once more. Even in the silence, and despite the cloying smell of tobacco, beer, spirits and engine oil, he felt he had come home.

And the best thing, of course, the very best thing of all, was that Molly was here with him too.

If she were with him, wherever he was in the world, he could never be unhappy, because she was the joyful song in his heart, his warm sunshine, no matter how dark the day.

In the end, wherever Molly was would be the only place where he could be happy, and no matter where he was, with her beside him, it would be home.

Rose must have dozed in the cosy quietness, because he was suddenly aware of someone shaking his shoulder gently.

He opened his eyes to see Kelly leaning down on his stick and one hand out, presumably to shake him again.

"Gosh! I must have nodded off, sorry, Adj." he smothered a yawn in embarrassment.

"Not to worry, Flash. We thought of someone as your operator, and I had to look for him. He came to us a few weeks ago, but his pilot was killed the day after they arrived, and the poor fellow's been at a bit of a loose end. Would you like to see him?"

Rose smiled. "Poor chap, bad luck! Well, I wouldn't mind a word, seeing as we're both in the same boat."

"Splendid! Well, come on then, old man, follow me." The adjutant limped back to the hallway outside.

Waiting outside was a young man standing stiffly at attention, clad in a filthy oil-stained boiler suit and dirty boots.

Rose looked at him dubiously. How come I always end up with the grimy ones? Even Granny was smarter (just about!) than this wee lad.

The thought of his dear old friend languishing far from the lights and delights of his beloved London as the CO of a Spitfire squadron in Wick did nothing to cheer him.

"Flying Officer Rose, this is Thomas White, Air Intercept operator. I thought I might be an idea if you both took a trip together?"

Rose saw the filthy and frozen-looking fingers and decided not to shake hands with White.

"Nice to meet you, White, stand at ease. I was wondering if you would like to conduct an air test, see if we could work together."

White kept his gaze on the floor, and he looked worn and dejected. "That would be great, sir, but has Mr Kelly explained that nobody else will fly with me?" He was well spoken, his voice educated and agreeable, but his manner cowed.

"Really? I'm not surprised, to be frank, White. You really ought to dress appropriately. I can't remember the last time I saw aircrew dressed so poorly," as soon as he said the words, the image of a very dear Squadron-Leader and his grubby uniform popped into Rose's mind, and he unwillingly suppressed a smile *(well, actually I do remember, but I'm not telling you about Granny),* "I'm surprised you haven't been put on a charge!"

He hated how prissy his words sounded even in his own ears and he made a face. *Oh my God, I sound like a proper martinet!*

White saw Rose's grimace and his eyes fell, flushing with embarrassment.

Kelly coughed. "He's on ground duties, Flash. Because he doesn't have a regular pilot, he's usually roped in to do things like sweeping the hangars, cleaning oil trays, latrine duties, temporary service policeman, that sort of thing."

Good grief…! Rose was appalled.

"What?" he stared at the slight figure before him, "An aircrew sergeant doing that kind of ground duties? Dear God! I don't believe it! In the RAF? Seriously? What did you do wrong, White?"

Oh Lord, listen to yourself! What would Molly say if she heard you flapping on like that?

White looked up hesitantly, blue eyes large in a pale and pinched face. Kind eyes, Molly would call them.

"Begging your pardon, sir, but I'm not a sergeant, I'm an aircraftsman."

Rose stared at him, flabbergasted. "Not a sergeant? But you're an AI operator, man. You've been highly trained! Why are you an aircraftsman? How did you lose your stripes?"

Oh Lord, what were they giving him? He felt a prickling of anger needle through him. *I may be the new boy here, but I'll be damned if I'm expected to adopt the squadron's rejects!*

He looked at Kelly, "I'm sorry sir, but I don't want to fly with this man if he has some disciplinary problems. I can't and won't fly with a troublemaker. I need someone reliable in my kite." He tried to ignore White's hurt, but couldn't, and felt rotten.

Harry Rose, angry with himself for hurting White so.

Kelly was obviously discomfited, "He isn't a troublemaker, Flash, not at all, and in actual fact, the Flight Sergeant says he's actually

58

quite a good worker. He has never been a sergeant. He was posted here as an aircraftsman."

Rose was perplexed. "After all his specialist AI training he's only an aircraftsman? What the hell is this? I don't understand; why isn't he an NCO at the very least? I had an officer as my operator in training. We did have some aircraftsmen, but they all got their stripes at the end of the course."

Kelly held up his hands soothingly to pacify him. "It's quite normal, Flash. Our operators all arrive here as aircraftsman, and get their stripes after a few trips. White hasn't done any trips here, yet. And because they are all general duties airmen, they get roped in to do whatever needs doing around the airfield. It's quite normal practice." He repeated uncomfortably.

He coughed again, "The CO thought they ought to prove their prowess before they were allowed to sew on any stripes."

Those dirty hands were being used to clean the loo or wipe up oil stains, which were essential duties certainly, but those hands with the chipped and grimy fingernails should be being used to operate an AI set! They were the hands of a highly trained specialist, damn it!

"My goodness. I've heard it all, now. This is wrong, sir. Right-ho, let's see what he can do, shall we? I want to take White up as soon as we can go. Could you please tell the Flight Sergeant? I'd like it if White was taken off ground duties immediately, and, of course, would you look into getting him some stripes?" Rose tried not to scowl, "He should be NCO aircrew, should be wearing stripes as a sergeant or corporal. Even an acting rank?"

He could hear something that sounded rather a lot like hysteria in his words, and he lowered his voice with an effort. It sounded as if he were giving orders to a senior officer, goodness only knows what White would think. He tried to soften his tone, "It's not right. Please, sir?"

Kelly nodded sheepishly, slightly shamefaced, "Of course, Flash. I should have done this myself before. I was NCO aircrew myself, once. Ought to know better."

White shifted uneasily, eyes on Rose, and held up a hand like a schoolboy asking for permission to speak.

Rose's voice softened further, "What is it, White?"

White's face might have been carved out of stone. "Sir, the thing is, the aircrews think I'm a bit of a jinx, ever since my pilot was killed. That's why nobody else has agreed to fly with me. It's only fair you know that before you decide. I'll understand if you change your mind." His eyes flickered to Kelly for a moment, "It's only fair that you know."

So the poor lad was being treated as a jinx as well as a general duties skivvy! It was grossly unfair, White was not responsible for his pilot's death.

Or was he? A thrill of disquiet passed through him.

Rose, like most aircrew, was highly superstitious, but how could he deny the boy a chance to do what he'd been trained for? It would be inhuman of him to deny the lad the chance.

Heroic Harry Rose, frightened of a boy in grimy overalls.

Damn and blast. Cursing inwardly, he cleared his throat. "Jinx? Why? Because your pilot died? What did you do? Are you responsible in any way?"

Rose raised his eyebrows theatrically, and leaned back on the balls of his feet, "Did you stab or shoot him? Poison him, perhaps?"

White looked shocked and shook his head, "Oh no, sir! He was run over by a bus in Piccadilly in the blackout. He was a very nice man, a good man, really keen to have a go at the Luftwaffe."

He squared his jaw stoically, "I miss flying with him." His eyes fell again beneath Rose's gaze.

There was something about the boy Rose liked, and he dismissed any superstitious fears from his mind. Besides, how could he exile the boy back into torment?

Oh well. In for a penny...

"Then let's not mention jinxes again, Hm? If you're any good, I think you should try me out, too, White. We'll see what you can do," *Oh Lord, I sound like Granny did when we first met!* "If you're any good, I intend to team up with you, so forget about everything else that's happened. We'll start afresh together, understood?"

Let's hope you don't live to regret the decision...

"Are you sure, sir?" White was astonished, and looked up again at Rose, and this time he kept his gaze raised.

"Yes, White. I'm absolutely sure." Rose smiled gently at the grimy young man in front of him, trying to ignore his inner doubts, "God willing, you'll get to know me quite well, soon, but let me tell you a little about myself. I flew Hurricanes last summer, and I got caught up in quite a few scrapes, I can tell you, had to force land twice, and then I actually managed to get shot down as well. I've lost some good friends, too. In the end my Hurricane blew up, but somehow I got thrown clear, my parachute opened, and now I'm here."

He lightly placed a hand on his hip, and tentatively felt for the little bump made by the little pink bear tucked carefully into his pocket.

"So either I'm pretty lucky," *Oh God, don't tempt fate!* "Which I would imagine should balance out any bad luck, or I've already used up all my good luck, in which case we'll find out together. Fly with me, White, and we'll find out. What do you say?"

White blinked, and his chin trembled, but his voice was firm. "Yes, please, sir. Thank you!"

Rose winced inwardly at the gratitude in White's eyes. *I hope we're both making the right decision, sonny.*

61

Kelly clapped his hands together, making them both jump.

"Excellent, that's all sorted out, then! Come on, White, old chap, come with me to my office. I've a few phone calls to make, and then I want you to go and put on your uniform and smarten up a bit."

He beamed wide like the Cheshire Cat of Wonderland, "We'll see the CO about getting some stripes up, eh? Things'll be a bit different, now,"

As White left, a determined set to his face, new hope burning brightly in his eyes, and his step lighter, Kelly squeezed Rose's shoulder gently, and winked gratefully, a relieved expression etched broadly across his features.

"Thank you, Flash. You're a good man. I can see why she thinks so very much of you. And again, welcome to Dimple Heath." The Adjutant nodded, "I must say that I'm very glad you're here."

Chapter 4

White arrived at the B-Flight dispersal hut in full flying kit, looking very much more like an RAF AI operator than he had at their meeting earlier. Even the dirt beneath his fingernails had disappeared; whilst a most welcome addition adorned his uniform sleeves.

On each arm he now wore hastily sewn on Sergeant's stripes.

Without the oil and dirt, the smooth cheeked young man before him now looked around twelve years of age.

Rose nodded approvingly, "Much better. Now you look a lot more like what you actually are." *Lord help us, the boy doesn't look as if he even needs to shave yet!*

White smiled hesitantly at him, "Sir, if I may, I'd like to say –"

Rose held up one hand, "You don't need to say a thing. Our turn to have a crack at Jerry, eh?" he said gruffly, "I want you to show me what you can do today. Everything before today is the past; it all starts now, just you and me, so do me proud. Don't let me down, chum."

"I'll do my absolute best for you, sir," The youngster replied earnestly.

"Good man." Rose encouraged him, "Come on, then, let's go and have a look at the kite we've been allocated. I have to say, I'm rather looking forward to this."

White coloured shyly, and nodded.

"But, I can't keep calling you White. What do they call you?"

White smiled again, "I've been called many things while I've been here, but I prefer 'Chalky', sir."

Rose laughed with delight. "I should have known! OK then, Chalky it is!"

In the armed forces it was common for those with the surname of White to be nicknamed 'Chalky', just as all those named Rhodes were often labelled 'Dusty' by their service contemporaries.

Rose glanced at White for a long moment, "You can tell me about that black eye some other time over a cuppa."

Startled, White reached up to touch his face, but said nothing. At least one score was now settled.

They had been given D-Dog, a veteran Mk IF Bristol Beaufighter in soot-black war-paint. Her designation letter, squadron letters and serial number all printed in medium sea grey.

She (of course, their aeroplane would always be a 'she') had belonged to another crew who had just completed their tour. They stood before it for a moment, admiring the aircraft under the anxious eye of the crew chief.

Rose sniffed in appreciation, savouring the heady and fragrant blend of metal, plastics, dope, canvas, machine oil and high octane fuel. Ah, the aroma of RAF fighters!

D-Dog was ten tons of solid fighting machine, and whilst not beautiful in the way his Hurricane had been, she had her own distinctive brand of loveliness.

A long-range heavy fighter, she squatted impassively on the hard standing, the snub nose and cockpit of the sturdy fuselage set equidistant between the two massive and powerful Bristol Hercules air-cooled radial engines with their huge three-bladed propellers.

64

D-Dog had a vicious, deadly bite, with four 20mm cannon in the underside of the forward part of her fuselage, and six 0.303 machine-guns in her wings (in a peculiar arrangement wherein four machine guns were situated in the starboard wing and only two in the port one, the landing light occupying the remaining place in the leading edge of the port wing).

She also incorporated arrow-shaped transmitting aerials in her nose, and complementary receiving aerials in the leading edges of her wings.

These had already helped her to account for at least four enemy raiders, and their scalps were painted in a proud line on her nose, beneath Rose's cockpit canopy.

They clambered into their fighter through their own respective entrance hatches in the underside of the fuselage, via the incorporated ladders, excitement buzzing in equal measure through them both.

Settling himself carefully onto the bucket seat and arranging his parachute pack like a cushion to be a little more comfortable beneath his backside, Rose looked around the cockpit eagerly.

Unlike the Blenheim, a veteran bomber in which Rose had completed his twin conversion, the Beaufighter cockpit was laid out carefully. It was designed so that everything seemed to be positioned in just the right place for the pilot, clearly visible and within easy reach.

The Blenheim, on the other hand, seemed to him to have everything in the wrong place, randomly arranged as if without thought, with things poking out all over the place, often catching against him as he moved around in the cockpit.

All of which now reminded Rose of the cautionary tale he'd been told by the stores clerk, a girl called Maisie, of how a dinghy had inflated in an airborne aircraft and caused the pilot of the Beaufighter to lose control and crash, killing both himself and his unfortunate operator.

For just such an eventuality, he'd been issued by the Stores with a wickedly sharp blade, and now he carefully checked that that it was still safely tucked away inside his flying boot.

Wouldn't want that flying around in the cockpit…

Outside, the engines were being readied, and he began his cockpit checks.

Rose relished flying again, but having flown Hurricanes, he had found the Blenheim sluggish and difficult during the conversion course, and it made him despair at his choice to fly night fighters.

During the course, there was much talk of evading Sir Isaac, a villainous personification of the rules of physics, the one factor which was constantly working against the students, and endlessly conspiring to bring about their downfall and death.

Having already survived Sir Isaac's evil intentions, Rose hated the Blenheim. He missed Hurricanes, and decided that he would visit the Air Ministry again to request single engine fighters again once he had completed the conversion.

However, flying the Beaufighter on the familiarisation course afterwards had been completely different, and he'd taken to the great brute of an aircraft immediately.

The strength and power that she possessed captivated him and reassured him that the choice had been right.

She was a fighter in every way, and he was a fighter pilot. What could be more right than the two be joined?

Then he smiled. There was nothing in the world more right and perfect than his being joined with Molly.

Now *that* was perfection, in every sense.

His eyes ran quickly, professionally over the controls, feeling at home. Arranged so that he knew where each was even in the dark.

"All set. Ready to go, Chalky?"

"I've been waiting to be asked that question for weeks now, sir, months even. Thank you for asking me. And, oh gosh, yes! I'm ready!"

Minutes later, Rose's left hand opened the throttles and they thundered along the main runway, whilst ensuring his right throttle was a little ahead of the left, to allow for and offset the dangerous swing commonly found in the Beaufighter on take-off.

And then, as the Beau bounded eagerly from the concrete like an unleashed puppy, he brought his hand forward to raise the undercarriage, then back again to hold the throttles in place. If they were to creep back he might lose power and speed when he needed them most.

He gazed out at the countryside around and ahead through the large bullet-proof windshield which afforded him an excellent all-round visibility.

He also wistfully noticed a black-painted Hawker Hurricane fighter of the Turbinlite flight parked to one side at dispersals.

There was no doubt about it; the Hurricane was a truly gorgeous aeroplane.

But today his kite was this much larger fighter, and he pulled the Beau into a gentle climb away from RAF Dimple Heath and towards the practice interception rendezvous.

"This is amazing!" exclaimed White excitedly. He was looking eagerly through the clear moulded Perspex bubble as they climbed upwards at more than 300mph.

Rose was pleased to hear the enthusiasm in the young operator's voice. White was in the right place at last.

Let the bloody loos look after themselves.

Rose also noticed that this Beau seemed to have a better rate of roll in comparison to the machine in which he had done his training and familiarisation.

"Chalky, are you sure that you want to start off with an interception? We could just as easily start off with a beacon identification and approach exercise?"

"It's OK, sir, let's go for an interception. I'm ready, and anyway, the other Beau will be waiting for us." T-Tommy had already preceded them ten minutes earlier for an air-test, and would rendezvous with D-Dog at the designated exercise area.

"Fair enough, my old son, if you're sure?"

"I am, sir, thank you."

A wave of apprehension swept over Rose.

Oh, dear God, let me have done the right thing! Please let me not be crewed up with a useless dud!

When they finally met up with T-Tommy at the meeting point, the other, more experienced crew began with a series of basic azimuth and elevation exercises which allowed White to describe to Rose T-Tommy's position relative to D-Dog from various angles and heights of approach, to ensure that the operator's AI set (better known to one and all as 'The Thing') was correctly configured for operational use.

Satisfied and relieved with White's performance in the basic exercises, Rose began a series of interceptions, wherein White actively gave Rose directions to turn onto a course that allowed them to finish up on the tail of the enemy aircraft, matching the enemy aircraft's speed and course.

If, however, the turn was poorly timed and executed, it could cause all sorts of problems to the nightfighter crew.

If the operator called the turn too early to his pilot, they would end up in front of the target, allowing the enemy aircraft to chase *them*.

Conversely, if they turned after the enemy too late, then they would end up in a position too far behind the target, resulting in a long pursuit in which they might lose the enemy bomber if it undertook evasive action or escaped beyond AI range.

It seemed night fighter flying and combat required equal measures of precision, ability, and good luck.

Rose was surprised and reassured by White's control as he repeatedly performed accomplished interceptions on the target Beaufighter from three different and varied approaches and speeds. He made some mistakes, but corrected them almost immediately.

Even with his hands around a broom for the last few weeks, thankfully, White had not forgotten any of the skills he'd been taught.

But it was one thing intercepting an obliging Beau in broad daylight, and quite another to intercept an evasive enemy bomber in darkness. White had done well, and shown Rose that he was an accomplished AI operator in these conditions.

Could he perform when it mattered, when all that stood between a British city and an enemy bomber was D-Dog? Operations might be a totally different story.

They would have to face the test soon, and Rose desperately hoped that they would not be found wanting.

With a steep approach and a flamboyant flare out, Rose stalled the Beaufighter into a neat landing onto the main runway at Dimple Heath. White said nothing as the wheels neatly touched the concrete once more, but Rose heard the sharp intake of breath over the intercom.

Rose was pleased with the landing, *when I was at my best I could land a Hurricane like that*, he thought happily. And indeed the Beaufighter was a sturdy, solid workhorse like the Hurricane. He would always miss his Hurricane, but the Beaufighter was a fine kite to fly.

Clambering out of the fighter, Rose felt tired but content. His muscles ached pleasantly and he had been comfortable handling the big fighter today. Of course, she was a great deal heavier than his lovely old Hurricane, but it had been a pleasure nonetheless. Perhaps she wasn't quite as manoeuvrable as a Hurri, and certainly she needed a lot more effort to fly by comparison, but they were both rugged and dependable machines that packed a punch and could take a bucket load of punishment.

Just as importantly, if not more, White had proven to him that he could do what was required when needed. Rose was more than a little angry that the young operator had been kept performing menial tasks when his very special skills were urgently needed elsewhere, in the sky.

Very angry indeed. What an inexcusable waste! While the cities were being bombed his skills were being squandered!

He would need to speak to Kelly and ensure there were no other aircrew languishing in inappropriate roles on the ground at Dimple Heath. They should be up there fighting the enemy!

White joined him near the tail, placing a gloved hand carefully on the stained metal of the tailplane.

"Was it alright, sir? Did I do OK?" His voice and posture were casual, but the blue eyes were anxious, face pallid with apprehension.

Rose smiled at him, "You'll do, Chalky. I'm afraid you're stuck with me." White looked away, but not before Rose had seen the naked relief and emotion on his face.

"I think you've earned a nice cup of tea and a bun, chum. Let's get back to the dispersals hut." Rose pulled at the sergeant's stripes, "Goodness me! These're a bit loose! I think you're going to have to put these on properly, my old son, because they're staying there."

White's voice was hoarse and unsure, "I wasn't sure I was going to get to keep them, so I just did a temporary job on them, sir."

"Well, you will be keeping them, Chalky. Perhaps you can get a friendly WAAF to sew them on properly for you?"

Surprisingly, White blushed and smiled self-consciously, "One of the Wing Commander's WAAF typists asked the adjutant if she could do them for me, actually sir." Inconsequentially, he added. "She's a blonde."

Interesting. "Hm. Sounds promising. I think you ought to take her up on her offer. Pretty?"

White nodded bashfully.

Rose cocked an eyebrow, "So, tell me more, blonde and pretty, that's a good start! So, Chalky, old man, what's her name?"

"Erm, I'm not sure, sir." White said self-consciously, "She did tell me, but the Adjutant was watching, and I didn't catch it. I didn't like to ask again."

Rose shook his head sorrowfully and put an arm around the boy's shoulders, "Oh dear, that's a bit of a poor show, Chalky. You're RAF aircrew! We're not backwards at coming forwards, you know! Don't let the side down, old cock!" he scoffed, conveniently forgetting his own bashfulness with Molly.

"You need to go back and ask her to sew on your stripes properly, Chalky, my lad, maybe try and find out her name, then, eh? Good man. Come on then; let's see if we can find that cuppa, eh? You can tell me all about the AI box thingie, although I should really be calling it 'The Thing,' shouldn't I?"

"Yes sir, it's a secret, we need to be careful whenever we talk about it."

"I'm not terribly good with technological things, so I think I'll leave all that in your capable hands, old son, you point me in the right direction and I'll just concentrate on doing the driving bit."

He smiled gently, "So here's to our team, *Sergeant* White."

White blushed with pleasure, and looked away, forwards to the snub nose, where the recessed gun ports of the four 20mm cannon were. "And the shooting bit, sir!"

Rose followed his gaze, and his eyes were hungry, remembering the *Luftwaffe* attacks and bombings he had experienced himself, both at RAF airfields and in the capital, "Ah yes, Chalky, of course, the shooting bit. I must say I'm rather looking forward to that!"

Chapter 5

James was waiting outside B-Flight's dispersal hut when they arrived, arms folded across his chest, pugnaciously puffing on a pipe, the stem firmly thrust between his teeth.

Rose was not allowed to smoke by a disapproving Molly, and now he gazed enviously at James' pipe, imagining what it would be like to smoke one...

"Back from practice, Rose? How did it go? Hm?" He looked shrewdly at the young sergeant, the youngster doing his best to merge quietly into the background. "And how did young, er, White do?"

"I think it went rather well, really, sir. The sergeant here did a good job of the interceptions, his patter was easy to follow, and I think he's definitely ready for operations. I'd like him as my operator, if that's OK?"

James looked visibly relieved, "Good show, alright then. I'll tell the Adj to sort out all the necessary. I'll include D-Dog on the operational roster from the day after tomorrow. We'll start your two days on operational duty then. In the meantime, lots more practice. Acceptable?"

"Perfectly, sir, thank you. We'll do some more practice flights later today and tomorrow."

James nodded in agreement, "Yes, I think that would be helpful. You seem to know how to handle a Beau, at least. It would be a good idea if you would carry out some dusk circuits and bumps just to make sure that you're comfortable with your Beau and your airborne awareness relative to Dimple Heath in the darkness, solo though, of course. I'd like you to carry out an air test later, and tomorrow afternoon as well. Make sure your kite's ready, yes? Have a chat with some of the lads on now so you get an idea how we organise and operate the two day duty period in conjunction with A' Flight. D-Dog will be allocated to you from now until the end of your tour." He removed his pipe from his mouth and looked into its glowing bowl.

"Thank you, sir. She's a lovely aeroplane."

"She's one of the squadron's better machines. You know how some fly sweeter than others. The last crew did quite well in her, and I thought with your experience, and a bit of luck, you might do the same."

He looked dubiously at White, "Uh, both of you, of course. Do your pilot proud, eh, White? Hm?" he jammed the pipe back into his mouth.

White, standing at ease, nodded respectfully but said nothing.

Rose held up a finger, feeling as if he were in class. "Sir, if I might I ask a question? I believe you have a blonde typist?"

James' teeth clenched dangerously on the pipe-stem. "What? Blonde typist? You mean Mandy? What do you mean? Why are you asking, man? I thought you were happily married?" James stared at him belligerently, chest puffed up in outrage.

"Might I ask a favour, sir? Could I possibly borrow her for half an hour?"

"What? What d'you mean, damn it? I don't approve of this sort of thing, Rose. I'm not sure that I can help you. I've a good mind to speak to your good lady. Borrow Mandy? You've got a bloody cheek!"

74

James tapped his pipe on the wall, and then emptied the contents into an empty cup. Not quite empty, as the dregs quenched the burning embers of tobacco with a slight hiss and a thin ribbon of smoke.

He waved the newly emptied pipe vaguely at Rose, "I can't believe the impertinence!"

Rose raised his palms in placation, "Oh, I'm sorry, sir, I don't think I made myself clear. My interest in, erm, Mandy, is purely platonic. I merely wanted to borrow her momentarily for her sewing skills. Sergeant White here is a little more accomplished with AI apparatus than with a needle and thread. I need to get his stripes sewn on properly, but I'm concerned that he may hurt himself, and I really need his fingers at their best if we're to fly practices and operations."

The confusion and indignation magically cleared from James's face. "Oh. I see. Hrmph! Well, if she would like to help when she's off duty, I see no reason why she can't. But not while she's on duty. She's not a seamstress, you know." He spoke to White, "Sergeant, you'll have to ask her yourself. I'm no bloody go-between. I've better things to do with my time!"

The young man looked as if he would faint with fear. "No, sir. Yes, sir. I'm sorry sir." White quavered.

"Yes, well…I'm sure she'll be glad to help. She's a nice girl, and a damn good typist, so keep your grubby paws off her, understood? She's no strumpet, damn it!"

Rose leapt to his operator's defence, "I'm sorry, sir. It was my idea to talk to Mandy. Chalky had no idea I was going to ask you."

James sighed long and hard. "No. No, no need to apologise. Chalky, hm? I'm here for a reason, actually. Ahem." James fidgeted with his pipe and sighed again, "It appears that there has been a bit of a bungle, Sergeant White, um, Chalky, and I must apologise to you. Confirmation of your promotion to Sergeant arrived some weeks ago, but it seems to have been overlooked somehow. It was actually young Mandy who found the message." James stared fixedly into the pipe's bowl and scraped at a dried shred, then looked back up at Rose.

"It had fallen behind a filing cabinet, you see. It seems that when the Adj brought you in, she decided to have a good check to see if there had been any communications regarding you. She bought me in the slip of paper not fifteen minutes ago."

He stuck the empty pipe back into his mouth, defiantly biting down on the stem with such force that Rose felt sure that the CO must crack a tooth on it.

"I thought it best to speak with you myself. It's unforgivable of course, and I must apologise. There's back pay and leave owing as well, so see the Adjutant or Mandy to sort out the paperwork, and erm, other stuff, alright?" James shifted his feet uncomfortably.

White smiled hesitantly; though his eyes still betrayed his anxiety, "Thank you, sir. It was good of you to tell me. I think I was fated to fly with Mr Rose here. If you don't mind, sir, I think I shall see Mandy about the papers a little later, and ask her to sew my tapes up when she gets the chance?"

James' voice was gruff. "Of course, um, Chalky. I'm sure she'll be glad to help. Well, must dash. See a man about a dog." He hesitated, then, "Welcome aboard and all that, eh?"

Looking mightily relieved and thankful to be able to go, James nodded companionably at them both and left.

"I'm terribly sorry, Chalky, didn't mean to drop you in it." Rose was mortified. "I really shouldn't have said anything. Sorry, chum."

White looked at him in surprise.

"Sorry, sir? What for? I owe you so much! I'm standing here with sergeant's stripes on my arm instead of sweeping out a hanger because of you."

76

He was silent for a moment, and then continued, his voice trembling, "I'm going to be the best operator this squadron has ever seen, and I'm going to do my best for you. You're already an ace, and I'm going to do all that I can possibly do to make you a night fighter ace as well, sir. Whatever you ask of me, I'll do gladly, I swear it. How can I ever thank you? For what you've done for me?"

Rose was taken aback and discomfited by the boy's impassioned outburst, and surprised by the burning intensity of feeling in the youngster's eyes.

He felt strange warmth prickling treacherously behind his own eyes and he blinked and cleared his throat. He couldn't think of anything to say in his embarrassment.

White rubbed his hands together to warm them, and his expression was thoughtful, "Actually, sir, I must say that it was really quite decent of the CO, to come and tell me what had happened in person, and to apologise. He could have sent someone else to do it instead."

He smiled suddenly, the naughty schoolboy inside appearing, "And best of all, I found out that lovely little blonde typist's name!"

Chapter 6

The Whitley bomber crew breathed a heart-felt sigh of relief as the darkened sprawl of Belgium's coast finally disappeared behind them, merging into the gloom, and praying hard that the starboard Merlin engine continued to run, albeit a little roughly.

It had picked up flak damage over Cologne, but the dear old kite stalwartly soldiered on.

"I'm heading back at low level, lads, but keep your eyes peeled for Jerry fighters." He spoke calmly, but the young Sergeant Pilot's heart was racing painfully hard.

Come on, love, keep doing what you're doing, you're doing it superbly.

He continued to mumble his refrain of reassurance beneath his breath, willing the Whitley to take his crew safely home.

She had already done so on seven separate earlier occasions, and (fingers crossed), she would do so again.

She always looked after them, and whatever anyone else might say, he knew that she could hear him and that she would do it again.

Come on, love. You're the best…

The navigator's voice over the intercom, "Fancy a coffee, skipper? How's she doing?"

"Yeah, good, mate. Just keep praying though. No coffee for me though, ta."

"A week's leave after this. I think we've bloody earned it this time."

"You're dead right there, skipper." The bomb aimer grimaced and bit his lip.

Poor choice of words.

The rear gunner, sitting alone and isolated from the other four members of the crew, in his turret at the end of the fuselage, piped up glumly. "Don't mind me, you rotten blighters. I'll just sit here quietly and freeze my bloody bollocks off."

The wireless operator, a Pilot Officer and the only officer in a crew of NCOs, tapped the navigator on his shoulder, "Here, give us the thermos, Ernie, pass it over, I'll go and give the old miseryguts a cup."

"No, John, don't worry, I'll do it. I need to go for a pee, so I might as well do it. Let me just get past you, cheers."

"Tubby, Ernie's on his way to you with a thermos. How does it look back there?"

Come on, keep going, girl.

"Can't see anything, Skip. We're a bit low, though; tell me if you decide to ditch. Be nice to have a bit of warning. Tell Ernie to get on with it, though, 'cause I think my meat and two veg have turned to ice."

"I'm sure the local girls will be grateful for small mercies," his pilot replied drily, a small smile cutting through tightly on his tense face, "But don't you worry, my old banana, I'll give you plenty of warning. I'll not leave you on your own."

"Thanks, Skip. How's she doing? Engine OK?"

I bloody well hope so. "Yes, chum. She's a beauty, and she'll not let us down."

The gunner grunted, "I dunno why you love this old bitch so

79

much, Skip. She's past her prime, but I have to say, she does seem to be a good 'un."

"For goodness sake! How many times do I have to say it, Tubby? Have a little respect for her. She's always done right by us. I don't like you flapping that sort of crap. And don't ever call her a bitch. How many times do I have to tell you? Call her by her name or not at all."

"Sorry, Skip, keep yer hair on. I'm really sorry. M-Millie it is." His gunner replied contritely.

"Apologise."

"Aw, Skipper…"

"I mean it!"

The gunner's voice was gruff, "Sorry Millie. Didn't mean it."

The pilot smiled and glanced mechanically at the engine temperature gauges again. Tubby was a very good gunner, the best, but he was such a miserable old bugger sometimes.

A kilometre to starboard, Rudi strained his eyes against the darkness.

"You must have the devil's own luck, *Herr Leutnant*. It's definitely a twin engine job. Medium bomber, I think. Droopy nose, twin tails. It might be a Dornier, sir! We need to get closer."

"My dear Herr Observer, do you note the thin line of smoke that comes from the engine of the aircraft? If it were a Dornier, it would it be heading the other way, would it not? Yet this damaged aircraft heads for England. Why should it do that were it not RAF?"

Rudi scratched his head and looked away. "Hmm. I see your point, *Herr Leutnant*."

"Brainless dolt," grunted Mouse.

Bruno grinned, "So less talk and more action, eh? And behind us? Anything, Mouse?"

"Nothing behind, *Herr Leutnant*, all clear."

As Tubby, the Whitley's semi-frozen rear gunner, turned to accept

80

the half-filled beaker of coffee, the Ju88C crept ever closer, concealed within the veil of night.

"So, Rudi, would you say that is a Dornier?"

Rudi shook his head. "No, *Herr Leutnant*, it's RAF. No doubts. I can see it now."

"And what can you see, my good Rudi?" Bruno von Ritter placed his fighter into position beneath and to one side of the ailing bomber.

"Um, Whitley, I think, sir."

Bruno took one last look, settled back to slip into position behind the enemy aircraft. "Stand by."

Yes, it was an Armstrong Whitworth Whitley alright, a medium bomber with a crew of five, droopy nosed in flight, a square long fuselage and two fins. Damaged, but still flying.

You bombed the Reich, but now revenge is coming for you... You may think you have escaped. And up until now, you had.

But only for a few more seconds...

The pilot squirmed in his seat. I need to take a pee, but it can wait. She was doing it; each uneasy second took them ever closer to home. Dearest Millie.

We may actually make it after all...

And then everything changed, and it all seemed to happen at once.

The Whitley shuddered and bucked as something tore loose in the engine, a sudden shower of sparks falling back from the starboard engine, then a thin tongue of flame licking back horribly from the wing. Suddenly he was fighting to hold the aircraft level.

"Cripes! Feathering the starboard engine." *Please, Millie, just for a few more minutes, please...*

And Bruno was pulling the heavy fighter into a hard turn, finger caressing the firing button lovingly, "Alert! *Firing...*"

The pilot of the Whitley flinched at the thunderous bellow from the rear turret, *"Fighter! FIGHTER! Turn to starboard!"*

The pilot almost groaned in despair. *No, no, no…*

And yet he was already dragging her into a skidding turn to starboard, exhausted muscles aching and straining, and she let him, the glorious, dreadfully wounded, beautiful aeroplane that she was…*Oh Millie…*

The cannon and machine guns in the Junker's nose spat vivid fire in a spreading fan that splattered across the Whitley from nose to tail, Bruno's hits sparkling bright on the bomber, and then in response there was an even brighter flash from the turret of the bomber, and Bruno felt the hits of .303 bullets against his Junkers.

Incensed, he turned back again and raked the Whitley again. *Schwein….*

The pilot of the Whitley painfully sucked in air through a mouth suddenly full of blood, and tried to speak. The cockpit was lit up by the flame from the burning engines, and already smoke was filling the space, making him choke. Hurt wracked him and he could feel the scream bubbling in his throat, and he clamped his teeth around it.

The guns in Millie's tail were silent, and he knew in the swelling anguish within his heart that Tubby was dead.

Dear dour, bucolic, womanising Tubby, blessed with incredibly skilful and artistic fingers which could convert a block of wood effortlessly into a little model aircraft in less than an hour, and a huge smile, rarely seen, which transformed his face whenever it materialised.

"Crew bail out, bail out…" It was an effort, but he managed to force the words, barely more than a whisper, out through his lips, his hands tightening on the controls.

Already he could feel his strength ebbing as another surge of overwhelming pain threatened to overcome his defences and claim him.

Got to hold her steady, give the boys a chance to get out…

"Bail out…" he cried, but it came out as a choking whisper, and the darkness was already crowding his mind.

Oh, God, it hurts so badly. His back felt as if it had been flayed, deeply laid open, as if it were on fire…

He was falling forwards, and with a superhuman effort he straightened his back jerkily, the stabbing pain coursing down dragging a whimper from his lips, wetting his cheeks.

And his heart was weeping too, for his beautiful Millie was burning, slowly disintegrating. She was dying.

But she was dying hard.

And despite it all, still she flew straight and level. Shattered and ripped, Millie continued to fly as the bomb aimer and the wireless operator jumped. The navigator paused, looking helplessly at the pilot through the smoke that filled the aircraft.

She was shaking now, her agony juddering viscerally, excruciatingly through his bones, the fuselage vibrating worse and worse as if in response to real pain, slowly coming apart, the icy blast of the airstream shrieking thinly through the cracked and holed windscreen.

But, incredibly, despite all the damage, she still continued to fly.

The Whitley pilot smiled sadly through pained eyes that were dimming fast at the stricken expression on his navigator's face.

"Ernie, go, get out…please," he gasped.

Behind the flying goggles, Ernie's eyes were filled with tears, and his pilot painfully turned away from him, exposing his torn and shattered back. He took one last long look, but his dear friend and skipper continued to face forward, and the vibration was worsening.

And then the navigator was gone, and the pilot was all alone on the Whitley, except of course for poor dear Tubby, lolling lifelessly behind him in the bullet-torn and devastated turret, his faithful companion in so many flights, and now sharing their very last flight together.

When the end came, Tubby would not be alone.

And even as the agony flayed his rapidly fading consciousness, a spark of pride glowed in what remained of him. Final memories of loved ones.

We did it! With a little luck, the boys should make it. I'm sorry, Mum and Dad, I'll not be coming home ever again. Thank you for all that you did for me. I love you so much.

Behind the goggles his eyes were streaming with tears as pain and overwhelming sorrow coursed unbearably though him.

His crew were safe, thank the Good Lord, and it was time. The young RAF pilot closed his eyes and opened his hands wide, releasing the controls.

Dearest Millie, thank you, I knew you could hear me, and you took care of us even when you've been ripped apart. You kept us alive.

Thank you. Dearest Millie…

Ernie the navigator swayed gently beneath his parachute, tears blurring his vision as he watched the sinking, downwardly curving comet that was his Whitley suddenly balloon brilliantly, absorbed in an eye-searing and angry expanding bubble of glaring light, as the fuel tanks in M-Millie finally blew her into oblivion.

He could not bear to look any longer as the glowing fragments of his friends and his aircraft gracefully twirled slowly downwards to the waiting sea, and he shut his eyes in pain and turned his face away, even though the sea was close.

I'll tell them, he promised, *I'll tell them everything, if I get back, no, when I get back, I'll tell them about how you held her steady to allow us to escape.*

I'll make sure they recognise your courage and your sacrifice. Your name will be remembered for ever more. You deserve a VC. And you'll get one if I have anything to do with it. God bless, Skipper. And you, Millie.

The three survivors were lucky; for they would shortly be picked up by a flotilla of Royal Navy Motor Gun Boats, hunting enemy shipping by night in the treacherously icy North Sea, fortuitously close to where they landed.

But the navigator would never forget the sight of Millie exploding, nor would he forget for as long as he lived the fleeting sight of the shadowy Junkers hurriedly turning away from them with a burning, smoking engine.

Tubby had drawn blood even as the stream of enemy bullets focussed and found him.

With a bit of luck, the Nazi bastards would end up in the drink as well, like their victim.

Bruno leaned against the wall of the debriefing room, trying to still the shaking in his hands.

So close. Painfully close. They almost had not made it back, and the landing had been a terrifyingly rough one.

As soon as they landed on the NNE-SSW runway and rolled to a stop on the large northern hardstanding at NJG2's Gilze-Rijen aerodrome, the Junkers was surrounded by fire support vehicles and the wing blanketed with foam, even though Bruno managed to successfully put out the fire on the flight back.

Their Ju88 had been immediately wheeled into the large northern hangar for repairs, the crew chief's long face a disapproving picture of gloom, whilst the crew were driven to the barracks for debriefing.

Rudi exhaled smoke forcefully through his nostrils and looked unseeingly at the shaking cigarette he held, "Well, we got him, boys."

Mouse stood with his back to them, hands in the pockets of his flying overalls, solid and unmoving. No trembling in that one.

"And he almost got us. Almost." He didn't turn. Must be used to facing the other way, Bruno thought with a spark of humour.

Mouse pulled gently on one ear. "That Tommy gunner was quick, fucking quick, a second or so more and he might have had us. Quick on the draw." He nodded to himself, "A proper gunner, a professional. He knew his business, that one. Almost a pity to kill him."

Fuck me, thought Rudi sourly, *he'll be crying into his coffee next.* He hawked and spat on the ground, wiped his mouth on his stained sleeve, "I'm not complaining." He stared unseeing at the splatter of mucus on the asphalt.

Bruno gazed at the oil stain on his boots, and with an effort, forced a rictus-like smile onto his frozen lips. He noticed the Intelligence Officer approaching, clutching his folder and pencils, and groaned inwardly.

"Ten victories now. They used to call those with ten kills an *Oberkanone*. Thank you, boys. I couldn't fly with anyone else." They were in double figures, now, but after the shaky flight back, he needed a break. It had been *too* close this time.

The IO smiled tentatively at them. Mouse returned his gaze darkly.

"You better not, *Herr Leutnant*, because I'll not get into any aeroplane unless you're behind the controls." Mouse continued to eye the Luftwaffe intelligence officer balefully. "Anyway, nowadays the correct term is *Experten*."

Bruno closed his eyes tiredly, "Good, decent Mouse, how could I trust another to guard my back when I have you?"

Rudi threw his cigarette stub to the ground, crushing it flat with one booted foot. "If you fly with anyone else, Sir, I'd kill the fuckers."

Bruno was surprised to see he was deadly serious. Rudi wiped his pale and stained face with a hand that refused to stop quivering.

"I need a big drink and a damned good fuck. Will you excuse

me, *Herr Leutnant*?" He glowered at Mouse, but the gunner said nothing.

Bruno nodded, "Of course, Rudi. I'll join you shortly. I could do with some *schnapps* myself. *Oberleutnant*, forgive me, is the debriefing complete? Have you finished with us?"

The Intelligence Officer shifted uncomfortably under Mouse's surly scowl, "I have all the details I need, *Leutnant*. I just wanted to applaud your victory. May I offer my congratulations?" He held out his hand. "Here's to the next one, eh?"

Bruno took it, conscious of the unsteadiness of his own limbs, and hoping the Intelligence Officer would not notice.

"Thank you, sir. Yes. Here's to the next one."

Chapter 7

"Well, my darling, you're back on ops again. I shan't ask you to be careful." Molly put down her cup of tea and placed her hand over his, squeezing it gently. Her words were spoken casually, but the rigid chill in her fingers betrayed her and told him of her fear.

Gently Rose placed his other hand over hers, feeling helpless and annoyed with himself that he caused her pain by his decision to return to the war.

Yet he knew there could have been no other choice. Who could stand idly by and watch as others fought? At least he was returning to the war with a decent young man alongside him to face the danger with.

Over the previous two days, Rose and White had flown many hours together, and formed a comfortable relationship that was rapidly turning into a friendship.

White was a quiet and deferential operator, and pleasant company on the ground. They worked well together and Rose was keen for his first interception, to put into practice what they knew and had learned together, to blood their partnership.

"Don't fret, Molly, I'll be careful, my sweetest, scout's honour. It's a sight safer than last year when we were flying in daylight. You know it's a lot harder to see the enemy and a lot harder for them to see us. It's a lot harder to see anything at all, to be honest. That's why I need Chalky, can't do it on my own, and at least we'll only be intercepting bombers, piecemeal, one by one."

He smiled at her tenderly, "There's no big massed formations for us to attack this time, my darling. No serried ranks of guns like some mobile fortress in the air. This time we'll creep up on the buggers, one at a time, hidden by the darkness. My D-Doggie's not quite as nippy as a Hurricane, but much better armed. She'll do nicely. Piece of cake." He said it reassuringly, voice gentle.

"Wanna give me a ride, mister?" she pouted her lips and fluttered her long dark lashes at him, even though her cheeks were colouring, eyes bright with unshed tears.

Molly was furious with herself, hating the fact that she was unable to remain composed and casual as her husband returned to the war.

He beamed and took both her hands in his, and like the rest of her, they were soft, slim, and a little warmer now.

"Any time that you ask, gorgeous. I'd love to take you up there. You know how often we do regular air-tests and practice interceptions, we could sneak you aboard. Show you the office."

"That would be so wonderful, my darling. I can't wait to take you up on the offer. I've always heard about your flying, I'd love to be flown around by you." She squeezed his fingers. "I'm always driving you around, be nice for you to return the favour and fly me about a bit."

Driving me around? At those insane speeds? Driving me around the fucking twist more like!

"Yes, my dearest." He replied meekly.

"I like Chalky, he seems a sweet boy." Rose introduced his new operator to Molly on the first day, when he took White to the HQ building for the formalities.

Mandy had been only too eager to sew on White's new stripes. Rose could not miss the shy way in which they looked at each other, and he was pleased for White.

"Yes, he's a nice lad, I like him too."

He picked a few of the brightly-coloured 'vitamin' tablets from the heaped bowl on the table and threw them to the back of his throat, before gulping down a mouthful of hot tea (*ouch!*) to chase them down.

"You're a sweetie, Harry, you like everybody. That's one of the reasons that I love you."

She leaned closer to him, "And the fact that you're thoughtful is another of the reasons. You *do* care about others. I heard about what you did from the Wing Commander. It was good of you to give Chalky a chance." She hesitated, trying not to let him see the doubt in her eyes. To say the words. "Jinx or no jinx."

He swallowed another handful with a grimace, but it felt as if one had lodged in his throat and he took another hasty mouthful of tea. Rose flinched as it burnt his throat.

"Oh Molly! He's not jinxed!" he croaked, "He's just been unlucky." *I hope I'm right, and what else could I do? Poor little sod. I couldn't just leave him in that agony…*

"Well, I'm not the only one who thinks he's sweet. I've spoken to Mandy, provided her with some helpful womanly advice, as you do, and apparently they're going to the pictures together at the next opportunity when they're both off duty."

She smirked at him, "that charming young man is a far faster worker than a certain timid young pilot officer I could mention."

"I was just a bit shy, that's all," Rose muttered grumpily, staring fixedly at the crumbs on the plate before him.

"Well, all I can say is that I'm actually rather pleased that you're not quite as shy as you used to be!"

90

Rose looked around anxiously to make sure no-one in the Officer's Mess could hear, but they were comfortably ensconced in a corner on their own, and no one was sitting nearby, and she laughed softly despite her inner unease at his return to combat.

"My darling man, do you remember the first time we met?"

He sighed with pleasure and nodded, "How could I forget? That was one of the greatest nights of my life."

Molly smiled fondly at the memory, and laughed softly, "That earnest look on your face, and the drivel you spouted! But even then, I knew there was something special about you."

"I knew you were special the instant I saw you, my love. I know I've said it before, but it's true. Who'd have thought then that I'd become a night flyer? I was prattling like a madman about clouds across the moon, now I'll be up there with the moon."

"I wish I could come up there with you, Harry."

"I know, my sweet and delicious flower, and I'd love to take you up there with me, take you to the moon and the stars and beyond if I could, but Chalky's champing at the bit, and he'll not give up his seat without a fight." He shrugged apologetically.

"Well, bully for him! If he wants a fight he might get one!" Molly's eyes widened glaringly and she bared her teeth, taking a mock-swipe at him with one clawed hand. She smiled, but showing rather more tooth than he was normally accustomed to.

Disconcerted, Rose leaned backwards slightly; just in case those fingernails came a little too close.

"Er, I don't think he's got much chance against you, my sweet little trinket. But he is a very highly trained operator, and, more importantly he's *my* very highly trained operator, and I'd much rather you didn't injure him too much, we've all got a war to fight, after all, and I'd like it very much if you were both in it on my side."

She flounced her hair and looked at him sideways, "Alright, naughty boy, I won't hurt him, but just you remember that when you're up there in the moonlight, all alone with that boy, I'm the one you love."

He grinned. "If it weren't against some darned regulation or other, I'd pull you across the table right this instant and plant a big slobbery kiss on your ridiculously beautiful mouth, you dazzling creature. Instead, it just so happens that I have something for you…"

Rose fumbled in his pocket and passed her a folded sheet of paper. She took it quizzically with raised eyebrows. "For me? What's this?"

"I wrote this yesterday, after we'd shared breakfast. Go on. Open it."

She took it from him. "Oh Harry, I've nothing for you!"

"I have your love, Molly, what else could I possibly want or need in the world?"

Carefully Molly unfolded the piece of paper. On it, Rose had written:

Between jug and cup, the bead of milk hangs suspended in that fleeting moment of time, expanded by recollections of you, a shining and perfect orb of white, shining brightly as if from within.

My cup of tea forgotten, in that instant I see only you, for reminiscent of that shimmering, faultless pearly droplet, you are perfection made real, excellence true, purity personified.

The shining whiteness reflects your inner purity, your luminous and virtuous heart, but in it I also see your outer exquisiteness, the perfect lines and curvature of your body's alabaster architecture.

My heart's princess, you are immaculate and praiseworthy, my only desire.

I allow myself stolen glimpses at your glory, as if caught from beyond the obverse of the mirror, within arm's reach,

*but impossibly distant, you are eternally desirable, o loveliest
of creatures.*

*Your grace caresses my eager eyes, quenching my thirst,
soothing my feverish heart, but leaving me ever incomplete,
wanting, unfulfilled and yearning, until you are once again
before me.*

Je t'aime, my Molly, Je t'adore.

"Oh Harry, it's charming!"

Phew. Not the best, but enough to please his love.

"You inspired me when you accidentally upset that jug of milk.
You looked scrumptious with that shocked look on your face, and
the droplet of milk hanging from the tip of your nose! I wanted to
laugh so badly! But then, you always look incredible."

Molly folded the paper up again and held it to her smiling lips.
"And where might flattery get you, you cheeky devil?"

"Yes, I know, I know. It'll get me nowhere. But I do wish I could
kiss you. I love you so much."

"And I you, my darling. I'll wave you off back to war with all my
love and wishes. Keep Genevieve close to you. She took care of you
before, and I pray that she continues to do so forever."

"I have her with me, and," he reached into his breast pocket and
pulled out a rather worn and dog-eared photograph, "And I have my
other good-luck charm, too!"

He held up the crumpled smoke-stained photograph, glancing
quickly at her picture.

Molly took the photograph from him, looked at it for a long
moment, a slight smile on her lips.

"Harry! You are such a silly sausage." She handed it back to him
and he carefully placed it back into his pocket.

"When I came to, floating down beneath my parachute, I was holding your picture. I must have snatched it up from the control console before my dear old Hurri blew. I don't know how I knew, and I couldn't see it, but I did."

Her voice was soft, "I know, my dearest, dearest love."

"You saved my life, Molly. I'm only here because of you. Else I'd be dead." He said simply. "You are the true source of good luck in my life."

She flushed self-consciously, but he could see she was pleased. "I didn't save you, my darling, The Almighty did, and for that I'm truly grateful. He saved you for me."

"Hullo, Hullo! Oh dear! Why the long faces? I'd have thought being married to the delectable Flight Officer here would leave a smile permanently etched onto your face, Flying Officer."

Being so immersed in their conversation, they had not noticed Rose's new flight commander, Squadron Leader Billy Barr DFC, walk up to them.

Rose stood and smiled, "Morning, my glorious leader. Didn't see you creep up."

Barr nodded amicably at them both. "Morning, chum. I'm on tonight with you, thought we'd head down to the dispersals together. I knew you'd be here canoodling with your missus. Sorry, Flight Officer, but I'm going have to abscond with your chap."

Molly smiled slightly at Barr, "Look after him for me, please, sir. Don't bend him; I quite like him the way he is, warts and all."

"I'll do my best, Molly." Barr grinned cheerfully, "'though I suspect that's easier said than done."

Rose scowled playfully, before darting forward and raising her hand to plant a hurried kiss on her fingertips.

"I'll see you soon, my beloved," he whispered. He was excited to be on his way, but did not want her to see that eagerness, did not want to add to her pain in this new phase of their life. Her lips moved to hide the stricken expression, not quite succeeding.

It was all there in her eyes, "Not soon enough for me, my beloved."

He could taste the oil from the fried bread on her fingers, and, oh, dear God! Was that marmalade? *Yuck!*

Rose groped in his pocket for his handkerchief to wipe his lips, but then stopped in mid-action.

What will Molly think? Her fingers weren't dirty. Don't wipe your mouth yet, old chap, wait until you get outside and she can't see you. Not very gallant wiping one's lips immediately after kissing a girl's hand.

Especially when the girl is one's missus.

He pushed the hanky back down into his pocket, and forced his oily, sticky lips into a smile.

Urgh, that marmalade was bitter. How could anyone eat such awful stuff?

"All my best wishes and love go with you, my heart, *ma bien-aimée*." Despite the brightness of her smile, Molly's eyes glistened lustrously. "*Je ressens un amour fou pour toi. J'appartiens à vous.*"

"*Et je suis à vous, très chers.*"

She watched him walk away, a young man so different from the one she'd first met and fallen in love with, yet somehow still unchanged and special, her heart sinking nauseatingly, but filled to brimming with pride and love and pain.

He was her man, the special man, her shining knight in armour, courageous and true and unyielding on himself, yet with the gentlest, kindest of hearts.

My beloved, my smiling and honourable hero. Oh, how I love you!

He felt her eyes on him. Harry Rose, trepidation and excitement warring in his heart, the taste of their parting and the breakfast marmalade horrid on his lips, but ashamed and humbled by the fear for him in her eyes.

At the door, he turned, and their eyes met for a moment, his stiff lips twisting into a smile that looked more like a grimace, and then he was gone, the door closing slowly into the empty space.

Molly picked up his still warm cup and held it between her hands, as if to keep him with her that little bit longer, placing her mouth gently against the rim, licking the smooth porcelain as if to catch the memory of his lips on it.

Her eyes unwillingly stole back to the closed door.

"I love you, wonderful man. May God bless you and keep you safe," she whispered.

Chapter 8

The B-Flight commander was a very tall, well-built man. A semi-professional footballer before the war, Barr had joined the RAFVR in 1936, learning to fly and the basics of night fighting the hard way, and a small scar on his cheek was the legacy of a dicey crash landing at night in a Boulton-Paul Defiant the previous year, rather than to any exploit on the field during his footballing past.

Like Rose, he too wore the ribbon of the DFC, a testament to having already successfully destroyed four German bombers at night. He was no virgin to combat, already a veteran.

"So, Flash, my old son, we've a full schedule of things to do before operations tonight, feeling keen?"

"I think we're about as ready as we can possibly get, and Chalky and I really would rather like to help add to the squadron's score." Rose told him dutifully.

Barr lit a cigarette. "Good man, the lads have told me that you two never stopped asking questions over the last couple of days. Apparently, the only way to get away from you was to hide in the ladies' loo." He blew a stream of eye-watering smoke at Rose.

Trying not to cough, Rose looked away. "Sorry, sir, we didn't mean to be a nuisance."

Barr chuckled, "Good heavens, I'm not complaining, old man. I'm pleased you made the effort to glean as much info and tips as you could. I think you two are as ready as you'll ever be, too. As you know, we'll all meet at dispersals first. It's a bit like school registration first thing in the morning."

"Right. Is it a discussion or a lecture this morning?"

"A general discussion about the events of our last two-day duty. As you might have heard, we got a couple of probables, but there were actually quite a few contacts, but they didn't turn into actual combats. We need to find out why we didn't do better. After that a chat on anything the crews want to talk about, then we'll check our kites after lunch. Preferably a spot of practice interceptions, and definitely an air test. Make sure your kite's tip top before you go up against Goering's boys. After you, Flash, old chap. Age before beauty and all that tosh."

With a last long pull on his cigarette, Barr stubbed it out against the side of their dispersals hut and flicked the stub expertly over his shoulder, turned, and pushed open the door for Rose, who murmured his thanks and entered.

Chalky was sitting shyly in a corner on a threadbare easy chair, next to Barr's operator, a Pilot Officer by the name of Trevor Dear, and he smiled in relief when he saw his pilot.

In addition to Rose and White, there were five other crews in B-Flight, Sergeants Williams and Heather in A-Able, Pilot Officer Herbert and Sergeant Trent in B-Baker, Flying Officers Barlow and Cole in C-Cindy, with Flight Lieutenants Clark and Jones in E-Emma.

Barr and Dear made up the sixth crew, in F-Flora.

Williams and Heather, the only NCO crew on the flight, had taken White under their wing and had ensured his acceptance in the Sergeant's Mess.

Williams rarely spoke, whilst conversely, Heather never seemed to stop, which was just as well, as he was the crew AI operator and needed to keep up a constant patter of directions during an intercept. It seemed to work, as they had already achieved four confirmed kills, with each of them also recently receiving DFMs.

Herbert had been an English teacher in Croydon before the war, whilst Trent worked as a trolley-bus conductor, the pair arriving at Dimple Heath a month earlier. They had been quite busy so far, having managed to score a confirmed kill, one probable, and four damaged. Herbert was always writing, making notes endlessly at dispersals, his intentions to write a book of his wartime air force experiences.

Barlow and Cole were an inseparable double act. They spent all their time together, on and off duty, and were quite well known throughout the airfield for the part they played in entertainment shows whenever ENSA (the Entertainments National Service Association, or more popularly known as 'Every Night Something Awful') visited Dimple Heath.

It was generally agreed (at least by Barlow and Cole) that the best part of any show was invariably one of their numbers. In addition to their vocal accomplishments, the pair had accounted for a pair of Dorniers and one Heinkel.

Clark and Jones were real night war veterans, having already completed almost ten months of night fighting, beginning in Blenheim fighters together, dabbling with Boulton-Paul Defiants, and then converting onto the first of the newly-introduced Beaufighters.

The pair had an enviable record of nine confirmed, three probables, and five damaged, and each of them had already earned a DFC, a DFM, and a MiD.

Both welcomed Rose genially, and recognised him as a fellow veteran of air combat, seeing mirrored in his eyes and face the same lines and grim resolve that existed on theirs.

To Rose, their faces bore the utter fatigue and grim determination worn by his friends during the height of The Battle.

Squadron Leader Barr and Trevor Dear were the senior crew in B-Flight. Like Barr, Dear was a regular, beginning the war as a corporal gunner, serving in both Blenheims and Defiants, flying both by day and by night, claimed a Heinkel bomber in daylight, and then shared in the destruction of four more bombers whilst flying with Barr. Along the way, he had been commissioned and earned himself a very well deserved DFM.

Rose sauntered to the tea urn, and turned enquiringly to White. "Fancy a cuppa, Chalky?"

"Yes please, sir." White stood, but Rose waved him back down.

"I'll bring it over, milk, no sugar?"

"Lovely. I'm sweet enough already, sir," the automatic response, pale face showing his anxiety despite his best attempts to conceal it.

"Yes, well, I'll need to ask Mandy about that, shan't I?"

White blushed deeply. He was understandably a little overwhelmed by the members of B-Flight, but was proud to be flying with Rose.

On their first day together, the youngster stared with unconcealed awe at Rose's impressive row of medal ribbons, and had then secretly made a promise to himself that before long, he would do everything he could to ensure that Rose's DFC ribbon was adorned with the gilt rosette of a second award.

He would ensure in his mantle of restored honour that he did everything within his power to see that Rose's position and honour was enhanced further.

For Rose had taken a chance on him when no one else would. White would now do his absolute utmost to see that kindness and trust rewarded handsomely.

Together, they would stand united with others as one in the defence of Britain.

'Corky' Clark and 'Toffee' Jones were the most helpful in terms of imparting experience and wisdom to the young Flying Officer and his young ex-skivvy AI operator.

The veteran pair had been in it from the very start, beginning their night fighting as sergeants on the outmoded Mark 1 Blenheim fighters, creaking up into the freezing skies night after night, searching the night skies over London and the Home Counties, their first kill coming on the darkest of nights when they suddenly popped out of cloud to surprise a Dornier.

The surprise had almost been on them as they emerged below and a hundred yards to the front of the slim pencil-thin bomber.

In the end it was the individual reaction time of the crews that made all the difference between life and death, with Jones just cranking up his aged Vickers K gun in the upper turret and pressing the trigger almost in reflex, automatically emptying the entire sixty round drum of .303 bullets into the nose of the bomber, leaving the shocked enemy crew dead and dying in a peppered cockpit following that fearful and vicious three second burst of fire.

With a dead pilot at the controls, the Dornier first reared up, and had then fallen into an uncontrolled yaw that quickly ended as the bomber, together with its bombload and crew smacked explosively into Hackney Marshes.

Clark and Jones were immediately promoted to Flight-Sergeants that very night, and also each received a deserved Mention in Despatches.

The job continued, a spell on Boulton-Paul Defiants, before being introduced to the wonderful magic of the new and secret Airborne

Interception AI sets that were being introduced, exchanging their battered, straining Defiants for the new Beaufighters.

In the following months eight more, hard-earned, confirmed kills had followed, as well as the ranks of Flight Lieutenant, and a Distinguished Flying Medal, followed by a Distinguished Flying Cross for them both.

But the long months of night fighting had been hard on them, their lined, drained faces and haunted eyes showed that they had done more than their fair share. With a little luck, they'd soon be rested, for a tour on night fighters was reckoned differently from those on bombers.

The average bomber tour of operations usually amounted to thirty, whereas a night fighter crew, flying only over friendly territory (for fear of the AI system falling into the hands of the enemy), in what was considered as a less risky role relative to flying over enemy territory, had to fly many more operational flights, and Clark and Jones had already successfully completed over a hundred operational trips.

Jones smiled gently at an anxious White. "I was an air gunner, originally. 'Joined up in '36 when old Adolf first got that angry bristle in his moustache and up his hairy arse. Started on Hawker Harts, classy kites, they were, and then we converted onto the dear ol' Blenheim."

"In fact, the first operational AI's were fitted to the Blenheim, and we were retrained on the job, so to speak by a group of instructors we called 'magician's', because they seemed to gaze into these two scopes much like the crystal ball gazers down Southend pier. It wasn't easy at the start trying to understand what showed on the scopes. We had so much difficulty trying to make sense of what we could see that we were all offered the chance of a transfer to another command as gunners, and some of my chums had had enough, and they left."

Jones took a sip from his cup and tapped his cigarette ash into the saucer beside him. "But not me. I'd been flying with Corkie here for

102

some time, and I knew he needed someone to look after him, poor old sod, so I stayed. Best thing I ever did."

Clark smiled wearily, "For both of us, Toffee." He'd given Jones the sobriquet 'Toffee' instead of the much more common 'Taffy' because: 'He's one of a kind, and if he ever got his guns trained on you, they'd stick like toffee. And surprisingly enough, considering his ugly mug, the girls seem to think he's quite sweet."

"Yeah, we've done OK, haven't we?" another sip, another flick of the ash, "You should have seen our first interceptions in Blenheims, kept flying around for hours with little to show, saw a Hun twice only. First time we weren't fast enough, and he just slipped through our fingers, because we just couldn't match him for speed."

He shook his head at the memory. "The second time we seemed to be doing some impossible speed as we caught up with him, but it turned out that we were coming at him almost head on, and he was past us like a blur. No chance of catching him."

Clark nodded solemnly, "Don't even know what type he was, he was gone so quick. I turned after him immediately, but the Blenheim is no fighter, whatever anyone says, and by the time we were heading the right way the bugger had dived away and gone. I guess we were lucky he didn't hit us."

Thinking back to his collision with the Bf109 the previous year, Rose could not agree more. He'd been incredibly lucky to survive that one.

"They taught us about that in training. I guess they learnt a lot from the experiences you chaps have had." White agreed quietly.

"Yes, they did, but the controllers can give you a lot more information from the ground as well, now, so if you lose it during an interception, you can often ask for help from the GCI people. Chances are a lot better now than they were six months ago. We had a lot less help before. "

"Then, when we converted onto the new Beaufighters, it was like the game had changed, and I still reckon they'd tweaked some of the AI stuff, too, because suddenly we were faster and the sets seemed so much clearer. It was pretty hectic because we were training and operations were still taking place, both at the same time. And then that 604 flight commander, Cunningham, got a Junkers in November. You know, the one who's famous in all the papers for the carrots he eats and his so-called Cat's Eyes, all bollocks, of course. The truth is that he's not only a phenomenal pilot but a damned good shot too. And his operator, Jimmy Rawnsley, is an ace with the AI. Carrots have got fuck-all to do with it, believe me, but you can't tell the public that, 'cause then Jerry'll suspect we're using something more, and if they look harder, they'll maybe find out we're using AI. Can't have that, can we?"

He yawned and rubbed his eyes tiredly. "Well, after that, it was as if we'd broken through some barrier, because the squadrons started to get kills, even a mediocre pilot could intercept and find a Hun in the darkness if he persevered." Jones waved at Clark, "he's an excellent example of that."

"Fuck off, Toffee," replied Clark good-naturedly.

"It's strange," Rose said, "When we first got to fly the Beau, we were a bit apprehensive, there were stories that the aircraft was a real beast to fly, and we actually lost a pilot in training."

A laughing boy from Liverpool with a fanatical love of motorcycle racing, dead in an unguarded instant.

Gone but not forgotten. At least not by his friends or his loved ones.

Clark's face was grim. "The Beau is no monster. She's not the easiest kite to fly, I'll give you that, and you need to keep an eye on things and watch out for the swing, but balance the throttles, manage the torque, treat her with a bit of care, respect her, and she's a beauty. I think the Air Ministry needs to look at the training program."

Toffee looked at his pilot glumly, "And at some of the instructors." He did not elaborate further.

Clark nodded. "Last year wasn't one I'd care to repeat in a hurry. We had some of your lot here, day jobs, and every evening there were fewer and fewer of them. I once sat down next to one at breakfast, a Hurricane pilot just like yourself, Flash. We'd had a bit of a rough night, so I was a going to have a pop at him, but when I turned to him all I could see was someone who look as if he'd died and been mummified for about a hundred years or so. He was all in, sleeping at the table, dead to the world."

He grimaced, "Sorry, terrible description. At least with us, it was only our own AA that was shooting at us. We weren't able to find Jerry in the darkness."

He picked at a tooth with one fingernail, looked at it, and then wiped it on his trouser leg, "The day jobs based here at the time weren't keen on our landings and take-offs because of the landing lights. After all they were going through in the daytime, we were showing Jerry where they could lob a bomb or two at night."

"Yeah," Toffee's eyes took on a faraway look. "They kept on going up, and kept on dying. They must have been shit scared, but they just kept on going. And all the time there was this dread eating away at me. I was so terrified that we were fighting and dying for nothing, that we'd not be able to stop the invasion."

Rose was surprised and reassured to hear that others, like him, had shared the insidious fear of defeat. It wasn't something one talked about easily.

Or even openly, for that matter.

Toffee smiled warmly, "I'm glad that you've joined us, mate." He turned his smile on White, "You an' all, Chalky, old lad."

Clark barked out a laugh suddenly and they looked at him in

surprise, "When we got the new Beaus it wasn't just the aircrews that felt the change, the groundcrews were a bit overwhelmed as well, and as for the WAAFs!"

He shook his head, "You know little Maisie, the stores clerk, used to be the driver for the crew bus? She used to love standing near a Blenheim when the engines were being tested, something about the way it made her feel as if she were flying?"

Dear and Barr, reclining comfortably beneath a miasma of cigarette smoke, guffawed together at the memory.

Rose tilted his head to one side in interest, "So, what happened?"

"She tried it wth a Beau, and of course it's a different kettle of fish with those Hercules engines. So there she is, hanging on for dear life to the rudder with both hands, hat, shoes, and hairclips gone, hair about to go the same way, and then, before you can say 'Blow me down,' the next moment the slipstream's caught her, pulled her off, and there she is, actually cartwheeling arse over tit, if you'll pardon the expression, through the air, skirt flapping around her shoulders like some weird parachute, legs kicking (nice smooth legs they were, too), and I swear she must have achieved an altitude of fifteen feet before she came back down to terra firma! She's lucky not to have broken something! The groundcrews there said she'd earned her wings so we nicked an 'AG' flying badge from Foster on A-Flight and we had an impromptu ceremony."

Rose chuckled, "No! I don't believe it! Was she OK?"

"She was alright, thank goodness, just a little shaken," Jones lowered his voice, "I was there, so I saw the whole thing, and let me tell you, that was one hell of a blast she was riding because I think it blew her drawers and stockings right off as well, and I should know, because I got quite an eyeful! Gave me quite a shock, I can tell you!"

There was laughter and a chorus of shouts, "Fibber!" "Line-shooter!" and "I don't believe it!"

Jones looked annoyed with himself, and lowered his voice conspiratorially.

"Look, I shouldn't have mentioned it, dunno why I did now, so please don't tell anyone about it, lads, because she shouldn't have been there, and if she gets found out she could be up on a charge, endangering RAF property or some such bollocks. Besides, she's mortified about the whole experience, that's why she stopped driving the crew bus. Couldn't face us every day after something like that. She knew I'd seen her lovely juicy pink bits, and she still blushes when she sees me. If she knew that you know about it, she'd be horrified, she'd really hate it, so please, please don't say anything. OK?"

Rose tried to dispel the image from his mind, feeling embarrassed on behalf of the cheerful young WAAF.

Jones looked around beseechingly, "Just keep it under your hats, fellas, OK? Please?"

Barr nodded, "Don't worry, Toffee, everything remains here, we won't breathe a word, right chaps?" he looked around sternly.

They all nodded, eyes averted, and quietly murmured their acknowledgement and agreement.

Barr looked at Jones censoriously, "Just don't repeat the story again, OK, Toffee? She deserves better."

Maisie was a nice girl, and very popular on the station. No-one on B-Flight would ever embarrass the pretty young airwoman.

Barr breathed out a long stream of cigarette smoke, and settled back with a satisfied sigh, "Good, that's settled, then. More tea, anyone?"

Chapter 9

Rose awoke with a jerk from his restive drowsing, heart clamouring and tongue plastered to his palate, as the telephone in B-Flight's hut rung jarringly. His hand struck the empty mug at his side and knocked it to the floor.

The mug made its landing with a dull *thunk!* But thankfully, it did not break. It did, however, make White jump, the youngster looking like some strangely futuristic half-human hybrid feature dressed in heavy flying kit and with his eyes hidden behind dark goggles.

They turned blearily to look expectantly at the operations NCO. With his own set of night goggles on, it was difficult for Rose to see that worthy seated in the shadowed gloom at the operations desk.

"There'll be some sandwiches coming shortly, gentlemen." The duty sergeant cautiously replaced the receiver amidst a volley of catcalls and shouts.

Barlow began to sing softly along to the music playing gently from the wireless. Barr and Clarke were already in the air, and being third crew on the roster, Rose was eager to get up there and begin his second operational tour.

"Sir?" White's voice was deferential.

Rose turned to him. "Yes Chalky?"

"What do you think of good luck charms?"

"I had a friend who kept a penny coin sewn into his hanky. He kept it in his underpants and would never fly without it. Seemed to work for him."

"Do you have one?"

Rose grinned, fondly remembering the day the girl had given him the little teddy bear.

"Actually, yes, I do carry one myself."

"Do you believe in it?"

"Yes," he said simply, and involuntarily placed a hand over the bump in his flying suit. He'd never dream of flying without Genevieve. "I'll bet all the others have one, too."

"Does it work, do you think?"

"Well, I'm still here, aren't I?" *Don't tempt fate, you silly sod…*

"I asked, sir, because, erm, Mandy gave me something to help keep me safe."

"Oh?"

In reply, White reached into the large map pocket on the left side of his Sidcot suit. "Don't laugh, sir, but she gave this to me," he held up his hand, and Rose saw that he was holding a little furry stuffed toy, a zebra.

Molly, you clever little thing! So that's what you meant when you said you'd given Mandy some advice. "Hm, looks like she's taken a shine to you, chum!"

White cautiously tucked the little toy animal back into his pocket and then smiled blissfully, "She's wonderful, sir. She's so kind and – "

The scramble bell jangled, making them jump again, and the NCO leapt up from behind his desk, "Flying Officer Rose and Sergeant White in D-Dog, scramble, scramble!"

White was a blur, leaping up like a greyhound from its traps, and was at the door and gone while Rose was still heaving himself out of the sagging armchair, cursing as he fought to free himself.

He almost lost his balance and stumbled, banging into the table and coffee slopped onto the floor, muttering an apology, he lumbered past it and somehow cleared the door frame to plunge into the darkness of the airfield outside, the good-natured raspberries and hoots of his friends chasing after him.

Already he could hear the crackle and grumble as the groundcrew started Dog's engines.

Luckily he knew exactly where D-Dog was parked and he ran as fast as was possible in the blackout, but, when he almost tripped over some unidentifiable object in his path, he remembered he was still wearing his goggles, and lifted them from his eyes and covered the remaining distance quicker, with one hand protectively over his right eye and finding his way to D-Dog with his left.

Cripes! It's hard enough just getting to D-Doggie in the darkness! Hope its better when we actually get up there!

It was important to preserve his night vision, but in the end he gave up and uncovered his right eye as well. It was dark enough outside not to impair his carefully protected night vision.

At last he was scrambling up the ladder and onwards into his dimly lit cockpit. The weak red light did nothing to interfere with his night vision, yet was just enough to his prepared eyes to illuminate the cockpit and controls sufficiently well.

Behind him, Rose could hear White settling down in his own compartment, and, as he prepared himself, he checked the controls once more.

You can never be too careful. He could almost hear Granny's voice and he smiled with fondness despite the tension taut in his belly.

Thank goodness the controls were arranged so sensibly and well.

So unlike the semi-chaotic arrangement found in the Blenheims on which he'd trained.

OK, wriggle onto the seat, stop that metal clip digging into your bum, get into a comfortable position and quickly run through the check-list...

Engine readings and instrument settings normal?

Instrument lighting and gunsight dim enough?

Control surfaces?

Yes.

Outside, the powerful engines snarled and bellowed their bellicose refrain reassuringly, seemingly eager to get into the hunt like leashed hounds.

Fifteen minutes later D-Dog was thundering powerfully upwards through the darkness to achieve the fifteen thousand feet of altitude required of them.

It was preferable to begin an interception with altitude in hand to allow them to have the advantage of height in an interception, and the extra speed available in a dive might prove useful if needed.

Ninety seconds behind them, Williams and Heather would form the other element of their Beaufighter patrol pair.

Instrument flying was the only safe and reliable method in minimal or nil visibility, and Rose concentrated on the controls before him, only occasionally glancing forwards and to each side out of the cockpit.

It was so dark outside that there was little to see. Despite all the training, it still felt strange to concentrate on the inside of the cockpit after all the importance Granny had attached of constantly checking the sky outside with the Mark 1 eyeball.

It was time to call Sector Control, "Hello Cowshed, Dagger 3 to Cowshed, what instructions?"

"Hello, Dagger 3, vector zero-nine-zero, what are your angels?"

"Dagger 3 to Cowshed, steering zero-nine-zero and climbing, presently Angels ten."

"Dagger 3, climb to Angels fifteen."

"Understood, Cowshed, Angels fifteen." The curling tendrils of excitement and fear gently clutched his heart and he forced himself to slow his breathing.

And strangely enough, for the first time in days, his leg was aching.

The speeding fighter rapidly gained height, achieving their target height within what seemed like record time. Control would have them on the screens now, but it was time to confirm they had achieved altitude.

Better just check again on White in the back first, though, "Chalky, are you still connected up OK? Check your oxygen flow, please. Make sure your tubes are clear, pal."

White answered buoyantly over the intercom, "Yes, sir, connected and working. No problems." His tone seemed to be saying, *of course*.

OK, sorry I asked. "Good man. Ready for a scrap?"

"Yes sir!" the young voice positively brimmed with confidence and enthusiasm.

Rose switched to the R/T.

"Hello Cowshed, Dagger 3 holding at altitude angels fifteen, steering zero-nine-zero, please advise further." He looked out of the windscreen. It was clearer at this altitude, with patchy cloud cover scattered between fifteen and twenty thousand feet.

To the south, he could see the outline of the coast through a gap in the low cloud, and a blacked-out Clacton-on-Sea. It felt wonderful holding the vibrating control column in his gauntleted hands, feeling the power of the aeroplane course through him, knowing the firepower that was available to him.

"Cowshed to Dagger 3, please hold in circuit around Dumpling. Please advise Lamplight Controller that you are in position."

Ah, so they were to orbit at fifteen thousand feet in a wide circle, keeping the Colchester beacon five kilometres to port.

"Thank you, Cowshed, understood." Rose contacted the Ground Control Intercept (GCI) Controller, code name Lamplight, advising him that they were in position.

"Dagger 3 to Lamplight, in position angels fifteen orbiting Dumpling, and awaiting directions."

"Thank you, Dagger 3, understood, standby, please." The GCI controller could only direct one interception at a time, and he was involved in one already.

They would have to patiently wait their turn, but it was unlikely their wait would be long.

Rose reached for his communications box again, and switched to intercom, "Control are keeping us on hold for a mo', Chalky."

"I'm ready, sir. I can hear you both clearly."

"Good, shouldn't be too long, chum."

As they circled, his eyes continued to scan the controls, trying to stay calm. They were possibly only minutes from their first combat together, and now they would find out if the training had been enough.

I hope Chalky is ready. But, more importantly, perhaps I ought to be asking myself if I am?

That poisonous little murmur of self-doubt again. But it was too late to be asking questions now.

Well, we'll find out the answers soon enough, old son. Any moment now…

It was time to take the fight to those murdering bastards.

"Lamplight to Dagger 3."

"Dagger 3 to Lamplight, receiving." His pounding heart began to race again, and his throat started to tighten.

Oh, fuck. Here we go…

"Please vector one-three-five, what angels?"

"Lamplight, be advised Dagger 3 at angels fifteen, steering one-three-five true."

"Maintain course, Dagger 3, we have some trade for you."

The blood pounded in his ears, and he fought to breathe normally as excitement raced through his body. "Good-oh! Maintaining course and awaiting further instructions."

Calm, stay calm.

"OK, Chalky, hear that? Keep your peepers peeled on The Thing, but keep an eye on the sky behind us, too." White was well briefed to keep an occasional eye on the airspace behind them. Rose felt better knowing he had a set of eyes occasionally checking what was happening to the rear of them.

Rose appreciated that the chance of being attacked from astern was minimal, visibility being what it was without an AI, but old habits die hard and he felt more comfortable knowing their vulnerable backside was being monitored.

"OK, sir."

"Dagger 3, vector two-one-zero, incoming bandit, below you. Flash your weapon, please."

"Understood, Lamplight, proceeding on two-one-zero. Flashing weapon."

Rose turned the Beaufighter onto the new heading, pushing her into a shallow dive, opening the throttles, so that the aeroplane sped eagerly downwards at over three hundred miles per hour, racing towards her destiny, and the bucking vibration of the airframe pulsing through him, dampened within his bones.

"Anything, Chalky?"

"Nothing yet, sir."

"Right-oh." He licked a bead of sweat from above his lips, and took another deep, sickly sweet breath of oxygen through his facemask. His face was wet but he daren't undo the mask to wipe it.

They continued careering powerfully downwards, Rose's eyes anxiously flicking from instruments to the enamelled night outside, the controller's voice crackling in his headphones, whilst behind him in the back, White eagerly pressed his face to the rubber visor protecting the cathode ray tubes of the AI, desperate for the first sign of their prey.

But still nothing showed on the scope, and tendrils of doubt began to surface.

After a few more minutes, which felt like rather a lot longer to both of them, there was still nothing, and Rose decided that a little more help would be useful. He called once more to the controller.

"Dagger 3 to Lamplight-"

"Contact!" Suddenly, White shouted from behind him, "Level out, turn gently to starboard by, um, twenty degrees."

A surge of electricity surged painfully through his body, and a thrill of excitement followed rapidly after it, the hunt was on!

"Dagger 3 to Lamplight, we have contact, will advise shortly."

"Understood, Dagger 3, good hunting." Then, more softly, "and here's hoping!"

"Where is it, Chalky?"

"Range about two miles, closing, maintain height, and turn ten degrees to starboard." Strained but calm.

Good lad.

Rose eased back slightly on the throttles, smoothly slowing the speeding fighter.

"Turn five degrees port, sir, maintain height, closing, range now one and a half miles."

His temples throbbed, "OK, Chalky, hang on to him, chum!"

Another moment, then, "Range still coming down, about one mile, maintain height and heading. Keep going as you are."

"OK, thanks." A quick check of the controls, check the reflector gunsight, dim enough but not too dim? Safeties off? Yes, good. Dear old Doggie was hurtling along at a good rate of knots.

"Range 2,500 feet. See anything yet, sir?"

Rose took another deep breath of oxygen, and felt the anxiety gnawing at him. "No, Chalky, damn it! I'm sorry, but –"

Wait! What was that? For a moment he thought he had seen movement against the lighter patch of cloud. He stared to one side of where he thought he'd seen the unknown something.

Use your peripheral vision, Barr had said, and gulp plenty of oxygen, get as much of it as you can into your bloodstream, and from there into your eyes.

Don't strain, let it call out to you.

The Beaufighter trembled imperceptibly, then began to shake endlessly, and Rose realised that they were now being buffeted by the slipstream of something flying ahead of them.

Dear Lord, they must be close!

"Sir? Contact is climbing, course unchanged, range now closed to 2,000 feet."

Yes! Good Lord! There *was* something! Before and a little above him, a vague, barely discernible shadow had appeared out of the darkness, twinned tiny pairs of blue flame, unearthly, faintly glowing pinpoints from the invisible exhausts of a still-invisible bomber, *ease back on the throttles, watch your distance…*

As if by magic, the enemy's outline suddenly began to materialise

116

from out of the blackness. One minute just a shadow, barely visible, and now more distinct.

It was a shape which was more visible, though, when he looked to one side of the amorphous blob.

Bloody hell! The blood thundered in his temples.

"Chalky! Have a squint outside. Ahead and above, tell me what you can see?"

White swivelled in his seat to look ahead. "Blimey! That's a bit close! Twin engine, single vertical tailfin, looks a bit chubby. I'd say it was a Heinkel, a Heinkel 111?" White's hesitant voice was filled with wonder and excitement, and quite possibly more than a trace of fright.

Or was Rose imagining it?

The enemy bomber continued to fly sedately before them. It was quite clear in profile now, and he wondered at the lack of reaction from the *Luftwaffe* aeroplane.

Surely, they must see the Beaufighter trailing them?

The hated enemy, and the first enemy plane he'd been so close to for many months! It felt strange to be flying so close to it, in close formation with an enemy bomber, without shooting it up, or getting shot up in turn.

They hadn't been seen yet, but that could change at any moment.

His heart was hammering madly like a kettle drum and white flecks danced before his eyes.

Rose licked his tight lips with a tongue that suddenly felt like cracked leather.

White spoke hesitantly, "I still have him on the scope, I'll stay in contact…" Rose could almost hear his thoughts, "*Well come on then, what are you waiting for? Get on with it!*"

Without realising it, he was automatically easing the fighter

117

into an optimal firing position, adjusting the controls carefully.

Rose nodded, eyes on the looming bomber, even though White could not see it.

"I agree with you, pal. It's a Heinkel 111 alright. Hold on to your hat, I'm going to give it a burst. Just look away or shield your eyes in case of flash or an explosion; I'll need 'em in a moment. Keep an eye on him in the set, just in case I lose him."

Line up on the chosen aiming point, throttle back just a touch, put the gunsight equidistant between those faint exhaust flames, don't look at the enemy directly, easier to see using indirect vision, allow for deflection, here goes…

Still no response from the enemy.

Stop thinking. *Finish it.*

"Firing…"

In response to his pressure on the gun button, the four cannons and six machine guns thumped and rattled with a deafening, shocking thunder, the airframe vibrating madly and the pungent, choking odour of smoke and cordite thick in his nostrils and clogging his windpipe. He choked, and dust swirled around him. It would be a great deal noisier in the back for poor White.

At the moment of firing, Rose involuntarily closed his eyes for a second but now he opened them, the limited flash from his guns hardly affecting the view ahead.

There was no tracer in that storm of flying lead, thereby protecting his night vision.

Thank God he had bags of previous combat experience in deflection shooting; with this darkness the whole business was a lot more complex and confusing, the target only half-seen, dancing wildly in the gunsight when he fired the guns.

He fired a full two second burst, pushing the nose slightly down gently, to counter for the recoil and to create a vertical three-degree fanning arc of gunfire.

Points of light flashed on the dancing image in front of him, was that the enemy gunner firing back at them?

Or were the sparkling flashes the result of his strikes on the enemy bomber? The darkness made it so much more difficult to see the effects, but it must be the latter, because no line of tracer lanced out at them.

This would take some getting used to.

But only if fate allows you the chance to do so, my old son…

The Beaufighter was roughly buffeted and swaying in the Heinkel's slipstream, gunfire spraying out with Rose grimly holding course, fighting to hold her pugnacious little nose on target and retain his aiming point as he pumped destruction at the enemy.

And then he lifted his thumb and the hammering, thumping guns fell silent.

Rose took a deep breath of the sweet oxygen and frowned out to see the effect of his guns,

"Break hard to port! Break! BREAK!"

A desperate scream from White, high pitched and bursting with fear, shocking Rose into an instant and automatic manoeuvre that dragged the sluggish Beaufighter into a sudden skidding, climbing turn, the controls seeming to resist him.

He gasped with effort, and his vision blurred, greyed, and then there was the irregular clattering of torn fragments of shredded metal from the Heinkel against the skin of the Beaufighter.

They'd hit it, at least!

And better still, it hadn't hit *them*. Or, at least, not with return fire.

He could hear White gasping and grunting over the intercom, "Chalky! Are you OK? What did you see?" Rose croaked drily.

Reassuringly, both Hercules engines continued to run smoothly, there were no abnormal vibrations in the airframe, and the instruments did not cry out doom-laden warnings of impending danger or damage.

As soon as the Beaufighter's guns stopped firing the Heinkel had suddenly slowed drastically, whilst also beginning to climb and turn to starboard.

With the distance between them rapidly shrinking, and the enemy bomber suddenly looming huge out of the darkness before them, White had foreseen the risk that they were going to run right into the enemy bomber, urgently, frantically calling the turn away, even as a catastrophic collision seemed imminent and unavoidable.

Rose's speedy response being not a moment too soon, and had been almost too late.

"Cripes, luvaduck!" White let out a big *whoosh* of exhaled breath nervously, "I was sure we were going to crash into him, sir; I think you must have hit him!"

"I've lost sight of him, chum, can you see the blighter?" Rose took another deep breath of oxygen. Was it him shuddering or was it the Beaufighter?

Had they themselves been damaged?

Worry gnawed at him again.

Rose fancied that White's voice was thin with strain. "Keep turning, sir, I've still got him on The Thing, heading two-nine-five, losing height."

"Two-nine-five, OK"

A moment, then, "Oh! Hallo! I just checked our tail, sir, and I think I can see a parachute just a bit behind us, sir. I think you must have hit him pretty hard if one of them baled out!"

Blood drubbing in his temples. "Turning two-nine-five, but, more important, are you OK, Chalky?"

"Right as rain, sir, thank you. It's quite fun, this, isn't it?" White chirped brightly.

Rose blinked. His heart was still hammering painfully, his throat and chest tight, and his shoulders ached abominably.

Fun? FUN?

Bloody hell! "Mm, it certainly is an experience." He turned his head to look along White's directions.

Couldn't see a blessed thing. Not a bobbin.

"Range?" he asked casually.

"Two miles, closing slightly, lose a spot of height, sir."

Put her into a shallow dive once more, push forward the throttles a touch, check the instruments yet again, peer out beyond the bullet proof windscreen.

The airframe was shaking wildly, engines howling, as she plunged after the enemy.

Where are you, you bloody Nazi bastard?

"Level out, sir, range down to one mile, directly ahead of us now."

"Is it manoeuvring at all?" Rose gasped, his face damp with effort, and wrists aching from the juddering in the airframe as he pulled hard on the controls as they began to stiffen with speed, but he did not dare to take even one hand off the control stick to wipe his eyes.

"Flying straight and level, range closing, throttle back just a smidgen, sir."

A moment, then, "A little more, sir," then, surprised, "Oh! I have something breaking away, sir…can you see anything?"

Something materialised magically before and beneath him, a pale mushroom-like shape, and then it was gone in an instant to one side as he looked ahead.

"My goodness, yes, I see it! D'you know, I think it's a parachute!

121

Is it the one you saw before, do you think?" his shoulders ached cruelly.

"Can't be, that was quite far behind, sir. Be well behind us now."

Two parachutes! The crew were baling out! It must have been hit hard by that first two second gunfire burst if the crew were abandoning it...

An outline began to materialise dimly before them again. Was that smoke that he could smell?

"I see it! I've picked it up again! What's the range, Chalky?"

The enemy visible once more, fresh vigour rippled through him in a scintillating wave.

"Five hundred yards and closing, sir. Our angels. Height constant."

The lad sounded quite controlled now, a consummate professional guiding his pilot in for the *coup de grace*.

"Yes, I can just make it out again," he reduced the throttles gradually as they drew ever closer, staring just to one side of the amorphous smudge before him. "I'm going to give him another burst, Chalky, can you see him?"

"Um, I think so, sir, wait, yes! I can!"

Rose sighted carefully, led, checked once more, and pressed down savagely again on the gun button.

"Firing..."

The cannon and machine guns once more barked out their song of destruction, and he held D-Dog's nose firmly in position as the Beaufighter bucked, again spraying the bomber's shadowy shape with deadly metal.

His heart was thundering still, yet he found with surprise that he was enjoying the destructive power in his grasp.

Another flurry of erratic flashing and sparkling registered their successful hits, a ribbon of flame licked hungrily back from one engine, followed by a sudden bright red flash within the body of the enemy bomber.

I wish I'd had this firepower last year, he thought, revelling in the destruction, *we could've knocked down a lot more of the bastards...*

And suddenly the raucous din from the nose gun ports stopped, replaced by the empty clattering of the cannon drums.

Their machine guns continued to chatter, the sound diminished and as nothing against the thunder from his cannon but he lifted his finger from the firing button.

No, no, no! His cannon had run dry!

Fuck, fuck, fuck!

He fought to keep his voice steady. "Chalky? The drums for the cannon are empty! Can you change them?"

"Flying Officer Rose, sir! I think he's going down, look! Off to starboard! You got him!" White was almost screaming with delight. "Oh my! Look at him go down! *Hurrah!* He's finished, has to be!"

Sure enough, the Heinkel was burning now, diving and turning away, bright flames streaming angrily from it, merging and creating a swiftly expanding and curving comet's tail as the turning and diving bomber quickly and precipitously lost height.

More burning pieces broke away, fiery streamers to mark its fall, lighting up the clouds beneath them with a falling constellation of flaring pinpoints of curving light.

The adrenaline pounded through him as he watched the enemy fall.

We got him! Bugger me, we actually got him!

"We got him Chalky!" He managed, his nerves were singing and he fought to control his voice, "Well done, chum, and thank you. Thank you for your magic. You got him right into our sights. That was superb!"

"*Oh God! Oh my God! Wow, look at him go down!* Congratulations, sir! *Oh my God!*" Rose winced as White triumphantly screeched his obvious pleasure ear-piercingly into his pilot's earphones.

The Heinkel was falling more steeply now, sliding steep out of control, slipping almost vertically, and their gleefully victorious eyes followed it down, until suddenly it exploded shockingly into an expanding and boiling ball of blistering white fire.

The searing flames must have finally reached the bomb load and the fuel it was carrying, blowing it into scorching, fragmented ruin.

Euphoria burst hot through him like a magnificent, glittering starburst, and he felt a sudden urge to throw the Beaufighter into a victory roll, but Granny's severe face appeared in his mind's eye (*'Never grandstand! What if your kite is damaged?)* and he restrained himself.

He'd done it! And that was number nine, ta very much!

But, much more importantly of course, it was the very first one for young Chalky. He remembered for a self-indulgent moment his own first time, that incredible feeling of victory in the friendless July skies of last year.

And now here he was, successful again, and one less of the enemy. Already the darkness rushed in to quash the scattered embers of the German bomber's death.

His heart was still banging hard and erratic against his breastbone.

Wish I could tell Molly we got him…

Rose clutched the bear gratefully. Lady Luck was flying with them tonight. After all this time, she'd not deserted him.

But how long would it last? Could he dare to hope…?

Rose exhaled long and hard as he struggled to calm himself.

"Well, that's our first. We've opened our innings in style, pal."

Nice. Keep calm, sound nonchalant, even though you may want to scream out your triumph.

"And heartfelt congratulations, Chalky my old son, you guided me perfectly. Could you reload the cannon? I'll hold her steady. If I need you to get back onto your seat, I'll rock the wings. Remember to keep checking in with me. Keep taking breaths, too."

"Yes, Mum!" laughed White elatedly, and with one last exultant look at the remaining glowing, fading remnants of the falling wreckage, he carefully unstrapped, took a quick and deep pull of precious oxygen from the mask, and began the difficult and dangerous job of reloading the cannon in the dark and rough interior of the Beaufighter's rear compartment.

Each of the four drums would have to be detached separately, put away carefully into stowage, and a fresh new drum loaded into place, mindful all the while of errant shell casings rolling underfoot.

In between each drum, White would need to continue taking regular breaths from his oxygen supply, and report he had done so in the pre-arranged pattern set by Rose.

What a bind.

And then he felt ashamed by his pique.

It was poor White who was the one who needed to crawl around the confined space to reload their cannon.

Rose had it easy by comparison. He just needed to keep her in level flight whilst White fought and struggled with the recalcitrant drums.

"Dagger 3 to Lamplight, please scratch one Heinkel north of Sudbury, possibly two crew parachutes, Dagger 3 now re-joining cab rank."

He could feel his chest swell with pride. *Scratch one Heinkel, God that sounded so good! Hope we get to repeat that many more times!*

Rose could catch the sound of the broad smile through the crackling in the other's voice over the R/T.

"Well done, Dagger 3! Understood scratch one Heinkel. Good work! Congratulations! Do you need to pancake?"

They still had enough fuel and ammunition for at least another hour or so, so Rose decided they would stay up. "No, Lamplight. We can continue, thank you, please direct."

"Dagger 3, please go to angels twelve and orbit Dumpling."

"Dagger 3 to Lamplight, received and understood, climbing to angels twelve and will hold at Dumpling."

As they flew back, the racing exhilaration of their victory steadily turned into a warm and satisfied glow in their hearts. They'd kept one bomb load from falling on their land. And they'd killed a number of the enemy.

"Reloaded, sir." Gasped White, at last.

"Chalky, can you see any damage to Doggie?"

White stretched against the harness to look carefully through his Perspex dome, checked the fuselage and wings, the engine fairings, the control surfaces as best he could. "Everything seems alright as far as I can see, sir."

"Thank you, Chalky. I'm ready for the next one, how about you?"

"Show me the way, sir! That was great! The best thing I've ever done! Let's do it again, please?" Was there a hint of hysteria in the boy's voice? Life could never be the same again for White.

Rose looked out at the darkness. During The Battle last year he and his friends would pray for the night, so that they might enjoy a few hours of rest after each tense day of fighting. And now, now the night was still his friend. It had hidden and protected him from enemy eyes and allowed him to triumph once more.

He gently patted the soft bump in his breast pocket formed by the little pink teddy bear, and touched Molly's photograph with a tender fingertip, wistfully imagining the sweet softness of her lips.

Thank you, dear God, for all the mercies you give me.

He smiled. *Still lucky!*

D-Dog stayed in the air on patrol for some time, but they were not called upon again.

An hour after their success, they landed safely at Dimple Heath, and taxied weary but cheerful to dispersals.

As they scrambled out, Rose quickly turned and held out his hand, "Here's to more, eh?"

White eagerly gripped it. "Hope so, sir!" his face was gaunt, and pale, deadly pale except for the dark rings around his feverishly excited eyes, the red marks from the rubber of his facemask gaudy against the white skin.

White spat out a few drops of blood, and noticing Rose's concern, shook his head ruefully, "Sorry, sir. It's nothing, I was so bloody excited when we downed the Hun that I bit my tongue whilst I was shouting."

Kelly was waiting with a big smile, matched only by those on the faces of the ground crew.

Even the crew chief was finding it difficult in maintaining his usual mournful expression. The leathery face kept crinkling around the eyes and the corners of his mouth continued to twitch and quirk upwards.

"Well done, Flash, old chum, one destroyed, confirmed, on your first combat! You've started off swimmingly! Here's to more, eh?" Kelly's face was animated, and he was rocking backwards and forwards, almost bouncing on the soles his feet.

"The Old Man's rather pleased, and the Intelligence bod's waiting to take an after-action report, after which I'll get you back to the crew hut. Billy damaged one and got a probable too, but they picked up a spot of German lead, nothing serious, but they did have a draughty ride home. They're thawing out in dispersals. You're the only two crews who were involved in actual combats."

"Thank you, sir," He looked at the stained and tired but jubilant face of his operator, and indicated him to Kelly with a gentle tilt of his head, "I think I picked a really good 'un! Most of the credit ought to go to Chalky here, without him the Heinkel would be on its way back to Hunland by now. I'd have had no chance of finding the blighter up there by myself. No chance at all."

Rose placed one hand on White's shoulder and squeezed gently.

Beneath the sweat, oil-stains and dust, his eyes red and hair plastered down with sweat, White bit his lip and blushed with embarrassment and pleasure.

Kelly nodded quickly. "Oh, yes, of course, well done, Chalky, old man, damn good show! One on your first trip! You lucky hound!"

White's beaming smile was so wide that it made the muscles of Rose's own face ache just by looking at it.

He tried to smile back but his teeth and gums felt as if they were stuck tight to his lips.

It was quite interesting to see the mixture of emotions chasing across White's face, fierce elation vying with the deflating flatness of anti-climax, and above all, the surprise and gladness of having lived to remember it.

I'll have to have a word with him about the nausea that comes later.

Was that what it was like for me? Is that how I looked? That young Pilot Officer Rose from a lifetime ago seemed like a stranger he no longer knew.

White was speaking, "Thank you, sir. I still can't believe that we got him. Mr Rose's a damned good shot, if you'll pardon my saying so, sir! Your aim was dead-on, the Heinkel was done for!"

Rose lowered his voice, "Just this once, Chalky, my old son. But I think we were a bit lucky too. That always helps. I think it might be a good idea to thank Mandy too, and you'll both have to come up with a suitable name for our little striped friend."

He could feel the knot of his stomach tighten, and he swallowed.

Rose nodded meaningfully at White's pocket, where a little bump showed that White still had the little cuddly zebra with him. He felt his own pocket discreetly. "Looks like it works after all, eh?"

White nodded enthusiastically, "I think it does, sir!"

Rose tapped the side of his nose, "Better hang on to it, then!"

"Oh, I will sir, I will." He said fervently. A moment's hesitation, then, shyly, "And sir? Thank you."

"Good grief, what for? I should be thanking you, my old son!"

"I'll not say it, but I think you know, sir." The boy's voice was trembling now, and his eyes were suspiciously bright.

Rose put an arm around White's shoulder, "Come on, then, you soft, silly bugger, let's go and fill out the action report with the IO, and get a nice hot cuppa, try and warm up a bit before we go back up again."

"Wouldn't say no, sir, I'm parched!" the boy's tummy rumbled loudly.

"Perhaps a quick bite to eat, too? I could do with a sandwich or a bun or something, I'm famished! One thing, though, Chalky, my old china?"

"Sir?"

"Would you say we're friends?"

"I would be very proud if you thought of me as your friend, sir." Surprisingly, White's eyes were wet now, and he pressed his lips tightly together.

Rose nodded. "Well, my friends call me Flash, and after what we've just accomplished together, I think I'd like it very much if you did the same. At least when the Old Man's not around. He might think it's contrary to military discipline or some such twaddle."

White's eyes were like saucers. "Oh, sir, I couldn't!"

"Why not, you silly sod? We're a crew!"

White sounded scandalised, as if Rose had asked him to sleep with a nun. "I'm sorry, sir, I couldn't possibly! It wouldn't be right! A week ago, I was clearing a blockage in the latrines, and tonight I helped you shoot down a Jerry bomber. I've never been so excited in all my life! Please don't ask me to, sir."

Rose blinked in surprise, and he tried not to smile. "Good gracious, alright, Chalky, my dear chap, don't get your knickers in a knot, old son. But, if it means that much to you, let's just keep things as they are!"

Before following White and Kelly to the car, Rose turned for a moment to the ground crew working on the smoke-stained Beau, despite the cold of the night, there were no gloves and their faces were pinched and sallow from the cold.

What a grand bunch of lads!

Already they had brought out the stencil and painted D-Dog's newest victory at the end of the line of swastikas on her snub nose, just beneath Rose's cockpit. She now proudly wore five of the victory symbols, and they looked *good*.

"Thank you very much, chaps," he called to them, "she was an absolute dream up there and everything worked perfectly. We got that one because of you. They hadn't even dropped their eggs. You earned that kill with all that hard graft. Good job! Well done!"

His stomach churned, and he swallowed hurriedly.

Whoops, time to go...

130

As Rose turned and walked away, the crew chief nodded approvingly at his men.

That Rose seemed a decent cove.

It looked like they'd been lucky and their Beau would once again be flown by a crew that got results.

He'd had his doubts over having that bloody jinx, that poor little bugger, ol' 'Shite' White, flying as an operator in his beloved D-Dog, but tonight seemed to show that things might not be as bad as he'd feared. He'd done alright by them.

If he weren't a jinx after all (and now the Chief had to admit to himself it really looked like the young operator might not actually be cursed after all), it was possible that Rose and White, with a spot of luck, and a lot of hard work from his erks, could become a top night fighter crew.

After all, a successful crew could only be effective with a good aeroplane, and a good aeroplane only came about from the hard graft of the boys on the ground. Can't shoot anything down with a bent kite, eh?

Yes, Rose and White might be worthy of dear Doggie.

He began to whistle tunelessly as he cast a possessive eye over 'his' Beaufighter, gaze stopping at the newly-added additional swastika at the end of the line.

His eyes caressed the new victory symbol lovingly, the smell of the paint still fresh.

Hm, now that was something worth looking at, Doggie had done for five of the enemy now. She was an Ace.

Good girl.

The newly-extended row of small white swastikas looked good on her, just as those silky-soft cream camiknickers fit just right around the missus' arse, and he felt the urge to gently stroke her metal skin, now cold in the night air. Lovely.

Good girl. He stuck his hands into his pockets, and cast a jaundiced eye over his team.

Struggling with the heavy and unwieldy ammunition belts, the machine gun loader grinned and furtively winked at his mate as the Chief ruined a very popular dance hall song with a tortuous rendition.

Cor, blimey! Sounds like the old bastard actually approved of the new crew! Would miracles never cease?

"Bates, you lazy little bastard, stop dreaming and move your fucking lardy arse!"

The loader stopped grinning and hurriedly picked up the pace, getting entangled in the ammunition belt and almost falling as he did so.

Watching him struggle, the crew chief allowed himself a secret moment of grim satisfaction. Couldn't let the cheeky beggars think he was getting soft.

The others began to work faster in grim silence, not looking at each other, or at him.

The chief's face was stony. "Don't rush it, fer fuck's sake! Do it properly!" he shook his head gloomily, "'Strewth, what did I do wrong to get lumbered with such a lazy, useless bunch of wankers?"

He coughed up some phlegm, and spat it disdainfully onto the hardstanding. "They must have made a mistake when they gave you lot to me. To think I queued on that fucking jetty in Dunkirk for this."

Wish they'd left you back there, you old bastard, Bates thought savagely to himself.

The pace had picked up, and the Chief nodded approvingly to himself.

That's more like it, thank you very much; he mused smugly with more than a little satisfaction as he watched his men strain.

"Come on then, girls, chop, chop!"

Merci beaucoup, madames et messieurs, normal service has been resumed.

Chapter 10

The following night, B-Flight's dusk patrol pair of Beaufighters, A-Able and B-Baker, were sent off first to get into position early over the North Sea. With luck, there might be a chance of getting in amongst some of the first of the nights raiders.

In the meantime, the remaining four crews of B-Flight remained on immediate readiness.

As they had successfully scored the previous evening, Rose and White were placed sixth on the duty roster, with Barr and Dear fifth.

Following their Heinkel kill last night, they had been sent up again for another patrol, but there had been no more action, and they had been able to enjoy their flying supper in the early morning as the sun crawled over the horizon.

With a coarse blanket draped over him, Barr was snoring fitfully on one of the camp beds in the far corner of the dispersals hut.

Barr's operator, Dear, was sitting beside the table, feet stretched out and head back, but he wasn't asleep, just trying to relax.

Barlow had bought a rather battered looking radiogram at a fleamarket in town, and both he and 'Icy' Cole were doing their best to get the wretched thing to work, but their efforts seemed to be having little, if any, success.

In the meantime, the hut's faithful old wireless continued to warble dance music peacefully behind them.

"You were pretty fast reloading last night, Chalky." Rose took a tentative sip from his cup.

The black coffee was very hot, and he put the cup carefully down onto the table, trying not to grimace, his lips smarting. "Those ammo drums are pretty heavy; I I'd never have done it so quickly. Particularly not in mid-flight in the dark."

White shrugged. "You're forgetting, sir, I'm used to hauling some pretty heavy things about. The canteen trolley bins are the heaviest things I've ever had to shift. Compared to those, the ammo drums were a doddle." He smiled cheekily and winked, "Piece of cake!"

They were quiet for a moment, listening with amusement as once more the radiogram refused to cooperate with all attempts to bring it back to life.

After an air test in the afternoon, the pair had shared a mug of tea and a currant bun, and Mandy found them still chatting as they gleefully re-lived their successful combat once more.

White's battledress tunic was in her hands, and shyly she passed it to its owner. It now sported his flying badge, the single wing of non-pilot aircrew, with the laurel leaves framing the letters 'AG', for an air gunner. Rose glanced with seeming indifference at it, but inside he was pleased with what he saw.

Rose had no idea what she was like as a typist, but, as a seamstress, Mandy's needlework was excellent, and the proud new insignia looked good on White's uniform.

He still thought it peculiar that AI operators had to wear an air gunner's badge, particularly since many of them had never fired a gun in anger.

Personally, Rose felt that all the back-seaters should wear 'RO' for radar operator instead.

As White quietly reminded him, however, "If we get shot down over water, and get picked up by Jerry, we don't want to spill the beans about 'The Thing', do we, sir? Better they think I'm a gunner and we're part of a Blenheim crew. Wouldn't do for Jerry to find out about our magic, would it?"

Rose nodded grudgingly. Hmm, it *did* make sense to hide the real function of the boys in the back.

Mandy was thrilled by their success, and the first thing she did was to quickly kiss White diffidently on the cheek. Rose smiled at the memory of their awkward embrace.

It was impossible to determine which of them had been the more embarrassed.

"You see?" White held up the little zebra delightedly, "You brought us luck, Mandy! Now you'll have to give me a kiss every time I fly!" he looked across at Rose and laughed, "Only me, though, mind! Not my boss!"

"But only when you get a Jerry, Chalky!" With burning cheeks and a fleeting smile at Rose, Mandy fled.

Rose adjusted the goggles preserving his night vision to scratch beneath one eye. "Mandy seems like a very nice girl. You both should have a meal with us one evening."

"Thank you, sir; I'll have to ask her. She always seems to be off when we're on, but then, I think you're sort of in the same boat?"

"Yes, I'm afraid so, chum." Oh, how cold and empty their bed felt when Molly was on duty!

"I saw you looking at that Hurricane, earlier, sir." White casually picked at a chip in the surface of the table with his fingernail. "D'you miss flying them?"

Rose picked up his coffee cup again, and blew gently into it, "It was fun flying them, I'll admit, the Hurri is a wizard kite, but there's something else really special about the Beau, and to be honest, it's actually rather nice having someone with me in the air."

He stared into the dark surface of the hot liquid, blew gently on it, whilst not really seeing it. "Sometimes I thought I was going to become cross-eyed trying to look at the controls, the mirror and the sky around the kite, all at the same time. God! My eyes used to ache something fierce, I can tell you. And staring into the sun wasn't much fun, either, believe me. Still seems a little peculiar not having to check my rear view mirror every couple of seconds or so. You wouldn't believe how quickly Jerry could creep up on you."

Pensively, he took another cautious sip, his goggles steaming up, "Mm, that's better. We were fighting against the bombers by day, defending Britain with all we had, and now that the Luftwaffe has switched to bombing primarily by night, flying with you, I'm part of that defence again. It's an enormous honour to be part of the main airborne defence again. You and I, a very essential part. Last night we proved just how important the night fighter defence is for Britain. We saved some lives, chum."

Reassured that his pilot wasn't going to desert him for single-engine fighters, White relaxed a little. "Last night was the greatest night of my life, sir. I want to do it again!"

Eyes still closed behind his dark goggles, Dear shifted comfortably on his chair. "Don't you worry, my old son, Jerry hasn't finished with us yet. You'll get your chance." With a sigh, he sat up, rubbing his neck. "I must say that the Hurricane is a fine-looking machine. What did the Turbinlite flight commander want? I saw ol' Toby sidle up to try and seduce you, Flash."

Rose had stopped earlier in the day to look at one of the Turbinlite

Hurricanes. It had appeared quite strange in black, like meeting an old friend after an absence of some years, yet those shapely, graceful lines were also heart-breakingly familiar.

Standing there, staring thoughtfully at the single-engine fighter, his head bursting with memories, not all of them good (and some actually bloody frightening), he was approached by Squadron Leader Tobias Black, the Turbinlite flight commander.

"I say there, Rose isn't it? Fancy a spin? I hear you're a bit of an old hand on Hurricanes?"

"Hullo, sir. Yes, flew them last year, got shot down, though. Hence the gammy leg."

Black's eyes took in Rose's ribbons. "Gave 'em a bloody nose at the time, though? Eh?" He waved one hand at the Hurricane. "Would you like to try a night flight, old man? We'd welcome having someone with your experience on an interception. Truth to tell, we could do with someone with a spot of combat experience."

Rose thought carefully for a moment, considering the suggestion, and then shook his head. "I could do it by day with ease, but I don't think I could manage at night. I think I'll stick with the Beau for now. But thank you for the offer, sir."

Black's moustache seemed to turn downwards in regret as he tried to hide his disappointment. "Fair enough, old man. If you change your mind…?"

Rose nodded agreeably, "Thanks, sir, maybe another time?"

White was irritated by what he perceived as an underhand attempt by the grotty Turbinlite brigade to poach his pilot. But he bit his tongue and said nothing, contenting himself instead with a murderous scowl at Black's back.

Dear, however, had no such qualms, "What a fucking cheek! Impertinent bugger! I hope you told him to piss off!"

138

"Well, it's not quite the done thing when one is speaking to one's senior officer, dear boy." Rose smiled sagely, "Could lead to disciplinary thingies and other unpleasantness, it could quite bugger up one's future prospects. I did, however, thank him most politely and declined gracefully."

Dear stood and scratched his crotch vigorously, "I should bloody well hope so! Well, I think he had a damned nerve asking. I can't stand poachers."

Barr hiccupped and the bed creaked precariously as he changed position. "No, I'd rather not, miss, don't like the colour of your knickers," he mumbled thickly, eyes still closed, and then the snoring resumed.

They all stopped what they were doing and looked at him bemusedly for a moment. To Rose, staring through the goggles, Barr looked like a beached whale wearing thick socks.

He sniggered.

Barlow pulled thoughtfully on his luxurious moustache. "That sounded quite interesting. Wonder who she was. Can't say that I've ever seen a pair of knickers that have put me off."

Cole piped up, "The colour doesn't matter, surely? I don't understand what he's flapping his gums about. The important thing is getting them off."

Barlow patted his operator kindly on the head, "Don't worry, Icy, you just try and get this damned radiogram thing to work. Leave talk of knickers to the big boys, OK? When your balls do finally drop, come and see me and I'll explain it all to you."

'Icy' Cole looked at his pilot with disdain. "Piss off, you silly sod." He turned back to his mysterious twiddling within the radiogram.

"You see?" Barlow shook his head and looked at Rose sadly. "See, Flash, old man, total lack of appreciation. Kindness is wasted on

139

dumb animals, chum. They just don't understand it. You have to be firm with the blighters."

He pointed at White, "If yours ever gets a bit lippy, just beat him with a stick. That's what I should have done. Too late now, he's turned feral. See the way he turned on me? If I wasn't made of sterner stuff, I'd have been scared shitless."

Rose grinned at him in the darkness, "Thanks for the advice. Jolly useful, I'm sure. Much obliged, I'll bear it in mind." He glanced at his operator and White returned his smile.

Jones, Clark's operator, stirred in front of the stove. "I'd like to see you find Jerry in the dark without your dumb animal."

Wisely, Barlow remained silent, eyes down turned and not meeting Jones' baleful gaze, instead apparently absorbed with the unfathomable problems of the radiogram.

White asked a little shyly, "So which do you prefer? What colour do you think is the nicest?"

The snoring stopped suddenly.

"Why, young Chalky! Talking about knickers? Didn't think you knew anything about ladies undergarments!"

White blushed bright red as Barr sat up with a creak of springs, and coughed hoarsely. "I need a fag. Anyone got one? Take it from an expert, Sergeant, colour doesn't matter." He put one stockinged foot on the floor, and then the other. "The important thing is getting the size of the drawers right."

Barr scratched his backside and coughed again. Dear tossed a cigarette onto his pilot's lap.

Barr examined it carefully, "Fucking hell, what's the point of me nicking your fags if you only keep the crappy ones? Anyway, going back to the matter of knickers, If it's too small it'll squash your crotch, turn your balls into pancakes and the cloth gets caught in the crack of your

140

arse. Bit like a cheese wire, doncha' know. It's a well-known fact that German troops wear 'em tight so that they can goose-step like that."

The B-Flight commander sniffed, rubbed his nose vigorously, and then yawned noisily, "Too large is far, far better than too small. Having bags of space is always better for one's own precious bag of balls. Personally, I'd get your pilot to stretch it well for you first. That's what Trevor does. Isn't that so, old boy?"

Dear reached for his pipe. "Good Lord. Must you tell everybody, Billy?" He looked around, "Normally I'd stretch 'em myself, but there is a war on. Can't do everything. Only human, y'know."

White looked at Rose in bemusement.

Cole stopped his twiddling for a moment and turned, "I'd heard that the tightest ones were best. Apparently the tighter they are, the more blood they push into your brain. The best crews have operators with the tightest knickers, y'know."

He pondered for a moment, eyed Rose and White, "But the smallest tackle, apparently," he added helpfully.

The blackout curtain swished back to let in a breath of ice-cold night air and a harassed looking orderly with a covered tin tray, "Sandwiches, gentleman. And there's some hot soup on the way."

He set the tray carefully down on the table and blew onto his mittened hands.

"Oh, Lor'. What flavour is it tonight?" Asked Barlow suspiciously, alarm written on his face.

The orderly thought for a moment, face scrunched up in concentration as he tried to recollect. "Um. Split pea, I believe, sir."

Barlow rolled his eyes and groaned in disgust. "Oh, Lor'!"

Cole beamed. "Marvellous! My favourite! I love pea soup!"

Barlow looked ill, "Are you sure?" he asked the orderly with an unsteady voice.

The Beaufighter was a superb fighter, but it had a number of idiosyncrasies, and one of these was that wherever an unpleasant odour emerged within the fuselage of the aeroplane, even if from the rear compartment, it invariably found its way forward and finished up in the cockpit, slowly bathing the pilot in an asphyxiating cloud of noxiousness.

If Cole managed to get hold of the soup, it would burble tempestuously through his system, and any resultant unfortunate emissions would ebb and flow to eventually accumulate in Barlow's office.

It would definitely add an additional experience to any interceptions in the next hours.

"Icy, I forbid you any soup, that's an order!"

Cole eyed his haughty pilot, tapped one finger lightly against his front teeth, eyebrows raised. "That's strange, Flying Officer Barlow, I thought Flying Officers couldn't give orders to other Flying Officers?"

"But it's Split pea, man! Split pea makes you fart incessantly like a damned motorised bellows", Barlow wailed despairingly. Cole smirked.

The telephone suddenly jangled, and the grin slipped suddenly from the orderly's face as he snatched up the receiver. "B-Flight Dispersals?"

He listened for a moment and the scratching of his pencil was loud in their ears. He put down the receiver abruptly and stood. "Four aircraft to angels fifteen, scramble, scramble, scramble!

Dear God! All four of us! A-Able and B-Baker aren't even back yet! Must be a big raid coming in.

Involuntarily Rose's hand went to check the bump that the little teddy bear made in his pocket.

White was straight out of the door immediately, but Rose was slower and was caught up in the jostling rugger scrum that was the stampeding mob of aircrew.

Cole grabbed a sandwich from the tray on his way out, yelling at the orderly, "Put the soup near the stove, Corporal, keep it warm, and don't let the other bastards eat it all!"

And then he was sprinting for his Beaufighter, arms, legs and heart pumping, pulling off the goggles and gasping at the sharp coldness of the air.

Four squat, tough Beaufighters crouched silently on the hardstandings nearby, as if ready to spring.

The night was quiet, but not for much longer, for the powerful Hercules engines would be started up when the crews were in their fighters, and their coughing, spitting and thundering would soon rip apart the still serenity of the night.

Chapter 11

Forty minutes later, they were still circling their beacon, griping and champing impatiently at the bit as they waited their turn *(and it came slowly, oh, so slowly!)* with the GCI controller.

The other three crews had already been vectored onto contacts, and D-Dog, being fourth, was last in line.

To their disgust and chagrin, Barlow and Cole had lost their bandit, were now on their way back, and would rejoin the 'cab rank' at the back of the queue, behind Rose and White, to await their next chance for another opportunity.

"Lamplight to Dagger 3, we have some business for you, please vector one-seven-five, confirm angels. Acknowledge."

Hurrah! It was their turn! "Dagger 3 to Lamplight, confirm course one-seven-five, angels fifteen."

"Lamplight to Dagger 3, climb to angels seventeen, course one-seven-five confirmed." The incoming bandit must be pretty high, if they were being told to climb higher.

It was generally accepted practice for the interceptor to be positioned at least at a fixed height greater than the bandit being intercepted, to allow for the advantages associated with height over an enemy which might be relatively faster when in level flight.

There was an almost unbroken layer of cloud below them, and Rose was grateful for the presence of White in the fuselage behind him. Without AI an interception even in broad daylight would have been a difficult, near-impossible task.

However, there were rumours of a RAF pilot flying an unmodified Hurricane over occupied Europe at night.

According to the rumour-mill, this incredible character had already achieved much success, accounting for a number of Luftwaffe bombers, flying and fighting over enemy territory all alone and unsupported. Personally, Rose believed the stories to be pure propaganda.

The thought of flying a Hurricane in the dark over hostile enemy territory gave Rose the screaming willies.

Whereas now, here at the controls of a potent Beaufighter at night, together with White over friendly Britain, he felt calm and cool and ready.

"Dagger 3, bandit will be crossing in front of you and below, vector two-six-zero, range fifteen miles."

Oh Lord, he was close, concentrate on turning the aeroplane, calculate his course, ease back on the throttle, let him catch up and pop down behind him...

"Dagger 3, vector two-seven-five, range three miles, bandit at angels fourteen."

"Understood, Lamplight, thank you. Course two-seven-five, descending to angels sixteen."

Then, "Chalky, anything?"

"No, sir nothing."

"Lamplight, any changes in the bandit's course?"

"No, Dagger 3, bandit now ahead and below, course unchanged."

A minute, then another. And another. "Chalky?"

"Nothing…wait…um, uh, yes - contact!"

Heart racing a little faster now, eyes staring into the blackness of the void.

"Contact lost, contact lost. Sorry sir."

Bugger. "OK Chalky, keep trying, chum." Damn, what a stupid, stupid thing to say. What else would White be doing?

"Contact! Contact regained, sir. Steer ten degrees port, range five miles, bandit below us, lose height please, sir."

Rose pulled back the throttles and pushed forward on the control column, nothing but darkness and emptiness before him.

"Level out…now. OK, sir, Steer five degrees starboard, range two miles, still closing."

OK, what was it Cunningham did; lower his wheels to lose speed? Maybe try it out?

No. No, I'm not brave enough to do that yet, just bleed off a little speed, watch airspeed, and check safeties…off? Yes. Quick visual sweep of the instrument panel, all OK.

"Range down to one mile; we're still gaining, but slowly now, sir. Bandit slightly above, course unchanged."

Each second strained past, and he continued to peer vainly into the murk of the night.

"Range now four hundred yards, still closing slowly, slightly above and to starboard."

Oh, for goodness sake! Where the fuck was it?

"Chalky, I'm sorry, I can't see a bloody thing, have a quick gawp. Can you see the bastard?" as soon as he had opened his mouth he caught sight of something moving.

Damn it! Spoke to soon!

"Oh, wait, I see it now, I'm going to slide in under the tail, can't make out what it is. What do you make of it?"

146

Every time he looked directly at it, the shape seemed to disappear, but then it would reappear when he looked to one side.

"Um, let's see, oh, my gosh, it's a bit close to us! Twin engine job, elliptical tail fin, single vertical stabiliser, it looks like another Heinkel 111 to me. About two hundred yards away, I'd say. Crikey! Never thought looking right up a Heinkel's arse could be so exciting!"'"

Good God, Chalky sounded so enthusiastic! The damned thing still looked like an irregular blob to Rose, but White's opinion was good enough for him. "OK, Chalky," aim carefully now, use the exhaust flames to help focus onto the target, "Firing…"

The Beaufighter shuddered madly as its cannon and machine guns hosed out a metal spray of death, Rose holding the nose firmly pointed grimly at the enemy aeroplane, but allowing a slightly irregular side-to-side spraying action to maximise the area of destruction.

One thousand and one, one thousand and two, arrowing, twisting grey smoke trails (imagined or seen?) converging hungrily towards the enemy, finger off the button.

Can't see anything, blink rapidly, try and locate that irregular smudge-like shape again.

Ah, and there it was…the bomber had somehow drawn a little ahead, no indication of any damage apparent, though. No smoke, no flames, nothing.

The Heinkel was turning away to port in a wide, flat curve, and then suddenly one wing dipped sharply and it was diving fast and hard to the cloud below. Rapidly the black shape fell away from them, diving for the sanctuary of concealment.

Blast! Throttles forward, wheel around and follow it down, calculate deflection, a tentative burst, no return fire, might the gunner be injured or dead perhaps? Was it too much to hope for?

A trio of sparkling hits, and an instant later something clattered against the leading edge of one wing, and he couldn't even tell which one it was. But the Beau shrugged it off and continued on after its prey.

And then the Heinkel had cut through the tattered sheet of cloud and was gone.

"Chalky, have you got him?"

"Lost contact, sir." White sounded distraught, "I've lost him. I've got nothing!"

He daren't follow the Heinkel down through the cloud. Without knowing where he was there was too great a risk of collision. Cloud may extend low, in which case there was a good chance of them hitting the ground.

Damn it!

"OK, OK, I'm breaking off the combat. We'll let it go, Chalky," he soothed, "At least we got in some good licks before it disappeared. I'm sure we hurt it. Did you see any damage?"

"I couldn't tell, sir, but you're right, you got in a lot of hits, 'cause he lit up like a Christmas tree. Sparkled from one end to the other. I can't believe he didn't go down. You hit him hard. I'm sorry."

The young voice was bursting with the same bitter disappointment that now filled his heart. Gone was the excitement.

"Don't talk such a lot of old rot, Chalky, you did a great job of the interception, I was the one who made a balls-up of the shooting bit. At least we can claim a damaged. Their dive was a bit steep, and it may not come out of it."

Rose sighed, "It could have been worse. I'm going to call up control and see if they still have the bandit visible. If not, we'll get back on the rank."

A little subdued, "Alright, sir."

Sod it. "Dagger 3 to Lamplight, contact lost. Can you help?"

"Dagger 3, contact lost our end. Bad luck. Did you manage to engage?" the controller's voice was thick with disappointment.

"Bandit engaged. Contact lost through cloud. We did manage to hit it and are claiming a damaged, Lamplight. Am re-joining rank, please advise angels."

"Dagger 3, confirmed damaged, well done. Please re-join cab rank at angels twelve. Can you continue?"

Rose thought of the glancing impact against the wing. "Dagger 3 to Lamplight, understood, angels twelve. We're OK to continue."

As they pulled up into a power climb to twelve thousand, a subdued Chalky checked the parts of the aeroplane that he could see (which weren't very many) and reported back that there was nothing untoward visible.

She felt alright, and the loss of their escaped prey rankled. Rose was not ready to go home just yet.

No need for them to refuel or rearm. They still had enough ammo and fuel. Might as well continue the patrol, and keep the old fingers crossed.

Better luck next time…

Chapter 12

A very long fifty minutes later, flying a wide circular orbit at fifteen thousand feet, a despondent Rose was still furious with himself at the mediocre results of the last combat, and thoughtful about tactics.

I should have been really close to that damned bomber, just as Granny taught me, so bloody close that there was no way I could miss. How did I forget that damned lesson? Granny kept bashing it into my head.

Instead he'd allowed himself to fall back before firing, had been bumbling about from too far away, and as a result he'd let it get away.

The damned thing had been trundling along in a straight line like a tram on Blackpool Seafront; flying in formation with it would have been a doddle.

I should have emptied the drums into the damnable thing rather than gazing at it like a fat old cow for so long, he thought petulantly for the umpteenth time, and the fire of despair burned deep.

It was one thing performing practice intercepts; the real thing was always different. The confirmed kill of the night before had made him over confident.

Granny had drilled into him again and again the danger of complacency, and he had thought himself better than he really was.

Enough, he thought sternly to himself, next chance we get, we'll formate as close as possible, and then we'll slow down as I fire a two second burst, start from in close with the distance opening safely as a result of recoil.

Poor old Chalky had been very quiet in the back, probably blaming himself, and now that Rose had decided on a tactic and future course of action, he decided he would share it with him to try and cheer up his dejected operator.

As he opened his mouth, the R/T crackled, "Lamplight to Dagger 3, fancy a spot of business?"

Excitement coursed through him, a splash of cold water through his veins. "Dagger 3 to Lamplight, oh yes, please!"

"Dagger 3, please vector one-zero-zero, angels ten."

"Dagger 3 to Lamplight, vector one-zero-zero, angels ten."

"Hear that, Chalky? Standby for a spot of action. There's another bandit on the horizon, chum!"

"Yes sir, standing by!" the possibility of action had even galvanised young White, and he now sounded a great deal more chipper than he had some minutes earlier.

As the Beaufighter dropped like a hawk swooping downwards with outstretched claws, Rose scanned the instruments as carefully as he had a scant sixty seconds earlier, and still he found no change, everything was as it should be.

The control column was vibrating like a live thing in his hands, he could feel the juddering of the airframe quivering through his fingers and into his bones, the thrill tingling through him, and could feel himself *joining* with the fighter once again.

Anticipation, excitement and terror surged strongly through his body in equal measure. He grasped the little teddy bear momentarily through the fabric with one glove.

Rose switched the gun-button back to 'fire', and for what seemed the hundredth time adjusted the brightness of the gunsight micro-scopically to get it *just* right. Not too bright, but bright enough.

Levelling out at twelve thousand feet, he asked, "Lamplight from Dagger 3, please confirm vectors."

"Hallo, Dagger 3, yes, please change heading to one-five-five, angels nine, range around ten miles."

"Dagger 3, understood, range now ten, heading one-five-five, angels nine." Then, "Chalky we're about ten miles back, the bandit's at angels nine and ahead of us."

"Checking, sir."

Push the snub-nose forward, throttles advanced, the snarling Hercules engines driving the Beaufighter through the cold night air.

"Dagger 3 to Lamplight, please advise, any change in the bandit's vector and angels?"

"No change, wait, vector one-six-zero, angels nine, range seven miles, you should see it soon."

"Thank you Lamplight, one-six-zero." OK, level out at ten thou-sand feet but maintain speed, even though the aeroplane was shaking madly as it raced after the enemy bomber at almost three hundred and thirty miles an hour.

And then White was in, "Contact! Contact at three miles, steer twenty degrees to port and below,"

Rose turned his fighter onto the new heading, *bloody hell, the range had closed fast!*

There was nothing visible, but White maintained a constant patter, "Contact now directly ahead, still below, range two and a half miles, reduce speed at one-mile mark, please sir. I'll warn you…"

"Dagger 3 to Lamplight, contact, thank you very much, will be in touch." Reduce the throttles a bit, but not too much, nose down a touch…

"Range two miles, contact five hundred feet below, still directly ahead, range closing."

Uh-oh. He was far too high, way too high, and they needed to lose more height.

Too late, because he could see it now, crawling slowly across the blanket of cloud like a swollen bug on a dirty bedsheet.

"I can see it now, Chalky, but keep an eye on it in the AI, oops, I mean in the Thingie, but have a look if you like. See it? I'm going to give it a three second burst." he would get them closer…

"Can't quite see it…*ooh!* Now I do! It's another fat Heinkel!" White whooped in delight.

Correct the aim for deflection, reduce the throttles just a touch more, lead the target's expanding shape vibrating in the windscreen, aim carefully and, "Firing…" and a boiling storm of bullets and shells fanned out once more, spat out in a deadly fan before the speeding Beaufighter.

Rose's aim was good, approaching from above directly astern of the enemy bomber; he dropped into position just slightly to port and behind the Heinkel, still firing.

And *again* there was no return fire to threaten them.

The solid burst of ravening metal hail impacted just before the enemy cockpit, stitching a destructive path backwards through the fuselage at an angle to come out first through the starboard wing root and then cutting into the vertical fin and starboard stabiliser of the tailplane.

At the same moment the rear upper gunner finally returned fire, his vision already failing and limbs weakening from the .303 bullet which slammed ruinously into his abdomen just seconds before, so that searing-hot red blobs of tracer leapt dangerously towards the Beaufighter, only to fall uselessly away even as the battered Heinkel checked, and slipped into a yaw to starboard as the damaged stabiliser and elevator failed.

The big Bristol fighter shuddered in the churning disturbed air of the damaged enemy bomber's slipstream, and Rose side-slipped to port as twisted, spinning remains of the Heinkel flicked past and to one side.

Flame began to sheet back from the starboard wing, lighting up the Heinkel's fuselage in silhouette from behind, and, lining up once again, Rose fired another burst into it, and there was the flowering burst of a small explosion inside the bomber in response.

And all the while the insidious little voice in his head was whispering, *don't let this one get away…*

The gunner was dead, possibly the whole crew too, and there was no more return fire, as suddenly the starboard Jumo 211 engine exploded shockingly into ruin, tearing ailerons and most of the outer part of the starboard wing completely off, the bomber slowly rolling into a dive, flames enveloping the entire fuselage from just behind the glazed 'fishbowl' of the cockpit.

They circled around to watch the plummeting and burning bomber as it continued to break up, finally disappearing from view into the expanse of cloud below, the light fading within it. A couple of seconds later and there was a monstrous flash that lit up the cloud from inside as the bombload in the fuselage of the flaming, falling Heinkel finally exploded.

They were silent for a moment, and then Rose spoke breathlessly. "Well, that was more like it, thanks, Chalky. Did you notice any parachutes, chum?"

"No, sir, none. Great shooting, sir." White sounded breathless but mightily pleased.

But not as pleased as me, matey. We didn't let that one get away…

"Thanks, pal. That's one more that won't be blowing up women and little children anymore. Best change the ammo drums, and have a quick shufti out, check the engines, see if you can make out any damage. I didn't feel any hits, but you'd better check, just to make sure. You might see something I can't.'"

He switched to the GCI controller, "Dagger 3 to Lamplight, scratch one big fat Heinkel, got any more?"

"Good work, Dagger 3, big smiles this end, very well done, and we have something for you, vector zero-seven-five, what angels are you?"

Rose quickly checked his instruments, "Um, angels eight, steering zero-seven-five."

"Dagger 3, contact looks like an empty," an 'empty' was an enemy bomber which had already delivered its bombload and was outbound, "Adjust vector to zero-eight-zero, maintain angels, range ten miles."

Damn it. On its way home it would be lighter and faster, harder to catch. Rose pushed forward on the throttles, nosing the fighter slightly downwards, got to try and catch up…

Uh-oh, better check that Chalky was belted up and secure before he began to throw the kite around…

He reduced the rate of descent to one that was gentler, and waggled his wings gently. "Chalky mate, are we reloaded, chum?"

"All four drums done, sir." White wheezed; he must have done the reloading at super fast speed.

"Good man, strap yourself in and hold onto your hat, we're in for a chase, I reckon."

"Gotcha, sir."

For fifteen minutes, with continuing guidance from the controller, they chased after the outbound enemy bomber, but it gradually drew away from them, and when they were almost thirty miles out over the North Sea, and no nearer the enemy trace, the controller called them off.

Frustration tempered with the success of earlier, Rose and White came off the cab-rank to refuel and rearm.

With a score of one confirmed destroyed and one damaged, they were greeted as heroes and once more another swastika symbol was added victoriously by the beaming 'erks' to the side of their stained Beaufighter. It was D-Dog's sixth individual victory, Rose's tenth and White's second.

Enemy activity in their area that night dropped off following their after-action combat report, and so a shooting-brake was called for them and they were taken back in it to dispersals.

The Flight was put on thirty-minute readiness, and the crews which had successfully engaged in combats were toasted with large mugs of sweet tea carefully prepared by the orderly.

The same night Barr and Dear also managed to successfully down a Heinkel 111 and damage another, Williams and Heather managed a probable, whilst Barlow and Cole had claimed two damaged.

The Luftwaffe had been out in force, alright. And the bastards had been bloodied badly by the defences.

However, the other crews of B-Flight were unable to manage a combat themselves, despite being vectored onto a series of contacts by GCI control.

Clark and Jones fruitlessly followed a phantom contact over Norfolk, before being illuminated by the searchlights at King's Lynn and being fired upon by the eager air defences.

The crew of E-Emma had sensibly beaten a hasty retreat, creeping home, smoke-stained by AA shell bursts from 'friendly-fire'.

To Barlow's utter despair, the container of pea soup remained untouched at dispersals, and Cole joyously half-emptied it into himself with great gusto and obvious pleasure.

No further raids appeared that night in their area, and they were taken off readiness at three in the morning. Barlow heaved a sigh of relief in his salvation from Cole; as did Rose, his only desire now to hold Molly close in his arms, to breathe in her fragrance, and find the peace and comfort that only she could bring to him.

Rose and White's first two-day duty stint had passed, and in that time, they'd scored two confirmed victories and a damaged that may not have made it home.

In that cruel and unforgiving unlit arena, they'd found success, and he was content that his fears of failure and cowardice were found to be unrealised. He and White had shown they were an effective crew.

White began his first two days off-duty knowing that he and Rose had effectively prevented two bomb loads, possibly three, from being dropped, and that they had saved many lives in the course of taking others.

He had also proved to Rose (and perhaps far more importantly, to himself) that he was not a jinx after all. Rose and he had faced and fought the enemy successfully together, and they had been gloriously victorious.

And now, with the taste of success sweet in his mouth, he knew that his life had changed once more and would never, ever be the same again.

In the two nights of mixed fortunes they had shared together, amidst the fire and blood and death in the cold wastes of the night, White was transformed from a nineteen-year-old boy into a veteran of war.

Rose had been instrumental in the making of that young man, and now he was everything to White, the extra-special older brother amongst their little band of brothers.

Watching Rose chat and joke with Barr, White felt a great wave of emotion wash over him. Gratitude, happiness and something akin to real love rushed through him.

He would go and eat his well-earned night flying supper, sleep for a short while, have a shave and a wash, and then look for Mandy. Perhaps share some elevenses with her?

The thought warmed him, and White smiled in pleasure as his inner thoughts turned to the girl.

What was it she'd said? "Get one for me, would you? If you do, I reckon you'll have earned a kiss."

And she'd smiled that shy smile at him and blushed a lovely shade of coral pink in wonder at her daring, to his great surprise and delight, and to her own mortification.

Well, he and Rose had accounted for two confirmed over the last two nights, so that must mean he'd earned two kisses, mustn't it?

Of course, it must. He nodded solemnly to himself.

Two kisses! The wonderful thought of her promise fulfilled gladdened him.

And might a 'damaged' warrant a third kiss?

White reflected wistfully on the memory of her soft lips, that sweet voice with the echoes of merriment in it, and the daydreams of her danced warmly and wonderfully through his mind like a pair of butterflies skittering and entwining through a sunlit meadow carpeted thick with bright spring flowers.

Chapter 13

The girl opened her eyes, squinting against the golden rays of early morning sunlight which flooded the room.

Her husband turned from the window, hair tousled, that easy, open smile that she loved so very much on his face.

"'Morning, my sweetheart, I'm sorry, didn't mean to disturb you."

She looked at him for a long moment, her sleep-filled eyes adjusting so that she could see the firm lines of his lean body, the scars on his leg a pale pink and thickly ridged line now, the nick on his forearm just visible.

She eased herself onto her elbows and winked at him, "I don't mind you, my darling, it's the others."

His grin broadened, and he waggled an admonishing finger at her in mock-disapproval, "So that's what you get up to when I'm flying, you saucy little thing."

"Oh, but you're my favourite one. I like you the best."

"It's only to be expected of course. Don't feel badly about being crazy about me, love, I'm me and you're only a mere woman, after all. You can't help yourself, not your fault, I'm simply irresistible. When they made me, they threw away the mould!"

She sighed softly and raised one eyebrow archly, "Is that so? I rather thought it was the mould that I actually ended up with!"

The young man gasped in mock-horror at her words, and then they laughed together, and he revelled in the blissful loveliness of the sound of her gladness.

She sat up fully, and the covers slid down from her shoulders to settle around her hips in soft folds.

Not a scrap of makeup, hair hanging loose and tangled and she was gloriously, incredibly, hauntingly beautiful.

He looked lower, and gazed in frank admiration and desire at her taut round breasts, their delightful brown areola and the proud, erect nipples. As always, the sight of her made the breath in his throat catch. "Wow! I thought it looked lovely out there, but I can see that the truly lovely wonders are actually in here with me!"

Despite the sleep still sticky in her eyes, she could not miss the twitch and stiffening of his penis as he stared hungrily at her naked body. How she loved that look in his eyes! Full of pleasure and wonder and weighty with raw need.

She tilted her head quizzically. "It's a bit chilly over there, why don't you join me?"

His eyes dragged reluctantly from her breasts to meet hers. "Is that an order Ma'am?"

"Yes, Flying Officer. I'm cold and I need someone to crank my motor. Seeing as you're here, I suppose you'll have to do. Why don't you do the honours? I'll give you a kiss and a cup of tea afterwards if you do."

He closed the curtains, and walked back towards the bed, "Well, if you put it like that..."

She pulled back the covers, and he slid in beside her, pulling them back over them both.

"I missed you so much, Harry."

"And I you, my dearest love. Young Chalky is a nice lad, but I'd

160

much rather spend my days and nights with you." He kissed her lightly.

"Just think about when it's all over…" she grimaced. It was stupid to think of that uncertain future when the world was once more at peace. She regretted the words as soon as she had uttered them. Even to mention it was dangerous, as if daring fate.

Oh, please keep him safe for me, she prayed, *I love him so very much.*

Even in the shadowed darkness he saw her troubled face and he drew her to him, "What is it, my sweetest?"

"Oh, Harry, I wish that I could look after you all the time. I want to spend my whole life with you, I wish I had a thousand years with you, ten thousand, more, even." and she hugged him fiercely.

"Only ten thousand?" he joked. Mm, her body felt very nice, very nice indeed.

Who's a lucky boy, then?

I am. *Very much so.*

He pulled her body gently against his, moving to clamber on top of her, revelling in the feel of her bare skin rubbing against his, the way her thighs opened wide to grip his waist and hips between them, welcoming his body into her intimate embrace, his fingers gently running along the uneven edges of the cruel scars in the small of her back, the terrible injuries she had endured at Foxton, now healed but never forgotten.

The dreams of what could have been only hopeless imaginings, with just the reality of now.

His Molly had truly earned her medal that awful day; more than earned it, of that there was no doubt.

Who else could boast of the fact that they made love to a wonderful and beautiful holder of the George Cross?

He could feel her heart fluttering, and he kissed her lips again, tongue licking against her smooth teeth, one hand sliding lightly down her back to the arc of her hip, his fingers cupping the firm and delightfully rounded curve of one taut, smooth buttock, and he felt her fingers lightly grasp and guide him to her soft, warm wetness.

Forget those lost dreams, for there is only now. How I love you, you extraordinary girl.

Her eyes gazed lovingly into his and they gasped together in unison as his eager penis eased smoothly into her, her body gripping him tightly, and then he was thrusting deeply into her, the only sound their gasps, the willing slap of skin against skin, and the squelching of his rhythmic plunging.

Molly closed her eyes in enjoyment, arms embracing him close to her as she opened herself wider to receive him, gasping and sighing with pleasure and longing.

The cottage they were renting was at the end of the little village's main street, not far from the parish church, and with a lovingly cared for rear garden that backed onto an open meadow.

They sat on the rugged grey stone wall that divided the garden from the meadow, and Rose gazed absent-mindedly up at the weather-beaten Saxon tower of the church. The air was fresh and raw, carrying the scent of the frost and grass into his nostrils.

"Penny for them?"

He awoke from his sated and peaceful reverie, and smiled gently.

"Oh, I was just thinking, sweetie, the church tower must have seen quite a few things in its time."

Molly turned to look up at the tower, "Apparently it's been here for over eight hundred years."

His eyes widened momentarily, "Good Lord!"

162

"Yes, just imagine, all the people before us who've looked at it, loved and lived near to it."

"And now we're doing the same." He took her cold hand in his, kissed it and then blew his warm breath onto it, holding it close to his mouth.

"Yes. Makes you wonder, doesn't it?" she squirmed closer to him. Unlike the stone wall in the fields near the Horse and Groom, this one was more evenly arranged, and his backside was quite comfortable as he drew her to him.

"What, my darling?" he placed her hand on his chest, shifting the lapel of his coat to cover it and protect it from the chill.

"About their lives, what was important to them, who they loved?"

"So many people, so many lives."

"Mm. And now it's us. We're the ones living here. And I'm the one loving you."

Despite the brightness of the day, it was still so cold, and he gazed at her flushed cheeks and the pinkness of the tip of her nose.

"No, my sweetest, I'm the one loving you. I'm the lucky one. Blessed by God with you."

She smiled gravely at him and kissed him lightly. "Whatever you say, Harry."

Molly looked back across the meadow. "Just imagine how they would have lived. Livestock sharing their houses, the stench! Phew! Can you imagine living like that, in a big shed with a goat or a cow?"

His lips quirked, "Must have been awful. But then, I don't need to imagine, my darling. I've got you, haven't I?"

She pulled away from him, "You cheeky devil! Are you calling me a smelly cow?"

He laughed, but said nothing.

With a pout and a severe look in her eye, she tossed her hair in his face and settled against him again.

"You're an absolute beast! And I don't know why I love you, you terribly horrid man, but I do."

"A fact for which I am extremely grateful, my dearest Molly."

There was a low grumble that increased in volume to a sudden howl, and a low flying Hurricane shot across over the trees that bordered the meadow at its far end like a thunderbolt and was gone in an instant.

She watched him as he stared to where it had vanished, eyes faraway and wistful. "Is it alright, Harry?"

He returned her gaze calmly, "Perfectly, my flower. I couldn't stand by whilst others were flying and defending us against the old Hun. What kind of man would I be? Not the kind of man a girl like you deserves. And in the course of it, I've made new friends. Young Chalky was so excited when we nailed our two Jerries. I was pleased as well, of course."

Molly's expression was thoughtful. "Have you seen the way he looks at you? If he was a woman I'd have pulled his eyes out by now. With a bent, rusty nail. Through his ears. I actually feel a bit jealous that he spends so much time with you. How odd is that? He adores you. I think you're some kind of hero to him."

Rose cleared his throat self-consciously, "Yes, well. He seems to think that I saved him from the life of a skivvy, but it was only a matter of time before he'd have been made operational. Just happened to be me he crewed up with. He's a nice lad, and good at what he does, thank goodness."

He changed the subject. "Tell me about Mandy, I can tell Chalky's keen as mustard on her."

She smiled fondly to herself. "Actually, I think it's mutual. Before I came off duty, I saw them holding hands beside the Turbinlite hanger. Chalky had a big silly grin on his face, but I think Mandy's was even bigger. Soppy old things."

"Well if he's getting a little bit of what I had a couple of hours ago, I'm not surprised he's wearing a soppy grin."

Molly coloured, and thumped his chest lightly. "Harry Rose! You are a very naughty man."

"That may be so, you fabulously gorgeous creature, but I'm the naughty man who gets to share your bed and to kiss your beautiful lips," and to prove the point he kissed her again, lips lingering against hers.

"I'll have to keep an eye on her." She mused, "I know how much being in love can rather upset one's whole demeanour and behaviour."

"Molly, love, Chalky doesn't talk much about himself. Could you do me a favour and check out his background, give me some idea of what makes the boy tick? Have a squint at his personnel file for me, would you?"

Rose picked curiously at a piece of yellow lichen. "I want to know all about him."

"Alright, Harry, but I shouldn't, not really." She looked ill at ease, "It's just a wee bit improper of me in my position as Dimple Heath's senior WAAF to read poor Chalky's file, just so that I can tell you what it says."

"You needn't if it concerns you, my darling." He soothed, "I daresay the lad will tell me about himself in time, if he wants to."

"No, of course I'll try and find out. It's hardly giving secrets to the enemy, is it?" she smoothed her skirt absently, "And he is your operator, after all. You ought to know more about him."

He hugged her and she smothered his face with light kisses, hugging him with a passion to match that of their earlier intimate embrace.

Her eyes were bright, and he marvelled at their beauty, the light iridescent in her irises. The eyes he dreamed of, the ones he craved to see when his own would not work.

Her voice was a whisper, "Oh, Harry, I love you so very much. I'm so happy that I could cry."

He gently grasped her chin, "Then I am the luckiest man alive twice, firstly because it is a girl like you who loves me so very much, and secondly because it mirrors the love that I feel for you. I could never love another. You are the best thing that could have ever happened to me. I adore you."

Rose looked up at the sky, and placed a hand over his heart, "Thank you, God."

The grass rustled as a light breeze whispered through it, as if in response to his heartfelt words.

She shivered and stood, "I think it's getting chillier. Come on, Harry, let's go inside, have some lunch and listen to the radio. I managed to appropriate some butter and a nice piece of cheese from the Stores."

He grinned easily, "Appropriate? Really?"

"Yes well, the Assistant Section Officer in charge of catering said she didn't need them anymore. Terribly kind of her, really."

He touched her cold cheek lightly with one finger. "Oh, I'll say, very!"

She took his hand and he followed her as she led him back into their little cottage. He switched on the radio, carefully stoked the stove, and sat down at the kitchen table as he waited for the wireless to warm up.

The fragrant smell of logs burning in the stove filled the warm room cosily, and he sighed with contentment.

While he waited, Rose idly watched Molly bustle neatly around the little kitchen, amidst the diligent clatter of crockery and cutlery.

Absently his fingers toyed with the corner of her brother's letter.

Edward had survived a tour of operations flying Hampdens, receiving an extremely well-deserved DFC and an equally deserved promotion to Flight Lieutenant in the process, and was now working in something 'hush-hush' at the Air Ministry. He wrote to his sister twice a week and adored her completely.

Perhaps even as much as I do.

She smiled her beautiful smile at him as she placed the butter dish and a bottle of milk on the table.

"You just sit there and relax, Harry. All that sitting down and pondering outside must have drained you. Take it easy, why don't you? I can manage by myself." She added pointedly.

"It wasn't the sitting down that's drained me so much, gorgeous," he countered cheekily, and Molly blushed.

"You horrid man, you're a brutish monster." She laid a plate of thickly cut slices of fresh bread before him, accompanied on the side by a generous dollop of mouth-watering pickle chutney.

The company and love of an intelligent and beautiful woman, delicious fresh food on the table before him, and the peaceful comfort of a warm and cosy room on a cold early spring day.

He closed his eyes and sighed in contentment, the smell of the fresh bread and her fragrance cheering him.

On the stove, the kettle began to whistle.

Mmm. I could get used to this…

Chapter 14

The sun was long set as Bruno von Ritter pulled back smoothly on the control column and lifted his Junkers 88 into the night sky, the dwindling airfield at Gilze-Rijen fading rapidly into the darkness behind them.

And then it was gone, as if it had never existed, just sea and sky and land blended together into a grey-black collage of indistinct shapes. Before them lay another flight, one that would hopefully be more productive than those of the last three days.

The leave in Paris had been delightful, the shows an eye-opening spectacle, and there'd been girls, plenty of them.

But they were instantly forgettable the following morning, for it was the girl on the base that caught his eye instead.

She was slim, petite and beautiful, a Luftwaffe nursing auxiliary, a *Luftwaffenhelferin*.

Her name was Anja, she was twenty three, and worked in the base hospital. He had met her at the awards ceremony when both Rudi and Mouse had received their Iron Cross first class medals at the hands of the legendary *Generalleutnant* Kammhuber.

Bruno had himself received his *Eisernes Kreuz*, his Iron Cross First Class, after shooting down his sixth bomber, and now had his sights set on a higher target.

Before the ceremony, Mouse suffered a metal splinter in one finger when checking the rear facing machine guns of their Junkers, and after the welcome ministrations of the nursing staff, invited a gaggle of them to the ceremony.

Bruno was listening to a tale of the previous war being recounted by some old fart of an *Oberst*, trying to look animated and interested, when he caught sight of her.

He was immediately smitten, by her sweet smile and the thick mane of dark hair swept back from her smooth forehead, arched eyebrows above smouldering eyes and a gentle but knowing smile. She was something special, and she knew it.

Anja enticed him from Kammhuber's side at the party after the ceremony had finished, and he did not even notice when the chief left the party later that evening, so entranced had he been in her company.

Whilst sweet faced and outwardly innocent in presence, the girl had not been shy in her approach, and he was quite flattered by her interest in him and in the way she monopolised his attention, whilst excluding all of the other girls in their company.

Strong and handsome in medals and uniform, Bruno was used to the approval and interest in women's eyes, but this one was different, and it helped that she was very attractive indeed.

He was captivated, and wanted to see her again desperately. Perhaps he might visit the base hospital on their return, and ask her to dinner?

As if reading his thoughts, Rudi now spoke from the seat to his right, "That girl seemed nice, sir, will you be seeing her again?"

In a voice that was harsher than he had intended, Bruno snapped, "Don't worry about girls right now, Rudi, you just concentrate on the task ahead of us."

Rudi stiffened, seeming to concentrate on the dials before him,

169

and Bruno mentally cursed himself for the unnecessarily severe tone in his voice.

Stupid, stupid, stupid.

Poor Rudi had intended no impudence, had just been making small talk. He deserved far better than that.

Bruno felt Mouse shift reproachfully in the seat behind him, and he sighed, eyes searching the darkness before the smoothly climbing fighter.

Better get that damned olive branch out. "We'll talk about girls when we get back, eh? Perhaps over some celebratory schnapps?"

There was a broad smile in Rudi's voice, "Yes sir! Hopefully celebrating more than one!"

Bruno turned his head slightly. "See anything, yet, Mouse?"

"Nothing interesting, sir, the sky's empty." Mouse told him grumpily. "I'm bored."

"Hopefully not for long, my friend."

"Let's hope, sir. The guns are getting bored and cold. And so am I."

All was well. Crisis averted, thank goodness.

Almost an hour later, lurking in the darkness, Rudi looked out into the night sky hoping to see the mouth of the Elbe in the distance, and instead caught sight of a moon glinting on something below them.

And then it was gone.

"I thought I saw something below us, sir, below and a couple of miles away in front."

Bruno craned his head, but could see nothing, "Surface or aerial object?"

"I'm not sure, sir, too far to tell."

"Heading?"

"Thirty degrees, last I saw, and quite low down, sir." Minelaying aircraft usually flew low at fifty or sixty feet.

In a moderate turn, the Junkers 88 turned its fearsomely armed nose like a shark catching the first scent of prey, seeking it out in the darkened depths of the cold night.

"Anything? Rudi, Mouse?"

They both answered in the negative.

"I'm going to level out at a thousand feet, boys, we'll head out for twenty kilometres, and then we'll double back. It might have been a mine-laying bomber or a low-level raider. Either way I want his scalp."

The fast moving Junkers fighter ate up the distance in a matter of minutes, and in no time at all they had flown twenty kilometres along the heading Rudi had suggested, but the search had been futile, and he cursed his luck.

"My friends? Anything?"

They both answered him in the negative, and he exhaled bitterly in disappointment.

"OK, boys, I'm taking it back along the way we came. Looks like we lost that one."

But even as he wheeled the heavy fighter into another wide and sweeping turn, there was a shout from behind, "Herr Leutnant, Sir, aircraft below and behind us, at your six o'clock, now moving into your five o'clock."

Bruno's heart leapt gladly. "Height, Mouse?" he asked quickly.

"Really low, Sir, it really could be one of those RAF mine layers."

He couldn't see it yet, "Rudi?"

"I see it sir, Mouse is right, it's really low, it looks like a surface vessel…but, no, it is an aircraft, no doubt about it, I see the wings now, oh my, I think it's a Wellington bomber, sir! They're mining the approaches to the Elbe, the damned wretches!" Rudi turned to Bruno, "It's about fifty feet up, head zero-six-five degrees."

171

Bruno snorted. "Hah, we'll teach the cheeky swine." He pushed down the nose and turned onto Rudi's heading, and sure enough, his eyes made out the cruciform shadow in the darkness ahead. A little part of his mind reminded him that the bomber carried a crew of six, all of whom would soon be dead.

Pulling up into the enemy's spreading slipstream, he caressed the gun button, aim for the rear turret and hose your fire along the fuselage, make it quick and clean.

Right then, you bastard swine-hounds...

Shockingly, the rear of the enemy bomber suddenly flared brilliantly, startling them and searing away their night vision, needles of light cutting out at them.

Instinctively Bruno violently pulled up and to starboard – *what the FUCK?* Beside him Rudi started in shock, gulped convulsively and grabbed for a stanchion.

And then fiery orange-red comets of tracer were pulsing past and then downwards as the bullets from the Wellington's rear turret raced after them.

They continued to climb and turn away and the enemy guns stopped firing, allowing the comfort of darkness to hide the Wellington bomber.

They fled into the safety of that darkness, pursued even out of range by British bullets.

"He saw us," There was grudging respect in Mouse's voice, one rear gunner appreciating another's craft. "He must have the eyes of a fox, that one."

Bruno said nothing, muscles straining and gasping, lights still sparkling in his eyes, damn it, how did Mouse manage to keep talking? It was hard enough to just keep breathing under these stresses.

The enemy fire evaded, Bruno tested the controls as he levelled out at a thousand feet further up, hidden from the enemy by the cloak of darkness.

Had the enemy gunner found them, and more importantly, had he damaged anything?

But no, she responded like the thoroughbred she was, and unconsciously he patted the side of his seat. They'd been lucky, very lucky indeed.

A second or two more, a few meters closer, and the unknown enemy gunner's expertise would have claimed *their* scalps. How easily positions could change in this black arena.

At last Rudi let out a shuddering breath, "Mein Gott!" he looked pale and sick, terrified eyes wide and staring.

My God. That's how I feel, do I look like that too?

"My God, indeed, Rudi. They almost got us! My fault, I'm getting too confident, too damned relaxed like some great fat sheep. I'm sorry. I should have crept up on him; instead I just went on in like some blundering dolt!"

He shook his head in disgust. "Did you see where he went? I want his head."

"I lost him sir; I was too busy trying not to shit my pants, I'm sorry, I lost all sense of direction." Rudi confessed, shamefacedly.

Mouse said nothing for a few seconds, and then, "I can't see him, sir, he should be off to port, but I can't see anything at all down there." He barked out a gruff laugh, "Fuck, Rudi, you're such a little girl."

"Shut your stinking hole, you big, brainless lout," Rudi replied, his voice quivering.

Bruno blinked rapidly trying to clear his vision, heart thudding and his guts still as cold as ice as he relived again the shocking flash of the enemy guns and the speeding web of light that seemed to reach out for the Junkers, to ensnare them within its mesh of death.

173

To ensnare him.

"Damn it!" He grated, "Keep looking!"

The cockpit was filled with a brittle tension as they searched for the Wellington bomber, but it had gone, making good its escape into the all-encompassing darkness.

The Junkers speed advantage was of no help now as it headed away from its prey. With every second that passed, the Jumos hauled them further and further from the British bomber.

Some miles away, cloaked by the comforting night, the gunner unscrewed his thermos and poured himself a beaker of stewed tea. The steam curled comfortably around his turret.

Lovely.

"Any sign of that Jerry, Des?"

"No sign of them, skip, I think ol' Jerry's given up. Shame, it would have been nice to shoot one down. I almost had him then, you know…"

The steam was fogging his turret and he hastily wiped the Perspex with the cleaning pad he'd been given.

"Yeah, OK chum. Maybe if he'd been ten yards away and as broad as a barn door, you might have hit him. I'll have a wee chat with the MO when we get home. Get you nice spiffy pair of specs?"

As the outraged gunner responded caustically to his sniggering pilot, the Junkers turned again in its search pattern, slowly widening the distance between them even further, and at the same time reducing the distance between the Wellington crew and their night flying supper.

Once so warm, but now no longer. Getting colder, colder…and colder still…and…gone.

Tonight the mine-laying Wellington had been successful in the deadly game of hide-and-seek.

After another half hour of unrewarded searching, fuel beginning to run low, they turned back for home, with Bruno seething and frustrated by the skill and vigilance of an unknown rear gunner RAF sergeant.

That was a crew that would live to fight another day, Bruno fumed.

Worse, there had been no other enemy mine-layer bombers they could hunt down before having to return home.

They had missed the one chance there was.

Another wasted night! Going home without even firing my bloody guns! How did we lose him so easily?

Bruno felt almost sick with anger, and livid that they'd not made the kill, but at least they had survived, and that was no small thing, for they had come precariously close to the end of everything themselves.

They were still alive, and life was precious.

And he still had the chance to see if Anja's knickers were regulation issue or not...

Mmm.

The thought of her gentle smile, those dark, beguiling eyes, and of what lay hidden beneath her uniform soothed him, and the sourness of the loss of their prey was lessened as his thoughts turned warmly to her.

And at least, their survival tonight meant there would be a next time.

Enjoy your egg supper tonight, my British friend, because the next time we meet, things will be very different...

Chapter 15

"*Cor!* Will you look at the Bristol's' on that!" 'Trolley' Trent held up the copy of *Men Only* and displayed the picture of the centrefold nude to the room.

His pilot, Pilot Officer 'Pepper' Herbert, looked up from his writing and peered at the picture.

"Hm. Yes. Very nice, Trolley. Very nice indeed." He agreed, and returned to his scrawling.

Billy Barr stared uncertainly at the magazine in the semi darkness for a long moment, then, "What is it, Trolley, a picture of a rabbit?"

"No Sir! It's a very tasty picture of a blonde. Nice piece of skirt. Or lack thereof, I ought to say."

"Well it's no bloody good showing it to us, is it, old stick?" replied Barr, indicating the night-vision goggles he and the other crews were wearing.

Being last on the duty roster, Herbert and Trent weren't wearing the blessed things.

Trent put the magazine back on the table and ogled the centrefold wistfully. "Well pardon me for leching. It's not my fault I'm a man."

Heather shifted his backside comfortably and the chair complained, "Good Lord! You're a man? Incredible revelations! I hadn't realised, mate. My congratulations. Do you know the names of each of the bits?"

Trent didn't look up, "Oh yes, my old fruit, of course I do. One may have the mind and body of a weak and feeble thing; but one has the rampant genitalia of a real man."

"Mm, how interesting. Where'd you find 'em, old cock?"

Trent shrugged. "Oh, there was some old bloke sleeping by the main gate so I pinched 'em from him."

They all laughed, and Dear stood up and checked the stove.

Rose continued to fear that the blessed thing would explode like a bomb because of the way in which Barr would insist on lighting it.

The B-Flight commander had discovered an insane way of lighting the stove from some questionable chum of his on 604 Squadron, involving the use of a disturbing mix of paraffin, coke and the phosphorous from a signal cartridge.

As Dear warmed his backside contentedly, Rose breathed a sigh of relief, it didn't look like the damned stove was going to blow anytime soon, although the flame was shot through with a rather peculiar greenish tinge.

White looked at Rose. "Talking of pictures, sir, Mandy gave me a picture of herself. Though not quite like the one in the magazine old Trolley was waving at us."

He patted his breast pocket. "I keep it where you keep yours, sir. I'll show it to you when we get a chance." He looked around surreptitiously, "I ain't gonna show it around these animals."

Rose raised an eyebrow questioningly, "Getting a bit serious, then, Chalky?"

"She's lovely, sir. Really sweet, and kind. She's the nicest girl I ever met, and she's a real looker, prettiest girl I've ever seen, um, excepting the Flight Officer, of course," White added hurriedly.

"Of course," Rose agreed, grinning amiably.

"We went for a bike ride yesterday afternoon, but the ground was a little bit icy and I slipped and took a bit of a tumble near the Post Office at Dimple village."

Rose sat up a little in concern. "Are you alright? Didn't hurt yourself, did you, old man? Any injuries?"

"I'm quite alright, sir, thank you. Honest." he grimaced ruefully, "I was just playing silly beggars, showing off, really, trying to impress her. Don't worry, I'm OK, twisted my ankle a little, but the MO has had a look, and he said it'll be right as rain in a couple of days."

"Are you sure you'll be OK to fly, chum? I could ask the CO to give you a day or two off?"

"Oh yes, sir, no problem. The best part was that Mandy helped me to the MO, gave me a chance to get my arm round her waist." He sighed dreamily, "She smells quite nice too."

"Oh dear, my blood-crazed fiend of an RO is besotted!"

"I like her a lot, sir. More than a lot, if truth be told. And, I'm not sure, but I think the feeling is reciprocated."

"Ah-ha." Rose nodded sagely, then asked helpfully, "Do I need to give you a lecture on the birds and the bees?"

White was mortified, and his lips pinched together furtively, an uncomfortable, hunted look appearing in his eyes, "Oh no, sir," And then, ever respectful, "But, thank you for asking."

Barr stretched and yawned bedside them, "Good God, man, there're so many lovelies to choose from, how can you settle on one already? Got to sample the field, so to speak, give 'em all a taste, doncha' know?"

White's lips pinched further, almost disappearing in chagrin, and he made no reply. It wouldn't do to cheek the flight commander.

Barr shook his head sadly, "You don't know what you're missing, old chap. Although, I must say that your young lady seems quite a catch. I'd hardly call her ugly. I suppose it's quite possible to see how she might have turned your head."

He pulled a crumpled packet of cigarettes from his pocket and looked at it pensively. "It would, of course, be most unkind to deny myself to all of womankind."

Rose leaned closer so no-one else could hear and lowered his voice, "Chalky, my old son, if you ever need a spot of advice from a married man?"

"Oh no, sir," White said quickly, "that's not necessary, Mandy's a nice girl, she's not like that."

Fair enough, mate, thought Rose blithely, *but just you wait 'til you're both caught up in the passion of the moment.*

Simple, chaste kisses swiftly progress before you know it, oh-so easily, into something more. A lot more.

Nice girls like a bit of the other as well, and I should know. I'm married to an incredibly lovely, super-terrific girl. And she's no shrinking violet in the bedroom, quite the opposite, thank goodness!

Trent put down the magazine with a sigh and looked around. "Anybody fancy a cup of coffee?"

There was a flurry of raised hands.

Trent sat back comfortably, "Wonderful! Make me one when you make yours, would you?"

Barr put down his hand. "Don't be a cheeky little basket, Sergeant," he huffed, "move your insolent arse, and don't forget, plenty of sugar in mine."

Trent jumped up, "Yes sir, pardon the insolence, who else wanted one?" he asked again.

The telephone suddenly jangled and they all froze. Rose felt a shiver of fear course through his body, but kept his features blank. White was immobile beside him.

"B-Flight dispersals? Yes? Oh, alright, thank you."

The orderly replaced the receiver carefully in its cradle. "E-Emma returning to rearm and refuel. Sector requests two aircraft onto standing patrol immediately."

Bollocks.

Reluctantly, Rose stood up, vacating the warm and comfortable embrace of his sagging couch.

"Cancel our coffee, Trolley, looks like we'll be busy for a while, come on Chalky, pass me my flying helmet, please, yes that's the one, thanks."

Barr got to his feet with a groan, "Make mine anyway, Trolley, my old son, leave it on top of the stove, that'll keep it warm, ta very much. Come on Trevor, my old lad, duty calls, don't dawdle."

The two Beaufighters orbited the beacon for over an hour, D-Dog maintaining a height of sixteen thousand feet, a solid layer of thick cloud below, talking desultorily, and Rose told White of the first time Molly and he met, of the fighting he'd taken part in the previous summer.

And of his precious friends of course, and especially of Granny Smith and Stanislaw Cynk.

Dearest Granny and Stan.

Two of the finest friends a chap could wish for.

"Granny was always moaning at me about checking the airspace around and behind me, and now I've got you to look after me." He laughed, "At least it's a lot harder for Jerry to bounce us in the darkness. I'm grateful for that, I can tell you! Just remember, though, when we're up there, keep a good lookout, my son."

They lapsed into silence for a little while, then, shyly, "I've asked Mandy to the pictures, sir. What do you think?"

"Sounds like a grand idea to me, Chalky. What're you taking her to see?"

"Well, I've heard that *Gasbags* is a bit of a laugh, and I like Bud Flanagan, anyway. What d'you reckon, sir?"

Rose nodded appreciatively, "Sound's great. And girls always love a good laugh. I remember the first film we went to see. It was *The Lady Vanishes*. I was so tired; I slept through the entire film. Still don't know what it was all about, but Molly said it was very good."

"Was Mrs Rose, um, a bit annoyed that you fell asleep?"

"No, Chalky, she knew how tired I was. Molly's a terrific girl. I'm very lucky."

"Yes, sir. I hope I'm as fortunate with Mandy."

"From what I've seen of her, I'd say she's pretty special, Chalky. Good luck to you, chum."

The first hour trailed grudgingly into the second, and still they weren't called for by the controller, slowly freezing in the bitter cold. The damned heating vent was about as useful as a pair of boots made from cheese.

Rose stared longingly at the hot exhausts mere feet away from him, and wondered again about the appalling heating system of the Beaufighter. How could someone design a machine as good as the Beaufighter and provide it with such a crappy heating system?

A thin stream of insipidly warm air played feebly across his right heel, doing little or nothing to dissipate the chill that was permeating his bones, despite all the gear that he was wearing. It was worse for poor old White, his heater produced a weak dribble of warmth that did nothing to heat the RO's compartment.

Rose thought longingly of a hot mug of coffee to wrap his cold fingers around. Better still, hugging Molly (preferably a naked Molly) was the finest way he could think of warming up, and, better still, it was lots of fun too.

Sigh.

Dear God, it was so *cold*.

He shivered. Come on, Lamplight, give us something, for pity's sake, before we die of boredom or the cold.

It looked as if the enemy weren't interested in raiding their patch this evening. But at least it meant no civvies were suffering.

"Lamplight from Dagger 3, you haven't forgotten about us, have you?" he asked plaintively.

Immediately they heard the controller's voice, "No, Dagger 3, I'm afraid we have nothing for you, no enemy activity for the moment."

But fifteen minutes later, the tedium was suddenly broken, "Dagger 3 from Lamplight, if you're not doing anything better, we might have something for you, please confirm your angels."

"We are at sixteen, Lamplight, repeat sixteen."

"Understood you are at sixteen, Dagger 3, vector zero-seven-five magnetic, incoming trade, angels six, range twenty-five miles."

"Angels six, Lamplight? Please confirm Angels Six, steering zero-seven-five mag."

"Lamplight to Dagger 3, confirmed Angels Six, zero-seven-five."

"Thank you, Lamplight, descending, please continue to vector us." He switched to the intercom, "Chalky? Wake up old lad, we've got some business, it's flying at six thousand, so we need to lose a lot of height, OK?"

"Gotcha, sir."

"Right then, turning onto zero-seven-five, here we go then, going down." Excitement coursed through him, and he patted his pocket, checking that the little teddy bear was still safely ensconced in there.

The thick cloud rushed up to them and then they were within it, engines purring loudly, powerfully, plunging rapidly through the murk. The altitude dropped off yet still they remained in cloud.

Tendrils of fear clammily encircled his heart.

Damn it, but how he hated low cloud. It wasn't particularly mountainous or even hilly around here, but it was so easy to fly into high ground, known by aircrews with grim humour as a 'crowded cloud,' and the thought terrified him.

"Dagger 3 to Lamplight, Please advise?"

"Dagger 3 from Lamplight, maintain current heading, range eighteen miles, angels four. Please confirm your angels."

"Received, Lamplight, Angels Four."

Inwardly, he groaned despairingly. Good Lord! That low down, tracking it on the AI set would be incredibly difficult if not impossible, the blip dancing seductively amongst the ground returns on the scope, and the effective range at that height would be half a mile or so.

Poor odds of picking up the bandit in such conditions.

It had better be a damned good interception by the controller.

More worryingly, the bandit was heading straight for Dimple Heath. Might it be an enemy raid?

Molly ought to be safe in the cottage at this time of night, but... What if he drops early? He could hit the village. What if...?

"Lamplight from Dagger 3, could you please advise home base that there might be an incoming raid? Oh, and how are we doing?"

"Dagger 3, will advise home base. Maintain heading, angels three, range ten miles."

Silently, Rose groaned. An altitude of three thousand?

"Dagger 3, we have lost contact, I'm sorry, repeat, contact lost."

This time Rose groaned aloud in despair. "Chalky, they've lost the contact, have you got anything?"

"No, sir, nothing. Is it an enemy raid?"

"God, I don't know, chum! It's really low down; I'm going to follow its heading from about fifteen hundred feet. I'll need you to keep one

183

eye fixed firmly outside, but just keep the other on The Thing an' all, in case we get lucky and end up close enough to it."

"Lamplight to Dagger 3, break off! Air defence have been alerted, observe five miles exclusion radius."

"Chalky, we're breaking off the pursuit, hang on to your hat, pal, I'm taking her up, we're climbing!"

Cursing foully under his breath, Rose pulled back on the control column and rammed forward the throttles so that D-Dog shot upwards again, his vision greying, the fighter suddenly erupting from the denseness of the thick cloud like some terrible marine monster exploding out from the depths of the ocean.

And then again, almost immediately, "Dagger 3, break off! Break off! Contact has been identified as friendly, repeat contact is friendly, please break off! Repeat, break off! Acknowledge, please!"

Rose closed his eyes, then opened them again and looked yearningly at Molly's photograph. *Oh Molly, we almost shot down one of ours! Dear God.* And then, *Thank God.*

They would find out later that the contact Lamplight had been tracking for them and directing them to, was in fact a flak-torn Wellington limping home, from Dimple Heath's very own bomber flight.

The battle damage done to the bomber included the destruction of the Identification Friend or Foe (IFF) system, such that the aircraft had been classified as an unidentified trace, and therefore, a probable bandit.

The Wellington had finally managed to identify itself, almost too late, belatedly via a hastily repaired shrapnel-torn wireless set to RAF Dimple Heath's air traffic control, and the frantic duty officer desperately phoned the news urgently through to Sector, thereby preventing a disaster in which Rose and White might well have downed a friendly aircraft (or vice versa?) in poor visibility.

Near to the end of their patrol time, all was still quiet, and with no enemy activity immediately apparent, Rose requested and received permission to return and refuel.

Wearily the two of them, frustrated, bored and half-frozen, traipsed back tiredly to the dispersals hut with the strange faintly green glowing smoke seeping resentfully from the jauntily askew chimney.

Rose and White made their way to the stove to pour themselves a well-earned cup of stewed sweet tea.

Half an hour later, readiness was relaxed, for there would be no enemy activity that night.

Nevertheless, the crews stayed up until dawn broke, waiting patiently, just in case, bolstered by endless cups of tea or black coffee, dreaming patiently of their fried egg 'supper' and the glass of refreshingly cold milk that often came with it.

They gratefully watched the sun crawl into the sky, the little band of brothers sitting and standing companionably close together, some smoking in the fresh glare, saying nothing but silently glad that once more, they had, each of them, survived another night.

Chapter 16

The following night, being third on the duty roster, Rose and White were airborne in D-Dog by seven thirty, arrowing cleanly up into the clear night sky at full power as they sought to gain height rapidly, a bright moon shining coldly down upon them from the south-south-east, indifferently illuminating the inside of the Beaufighter's cockpit with its cold shine.

But Rose was not even remotely interested in admiring and enjoying the moonlight; he would appreciate it only when Molly was with him. Right now, however, it was a useful tool, a weapon even, to be taken advantage of and used to assist him in any coming interception.

Once they had reached their directed height of fifteen thousand feet, sector control told them to circle the Sultana Beacon on the east coast, and then they were once again assigned to their GCI controller, Lamplight.

They were not kept waiting for long, and Lamplight was soon passing them a set of vectors, but the range was far too long, and White was able to hold the fleeting blip only briefly, helplessly watching it slowly slide off the scope as the distance between them and it gradually increased over the next ten minutes.

White clenched and ground his teeth together in frustration as the trace gradually crept away from them, flittering timidly at the edge of the screen for a teasing moment, and then it finally disappeared from his scopes altogether.

Whatever they had been chasing had a far better turn of speed than they did, and easily outpaced the battling Beaufighter, even with the powerful Hercules engines driving them after it at maximum speed, the controls trembling and stiffening in Rose's straining hands.

Grimly, they returned disappointedly to the cab rank holding point, but the night was not yet over for the crew of D-Dog.

Half an hour of circling later, in the far distance, a pair of searchlights suddenly lit up, the thin white fingers of light criss-crossing slowly.

The lights wandering apparently aimlessly intrigued him. "Fuck this for a game of soldiers. I'm fed up with all this stooging around," muttered Rose, half to himself, "Shall we go and see what those lights are all about, Chalky, my old bag of pants?"

The boy's voice was eager. "Yes please! Go on, sir!"

"Hullo, Dagger 3 to Lamplight, there're a couple of lights on the coast or thereabouts, permission to investigate, bearing zero-eight-zero relative to Sultana."

"Dagger 3, permission granted, things are a bit quiet in your area at the moment. I've nothing for you at the moment. See what you can find. Good hunting."

"Thank you, Lamplight, will advise soonest." *Here's hoping...*

Rose dropped the Beau down to twelve thousand feet and headed straight for the lights. One of the thin pencil-like beams went out for a second, but almost instantly re-appeared.

"Nothing so far, sir." White thought his eyes would pop as he stared unblinkingly at his set, face stuck against the visor, willing a blip to appear amongst his wavering lines.

187

As the spidery threads of white cold light wavered before him in the night, Rose's eyes turned to one side to protect his night vision, and then White suddenly called out urgently from behind him, "Contact! Contact, vector zero-seven-zero, range five miles, erm, angels twelve thousand five hundred, he's above us, range closing fast! *Oh shit!* He's coming towards us!"

Instantly Rose pulled back further on the control column, turning the snub nose of D-Dog directly onto the line of approach of the enemy plane.

White was still babbling, "Range one mile, he's to port of us and still above!"

"Stay in your seat, Chalky!" He thought he saw movement fleetingly, just for an instant, and then quite suddenly a sparkling necklace of tracer reached out, hurtling down and towards them, but then curling away below and behind as the nose gunner of the enemy bomber blasted away at them, the grey blur of the enemy bomber streaking past in the wink of an eye.

And then they were turning again, turning, turning hard after the enemy, the Hercules snarling and snapping as he pushed forward hard on the throttles, pressed back hard into his seat in turn as they fought to pursue the German bomber.

The turn was not one of those gentle Sunday-afternoon steering manoeuvres more common with an AI intercept, but rather a muscle-twisting, chest crushing, vision blurring and breathlessly wheezing one, much like those he'd performed when dogfighting with nippy little single engine fighters the previous summer and autumn.

"Cripes!" Rose gasped, surprised that he was actually *enjoying* the manoeuvring. He felt so *alive!* "Do you have him, Chalky?"

"Contact, three miles, vector two-two-five, same angels as us." White panted beneath the overwhelming forces as the Beaufighter wheeled after the enemy, "Range closing! Two miles! He's coming back! *Oh Fuck!*"

Rose felt like laughing madly at the gulped fear and surprise in White's voice, despite the circumstances. He felt exactly those same feelings mirrored perfectly in his own thumping, thrashing heart.

Bloody Hell! This one was going to fight it out with them! A dogfight with an enemy bomber!

And then the darting enemy was zipping close by once more, and this time the deadly line of boiling red blobs of fiery lead passed below them, and then the bandit shot past once more, and again Rose pulled the fighter hard into yet another straining turn, the world tumbling around them.

"Still in contact, *whoops!*" squawked White in discomfort as his stomach lurched and reeled violently, and he struggled, neck and spine straining, to keep his head from being pulled to one side as Rose violently wrenched the Beaufighter around after the enemy aircraft.

White's voice was thin and reedy as he gasped, "Keep turning, heading one-zero-zero, range two miles, bandit now descending! Reduce angle of bank."

"Thanks, Chalky." Rose wheezed and strained as the forces punched against him roughly, turning the Beau onto the new heading and pushing the nose down, "Angels?"

"Nine thousand and still going down, sir, maintain heading."

The airframe was quivering eagerly like a hunting dog as they shot after the enemy bomber, and Rose realised with some irritation that he still wasn't even sure what type of aircraft it was.

They snapped through a thin, filmy, patchwork of cloud, ripping a ragged, swirling trail though it as they chased once more after their enemy.

"Angels?" asked Rose again; carefully scanning the sky ahead, but nothing was yet visible.

"Seven thousand five hundred, still going down mighty fast, sir, still one-zero-zero, range three miles."

Oh Lor'! It was going to get away! The AI set at this height had a reasonable range of seven miles or so under ideal conditions, but if the bandit got outside that, they might lose it in the darkness...

Come on! Come on! Come on! It felt as if his heart would burst. The Hercules' were bellowing with effort.

They passed through six thousand feet, "Chalky?"

"Still going down, sir, four thousand, one-zero-zero, range just under three miles."

Come on! Come on! Come on!

D-Dog was straining and rattling, but they weren't getting that much closer, and that damned bomber was going down really fast! His arms ached holding the stiffening controls and his face was clammy.

Damn it! Come on!

And then, at three thousand feet, those dreaded words, "Contact lost, sir. Contact lost. Sorry..."

White sounded sick.

This close to the ground terrain, the enemy's return on the scope had disappeared into the ground clutter. Reacquiring would be nigh on impossible.

He swore. *Damn it!* He'd lost an enemy bomber over which he should have had a performance advantage on a perfect moonlit night! He felt an absolute chump.

"No, no, Chalky, not your fault," Rose said quickly, reassuringly, even though he could feel the same anger and frustration gnawing at him, "He was quick, Chalky, damned quick, and he didn't hang around. He threw me onto my back foot straight away, kept us flapping and then scarpered sharpish, while I was still trying to get after him. He was good."

Very good, bloody good. And damned lucky.

The lucky, *lucky* bastard.

But then his fury relented.

At least they themselves were still alive too. They had survived the encounter.

And there might still be a chance of making good…

"Cheer up, pal. Let's see if Lamplight still have him, eh?"

"OK, sir." Chalky replied doubtfully.

God, the poor old thing sounded so miserable, and Rose could understand and sympathise utterly.

Against all the odds, they'd actually found a bandit for themselves, but then lost it without even getting a shot in.

The same couldn't be said for the enemy, sod him.

If only Chalky had a gun in his Perspex dome, or better still a gun turret, things might have been different.

If only…

"Dagger 3 to Lamplight, I'm afraid we lost him. Can you help?"

"Rotten luck, Dagger 3. I'm sorry to hear that, but we only got a fleeting contact and we don't have him at all now. Please rejoin the cab rank. We'll try and find something for you."

"Thanks, Lamplight, am now re-joining cab rank, please advise angels."

Fuck it! Rose closed his eyes for a moment in pain as he pulled hard back, pushing them up into a steep, soaring climb.

They'd not managed to stop that one. How many lives would that German's bravery, luck and aggressive tactics cost?

The thought of their failure made him feel physically ill, and in his mind's eye he saw once more the long lines of dead girls clad in RAF blue.

But what else could they have done? D-Doggie wasn't a Hurricane, they hadn't been able to turn inside the turning circle of that mysterious bomber, and weren't able to get into a good position at any point before the enemy pilot had managed to escape.

He'd been good, alright.

Fuck!

A dejected and lengthy quarter of an hour later, Lamplight called for them, "Dagger 3, we have business for you. Please steer one-eight-zero magnetic, angels ten, range twenty miles, bandit will pass from west to east."

Ah, one heading eastwards, probably an 'empty,' a bomber that had already dropped its load and it was heading for home, now lighter and faster.

OK then. They had been another chance to make good. Better not mess this one up.

"Received, Lamplight, one-eight-zero, angels ten." Then, "Chalky? Looks like we've been given another go, an empty probably."

"I'm not fussy, sir."

For ten minutes they followed the vectors fed to them by the GCI controller, losing height and finally settling on a course that would take them out over the North Sea via Cromer.

And then White called out in satisfaction, "Contact! Got it! Bandit three miles ahead, five hundred feet above, same heading."

"Well done, Chalky! Lamplight, contact established, thank you for your help! Will be in touch."

"Understood, Dagger 3, good luck!"

With White's guidance, they rapidly cut the distance between the two aircraft to a thousand feet, and soon Rose caught the fleeting red tell-tale flicker of the enemy bomber's exhausts, around which the smudged shape of the bomber progressively materialised.

Playing with the controls deftly to slide comfortably into position below and behind, the dark shape above gradually increasing in size as they drew nearer, until they were less than three hundred feet from the enemy bomber.

Rose eyed it nervously, thumb hovering close to the firing button, "Chalky, we're really rather close now, you can have a bit of a leer now. What do you make of it?"

Excitedly, White swivelled his seat around to look, detaching his harness. "Ooh! Looks like a Dornier, um, a Dornier 17, very thin fuselage, two radial engines, twin tail fins, definitely a Dornier 17, I'd say."

"Thanks, Chalky, I agree with you. Tie yourself in and keep it in the scope. I'm going to give it two bursts."

"OK, sir, still got it on the set. Fire away."

"Firing." He depressed the button and the cannon thunderously spat out their focussed spray of hate. He was sure of the deflection, but nonetheless Rose pulled and pushed the control column backwards and forwards slightly, see-sawing the gunfire pattern generously across the target.

The flaring light from the guns reflected against the underside of the cowlings, making him squint against the rhythmic glimmer, and the bitter stink and smoke from the cannon crammed into the fuselage and into his lungs.

The raw torrent of shells and bullets from the Beaufighter viciously cut up through the port wing of the Dornier, destroying the port Bramo 323 engine and igniting the wing fuel tanks in a violently flaring, strobing, coruscation of blinding white light that suddenly flung the enemy bomber onto its side.

As the Dornier reeled wildly to port, the self-sealing tanks partially closing off the guttering stream of white fire pouring from them, the rear-facing upper gunner desperately opened fire with his MG15s, and a hose of well-aimed 7.92mm rounds pumped up wickedly towards D-Dog.

Rose lifted his finger, adjusted his aim and fired again, his fire cutting another swathe through the air to batter at the Dornier, an aileron flicking back, angry spots of light where the metal skin of the bomber was burning, striking heavily at the German even as the enemy tracer whirled up to them, whipping off first to one side, then connecting with the Beaufighter, and they felt the heart-stopping *thump-thump-thump* of bullets striking against the fuselage and wing before the stream passed across and away.

Damn! Heart racing, Rose threw his aircraft into a vicious turn to starboard, yanking back on the control column, and the heavy fighter began to yaw adversely so he immediately corrected and brought the aircraft out of the turn.

Damn it! He checked the controls, "Chalky! Are you OK? Are you hit? Chalky? Chalky! Talk to me!"

White's voice answered immediately, "I'm OK, sir, don't worry, how about you? I heard the hits, how's Doggie? Is she OK?" White was looking out of his little dome, watching as the enemy machine dived steeply downwards.

There was a bright flash, then several more, one after another in rapid succession, before the Dornier finally disappeared from view.

Something felt wrong to Rose, but what the hell was it? "Just checking, chum…there's a really strange vibration, maybe the port engine's running a tad rough, oil pressure and temperature are OK, though. I'm going to head for home, get the ground boys to have a look. I'm breaking off the combat."

White sounded unconcerned, "OK, Sir, sounds like a sensible idea. Old Doggie does feel a bit funny. I can't quite put my finger on it but I can feel that weird vibration too. I think you hit him hard, looks like he's going down."

"Dagger 3 to Lamplight, I think we got a probable, but we've picked up a bit of lead from our German friend, and may have received some damage. We've broken off the combat and are RTB."

"Thank you, Dagger 3, understand you are claiming probable and are returning to base, well done and good luck."

Nursing the unsteady Beaufighter gently, sweating despite the bitter coldness of the fighter's cockpit, eyes anxiously checking the controls, Rose flew carefully back to Dimple Heath.

Mouth sticky with fear, and nervously maintaining his flying speed whilst his heart battered painfully against his ribs like a trip-hammer, Rose gingerly touched down a very long twenty minutes later, breathing a sigh of relief as he finally taxied into his hardstanding and gratefully switched off his faithful engines.

Shaken, he allowed himself ten seconds with his eyes closed, relief washing over him, before releasing his harness and turning for his exit.

That had actually been pretty dicey at the end, even though Doggie had behaved perfectly well on the flight back to Dimple Heath, the strange, inexplicable vibration had remained.

Kelly and the ground crew were waiting excitedly for Rose and White in front of the fighter. White's face was pallid and drained, his smile sickly, the livid pressure marks from his facemask standing out darkly.

Lawks! Chalky looks a bit ragged. Do I look like that, too? He looks shattered, poor sod.

The adjutant was exultant, "We just got word, Flash, good news! Sector phoned it in a few minutes ago, a Dornier came down a mile off the coast near Cromer, almost hit a fishing trawler. It was seen by a shore battery and the local coastguard too. There weren't any other combats in the area at the time and the AA bods aren't claiming anything either."

He was beaming with pleasure, "It sounds to me like your probable just turned into a confirmed kill! Subject to approval from Group, of course, but I'd say it's in the bag, old man. Well done!"

Trying to adjust their weary eyes, Rose and White exchanged a tired but jubilant smile. "That's great news, sir! I'm sorry, excuse me for just a minute; Chief, could you just check the port engine, Jerry gave us a burst and she felt a bit strange. Thought the port engine may be a bit knackered, but the pressures and temperatures were fine up to the moment when I was switching off."

Rose raised his voice, "Thanks lads, that's another one down to you all. Well done! You gave us a fine aircraft. She'll do us nicely!"

Already the ground crew were swarming over the aircraft, and whilst the cowlings were removed and the engines checked, they grinned and winked and nodded with pleasure at his words.

"Come with me, lads, let's get a cup of hot char or two into you and we'll fill in an after-action report. Heard you also had a bit of a scrap earlier as well? Tell me about it. And I'd like to hear about the Wellington."

In the darkness, his voice was thoughtful, "Don't say anything, hush hush and all, but intelligence believe that the Germans might have captured at least one of our bombers, and might be using them as pathfinders for the raids that come after. It's going to be a bastard of a job identifying something like that. Leave that for the boffins to sort out. God knows enough of our bombers are coming back from raids with damaged friend-or-foe systems."

As they turned for his service car, the chief walked up to them, "Sir? A quick word if I may? The engines are OK, there're a few bullet holes, though there's no serious damage, but there is a bit of a hole outboard of the engine and the port leading edge and aileron looks a bit dented, probably down to bits of Jerry hitting you? 'Course, it would've buggered up the airflow. Anyway, that might explain why she felt wrong to you. Oh, and one of armourers noticed that a bullet had hit the barrel of one of your cannon. If you'd fired it again a shell might have gone off inside the barrel. Could've made a bit of a mess of the kite. And, er, of you as well, of course, sir, if you'll excuse me for saying so." He added hurriedly, "We'll get it replaced straight away."

The Chief looked back at the Beaufighter fondly, "Looks like it really was your lucky night, sir."

He suddenly grinned widely like Alice's Cheshire cat, his tea and nicotine-stained teeth almost invisible in the gloom.

"And very well done, Sir. That's another of the bastards who won't be coming back to our shores any time soon! Don't worry about the kite, we'll work as fast as we can, and should have her ready in about ninety minutes or so."

I'm going to fall asleep on my feet. He blinked his gluey eyes blearily. "Very good, Chief. Thanks."

There was a very good chance that by the time the damage and other issues with dear old Doggie had been sorted out, the Flight would be on half hour readiness, and (with a little luck) they might not need to go back up again tonight.

God willing. Fingers crossed.

Rose smiled his thanks as the Chief turned away, and fumbled with stiff fingers for the little pink bear in his pocket before turning back to Kelly and White.

The hairs on the back of his neck had risen, and his limbs were trembling in reaction to the stress from the combat and the flight back, and he wasn't sure if he could speak without his voice quavering. Poor Chalky looked washed out.

They were lucky to be alive. If he'd fired the cannon again, it might have brought them down!

Even if it hadn't, he himself sat pretty much directly above the cannon's gun ports, and he could have been injured or killed. And if he'd been killed, Chalky might have died too.

Rose felt relief wash over him again.

Lady Luck again. Thank you.

Lady Luck flouting Sir Isaac's intentions again! He wiped his stained face with one stiff, gloved hand.

They'd lost one, but they hadn't lost, not really, because it had been the Dornier crew who had been the real losers in tonight's struggle against the Black Knight. His thigh and calf muscles were trembling uncomfortably, and he felt he could sleep for a week. He yawned.

I need a strong cup of tea and to sit down for a minute or two.

Strangely, his eyes were wet with tears.

I'll have a little rest. Just for a minute or two.

Chapter 17

A couple of hours later, suitably reinforced with strong sugary tea, the after-action report safely filed, and with the level of readiness relaxed as there was no more enemy activity apparent in their sector, Rose and White were sitting down in front of the stove in the dispersals hut, exhausted but thoroughly warmed and highly satisfied with their busy night's contribution.

Furthermore, Rose was comforted to see the hand he was holding his cup of tea with was still once more, no sign of a tremor at all now.

Kelly had just telephoned from his office, having discovered that one of the enemy crew from their Dornier had survived, and he suggested to Rose that they might want to visit him.

Rose responded curtly that he did not have anything useful to say the enemy crewman, but that he would be more than happy to form a part of a firing squad for the bloody man.

The others looked startled, and even he was surprised at the harsh words that came from his lips. He clamped his mouth shut, lest he say anything else.

Kelly sensibly had no more to say after that, gently putting the phone down at the other end.

Rose finally managed to order his faithful operator to go to bed, but remained in dispersals himself, grabbing an hour's troubled snooze, because he had a breakfast date later with the most beautiful girl in the Women's Auxiliary Air Force.

In fact, the lovely girl was the most beautiful woman in the world.

And nothing would make him miss that rendezvous, for no matter how tired he was; he intended to keep their date, come what may.

With the difference in their 'working' hours, it was one of the few times they could share when both were on duty, and each and every second he could spend with the wonderful girl he loved so very much was precious.

She was the one who brought him joy and calm.

Molly tapped a piece of crisp fried bread on the side of her plate and pouted sorrowfully, "Oh, Harry, I wish I could go home with you, but something's come up and I've got to be here for a while."

Rose put down his cup of Camp coffee and wiped his lips, trying manfully to keep his eyes open, "Why? What's happened, my darling?"

"Some of my girls are up on a charge, and I've got to have a word with the WO of the Service Police."

"The SPs! Oh dear, what've they been doing now?"

"It's silly, really. This morning two of them on duty in Maintenance were invited to share a meal with some of the airmen from Technical Section, and they were all sitting down for some reconstituted egg on toast when the SPs caught them."

Rose laughed, but inside, a part of him was irritated at the monolithic stupidity of regulations and procedure.

How completely absurd!

"On what charge? Eating reconstituted eggs? I can understand how it could be considered a crime to have to eat the bloody stuff, but– "

Molly put down her piece of bread, "Honestly, Harry, why are men so obtuse?" she scolded, "My girls were put on a charge for sharing supper with their oppos, their shift counterparts. It happens every day, it's not really counterproductive to service discipline, in fact I believe that it helps strengthen it and I'm going to have a stiff word with the SP Warrant Officer."

Rose smiled wryly. "Ooh-er. I better wish him good luck, then. Just assure the poor fellow that they'll be paragons of virtue from now on, and perhaps he'll let them off, the little angels. Oh, and don't kiss him, whatever you do, even to get one of your girls off a charge, remember you're mine."

Molly grimaced helplessly and cast her eyes to the heavens. "You cheeky brute. Paragons of virtue? Little angels, you say? Some hope, one of them is Elsie Dyer. Might as well try to stop the sun from rising."

Rose stopped crunching his overdone slice of fried bread.

"Oh my God." He shook his head sorrowfully, "Elsie Dyer? Oh no. Oh dear. Oh Molly. Cripes."

"I know, but what else can I do? She's one of mine, and I'll always be there for her." After 'failing' her girls the previous year at RAF Foxton, she could no more abandon one of them than she could stab James with a bayonet.

Elsie Dyer, known to one and all throughout the station as 'Jankerella,' was the female nemesis of the station's SPs.

If amassing punishments were an Olympic sport, Elsie would be a Gold medallist many times over.

Whenever there was a WAAF up on a charge, there was a better than even chance it would be Elsie Dyer, being punished for having her hair hanging below her collar, cap at a jaunty angle like a Clippie, wearing non-issue silk stockings rather than the thick Lyle Grey stockings, sometimes no stockings (and even no knickers at all according to popular rumour), or some other minor, piddling transgression.

Elsie was a semi-regular fixture in the kitchens on 'Jankers', peeling potatoes in punishment for having commited some infringement or other, and some of the men swore blind they could tell when she was on Jankers by the cut of the chips.

The problem was that she didn't take well to service discipline, and Molly was at her wit's end in trying to control the girl (or at least to keep her out of trouble).

"Perhaps you can get a 'Confined To Camp' order for her?"

"Oh no! you must be joking! Can you imagine Elsie confined to camp? I couldn't bear it! Just think of the infringements she might make! She'd drive me mad! I'd much rather she was outside doing whatever naughty things she does. The less likely she is to doing them in here if she spends some time out there! I'd rather get her an admonishment or dismissal of charge."

"How about dismissal from the service? Get rid of her altogether?"

"Oh no. No, I couldn't do that. She's actually quite a nice girl, just a bit scruffy and more than a bit fond of the boys. But she's essentially a good little worker."

"Talking of scruffy, how did Granny always get away looking the way he did at Foxton. I'd have thought he'd have been on a fizzer every day?"

"Everybody loves Granny, he's so irreverent and chirpy to everybody. I think he's quite hard to dislike, even when he's being rude or outrageous."

Molly smiled warmly as she thought affectionately of their friend, "And to be honest, I think all the SPs loved him too. You saw how AVM Park was with him? If the AOC doesn't put him on a fizzer, who else is going to?"

He nodded sagely. "Hm. I take your point. He was going to tell me how he first met the AVM, but he never did."

"Well, I heard it was at Tangmere in '37, but I don't know the details. Next time we see him, we'll have to ask."

"Who? Granny or AVM Park?"

"Either of them, neither of them, both of them, who cares? I don't. Not in the slightest. They're wonderful men of course, but all that matters to me is being with you." She took his hand and wiped his oily fingers with her napkin. "You could be as grubby as a tramp, but I'd still love you."

Molly looked closely at his face, there were fine lines there now that hadn't been there in January, and his eyes were weary and red-rimmed. "How are you feeling, my darling? You look all-in, you must get some rest."

"Yes, I'm fine, my gorgeous. I'll go and get a bit of kip later; I want to be with you right now, these nights on duty mean I hardly get to see you for almost two days. I really feel it when I'm not with you. It's a lot safer than flying over France every day on those Circus operations. That's crazy, and it's a waste of good crews. At least the Luftwaffe fighters can't escort the bombers at night time. Last year it was so difficult getting through the screens of fighters to get to the bombers," he shuddered, "but now it's just a matter of finding the blighters, their single-engine fighters are no good in the darkness."

Hope that's still true...

Best not mention that old Doggie had been on the receiving end of a German machine gun, nor how difficult it was to actually find a target or to be able to stay in range. This night fighting lark had its own hazardous set of peculiarities and difficulties.

"I'm glad the two days are over. I hear that you did well, got another one? That's eleven confirmed now, isn't it? And, um, three for young Chalky?"

Rose smiled slightly, she knew exactly what his score was, but she'd let him confirm it and then accept her admiring glances. What a terrific girl she was.

"Yes, sweetheart, we managed to down a Dornier last night. Had a real fight with another bandit earlier, but he was a wily fox and we lost him, and you know about the Wimpy we almost shot down the night before?"

"Goodness, yes. It's a good thing it was identified as a friendly in the end."

"Yes, I couldn't bear it if we'd shot it down. Thank goodness we didn't catch it, although its par for the course to be vectored onto friendlies, they're not always that easy to identify on our equipment. We often tend to chase a couple of our own every night, that's why it's really important to identify what we're chasing before we try and shoot it down. That's why I always ask Chalky to have a look and see if he sees the same thing as I do."

Molly lowered her voice conspiratorially, "I hear it's actually quite easy to do. Apparently, a pilot from 604 shot down a Beaufighter from his own squadron, but don't tell anyone, for goodness' sake. All a bit hush-hush."

His eyes widened in shock and surprise, "Cripes! What rotten luck, poor chap. And the poor blighters in the Beau. God, what a mess. What a nightmare. Did you hear if the crew get out OK?" A chill swept over him at the thought of shooting down one of their own.

"Don't know. I'll try and find out. Just be careful, Harry. For me. Maybe you don't need to worry about being bounced by 109s anymore, but you need to watch out for our own. I don't think some of them are actually that careful about identification, there're always a few press-on types, aren't there?"

"Don't worry, love, the controller gives us permission to attack, so it must have been some breakdown in the system. Unfortunately, this sort of thing happens in wartime."

He thought pensively for a moment, "Actually, it happens in peacetime, too. Just a bit of ghastly rotten luck. I've got Genevieve with me, so you've nothing to worry about, alright, my sweetest morsel?"

Then he remembered something that Kelly had mentioned earlier in passing, "The Adj told me that the Sadlers Wells Ballet will be visiting us next month!"

Molly adored ballet. Rose found it monstrously boring, but endured it for her. Anything for her.

"Oh, how wonderful! I'd love to see them perform!"

"Don't worry; my sweetest of girls, we'll get the chance to do so together. I'll make sure we get the best seats in the house."

She touched his face then, dark eyes filled with adoration and tenderness. "I think you're simply wondeful, my darling, *et Je t'aime.*"

Oh Lord, time to dredge up his French again…

Erm, um…

"*Je t'aime plus, mon cher fille.* I wish that I could just lie down and sleep in the sanctuary of your arms. The warmth of your body is like the heat of the sun."

She smiled beautifully, alluringly, entrancing him. Their ankles were already interlocked beneath the table, and now she took both his hands in hers.

I must've said the right thing. Wish I could take her into my arms and give her a kiss, or something much more. Ooh, rather a bit more. But if I did, I'd probably be up on a charge as well.

Oh well. Even just holding hands with Molly was really rather nice too.

Her chin tilted slightly, "Harry, you're having lecherous thoughts again," she admonished him reprovingly.

"No, no, my sweet girl, I was just admiring your glorious beauty and the clear purity of your soul." He mumbled defensively.

How can I look at you and not have lecherous thoughts? You're bloody gorgeous! I want to undress you and have you splayed open and welcoming beneath me…

One perfect eyebrow arched. "Don't fib, I know you too well, you horrid, beastly man, I know exactly what you're thinking, and I'm surprised you have the energy after all that flying and combat last night."

Molly sighed regretfully, "But I'm afraid that you'll have to wait until this evening to have your wicked way with me, because I've got to sort out Elsie today and that other poor girl who was caught with her by the SPs."

"*Je veux vous lécher et vous embrasser partout, je veux te goûter, à lécher les ouvertures douces,* but I'll wait, because you're more than worth it."

She laughed softly in delight at the rather saucy promise, and then shyly glanced around to make sure no one was close enough to hear them.

As usual, they were considerately given a little space to themselves by the others. "You nasty, naughty boy, I'll hold you to that."

He was exhausted, and he could feel his eyelids drooping and his mind dulling, but still he managed to reward her with a bright smile, "You'd better, lovely girl, because I can't wait!"

But first, I need a damned good sleep, I'm completely bushed.

Chapter 18

With the rearmost part of the Junkers 88's gondola opened, Bruno scrambled swiftly up the ladder that led inside the cockpit, grabbing the handholds carefully, making sure that none of the switches or adjustable controls was snagged by his clothing.

Before settling onto his seat, he quickly checked his controls, making sure everything was in place and as it should be. Then he checked the automatic fuses in the box. He did not switch them on as he would pre-flight, but ensured all was in place, then checked the valves for the oxygen bottles, ensuring they were in the 'off' position.

All seemed in order, and as the fuse box to the left of his seat was close enough to easily toggle his other switches, and allowed himself to relax with satisfaction.

Bruno checked his seat *(mind the bomb release lever!)*; the position was just right, feet onto the rudder pedals. He closed his eyes and thought about the previous night, ignoring the ground crew performing maintenance of the starboard motor.

The opera *Elektra* in Amsterdam the previous evening had captivated Anja, but his own performance later at her friend's apartment he felt certain had impressed her more, and he'd even impressed himself.

Leutnant Bruno Von Ritter. Master of aerial combat, champion of the bed chamber.

Opera meant nothing to him, the impressive repertoire and skills shown by the lead in this most complex of operas, but it was Anja's great love, and she had adored the show.

The sight of her slim, lean nakedness on the soft sheets was indelibly imprinted onto his mind, and he relived with pleasure the way her skin felt beneath his palms, warm and smooth. Her easy smile and her little gasps and cries of pleasure as he mercilessly ploughed himself into her, her desperate need matching his as she rhythmically thrust herself up onto him in turn, the shared climax flinging them into a tempestuous world of pleasure that was finally stilled in the deep and dreamless sleep of total exhaustion.

They'd awoken and loved one another twice more that night, more tenderly than the first time, gently, and he realised that he was lost completely, totally besotted by the softly spoken, long-limbed lovely girl with the cheeky yet enigmatic smile and the thick mane of hair.

And he had found that she didn't wear uniform-issue knickers after all, but instead a sheer confection of delicate lacy black French silk.

It was but a few hours since that hot, prolonged farewell kiss at the entrance gate to Gilze-Rijen, and he pursed his lips with enjoyment as he remembered the softness of her lips, the taste of her mouth..

Bruno had had more than his fair share of women, but Anja was somehow completely different.

Not just was he in love with her, he was quite simply totally obsessed by her.

He sighed and opened his eyes. Staring back at him with interest through the windscreen was a member of the ground crew, wiping the clean Perspex industriously with a piece of cotton.

208

As soon as he realised that Bruno's eyes were open, and staring back into his, the *Gefreiter* averted his fascinated gaze but continued wiping.

It was time to go. He got up and carefully made his way back out of the aircraft. Walking slowly up the flight line, he stopped to look at *Oberleutnant* Stein's machine. The groundcrew had removed the propeller and were refitting the oil-cooling annular radiators of the starboard engine.

Stein had ventured over a Tommy airfield last night, bagged a Wellington in the landing circuit with its navigation lights on, and then shot up what he could see of the hangars. On the journey home, he'd also managed to claim a second British bomber, a Blenheim.

Despite basking in the memories of the night before, Bruno felt a spark of irritation and resentment. Stein had a score of eight now, and he was close enough to vie for the *Gruppe's* plaudits as top scorer.

Doubtless he, too, had a chronic case of the 'throatache', the all-encompassing desire to be awarded a *Ritterkreuz*, but Bruno would be damned if he allowed that hide-bound Swabian bastard Stein to beat him in the race to the Knight's Cross.

He stared morosely at one of the newly arrived Dornier Do 215B-5 fighter conversions that they were supposed to be trialling. With four machine guns and two cannon, the sleek converted bomber looked every inch a deadly nocturnal hunter.

I have to get another, he thought petulantly, *at least one more tonight. I'm going to attack a Tommy aerodrome tonight, but unlike Stein, I shan't forget to drop my bombs on the swine.*

Despite his successful night, Stein had been mortified to discover on his return that he'd forgotten to drop his bombs in the adrenaline charged excitement of his daring raid, instead bringing them safely home to his immense chagrin.

Bruno looked around; saw his crew chief watching him quizzically, "Petersen! Petersen, you old hound! Load her up with some eggs. I'm visiting our English relatives and I want to leave them a present to remember us by."

The lined and greying *Oberfeldwebel* snapped to attention with a smile. He was covered in oil and dust, so that even his lapel tabs, originally a bright golden-yellow, were now a dull and tarnished orange. "*Leutnant* Von Ritter, sir?"

"My dear fellow, I want some 250kg bombs loaded on her tonight, we're going to visit *Frau* Tommy at home, and I want to leave her a nice present."

The senior NCO nodded respectfully, "Yes, sir. Would four be acceptable? Two and two underwing grouping?"

"Thank you, Petersen, sounds perfect. Will she be ready on time?"

"She'll be ready, sir. I'll go and do it now. If the *Herr Leutnant* will excuse me?" the crew chief saluted and strode off to make the arrangements.

Bruno turned to look back at his aircraft.

Damn Stein! Tonight *we* are going to give Tommy a beating that he'll not forget.

And when we return, if she's free, I'm going to give my lovely Anja an evening that *she* won't forget.

One hour after sunset, the Junkers 88 passed low over the rocky cliff face of the coast of Yorkshire, nose pointing directly at the target Bruno had chosen after consultation with the *Gruppe* Intelligence Officer, *Hauptman* Baum.

RAF station Driffield was a Bomber Command base located south-west of Great Driffield, on the northern side of the road running between Great Driffield and Market Weighton.

The Aerodrome consisted of closely grouped RAF station buildings and wide runways. As with standard RAF practice, the munitions storage area was sensibly placed some distance from the main buildings, at the North West corner of the airfield.

A raid by the Luftwaffe the previous summer damaged the base badly, crowed intelligence, killing countless RAF personnel and destroying many Whitley bombers.

A huge success.

Badly damaged, the airfield became non-operational following the attack, but Baum had recently received information that RAF Bomber Command had now assigned a squadron of Wellingtons to Driffield, and that they were working up for operational readiness.

It was Bruno's intention to take advantage of the inexperience of the fresh bomber aircrews.

A short while later, the large German fighter was circling the RAF airfield at a distance of five miles.

"Boys, keep a good lookout, we should get a customer shortly. The night-flying program here should be quite busy as they work up."

Rudi snorted, "It's as black as a witch's tit out there, sir. It's not going to be easy to catch them this low down."

"No Rudi, they're not operational yet, I expect to catch one of their crews blundering around up here getting accustomed to night-flying from Driffield…"

Even as he was speaking, the Junkers was suddenly buffeted as it passed through the slipstream of another aircraft.

"That was something! Can you see it? It's got to be close by…"

Almost immediately, slightly to port and below, a set of navigation lights winked on about a kilometre ahead. They had crossed paths so close with the other aircraft; it was incredible that they had missed one another!

"There! I see him!" increasing the throttles, Bruno rapidly closed the distance between the two aircraft, to reveal a Wellington bomber, wheels down as it gradually descended, losing height every second, but he held his fire, the enemy aircraft now framed by and seeming huge and looming in the windscreen.

"In range," breathed Rudi imploringly, staring at the machine guns in the rear turret of the looming Wellington, but the gunner was looking down, caught in some inner reverie.

"No," replied Bruno, caressing the firing button lovingly, "Not yet, I'm waiting until the runway lights up for this wandering sheep. I want to see the Tommy base."

He reduced height and speed to keep station with it as it bumbled slowly downwards, and then ahead of them two parallel lines of lights winked on as the bomber began its landing approach, guiding their British enemy onwards to safety.

The Junkers 88C was now less than a couple of kilometres from the airfield perimeter.

"Now?" asked Rudi again. *Oh God, what are you waiting for?*

"Yes, Rudi, now," Bruno checked once more that the large twin-engine bomber was centred in his cross-hairs, pushed down hard on the firing button, and poured a vicious fusillade of cannon shells and bullets along the length of the bomber's fuselage, simultaneously ripping through delicate instruments, flying controls and fragile human beings.

Small explosions erupted violently within the bomber, one detonation ripping out a section of fuselage to flick down, and it sparkled and shook with hits and puffs of smoke and burning flecks of metal.

With its crew dead or dying, now no longer under control, the Wellington reared up like a startled stallion, and as its speed bled off and it lost lift, it yawed to port and spun downwards into the ground. From a height of five hundred feet it only took a few seconds for it to smash into the ground in a boiling eruption of fire and light and sound that they could see and hear and feel.

Mouse looked with satisfaction for a moment at the conflagration as it passed behind them, then resumed his careful searching of the sky behind, even though the flames had damaged his night vision.

"Good shooting, *Herr Leutnant*. Can you give me something to shoot at for a change now, please?"

They were passing over the perimeter fence now, the flaming ruins of the bomber left behind now.

"Thank you, Mouse. If you see targets, give them a good long burst. There'll be buildings to my starboard, give them a squirt."

Already he was turning slightly to starboard, lining up on them, "I'm going to bomb the hangars, give them and the buildings a good long burst."

And still no flak. The lights of the runway were still on, giving Bruno an excellent reference point in his rapid approach to the hangars and airfield buildings.

Even now, the people on the ground were confused and the defences remained silent.

There. He had chosen the paired hangars as his target, difficult to miss. As they loomed closer, he rested his fingers on the lever.

Still no flak!

At long last the runway lights flicked off, but it was too late, for he knew exactly where he was in the darkness, and where his intended target was.

Here goes… push the bomb jettison lever, and then the Junkers seemed to lift as it was relieved of 1000kgs of weight, and he struggled with a racing heart to keep her down as the bombs were falling.

"Bombs gone!" the Junkers bounding up, pull to full throttle, run from the blast, head down and run, run fast…

As soon as he heard Bruno's shout, and felt the lightening of the night fighter, Mouse opened fire indiscriminately into the darkness below without sighting, spraying the unseen enemy airfield.

Sweeping down in a wide arc, all four of the falling *Sprengbombe Cylindrich 250* bombs landed on the far side of the paired hangars Bruno had targeted, exploding to rip great craters in the open ground between the hangars and the operations block; stones, earth, fragments, shrapnel and airslap blasting outwards, tearing and thrusting rents and dents into nearby structures, the airslap pushing down hard, pulling out and shredding shrubs and trees, flinging nearby vehicles in the air, and dropping an asbestos profiled sheet onto an aircraftsman in the empty hangar as he worked on the dented mudguard of his bicycle.

In another hangar, the groundcrew working on one engine of a Wellington cowered and fell as the air pressure blast slapped against the wall, the steel frame ringing sonorously, windows and asbestos tiles and concrete chipping and cracking, ground shock knocking them down like ninepins, dirt and dust wildly swirling and soaring as if in celebration.

Shaken but unhurt, the airmen unsteadily got to their feet and stared at one another in shock.

Mouse scrutinised the great cloud of dust and smoke and dust expanding, shot through from within with bright flame.

"You hit the big hangar, sir! You must have destroyed at least one more bomber inside it! You *must* have! We've destroyed at least two bombers tonight! Maybe more!" He was almost shouting, "That hangar was big enough for three or four bombers. It's a great victory! You must have killed hundreds of the bastards!"

The air raid siren was belatedly wailing the alert, but the drone of the Junker's engines was already fading, Bruno making good his escape into the sanctuary of the night.

Pleased, Mouse dispassionately watched the sullen, flickering flame-lit smoke cloud hanging heavy and low over Driffield, and to one side, the burning embers of the smashed Wellington.

He himself had emptied his guns onto the area where he thought the operations block was, and he felt satisfied with his efforts. Hopefully he'd accounted for a large number of the enemy. He felt satisfied that he'd blooded his guns this night, and his chest puffed out with pride.

"Good work, sir! That was an excellent attack. Smooth."

"Glorious, simply glorious!" Rudi pumped the air with his fists in excitement, eyes huge behind his goggles, terror forgotten as they regained the safety of darkness, some distance now between them and the enemy airfield.

Bruno was bathed in sweat and he kept glancing nervously at the sky around them, whilst behind them the damaged airfield and its fire-lit clouds of smoke faded into the blackness behind them.

"Thanks, boys, that was something incredible, wasn't it? We certainly caught them with their drawers around their ankles!" he pulled the throttles as far as he could, *time to get out of here…*

"They didn't even shoot back at us!" gasped Rudi in astonishment and heartfelt gratitude. "Why didn't they shoot at us?"

Mouse rudely blew a raspberry, "Who cares? Thank goodness for that! They weren't expecting us at all, sir, you took them completely by surprise! Incredible! We must have killed many, maybe at least a hundred? Two? And in addition to the bombers we must have destroyed in the hangar, we got that Tommy bomber in the air too!"

Bruno checked the throttle position with his fingers again, eyes still searching anxiously, switching on the window heating panels as the glass began to mist slightly as they recovered, "And now, dear friends, we are getting the hell away, as quick as we can, while they are still wondering what happened. Keep an eye open for their fighters, boys, they'll be as mad as a mule with a stung arse with us!"

Time to get out of it...

Chapter 19

Bruno finally began to relax when they were twenty miles from the Norfolk coast. Intelligence reports suggested that as a rule RAF night fighters did not fly far from the coast of Britain, so there was a much reduced likelihood that they were going to be intercepted now.

The others, however, were quite cheerful, and seemed, at least to him, far calmer than he himself was. "Mouse, anything?"

"Nothing sir, we got away cleanly, it's been a great mission. A great mission."

Satisfied, Bruno pulled back and the aircraft began to climb, watching thankfully as the altitude increased.

He tried to slow the frantic beat of his heart, to still the tremble which remained, making it appear as if the fighter were flying through unsettled air.

The fighter shuddered alarmingly, and Bruno tried harder to hold the control column firmly.

Damn it! Get a grip on yourself!

"What the…?" there was surprise in Mouse's normally even voice. "*Herr Leutnant?* We just passed behind a large aircraft!"

"What? Mouse, give me a proper report, damn you!"

"Sorry, sir, unidentified large aircraft behind, heading away on an opposite course."

Even as Mouse was speaking, Bruno had levelled out and was hauling the aircraft around back the way it had come.

Dear God, that was the second near-collision in the space of less than an hour! Luck truly was smiling on them this night!

Might they get yet another of the enemy this amazingly wonderful night?

"Thank you, Mouse. Keep an eye open," He grinned humourlessly, for the words were unnecessary. Nothing could creep up on them from behind with Mouse protecting their backsides!

"Rudi, eyes open, let's see what it was…"

One minute turned into two, and then, "*Herr Leutnant!* Aicraft above and to starboard! My God, it's big!"

Bruno leaned forward to look better, "What is it? A Wellington, maybe?"

"I'm not sure, sir, big, bigger than a Wellington, four engines? Yes, four engines, single vertical stabiliser."

"Four engines? A Kondor, perhaps?" Certainly, the long-range Focke-Wulf Fw 200 fitted Rudi's description.

"Maybe, sir…" Rudi sounded uncertain.

"Hmm. Alright, I'm going to approach it, can you see a gondola?"

"Um, not sure, wait, oh I can see it better now, let's see now." Rudi cocked his head, "Well, I don't see a gondola, sir."

His hands had somehow become rock steady, and he carefully drew underneath the large shape, noticing the rear facing gun turret for the first time. Kondors don't have those. He was sure of that. They were lucky not to have been seen by the gunner, but then, luck had walked hand in hand with them since they'd left Gilze-Rijen.

Working the controls carefully, Bruno expertly maintained

position beneath and just behind the four engine bomber, studying the underside of the enemy aeroplane carefully through his clear canopy.

"I agree with you, Rudi, I don't see one either. I don't think it's a Kondor. It looks familiar, but I can't think what it is."

"With your permission, sir?" without waiting for a reply, Mouse continued, "I seem to remember that the British have a four-engine bomber. Might it be one of those?"

Rudi punched one fist into an open palm, "Oh God! Of course, the Short Stirling!"

Mouse sounded smug, "Some of us go to the aircraft recognition lectures."

Both amused by Mouse's comments and annoyed at his own ignorance, Bruno cursed himself.

It didn't look good to be less well informed than his men. "Well then, it's settled, we're going to add him to tonight's score. Ready? Standby." And then he had a thought, "Mouse, you saw it, do you want a shot?"

"I'm sorry, sir?" Mouse asked in surprise.

"I'm going to pull ahead a little, he's on a steady course, so I want you to shoot up his nose section, kill the pilots."

"*Herr Leutnant*, he has a nose turret, he could shoot at us while you're getting into position."

"Well, shoot the gunner first, then. He'll be looking ahead, not below. Now stop talking, we're almost back at Tommyland again. Fire as soon as you can. I'll go down to increase your accessible arc of fire."

"Yes, sir!"

Rudi grimaced. *What on earth?* If Mouse didn't get the enemy gunner quick, there was a good chance that they'd be the ones floating in the water in the next few minutes.

"And thank you, sir!" Mouse was a lot less concerned.

Bruno pushed the fighter into a gentle descent to port, pulled the throttles gently, and the Junkers began to pull ahead on a divergent course.

Rudi hunched apprehensively into his seat, closed his eyes and began to pray.

Mouse was ready, and as soon as the front of the Stirling entered his sights he pressed his triggers, "Firing now…"

The machine gun clattered wickedly behind them, and a bright line of tracer played across the nose section and inboard part of the port wing. He vaguely remembered being told that the inboard fuel tanks were the only ones on the new bomber without a self-sealing capability.

Or was that on the new Halifax bomber?

Whichever it was, there was no reaction from the bomber as Mouse's three second burst ripped wickedly into it, a pattern of hits sparkling and flaring brightly on the nose section and wing roots of the great bomber.

As soon as he Mouse's gun fell silent, Bruno jinked and then pulled into a diving turn to port, curving the big fighter into a wide turn, "Mouse, keep an eye on it, I might need you to guide me back in, what's it doing?"

His gunner craned his head around to keep an eye on the bomber as the forces of the turn pulled at him.

"Nothing, nothing at all, sir," he said in disgust, "I'm sure I hit it but I'm not sure I did any damage. It's still on course, no change in height or heading."

Bruno positioned the Junkers carefully a safe distance behind and below the Stirling. Certainly there appeared to be no damage done, but then he noticed the faint trail streaming in a thin, pale cloud behind the bomber.

"You hit it, Mouse! There's a vapour trail streaming back! I don't know why your tracer didn't set the bastard alight. Rudi, would you like a go?"

"*Herr Leutnant*, will you stop messing about and shoot the Englander down? I want to go home!"

"Alright Rudi, keep calm, man. I'll get a bit closer then we'll hammer him with the cannon…wait! What the hell's that?"

Something flew back from the bomber, falling away, rapidly followed by a second. Bruno leaned forward to watch the objects fall away. What were they? Another of the mysterious objects flew back, just as the first suddenly bloomed into the shape of a parachute.

The crew were baling out!

Bruno noticed that the enemy aeroplane was slowly losing height. "Mouse, you did it! The enemy's losing height! It's going down! You must have killed the pilots and front gunner. Good shooting my friend!"

Mouse gazed at the four parachutes that fell behind and disappeared astern into the darkness. "Four got out, sir. The rest of the crew must be dead, after all."

In morbid fascination, Bruno and Rudi watched as the massive four-engine RAF bomber started to slide into an ever-steepening descent. "Well, we did get another one then, my friend, this wonderful night!"

"Can we go home now, please?" asked Rudi plaintively.

"Oh God! Patience, Rudi. Just a moment longer, it's so big, I want to see it hit!"

Rudi turned away with a grunt of disgust and began to rummage in his satchel, he would have some coffee as they waited. And it might help to calm him.

"Don't pour it yet, Rudi, I'm going down. We're pretty close to the English coast." Already the coast was visible as a dark line ahead.

With a sigh Rudi sat back, casting anxious glances out of the canopy surreptitiously. Surely they'd done enough for one night? It had been a dream mission. The English coast was so close! Too damned close!

And still the Stirling bomber was descending, the only sign of damage the dispersing hazy plume of petrol spewing from its fuel tank. How is it that the blasted thing wasn't alight?

And then suddenly there was no more height, the long plunge was over, and the Short Stirling crashed nose first into the waves just offshore. One moment it was whole, a huge dark weapon of war that had flown against their countrymen and dropped bombs on them not long before this very evening; and the next it was shattered and torn asunder by the impact.

In the darkness the crash was a vague disturbance, a pale spray and fragments being flung forwards, amongst them one engine cartwheeling just seen; the sights abruptly extinguished by a long streak of boiling white flame, the eye-aching light equally suddenly snuffed out, leaving only disturbed boiling water strewn with tiny floating pieces of burning wreckage, lighting the great airborne stain of steam and dirty, oily smoke.

Bruno shivered involuntarily as he contemplated the final resting place of at three or more of the enemy. But at least they had been dead, or so a part of him hoped.

Dear God, might they have yet lived? Might they have been conscious in those last moments before the bomber hit? Knowing that what remained of their lives was measured in scant seconds, knowing and yet being unable to do anything about it.

Again he shivered. No, the others would not have parachuted from

222

the bomber had their crew mates been alive. There can't have been any survivors still aboard the huge bomber as it hit the sea.

Then he frowned to himself. What was he thinking? They were the enemy, and had likely killed many of his countrymen themselves! It was an honour to have killed them, damn it!

"Two tonight, Herr Leutnant, double kills! It's been an incredible night! What a trip!" the normally impassive gunner actually sounded quite cheerful!

But he was right, it *had* been an incredible trip. Everything had gone perfectly, just as well as he could have wished.

"Perhaps we ought to go home, *Herr Leutnant?*" Rudi's spoke solicitously, "Or shall we go on a trip to see more of the English coast at night? Do we have enough fuel?"

Bruno belatedly realised he was still circling the crash site, perilously close to enemy territory. Hastily he pulled the aircraft onto a course for home, their airfield in Holland.

"I'll forgive your impertinence, Rudi," he said coolly, "but stop being such an old woman. It's been a good night. You should be pleased."

"I'll be pleased when we're sitting down to a nice hot cup of celebratory coffee, ersatz or not, *Herr Leutnant*, if you'll excuse my saying so."

"Yes, yes, you'll notice we are on a course for home, stop moaning so, you old misery. What's our score now? Have either of you been keeping count?"

"My wonderful leader, of course! Tonight makes twelve! I wonder how many we destroyed in the hangars. Three or four perhaps? Will they let us count those, do you think?"

Twelve enemy bombers destroyed, confirmed! Let Stein suck on that, the dog!

The sound of the Junkers 88C night fighter diminished into the distance, its jubilant and weary crew in a mood far brighter than the dying, glowing embers that were all that they left behind them of the men they had just killed.

Chapter 20

Rose stared through the windscreen glumly.

Bored, bored, *bored.*

Apart from the backs of his flying boot-clad ankles, upon which a painfully thin stream of warm air from the heating tube played rather diffidently, he was freezing and hungry and they had not yet been called upon by the GCI controller.

Worse, the escape hatch behind him must have something accidently caught between it and the fuselage, because an icy draught of air curled up through the cockpit and kept wafting horribly across his forehead, making his eyes water and his head ache. He jiggled the goggles around to protect his forehead.

Bored.

It was almost an hour and a half since they'd taken off on patrol, and whilst a 'customer' had been selected for each of the others on patrol, there'd been nothing left over for them to chase.

It was surprising, because the night was clear, with a luminous bomber's moon glowing bright and round upon them.

Bored.

For about the tenth time in an hour, he called the controller. "Dagger 3 to Lamplight, anything for us?"

225

"Lamplight to Dagger 3, sorry, nothing doing. No customers at the moment." Even the controller sounded fed up. The last thing he probably needs right now is idiot Beaufighter pilots calling him every few moments.

He sighed and wiped his icy forehead.

Bored.

Stifling a yawn, Rose switched to intercom, "Are you sleeping, Chalky?"

"I would be, sir, if you didn't keep gabbing on about the good old days when you were a lad!"

Rose grinned, and shook his head. Impertinent little puppy; conveniently forgetting that he'd been rather like that himself not so very long ago.

White actually sounded quite chipper and not even the slightest, teeny-weeny bit drowsy or bored.

How does he do it? It's indecent.

I hate him, cheeky wee bugger.

But of course, he didn't. Not really.

Well, perhaps just a tiny little bit.

Bored-bored-bored. And fucking frozen.

It had been almost a month now since their first trip together as a crew, and although they'd bagged three on operations since then, the two Heinkels and the Dornier had remained the only confirmed kills they'd achieved so far.

There had been chases and combats aplenty since, but all that they had been able to manage in the time since those early combats had been one enemy bomber badly frightened, three damaged and two probables.

Both of the latter enemy bombers had received a good pummelling by their guns, and both had dived away quite steeply at an angle from

226

which they'd quite likely never recover. But without any combustion, and unable to follow the steeply diving enemy bombers in what were most likely uncontrolled dives, there had been no indication of the seriousness of damage they'd suffered.

The only way of knowing would be the sudden flash of a stricken enemy smashing into the ground or sea below.

Without this, the combats had ended inconclusively, no proof of destruction, allowing them only probable kills on both occasions. No matter how unlikely it might be, recovery from a steep dive at low level was not impossible, and quite possibly those diving aircraft may have made it back to their airfields.

On one particularly frustrating occasion, after a text-book interception brilliantly performed by a terribly smug sounding White, one in which everything had gone right, and when they'd been perfectly placed behind an unsuspecting, lumbering great Heinkel, the guns had inexplicably jammed after firing only seven rounds that appeared (unsurprisingly) not to have had any effect whatsoever.

It had been one of the most galling experiences of Rose's life to watch the bomber dive safely away and disappear into the black night. The enemy gunner had squirted a short burst at them and then fallen silent as the enemy bomber disappeared safely into the dark.

Later, on the ground, a grim-faced crew mechanic had silently shown Rose and White a detached connection in the control wires, a tiny little thing which caused a break in the circuit and prevented their guns from firing more than a handful of shells.

On yet another occasion, Rose and White successfully intercepted an enemy bomber on its way home, a fleeting contact diving towards them, hurtling for the coast on an opposite heading, a little scrap of Rose trembling inwardly as the German had loomed towards them in his mind at their phenomenal combined speed, awful memories still sharp of a horrific collision between his Hurricane and a Bf109 the previous year which almost resulted in his death.

This time, though, the enemy zipped past them unseen, not even close enough to feel the other aeroplane's slipstream, and even as he turned after it, muscles straining and vision blurring, the contact on White's scope was lost almost immediately in the 'grass' of the screen's background returns.

Rose and White then spent a fruitless and frustrating quarter of an hour hoping to catch it again on the scopes, but were unable to reacquire contact, and the wily enemy pilot scurried home at low level, scared out of his skin, grateful for the lucky escape and looking forward to a furlough in Paris with his new French girlfriend.

There were also plenty of wasted chases in which the bomber had been either too fast or they had been seen by sharp-eyed gunners whilst still out of range, and the enemy would evade by diving before they could get close enough to shoot.

In one instance Rose attempted a few tentative bursts as the enemy bomber drew away, but none of the rounds had connected and all he could do was swear impotently into his mask and break off as his controls began to lock at the high speeds.

And when there was no custom at all and they were on long hours of dreary patrolling, the time dragged as they waited for directions onto an enemy aircraft.

Initially, the first couple of patrols Rose had flown with a little underlying tension as he worried about staying on his allotted circuit, but with time he learned to step back and manage the tasks automatically, and easing the tension and concentration.

There was something soothing about maintaining position by the stars when the nights were clear and dark or even when well-lit by the moon.

He hated the dirty weather, lashing rain pounding at them and the flickering electrical discharges that danced, slipped, crowded and squirmed over D-Dog, just as fleas would over a real dog, and just as uncomfortable for them both, faces lit eerily by coruscating waves and headphones hissing and popping.

Rather than fly the fighter with an effervescent but harmless and glowing electric cerulean overcoat, a discomfited Rose usually descended to less ionised air.

A fortnight before, the cloud had been deep and all-consuming, opaque swirling thickness and buffeting gusts. Despite the aerial roughness of the interception on which they were, the GCI controller expertly brought them into contact with a bogey, and White did the rest, closing the distance with the contact to a few hundred yards.

And after all of that the job was his to complete, Rose had merely to place the enemy within the gun sight and let rip.

Yet he could not do so. Despite closing with the other aircraft as close as he safely could, he was unable to pick it out in the dirty murkiness.

And without a positive identification, Rose was forced to hold fire. What if it were British? If it was a friendly it would be fratricidal to shoot it down, and if it weren't, how could he aim? What would he aim at? And then of course if he fired there was the danger that they would fly through debris or get too close and collide with the bogey.

Despite a lengthy pursuit (from a respectful distance), the cloud had not thinned appreciably, and they never once caught sight of the enemy (if that was what it was) and finally were forced to break off the pointless hunt. It had been a bitter but unavoidable pill to swallow.

They'd done the best possible, but that did not help to ease the deep despair in their hearts. The best had not been enough. Would that unidentified aircraft be back tomorrow to drop bombs on their country folk? They could never know for sure, but it was likely.

And then there was the ice. Insidiously, silently, gradually, it would gently build up to form a second skin, weighing down the Beaufighter, affecting the flying surfaces, obscuring the cockpit windows and White's observation bubble, and straining the Hercules engines as they strove to drag the encumbered aircraft to height.

Chunks of ice large and small would break off to disappear in their turbulent wake with unnervingly daunting cracking sounds, sometimes tumbling back to whack and clatter violently against the aircraft nastily, like monstrous lumps of sleet.

After one such flight Rose inspected the fuselage and was disconcerted to see deep indentations left on the skin of the aeroplane by the lumps of ricocheting ice.

Ice building up on the aerials a couple of days ago damaged them badly as D-Dog was climbing after a scramble, cracking them and rendering the AI totally unserviceable.

Returning to base so soon after take-off because of damaged equipment had been infuriating to say the least, and recalibrating and repairing the damage had meant that they were forced to switch aircraft and fly G-Gertrude instead, the squadron's hangar queen.

And dear old Gertie continued to act true to form.

It had taken them the best part of an hour to drag 'Dirty Gertie' (as she was unkindly known by all the ground crew and aircrews) to their operational patrol altitude at fifteen thousand feet, and almost immediately she began to lose revs in her port engine, forcing Rose to lose height as he fought to hold altitude.

Finally being able to maintain altitude at eleven thousand feet, with both of the Hercules engines behaving normally, Lamplight had found them a customer, and began to direct them to an intercept.

As soon as Gertie was within twenty miles of the bandit, as was normal practice, White switched on the set and almost immediately his compartment was filled with the awful stink that indicated all was not well with the set. Hastily, he switched it off and shared the bad news with Rose, who in turn would have the unenviable task of passing on the gen to Lamplight.

Rose closed his eyes wearily and keyed the R/T to advise the controller of their predicament, "Lamplight, I'm afraid that my Thing is unserviceable." He wouldn't use the words 'My thing is bent', with all its unfortunate connotations, but he needn't have worried, for the girls in the control room had heard the words so often over the previous months, no one would bat an eyelash.

They tried hard, assisted very ably via direction from the ground to intercept the raider, but it had been a fruitless search without a functioning AI, and Gertie had been brought back to Dimple Heath without further ado. Luckily the flight back and the landing was one that was (fortunately) without excitement or incident, although Rose watched the controls like a hawk throughout.

An exceedingly fretful hawk.

Once the fighter had rolled to a stop, and safely on the ground, Rose laid one palm gently against the stained skin of the fuselage, and pursed his lips thoughtfully for a moment, but the crew chief merely stared darkly at Gertie, had shaken his head and ordered her wheeled away back into exile at the back of the hanger.

Once more the groundcrews and technicians scratched their heads unhappily, and wondered what to do with her.

It was suggested unkindly by some wag that she be rolled out and left exposed on the hardstanding until their occasional and inept enemy night raider (derisively named 'Von Plop' by all and sundry, to differentiate Dimple Heath's gormless intruder from Manston's 'Von Plonk') obligingly dropped a stick of bombs on her and put

231

Gertie out of her misery, but the suggestion was rejected because it was generally agreed that Von Plop's aim was rotten (thankfully he'd yet to hit anything other than open ground with his bombs) and poor Gertie might have to wait a very long time to be hit.

Furthermore, it was felt that even an aeroplane like Gertie did not deserve such an ignominious fate at the hands of Von Plop.

To provide her as an easy target for him would be unpatriotic.

Toffee sighed when he heard the news. "She'll be sent as a training aircraft and shred some poor new crew's nerves," he predicted acidly.

Chapter 21

With a disgraced Gertie banished back into obscurity, back in her usual resting place in the darkest recesses of a hangar again, Rose and White were assigned the shared use of A-Able with Williams and Heather. When one crew landed, the other would take off.

It was a prickly arrangement (no-one wants to share *their* aircraft if they can help it), and the next day there was a collective cheer when a brand new replacement Beaufighter appeared in the circuit overhead.

The pilot expertly turned the heavy fighter into a steep landing approach, smoothly pulling up at the last moment to perform a neat three-point landing, the wheels hardly even kicking up a slight fuss of dust as the Beau settled onto the ground.

Once on the ground, the aircraft was quickly marshalled into a vacant hardstanding.

A little group of pilots had gathered behind them.

"Hm, that was a bit flash, no pun intended, old man," murmured Barr, grinning apologetically at Rose, "Must be an expert pilot; that was a neater landing than I'm used to seeing around here."

He ignored the dirty looks and the derisive muttering from his companions, "Perhaps we could get the fellow to join our little band?"

The pilot of the machine ran up the engines at maximum revolutions for a moment, blipped them, and then, safety checks done, switched off. A moment later a slim figure bounced down the ladder to chat with Chiefy.

Meanwhile, the ground crew fell on the fighter eagerly, inserting the locking components in the undercarriage and opening up hatches, ensuring that the aircraft was readied for operations as quickly as possible.

"Oh dear, the chap's a bit on the small side," Barr grinned contritely once more as he looked down at Rose. "Not that there's anything wrong with that, of course."

Rose beamed back good-naturedly, "'Course not. It's not all bad being small, y'know Billy, because I'm actually perfectly placed down here to punch you in the balls. Fancy a demonstration?"

The Beaufighter pilot finished the discussion with Chiefy, looked around the airfield with interest and noticed the little group of pilots including Rose and Barr, and with a final nod at the grizzled sergeant, turned and walked towards them.

Pulling off the flying helmet, to the onlooker's astonishment, the pilot shook out a wavy thatch of shoulder-length fair hair and pulled off her goggles to reveal a very feminine face.

Despite himself Barr whistled and Rose was amazed to see Toffee Jones gawp in surprise.

"But she's just a girl!" muttered Cole in surprise, looking past the figure approaching them. "Where's the pilot?"

"Hardly a girl, Flying Officer. And I'm the pilot. Who were you expecting? Trenchard? Hermann Goering? George Formby perhaps?"

The 'girl' stopped before them, and her voice was light and cool, eyes flinty.

"My name's Wilcox, *Flight Captain* Connie Willcox, and I'm with the Air Transport Auxiliary. Surely you must have met some of my colleagues before?"

On Willcox's shoulders were the two and a half gold stripes of her rank, and on her flying overalls were her 'wings', bearing the legend ATA. She was senior in rank to all of them (but equal in rank to Barr), despite her girlish freshness.

"You're the first ATA pilot to deliver an aircraft to us, Ma'am," Rose smiled but his words were respectful, "I must say you caught us all quite by surprise!"

Willcox smiled warmly back at him, face and voice softening as she expertly shouldered her satchel, helmet and gasmask. "Oh. I didn't realise. I'm the first?"

Barr jumped in smoothly, "The first any of us have seen, Miss Willcox, but well worth the wait, believe me. But enough of this. You must be parched after flying that Beau, they aren't the easiest of kites to fly; it must have been quite a flight for a delightful young lady such as yourself. Would you care for a cup of tea? I could show you around?" he gave her his best, most charming smile, his 'Knee-trembler', and immediately hers disappeared.

"I found it quite a pleasant trip, Squadron Leader, and she was an absolute delight to fly, even for a mere little young lady such as myself, quite the sweet little kitten, in fact." She smiled, a thing of slicing ice, "And I will have a cup of tea, but I think I can find one all by my own, helpless little self. I did manage to fly and navigate my way here all by myself, of course."

They were agog, and Cole's jaw hung open. It was the first time any of them had heard of a Beaufighter being called a sweet little kitten. Usually they behaved like anything but, and had more of a reputation as a monstrous brute.

Recovering quickly, Barr swept off his cap and smiled winningly at Willcox, charm and magnetism personified, "Oh, but I must insist, miss."

Willcox shook her head, "Thank you for the kind offer of your company, Squadron Leader, but I'm not looking for it. And even If I were, I'd not be looking your way. Understood?"

Ouch! That's cut you down to size, my old mate!

Barr's mouth opened and closed helplessly like a landed fish, and Rose tried not to laugh at his bewildered expression.

Willcox noticed his amusement, and her smile returned. "Perhaps you could point me in the right direction, Flying Officer?" her eyes danced, "Care to show me the way?"

He could feel his cheeks colouring. "I'd love to, Ma'am, but I'm afraid the Squadron Leader and I were discussing the flying schedule for later. However, I'm sure my navigator, Sergeant White here, would be more than happy to take you. Chalky, would you mind, old chap?" he held up a finger, "But first best nip into Operations so they can sort out the Flight Captain's paperwork and a travel warrant, OK?"

White's eyes were like saucers, "Oh, um, yes sir!" the young NCO almost tripped in his eagerness.

"Right-oh, then, lead on, Chalky." She inclined her head solemnly to Rose, warm eyes curious, "Thank you, Flying Officer…?"

"Rose, Ma'am, Harry Rose."

Willcox smiled playfully, one hand brushing back some errant strands of hair, "My friends call me Connie, Harry Rose, and so must you. Next time, perhaps?"

Rose nodded in agreement, "Next time."

But not if my lady wife has anything to do with it, Flight Captain, he thought regretfully, before instantly reproaching himself for even thinking it.

He was happily married for goodness' sake!

The eyes of the little knot of B-Flight aircrew collectively followed

Willcox's jaunty step as she followed after White, and a silly little limerick began to silently form in Rose's mind as he watched her walk away from them.

'Today an angel delivered our newest kite,
A porcelain butterfly born into flight,
Soft eyes of grey, lit bright from within,
She smiled and my world began to spin,
And I no longer knew my left from my right…'

"You cheeky beggar, if you hadn't spoken up I'd have hooked that delicious little fish. Had her eating out of my hand, mesmerised, she was." Barr huffed, eyes still fixed longingly on the girl, dragging Rose from his musings.

Rose laughed, "Yeah, Billy, I could see that you'd captivated her completely!"

"Couldn't get a word in, with all that purposeless jabbering you were doing, all your bloody fault, you scallywag," Barr whined plaintively, "A real corker, wasn't she? Be wasted on you, Flash."

Toffee let out a long, low whistle, "Whew…!", and Barlow wistfully hummed a line from a song.

Indeed.

With a sorrowful sigh and a shake of the head, Barr turned to glower at Rose. "You'll be sorry, you damn disgraceful donkey. I'm going to tell Molly that being married to gorgeous senior WAAF Totty isn't enough for you, now you're running around chatting up gorgeous senior ATA Popsie!"

Barr grinned suddenly, "I ain't blind, I saw the way you were drooling at the lovely Flight Captain, though I think she needs her eyes checked if she liked the cut of your miserable jib!"

237

Rose laughed again and waved his hand at Barr, as if warding off a troublesome fly.

Four days later, Clark and Jones left B-Flight.

Their tour of operations finally over, the pair, after a very long tour of ops were being 'rested' at long last.

Almost eleven months of continuous operational flying and fighting later, eleven confirmed kills, ending their tour with a very well-deserved Bar added to their DFCs.

Pre-war regulars initially flying Hawker Harts, the pair had begun their fighting war as NCOs under the most primitive of conditions, finally finishing their tour at the forefront of the RAF's night defence umbrella as officers, with a DFC and Bar, DFM, and a Mention in Despatches each to show for their experience, expertise and sacrifice.

After all the stresses of front line fighting, learning that they were being rested left Clark and Jones looking simultaneously lost, melancholic, relieved and euphoric.

The resulting massive celebrations left all of B-Flight (and more than a few friends and girlfriends) with tender heads the following day, and finally waving off their friends was a bittersweet moment.

Clark and Jones had more than earned their rest, and it would be one of performing administrative duties at Group.

In his heart Rose felt that their skills would be far better employed in training new crews, but the veteran crew had faced more than enough danger already.

It would be unfair to strap them along with a student or two into an aeroplane that was not the easiest to fly at 81 Group, Fighter Command's training component.

The fact that many of the training Beaufighters were underpowered with Merlin engines made the aircraft that much more of an undertaking to fly relative to the Hercules-powered Beaus, and consequently made night fighter training more fraught and complex for students and staff alike. Whoever was behind it, the decision to use Merlins in the Beaufighter II was a badly thought one.

Indeed morale on these units was at rock bottom and the Beaufighter was getting an undeservedly bad name amongst the trainee crews.

Nonetheless, trained crews of quality with operational experience needed to be assigned to train the newcomers for long term success.

In a field of warfare that was continuously developing, experience would pay huge dividends in the production of future night fighter crews.

Molly put down the piece of paper, and rubbed her eyes tiredly.

The CO, Wing Commander James, wanted a badminton competition organised between teams from the various units at RAF Dimple Heath, and the competition was to include at least one (but preferably more) WAAF team.

Molly sipped from her cup but the tea had cooled and she grimaced at the taste.

Unbidden, the memory of the morning they returned to her friend's London flat after a night sheltering on the London Underground platform, their bodies stiff and dusty, the memory of humanity packed tight together on the platform of the dank and reeking Underground station stark and still fresh in their tired minds, the stench seemingly permeated into their clothes and skin.

Following the bombing, there had been a gas mains leak nearby, and there could be no lighted flames that morning.

The exhausted couple breakfasted on cold, and stodgy powdered egg, crusts of bread and cold stewed tea, their nostrils filled with the smell of brick dust and bitter smoke, but grateful to have escaped the dank enclosed space, and that they still had somewhere to stay.

At least for one more day.

The experience unsettled them both, and Molly was unable to forget the sight of the frightened little children, apprehensive and pasty in the poor light as the earth shook and rumbled.

How did Humphreys do it every night? What kind of superman was he?

Another everyday hero who gave everything they had for little, if any, recognition.

She yawned hugely, jaw popping, then covered her mouth delicately, and wondered wistfully if it might be possible to arrange some leave for Harry and herself.

How she yearned to have him all to herself, away from all this, just the two of them, even if it were only for a few days.

It would be just wonderful to see the Isle of Skye again. This time she'd get that wonderfully naughty boy of hers to visit and enjoy the sights properly.

And then another vivid memory flashed suddenly into her mind.

Early evening in a candle-lit Portree hotel bar, the ravening wind howling angrily and rain slashing and thrashing viciously at the windows, dimming the greyness of the day with its intensity, whilst the two of them were comfortably ensconced before a roaring fire, a delicious dinner of rich mutton and barley broth with fresh-baked bread laying comfortably warm in their stomachs.

At the bar, one of the patrons was reciting John Stuart Blackie's epic poem 'The Death of Haco', recounting the fate of the raiding expedition by King Hakon's massive fleet.

His face lit eerily by the flickering light of the roaring fire in the hearth, the bar silent except for clink of glasses and the logs crackling and popping in the fire, the angry sound of the weather muted outside.

The man was as drunk as a lord, but fervent and tearful with emotion, he enunciated every word slowly, clearly and loudly.

Molly listened with frank interest, immensely enjoying the classical verse, but a sleepy Rose was finding it hard to keep his eyes open.

"They took the body of Haco, in a ship across the sea—", intoned the well-oiled narrator solemnly, and he raised a filled shot glass blearily to Rose and Molly.

Rose had sighed glumly and shifted in position, pushing his buttocks comfortably against her, "God! Will it never end? He's as pissed as a fart, how does he remember it all? I wish someone would take that silly old bugger away in a ship across the sea."

The 'silly old bugger' blinked groggily, before beaming a brown-stained smile at Rose.

And then continued on with his monologue.

Molly giggled at the memory. Those ten days with Harry had been a delightful, idyllic time, and one that she remembered with great pleasure.

Her tears on the last day as they watched the island fade into the mists from the open deck of the ferry were for a wonderful time that might never be repeated, for the war was waiting for them.

Molly sighed and picked up the piece of paper again, she could only hope and pray that one day, some wonderful day, there would be a peace, and they might be able to enjoy the future together without the threat and terrors of war.

Would it ever come? Was it too much to ask for?

Dear God, keep my darling Harry safe. Please grant us our happiness...

Outside, on the parade ground, an NCO began to harangue some unfortunate erks, his shrieks punctuating the quiet with raucous sound; reminding Molly the real world was still out there, wanting to be let back into her innermost thoughts.

Molly leaned back comfortably in her chair, crossed her legs, and scrutinised the partial list she had prepared.

Now was not the time for memories, no matter how wonderful they might be.

They would still be there when she wanted them.

It was time to put them carefully back into the little safe place in her mind, because there was a WAAF badminton team (or two) to organise…

Chapter 22

Their honeymoon had been in Scotland, a perfect and blissfully happy ten days in December, in which Rose discovered first-hand both the beauty and delight of the Trotternish Peninsula on the Isle of Skye, and (infinitely better!) the sheer beauty and incredible delight of Molly's slim, smooth and shapely body.

The destination had been Molly's decision, and there had been a method to the madness, as she planned to nurse her beloved new husband onto that final stage of recovery from the injuries he'd experienced.

The ecstatically happy couple stayed at the large and impressive Royal Hotel in Portree (where they were daily reminded by the nice lady on reception that Bonnie Prince Charlie met Flora Macdonald for the last time at the hotel, back when it had still been MacNab's Inn).

Every morning, Molly coaxed Rose out of their warm bed (no mean feat when all he wanted was to undress her and get her back into it with him), down to a delicious and filling hot breakfast that seemed little affected by rationing, and then out for a gentle stroll around the harbour and onto Thomas Telford's pier.

All the while, as Molly chattered gaily beside him, her face shining with happiness and her hand in his, she gradually led him further and further afield, the walks longer and brisker, so that his poor leg and his strained mind progressively healed and strengthened.

Rose had never known so much happiness, and as he revelled in the wonder of his good fortune (*how on earth had he survived the savage fighting and then gone on to net such an incredible girl as well?*), he could not quite ignore the fact that his countrymen and women were fighting and dying whilst he enjoyed this idyll.

As Rose grew ever stronger each day, his beautiful wife, herself haunted by the memories of RAF Foxton's bombing and the losses she had suffered, continued to bestow upon him her complete love, until Rose reached the point where he could manage without the walking stick. Of course she knew that it meant that he would become fit enough again to fly, but understood that he could not stand idly by whilst others fought and died.

On their first Saturday there, a day that promised clear skies and excellent visibility, Molly and Rose hired a taxi cab to take them north to see The Storr, and to marvel at the savage beauty of the jagged rocky outcroppings and the moody great Gyrolite rock formation.

The Storr was almost seven miles to the north, on the road from Portree to Staffin.

As a child she'd visited the Isle of Skye and the sight of the dark majestic ramparts wreathed in the mists, like a mysterious fortification, left a lasting impression on her.

Her father had laughed gently when the fearful eight-year old, clutching his hand so tight that it hurt, had asked him if it was home to some dragon or evil wizard; his reassurances only half convincing her younger self.

244

It was a precious memory of a magical time in her childhood, and Molly wanted to share the unearthly experience and her memories with the man she loved.

Just before she took the long train north with Rose, Molly told her father, a station commander in Bomber Command, of their trip, and again he'd laughed. "It's a place you never forget, my little one. Have a lovely time and enjoy yourself. Take some pictures with Harry for my album."

On hearing that they were heading north by rail, and even though the trains were packed and uncomfortable in wartime, Rose rejoiced. He was certain that going by road in Molly's little red car would be the end of him. There was no way that his heart could survive in the passenger's seat over such a lengthy journey.

This time, the little red car stayed at home and Rose could breathe easy.

Wisps of mist began to materialise as they made their way northwards, slowly thickening until the surrounding rock faces drifted in and out of the milky skeins of icy haze.

"Wow," breathed Rose, "It's like a fairy-tale landscape. It's a bit scary isn't it?"

Molly giggled, "Don't worry, Harry, I'm here, I'll take care of you."

"How dare you, Ma'am," he answered, eyes still fixed to the sights as they came into sight before drifting back into the white, "I'm here to look after you, y'know."

"Look after your lady well, sir," piped up the little driver, a man called only 'Sporran' by everyone in Portree, bright brown eyes and a ready smile set in a tanned and lined face. "There're fairies around here, and they can't always tell the difference from right or wrong. Don't get too close to the edges either, don't want to get pushed off, eh? Och, and beware the Glastigs."

Rose turned to look at him, voice steady and cautiously nonchalant, "Glastigs?"

Sporran nodded sagely. "Oh, aye."

Rose tried again, "What're Glastigs?" Molly squeezed his hand comfortingly.

"Ah, dearie me. Glastigs're howling wee beasties, bit like goats but no' as friendly. Dinna worry, though, I'll be wi' ye."

Rose licked his lips, eyes flickering between the view outside and the back of the cabbie's head, "Do they, erm, attack people?"

Molly giggled again, and Rose glowered at her.

The cabbie waved a dismissive hand floppily, "Och, never, sir." He thought for a moment, "well, hardly ever, that is."

Bloody hell... Rose fearfully gripped his walking stick tighter.

The cabbie pulled out the knapsack carrying their picnic lunch and passed it to Rose.

"Are ye sure, now?" he sounded disappointed. "I'd be happy tae show you the way."

Rose nodded, settling the knapsack comfortably over his shoulder. "Yes, thank you, er, Mr Sporran. No need to accompany us. I'm sure we'll be alright, the pathway looks pretty clear. And it's just about two and a half miles round trip, isn't it?"

"Aye, but no need to rush, enjoy the walk. I'll be waitin' for ye here. Dinna wander off the path, it's a bit wet, don't want ye takin' a tumble, 'specially with the gammy leg and all, ye ken? Remember, bear right where the path splits, then left at the next split. Ye'll see the Old Man as ye go higher."

He smiled at Molly, then winked at Rose, "Watch out for the Glastigs, mind."

* * *

246

"I'm not sure your father likes me, Moll." The wooded area was behind them now, an open gentle slope leading them onwards.

Molly shook her head, her hand warm and comfortable in his. "He's a bit shy, Harry, always has been. He might seem a bit taciturn, but he knows that you love me and that I love you."

The path was getting a little rocky and Rose's pace had slowed. "Plus, you're a fighter boy. I come from a bomber family. Not quite the Montagues and the Capulets, but you get my meaning."

"Hm." His ankle was beginning to ache a little now. "D'you think we could stop for a moment?"

She stopped, concern in her eyes. "Is it your leg? It is a bit rougher than I remember."

"Ankle's a little sore." The bloody thing was sore as hell, but he was a man, and a RAF fighter pilot to boot. He'd be damned if he let the girl he loved know how bad it hurt.

"We'll find somewhere to sit down, Harry. Can you manage a little more? The path goes left here, let's go a few more yards and we'll find a nice rock to sit on."

They made their way a little further uphill, a tad more slowly, and Molly espied a likely looking rock.

"Here we are. Pass me the knapsack, my love. I'll pour us a cuppa. Would you like a sandwich?"

He placed an arm around her. She felt so *good*.

"No thank you, lovely. A cuppa would be nice, though."

"I'll pour then, and you keep an eye out for the fairies and the Glastigs." There was a mischievous smile on her lips and he leaned forward to kiss her.

Her lips were cool and supple and delightfully responsive, and his penis twitched involuntarily with desire. "He was pulling our legs, the old rogue." He shifted position to ease the pressure on his groin.

247

Molly passed him a little tumbler, steaming in the cold air, the aroma of hot tea mingling with the fresh scent of earth, wet rock and grass.

She sighed. "Isn't it quite beautiful?"

The mist drifted across the landscape before them. "I'll say. Is that The Old Man, over there, to the right?"

She sipped carefully from the tumbler and nodded. "Yes, that conical rock, set between the jutting rocks? Apparently, legend has it that the Old Man was a giant who once lived in Trotternish. Isn't it just grand?"

She sighed again contentedly.

Whilst it was impressive, Rose was more aware of her nearness, the softness of her lips and the fragrance of her body merging with her perfume. "It *is* lovely, just like you said. It's made a great deal lovelier by you being here, though. You are so very beautiful, my darling."

She fixed him with a gimlet eye. "Hm. I know that wheedling tone. What're you after, you cheeky boy?"

"I was just thinking, what a beautiful place this is and what it might be like to make love with you here." His penis throbbed urgently.

She smiled. "My, my, young man, your poor leg seems to have recovered a bit. I think it would be lovely, my darling, but it's a bit chilly, this rock's a bit hard and wet, and the floor's a bit rocky. We don't have a ground sheet and I'd rather not have a badly lacerated bottom. You can be quite potent when you get going, not that I'm complaining. It's really rather agreeable."

The beautiful smile widened mischievously, "I'd rather lie on something a bit softer, and I'd like it if you lay on top of me. Fancy heading back? We could have a picnic in our room."

His penis was already engorged and stiff with desire, and a part

248

of his mind wondered if the sight of The Old Man jutting proudly upwards had been a suggestive influence.

"D'you mind, my honey? I know how much you looked forward to seeing Storr again. Wouldn't you like to stay a while longer?" he looked at the barren rocks, "We could sit here for a while, yet?"

"No, I love it here, but I love being wherever you are. I love you so much, and you make me feel so happy."

She lowered her voice and leaned close, quickly glancing around, even though they were quite alone, to breathe into his ear, "And I simply *love* it when you fuck me."

His breath caught in excitement, as it always did when she spoke words like that one, and he hobbled to his feet eagerly, shifting his penis carefully to one side with his free hand to ease the tightness of his groin.

And then he stopped.

"What on…?" He peered uncertainly into the mist uphill, "Did you see that?"

She turned to look, "See what?" the path ahead was empty, just mist rolling fitfully.

"I thought, um, I thought I saw someone up there…" just for a moment, Rose could have sworn there had been a grey and shadowy figure standing still and unmoving in the ebbing and flowing mist, further up the pathway's steep gradient, quite near to the rock face.

But now there was nothing. The hair stood up on the back of his neck. This place was so spooky…

"I can't see anything," she said uncertainly. "Are you quite sure? One of Sporran's Glastig's?" Molly laughed nervously, still eyeing the spot Rose indicated, "You're pulling my leg. Don't mess about, Harry."

His heart was thumping, "No, love, honestly. I'm sure I saw someone standing there."

What was it that he had seen?

She gripped his arm, "Come on, then, let's go Harry." She reached for the flask and the tumbler, still half full.

Above them there came the faint sound of gravel shifting and slipping. Rose felt a sudden overwhelming feeling of foreboding and menace slip heavily onto him. It was as if they were being watched by invisible eyes.

Something felt wrong, really wrong.

Relying on his instincts had saved Rose's life on more than one occasion. There was no way he would ignore them, he was sure there was some kind of danger here, and he needed to get Molly away as fast as possible.

"Leave it, Molly, let's go, come on, sweetheart, come on, quickly." An inexplicable fear prickled along his spine.

Grabbing her sleeve and pulling her after him, he started to half run, half walk back down the way they had come, his erection had disappeared completely, and he ignored the faint objection of discomfort from his ankle.

At least the going was good downhill. Any minute, Rose expected a huge monster with slavering jaws and mad glowing eyes to come bounding out at them from within the mists, like a scene from *The Hound of the Baskervilles*.

Luckily nothing monstrous appeared behind them as they fled.

His heart was pounding like a gong against his ribs by the time they got back to the cab, to be greeted by an astonished Sporran. "My goodness, folks, that was quick. Did ye see any fairies?"

Rose leaned against the car to catch his breath for a moment. Molly was panting and her face was flushed, but she was smiling. "Wow! That was exciting!"

His heart was beginning to settle, and he stared back up at the slopes.

"No fairies, Mr Sporran, but I think we've seen enough, thank you." He took a deep breath, "Could we go back to the hotel, please?"

Sporran nodded slowly, "Aye, well, hop in, then. Let's be off." *Shouldn't have told these folk the fairy tales*, he thought to himself reproachfully.

As they clambered breathlessly back into his cab Sporran shook his head. The most beautiful place in the world and they didn't even stop to enjoy it.

They'd run back down all the way, and him, with a dodgy leg!

These English were such a peculiar folk…

Uphill, beside the rock upon which they had so recently been seated, there was a shifting of gravel and brush, and two figures emerged slowly as if from nowhere from the rocky ground.

One called up, "Bamford, you fucking twat, they saw you! If they'd been Jerry, you'd have a perforated pair of bollocks! Get that useless arse of yours down here right now!"

The other figure, huge and broad, brushed earth from his battle-dress, and swung his Lee-Enfield onto his shoulder.

"Shame, that, thought he was going to roger her right there on the rock. Would have been a nice show to break the monotony. She was a bit of a looker, wasn't she, sir?"

"Chubby, you rascal, I'd have announced our presence well before he'd got her knickers off. Wouldn't have been right to have 'em go at it hammer and tongs in the middle of the platoon. Even if he was RAF."

The officer raised his voice to a bellow, "OK, then, gentlemen, it's time for a bite to eat."

All around them, as if by magic, camouflaged figures appeared from their hidden positions in this mock-ambush site. The officer always found it useful to see how well his men could hide, and unsuspecting walkers never realised how many rifles were pointed at them as they used the path.

A shamefaced Bamford made his way downhill to the little group of Commandos.

The officer's voice was stern, "Well! Why did you break cover, you simpering idiot?"

Bamford's broad face was defiant. "Sorry, sir, I was dying for a piss. I didn't know they were there. Once I saw 'em I stood still."

"In plain sight? Fuck me. A genius. How're we going to win this shitty war?" The officer scowled, "Didn't know they were there? Couldn't you hear 'em? Could have heard them a mile off." He shook his head, "'Strewth! We'd have been dead if it were the real thing. You're lucky it wasn't."

His NCO took a swig from the tea, now somewhat cooled, pulled a sandwich from the abandoned knapsack, and took a huge bite. "Mm, Ploughman's, delicious."

Still chewing with enjoyment, he emptied the warm liquid from the tumbler into his mouth, and then threw it at Bamford.

His aim was true, and it hit the Private on the back with a dull metallic *Cluuunk!*

"Owww! Why'd you do that, Sarge?" frowned Bamford.

"To knock some sense into you, you silly cunt!" roared the NCO, "Next time, you thick wanker, I'm going to stick that ruddy rifle right up your fucking jacksie! We'll see how still you can stand with that rammed up your useless fat arse!"

Bamford looked hurt, "Ain't no call for that kind of talk, Sergeant. Can't help it that I was busting. Couldn't lay there and piss meself, now could I?" he replied reasonably.

Ignoring the reproving Private soldier, the grizzled mountain of an NCO turned his back and threw the remains of the sandwich into his mouth and chewed it furiously before it could make any attempt to escape.

Grinning and shaking his head, their officer checked his watch. "Fifteen minutes, brew up, eat up, take a piss, then back into your positions again, lads."

As his men groaned dutifully, the officer turned back to his NCO, "Hey! Save me a sandwich, won't you? Don't you scoff the lot!"

Down below, Rose looked back fearfully at the mighty rocky parapets through the cab's rear window and breathed a sigh of relief.

That was close. I'm not going back there ever again. Molly's going to need a team of bloody Shire horses to drag me back up onto those bloody haunted rocks again.

He shivered suddenly, remembering the primitive terror he felt grip him whilst up on those mist-shrouded rocks. Molly, warm and soft, snuggled closer and giggled, "My hero!"

Harry Rose, champion of the air, destroyer of the enemy, and decorated by His Majesty the King himself at The Palace, for once vanquished and thrown into undignified retreat by the unearthly mists of Skye.

Give me the Luftwaffe any day, he thought grumpily, embarrassed and unable to meet her eyes, feeling feeble and useless, not at all the kind of man such an amazing girl truly deserved.

You know where you are when Fritz is trying drill your arse with lead. It's quite another, being chased by the ghosts of otherworldly beasts amidst the silent mist-blanketed slopes.

Yes. I'd much rather face a Staffel of Bf109s on my lonesome than go back up into those haunted hills, he thought fervently.

Those bloody rock monsters and goblins and glastigs and other assorted beasties can stay right where they are, thank you very much.

Chapter 23

The indolent snuffling of the exhausts on either side of the cockpit was lulling him into a dangerous state of drowsiness, and Rose shook his head again, trying to clear the cobwebs of stupor and dispel the daydream he'd been in with Molly. The GCI controller remained silent, reflecting the emptiness of his screens.

He stifled a yawn. "Shall we see if we can find one for ourselves, Chalky?"

Now entering their fourth week on operations, the *Luftwaffe's* campaign seemed to have run out of steam, and the enemy currently seemed to be taking a holiday from operations. Certainly the raiders continued to come over, but the numbers had fallen off sharply.

With the availability of custom currently patchy, it had been agreed by The Brass that, provided enough aircraft were available for interceptions, free hunting would be allowed for those not being gainfully employed. As a result, experienced crews would be given some autonomy to go hunting.

"Yes sir, do let's!" White blared, "I've eaten all my sandwiches and finished off the tea, and I'm bored stiff! You're the absolute best, ace pilot an' all, but you're not as pretty as Mandy! Way too hairy for a start!'"

Rose laughed, "You cheeky so-and-so! You're no oil painting yourself! OK, then, matey, I'll ask the Controller for permission!" Then back onto the R/T, "Dagger 3 to Lamplight, if there's nothing for us, would you mind awfully if we tried to find one for ourselves?"

"Dagger 3, wait a moment, I'll check..." and a moment later, "Permission granted, but be back in time for tea!"

Rose laughed, "Dagger 3 to Lamplight, understood. Thank you."

"Lamplight to Dagger 3, I'll call you if I have anything or if there's a friendly fighter sniffing around you. Take care, good luck and good hunting!"

"Dagger 3 to Lamplight, Thanks!" Already he was turning for the coast, "Chalky, we're going to head for the coast, see if we can catch one on their way in or going out. Perhaps we should go down a touch? Might even catch one of their blinkin' mine-layers."

"Good idea, sir. The bastards may be coming in or going out at low level. Be nice to catch one."

"Mm-hm. We'll get down to four thousand feet. You keep an eye on The Thing, chum, and I'll see if I can catch anything with moonlight glinting off its upper surfaces. You never know, might strike lucky."

"Sounds good to me, sir, fingers crossed."

Relatively few Heinkels were needed for the mine-laying operations around the British coastline, but their efforts wrought havoc with the systems of defence.

The mine-layers generally flew well below 1,000 feet, so the only way that Rose and White might find them would be fly almost directly over them at more than 5,000 feet to cancel out the effect of the returns from ground clutter.

Once a contact was obtained, the night fighter would have to lose height in steps whilst trying not to lose touch.

And all the while they would be visible to the enemy gunners below.

Rose decided to fly the Beaufighter twenty miles out to sea, and then return via The Wash, turning back to their starting point as soon as the first of Peterborough's searchlights flicked on, still well out of range.

Notoriously trigger happy, the AA Command gunners of Peterborough shot at whatever came close, no matter what markings it carried, so pilots with even just an ounce of common sense maintained a safe distance.

Twice they performed the circuit, and after a hurried discussion, White and Rose decided that they would try it just once more before heading back for refuelling.

Half way back across The Wash, White suddenly stiffened in his seat and stared carefully at the twin scopes, pushing his face harder against the visor, concentrating hard. Something undulated and bulged on the 'Christmas tree' on his screens.

What was that…?

"Sir, I've picking something up, just appeared to port, a bit faint, but it's definitely there. A thousand feet above, crossing slowly from port to starboard. Range about four miles. I think it might be on a course at an angle to us. It's not parallel. Yes, it's indistinct, but there's definitely something there. Steer one-four-five and climb to angels five, sir, please."

Rose felt a thrill of excitement and fear course through him urgently, and the cold and frustration was suddenly forgotten. "Tremendous! Thank you, Chalky, steering one-four-five, climbing."

Already he was pushing forward the throttles and staring into the darkness, but at the moment, despite the striking presence of the moon above and the clearness of the night, he could see nothing.

Wait a minute, though…were those navigation lights?

"Still ahead of us, sir, steer one-six-zero, range closing, still above." There was a pause, then, "Hullo! This looks a bit strange…"

"What is it, Chalky?"

"There's another blip. It's actually a bit clearer. I think there might be another aircraft behind the one we're chasing. Do you want a heading, sir?"

Two separate aircraft? What was going on here? "Yes, for the second one, not the leader, please. Height?"

"OK, sir. Steer one-four-zero, angels five, range one mile."

God, they were drawing close! "OK, angels five, one-four-zero. Look, I'm going to make sure we don't get caught in an interception. Follow the second trace, Chalky. I'd rather be behind those four cannon in a Beau than in front!"

Back on to the R/T, "Dagger 3 to Lamplight, do you have anything in our location?"

"Dagger 3, flash your weapon, please." And then a moment later, "Negative, we have no intercepts currently in your location. Repeat, no friendly aircraft in your vicinity, you have permission to slap."

"Dagger 3 to Lamplight, understood, will engage."

And then back to White, "Chalky, permission received to engage. I'm going to identify and hopefully attack the rear contact first. The one in front might be bait." Their Beaufighter bounded in the other's slipstream.

"Yes, sir, steer one-five-five, stay at this height please, range now down to half a mile."

This one had no navigation lights showing after all, but once again, judiciously using his peripheral vision, Rose soon could make out the vague ghostly reflection of moonlight on upper surfaces, and then he could also make out the exhaust flames of the other aircraft.

"Range, Chalky?"

"Five hundred yards, sir, What do you make of it, sir?"

Rose's forehead creased, "Looks like an 88 to me," he said uncertainly, "fancy a gander, chum? Tell me what it looks like to you."

"Ooh, yes! Slim fuselage, twin engine, single vertical stabiliser, glasshouse cockpit, it's a Junkers 88 alright!"

And then light flared in front of the Junkers, and luminous whiskers of tracer shot forwards from its nose.

"What on earth?"

White spoke urgently, "He's shooting at the other contact! Quick sir, shoot him! The one in front must be one of ours!" His voice rose to a shout, "Shoot him!"

Rose did not need to be told twice. The enemy night fighter was already dead centre in his sights and with blood throbbing madly at his temples, he reflexively squeezed the button, completely forgetting to declare his action to White.

With a thunderous banging that made him jump even though he was prepared for it, the firepower from the cannon and machine guns lanced out and tore at the German fuselage, the familiar heavy stink of cordite and smoke sharp and bitter in his nostrils and mouth as a constellation of flashes and small explosions sparkled and glittered and died along the side of the darkened shape.

Finger firmly down, he emptied his four drums and machine guns into the other aircraft, watching his fire rip deep swathes of ruination into the enemy.

The haphazard pattern of twinkling flashes continued to light up against the length of the Junkers, one engine beginning to smoke badly, and a thin smear of dirty flame licking back as the German aircraft lost airspeed and shook beneath the impacts of bullets and shells.

There was a sudden burst of an explosion within the enemy's interior, larger this time, closely followed by a second, then a third and a fourth, and the Junkers slowed down further, slowing almost to stalling speed, wobbling uncertainly with the nose slowly pulling up and tail falling.

As the Junkers teetered on the edge of a stall, the port motor flared explosively white, searing and clawing painfully at their vision.

The distance between them shrank quickly and he saw they were quickly overtaking the enemy aircraft and in danger of colliding with it as it continued to slow, and even now they were almost upon it.

Rose hauled back sharply on the stick, pulling D-Dog up into a steep climb, soaring straight over the slowing, stricken Junkers, now teetering in a stall, seemingly close enough to touch.

They came so close that for a moment he could hear the wickedly sharp crackling pop of the rear gunner's machine gun '*pop-pop-pop-pop-pop!*'

Luckily (for Rose and White) the enemy rear gunner, already wounded in the head and arm by their telling burst, was firing at the Beaufighter wildly as it materialized from within the darkness like some evil presence and soared terrifyingly close over them, but his burst was hopelessly off, coming nowhere near the big RAF fighter, but blistering off to one side.

Shooting up almost vertically, Hercules engines howling and airframe vibrating crazily as their airspeed bled away, Rose, fighting the greying of his vision, struggled urgently with the Beaufighter's stick and gasped out, "Chalky, are you OK? Chalky! Speak to me!"

As Rose levelled off, White blinked rapidly a few times, seemingly-squashed eyeballs gradually regaining vision, stars still dancing before him. "It's OK, I'm OK. I'm OK, sir." He gasped, "Don't worry, I'm OK. Whew! What about you? Are you alright?"

Rose sighed with relief, heart jangling. "Yes, my old son. That *was* a bit close. He lost speed really fast, then. We almost crashed into him; I really thought we were a goner for a moment." He fought in a breath.

"Oh my God!" He wheezed, sucking in more oxygen deeply, the weight gradually easing from his chest. "Can you see him?" one hand stole down to the bulge that was the little pink bear safely tucked into its pocket.

"I watched the whole attack!" White burbled breathlessly, "It was great! I think he was a night fighter, too! The other kite in front must be one of ours!"

White, still panting but grinning with excitement, rubbed his head where he had caught it on the edge of his Perspex dome when Rose pulled the Beaufighter into the climb. It had one hell of an edge - *Ouch!*

They were turning gently now, the engines throttled back, mumbling and cracking fretfully, the big fighter wallowing uncomfortably while Rose tried fruitlessly to locate the enemy fighter in the gloom below.

Calm down, calm down! Deep breaths, slow down...

"Chalky, tell me what you can see; where is he? I don't want him crawling up our arse with his cannon!" And then he remembered, "Oh crumbs! Can you change the ammo drums, Chalky? I emptied them in the attack."

And then he changed his mind, "No, hang on a mo', we better find out where everyone is before reloading. Better make sure we're safe before flying straight and level. Can you check in The Thing for me? See anything?"

"I can't see him, sir, either outside or on my, er, Thingy."

"Damn! OK, what about the other contact? The one our bandit was firing at?"

"I've got bugger all on the scopes, sir. I'm sorry. I reckon he was one of ours, though."

"Don't worry, chum, stay in your seat, let's get help from Lamplight. Have a quick squint outside and check if you can see any damage to Doggie." Back onto the R/T, "Dagger 3 to Lamplight, some help, please."

"Dagger 3, we've lost contact, I'm afraid. We had you both, but when you went up, the bandit went down."

"What, both of them? You lost them both?" asked Rose in surprise.

The controller sounded equally startled, confused, and just a touch mortified, "Pardon me? Dagger 3, both of them? What do you mean, *both* of them?"

Rose's brow furrowed in confusion. "Apologies, Lamplight. I thought you knew. We intercepted two aircraft, the second being a bandit. He was a Junkers 88, We are claiming the bandit as a probable. We hit him pretty hard."

"Well done, Dagger 3, good shooting, congratulations! Do you need to refuel and rearm?"

"Thanks, Lamplight. I'm just going to stooge around for a little while longer. Might get lucky. Will advise when we return to base."

"Dagger 3, understood."

Rose sighed. "Chalky? Lamplight lost him too, I'm afraid. I'm going to circle for a while on the off chance, we got lucky, might do it again. Please change the ammo drums, chum. We'll hang around for a quarter of an hour or so, just in case."

"Right you are, sir. I'm going to unstrap. Waggle your wings if you need me back at the Thing."

"Thanks, Chalky. I'd prefer you to keep your oxygen mask on though, chum."

"The tubes and leads always get in the way, sir. Don't you worry, I'll be done in a tick. Talk to you in half a mo'."

I'll check again with Lamplight, thought Rose to himself, whilst behind him White unlatched the first ammunition drum and transferred it into the storage tray.

"Dagger 3 to Lamplight, any help?"

"Sorry Dagger 3, we've nothing for you. No custom I'm afraid. No sign of yours, either."

"Oh well. OK, understood Lamplight, thanks anyway."

Frustrated, Rose swore quietly. Had they got the enemy kite or had it managed to get away?

It was just possible that the enemy had recovered from their attack? What if he was still out there, curving around behind them, maybe?

He turned the Beau gently, searching the night outside with anxious eyes, and mindful of his friend clambering around inside the narrow, shadowed interior of the fuselage behind him with weighty sixty pound ammo drums clasped in his gloved hands.

Damn and blast! "Chalky, you there? Are you done yet chum?"

"Not quite, sir," White gasped heavily, "Done three, but I'm just about done in. I'm sorry sir, but I felt a bit worn out after the third one, and got a bit breathless," White took a deep breath, "so, I thought I'd have a quick sit down, just for a few seconds."

"That's quite enough, my old lad, leave it, please. Strap yourself back in. Three'll do very nicely. Are you sure you're OK?"

"I knocked my head a bit when we pulled up, but I'm OK, sir, don't fret."

"Oh God, Chalky! Why the bloody hell didn't you say something you, silly sod?" Rose's blood turned cold, White didn't sound at his best.

"Strap your arse back in your seat right away, Chalky, I'm heading for home, hold on, chum."

"Sir, stop being such an old bag. I'm OK, don't worry, please. We should stay on patrol for a little while longer. We might have the chance to get another one. Let's stay for a little longer, please?"

"Shut up and do as I bloody say, you impertinent sod. I'm not fucking asking. We've done quite enough for the minute, we're going back .""

"I'm strapped in, sir. And I apologise for calling you an old bag, your senior master pilotship, sir. I should have had more respect and said 'old woman'." Grumbled White.

Despite his concern, Rose sniggered, because the disrespectful bugger sounded like he was OK. He felt an overwhelming surge of affection for his young operator.

"Thanks, Chalky," he said softly, almost to himself, as he turned the aircraft for home.

Please God let him be alright. It was strange, but he couldn't imagine what it would be like to fly without him now.

An anxious thirty minutes later, a hugely relieved Rose was sitting with White at dispersals over a steaming cup of tea.

The senior base medical officer, Squadron Leader David Thomas, was waiting for them when they landed, and after asking a few questions, followed by a quick physical and neurological exam, he declared the young man fit, but requested that they do no more flying that night, just to be on the safe side.

As the dregs in their cups turned cold, no bombers to intercept, and with only the two patrol Beaufighters turning drearily on their airborne beat, the state of readiness was relaxed.

And then the phone rang.

They all stiffened, even Rose and White, even though they would not fly now until the following night, expecting a late scramble for a last minute raider (Von Plop had made an appearance earlier, skilfully bombing an empty field beside the airfield before heading for home at high speed and low level).

The phone call was from the senior intelligence officer of an RAF bomber base, calling to ask if one of Dimple Heath's fighters had intercepted a Junkers that had been attacking one of their Wellingtons.

It turned out that the Wellington crew witnessed D-Dog's entire attack, and confirmed that the Junkers went down vertically, fuselage and both engines burning, a flaming torch spiralling out of control and shedding pieces after D-Dog's attack. The bomber's rear gunner and navigator both confirmed the victory and extended an invitation to their rescuers for a pint (or ten) and a flight in a Wellington.

As usual, Dimple Heath's grapevine was faster than the telephone lines and a jubilant and gloating crew chief knocked on the door to offer them his congratulations and to confirm that their latest victory swastika had already been painted on the side of D-Dog, followed in turn by the apologetic Intelligence Officer requesting their amendments to the combat report.

At last they were left alone and Rose sat back with a fresh cup of tea, White snoring like a tractor on the camp bed beside him. He would keep an eye on White for an hour or two, then wake him and send him to his bed, before meeting with Molly. She would be coming in early this morning to share breakfast with him.

Sharing his operational fried egg with Molly was one of the best parts of a night on operations, even though the local farmer regularly provided the couple with fresh eggs for their own kitchen.

For Rose, sharing his flying supper/breakfast with Molly was something extra special, and his friends would leave them alone on these rare occasions, and eat their own eggs at a different table.

Molly, not wanting him to deprive him of his prize, ate slowly and took smaller pieces, but somehow, she always ended up with most of the rich yellow yolk.

Seeing those tired eyes light up with pleasure as she ate his egg made her want to weep with love and pride.

With their successful combat against the Junkers, and the bonus of having saved the Wellington, Rose and White would have more cause to celebrate this morning.

With another 'kill' they'd finally broken the dry spell, thank goodness! Rose was beginning to fear the enemy had found a way to avoid detection.

And dear Chalky had gained his fourth kill!

The lad was the one who deserved all the luck, with his decency, quiet courage and endless bubbling enthusiasm.

His young friend had gone far in so short a period, and with one more kill, he too, deservedly, would be an ace.

Mandy would be pleased.

But not as pleased as the young operator would be, if what Molly had shared with him was true.

Apparently, White was promised a kiss for every kill he scored, although as far as Rose could tell, during their dry spell of the last few weeks, White had not been deprived of such favours in the slightest. Quite the contrary, in fact.

Rose took a last sip of the sweet dark brown liquid, savouring it for a moment, and noticed the sky was lightening ever so slightly in the east, heralding the coming of the dawn. The Beaus still on patrol would be returning soon.

He yawned jaw-achingly and stretched out with the last of his strength.

There was still a little while to go before breakfast, and he was totally exhausted after the events of the night. He'd close his eyes for forty winks.

A nap would leave him feeling at least semi-refreshed before his early morning flying supper with Molly. The rumble of the returning fighters would rouse him as they came in to land.

Feeling as helpless as new-born kitten, Rose nestled further back into the chair and tipped his cap forward over his eyes.

Instantly, he was asleep.

* * *

At the same time on the other side of the North Sea, Bruno von Ritter was celebrating with Rudi and Mouse.

They had successfully intercepted a mine-laying Whitley bomber and shot it down into the sea, and he was certain that the *Ritterkreuz* would be hanging proudly around his neck any day now.

Stein has a bit of catching up to do, he thought smugly, and with more than a little satisfaction, not knowing that his rival was overdue from patrol.

He did not know it yet, could not know it, but his rival *Nachtjager* pilot and crew lay dead in the burnt out remnants of their Junkers, pieces of exploding cannon shell from Rose's guns embedded in his corpse.

There would be no Knight's Cross for Stein, after all.

Chapter 24

One late afternoon, not long after Rose and White's interception of the German night fighter, the flight were driven down to see 'Lamplight', the Ground Control Interception station dealing with their sector, to see first-hand how things in the AI war worked from the ground.

They arrived at dusk in a rutted and muddy field in the middle of nowhere, where all there was to see in the gloaming were a rather shabby collection of wooden huts, a nondescript brick building at the edge of the field, and a motley assortment of vehicles which included some grimy Bedford, Matador, Crossley and Dennis trucks.

In the midst of it all was a dilapidated trailer, covered over with a muddy canvas sheet, and a rather strange rotating, metal-framed structure set to one side.

No defences were visible, although there were a small number of army sentries present, and their identities were carefully checked, verified and recorded.

As their papers were examined, Rose tried anxiously not to look at a huge chained guard dog which fixed its gaze on him, and he furtively moved to stand behind Barr.

The evil-looking beast had a mouthful of sharp yellow teeth, rabid eyes, looked horrifyingly ravenous and seemed very eager to make his acquaintance.

In the last of the waning light, and closely escorted by a pair of alert looking armed soldiers acting as their guards, they struggled across the glutinous mud to the metal walkways between the vehicles that led to the trailer.

Barr, ever elegant, and expecting the GCI station in a far more salubrious location, lost a shoe and both he and it had to be rescued by Trent.

Slipping cautiously under the grubby mud-spattered canvas sheet, guided by torch light, they silently clambered up to emerge in a large and shadowed room.

The controller himself was seated behind a great flat console-like structure, in the centre of which was situated a large vacuum tube with a phosphorescent screen containing a rotating trace, onto which had been marked a section of the British coastline for which the station was responsible. B-flight would shortly learn this scope was formally termed the 'Plan Position Indicator'.

A loudspeaker on the wall crackled softly.

There were a large group of people, airmen and airwomen packed into the dim room, well wrapped in regulation and non-regulation mufflers and other heavy clothing against the cold, with conversation limited and terse.

At first glance it was like a soup kitchen without the soup or the despair.

The controller, a tall, thin squadron-leader, looked up as they walked in, and Rose was surprised to see that he knew the man well. Knew him very well, in fact.

The thin, ascetic, face beneath the woolly cap also registered momentary surprise when he saw Rose, and then he smiled delightedly, "Flash, my dear fellow!"

Rose held out his hand, "Good God! Hello, David, or should I say sir?" seeing the bemused expressions on the faces of his colleagues, Rose explained, "Folks, this is Professor David Morrow. Squadron Leader Morrow and I trained together as pilot and operator." He smiled ruefully, "Last time I saw you we were both Flying Officers, though."

It wasn't the first time Rose had seen such a rapid promotion. Dear old Stan had been a Sergeant-Pilot one month, and a Squadron-Leader in command of a Polish fighter squadron the next; whilst dear Granny also achieved something similar the previous year, Pilot Officer to Squadron Leader in a matter of months.

Despite Smith's rapid rise in the ranks, however, his sartorial skills still needed a lot of improvement.

The ex-university tutor and Rose's one-time airborne intercept operator nodded, with no sign of his previous absent-mindedness apparent, "Yes, I was commandeered and kicked upstairs to command this station, and we're the ones who guide you onto the Nazi bombers. Because I trained as an operator the powers that be thought it would help me in the job. I'd love to be up there with you too. Flash, how's the tour going so far? Any luck?"

"I'll say!" he laid a hand on White's shoulder. "This is Sergeant 'Chalky' White, he's my AI operator now, and so far we've managed four confirmed."

"Goodness me!" Morrow smiled at White, "Very well done, young man! I envy you! Wish it was me up there, if you'll pardon me for saying so, Chalky! Always the bridesmaid and never the bride, hey? Flash, my dear boy, if my memory serves me properly, you had eight to your name already when we were in training, which means you've managed twelve confirmed all told, now. Am I right, old man?"

"Yes, sir, you've got a great memory as always. I think we've you to thank for that, though!"

Morrow winked at him, and faced the group. "It's what we do. And we wanted to share it with you, so you realise that we're doing our best for you,"

He indicated the large scope before him, "We have the Nazi buggers' positions on this screen when they enter our airspace, and my people plot their locations as they move across the screen, relay them to the boffins over there," fingers waved casually to a knot of individuals clustered around navigating and calculating machines, "And they calculate speed and course for us. That way we know where they are going. Those others," another languid wave, "determine the bogey's height from the scope they're operating. Combining speed, direction and height allows us to direct you on to them. These good people keep monitoring each bogey carefully, and we relay the info to you until we bring them together with you, and then when you have them on your AI sets, Bob's your uncle."

Barr whistled, "Blimey, it's a bit complicated!"

Morrow took out an empty pipe and tapped the mouthpiece on his scope. "Complicated doesn't even begin to describe it. If we bodge it, we lose it and so do you. It's an exact science, anything less and no coconut. And of course, we have the same problems as you, for example, the equipment occasionally misbehaves, or if the bogey is too low, we lose it in the ground returns. But be assured, we do our bloody best for you. There's no trade at the moment and there aren't any practice interceptions quite yet. Just a matter of time, though. Should be something along soon. The enemy pathfinders, the 'fire-lighters', are usually the first, so that they can mark the targets for those following behind. They usually nip over around dusk."

Rose looked at his ex-operator with compassion and understanding.

Merciful God, what a load to carry! Rose and White were responsible for a small part of their sector, but poor Morrow bore the full responsibility of every interception! It was he who had to actually guide each night-fighter into position behind the enemy bombers.

One of the two Norwegian crewmen which had replaced Clark and Jones on the roster held up a hand, "Sir, how do you distinguish between us and the Luftwaffe?" Rose tried to remember his name. Peter? No, Petter, Petter Alstad, yes, that was it.

The young Norwegian pilot was pale, tall and thin with a ready smile and blond, almost white, cropped hair. Petter and a small group of his Norwegian Army Air Service friends had 'appropriated' one of the Royal Norwegian Naval Air Service's He115N floatplanes, and flown it from the floatplane base in Sola to the UK.

Originally a Gloster Gladiator pilot, Alstad had followed the same route as Rose from single-engine fighters to twin-engine ones.

Morrow put the empty pipe back into his pocket. "Good question. As you know, there are a number of mysterious boxes in our aeroplanes, and one of those performs a special function that tells us who you are. It's called Identification Friend or Foe, or IFF for short. That way, we can differentiate between you and the bandits." IFF was an arrangement whereby interrogation by Chain Home systems created a response signal that allowed a 'friendly' to be identified as such.

"I did wonder," Remarked Dear dryly, "Because we do seem to be vectored onto the odd Whitley or Wellington. Are you sure it works all the time?"

Morrow's brow darkened, "As you might well be aware, there may be the occasional hiccup in any device, just as an AI set on a Beaufighter can get 'bent'. Flying is a rough business, and being thrown around in stormy weather over the North Sea isn't always terribly helpful for a delicate piece of technology, neither are the effects of hits or near hits by flak. You'll appreciate of course that machinery installed in a combat aeroplane will not always be asked to operate under the most ideal of conditions. Quite a few of our bombers have been handled a bit roughly by the Hun, and it does tend to make the aeroplane a bit shop soiled. It is unrealistic therefore to expect the IFF device to work perfectly each time."

Morrow's eyes were cold in the gloom, "We always do our very best for you, please do be assured of that."

Looking abashed, Dear bobbed his head apologetically and said nothing more.

Rose had to look away, hiding his smile; Morrow seemed to have lost his absent-mindedness but none of his rather cutting means of delivering comments. But then, David had never been one to suffer fools gladly, particularly if he felt that his own expertise was being questioned.

White held up a hand hesitantly, "What happens if the revolving, um, array thingy outside breaks down, sir? Do you have an engineer here?"

Morrow chuckled quietly, but his eyes were serious. "Yes, we do have an extensive team of highly trained maintenance personnel, ready for every eventuality, but our array hasn't broken down so far. It isn't turned by a motor, you see, rather, we have a large team of volunteers who take it in turns to pedal the tandem bicycle that rotates it every night. We call them 'Binders', The Lord only knows why."

Billy laughed, "The poor sods probably find the job a bit of a bind, I should imagine!"

Morrow looked startled at the interruption. "Oh! I hadn't thought of that…it does make sense, I suppose."

He sniffed, "Hm. Well, anyway, the bicycle is in the aerial trailer, and the ensemble is termed a Type 8. The Crossley trucks hold some of the other important elements of the system."

He indicated a push button on the surface before him, "With this button, I can get the cyclists to pedal the other way. That way we can direct the system as required, when required."

"Are you here every night, sir?" asked Barlow respectfully.

Morrow looked at him as if he were mad, "Every night? Good God, no! I'm the Senior Controller, but I've got a pair of other controllers, understudies if you will, with whom I share the duties. If I did this every night, I'd have gone stark, staring, bonkers weeks ago!" he blinked and shook his head. "No."

Outside the tarpaulin creaked as a sudden gust pulled at it. Rose noticed how cold it was in the trailer, how their breath became pale clouds that rapidly dispersed, and how the pitted walls behind the noticeboard, posters and the official notices was stained with mildew and damp.

Life at the GCI station was clearly no easier than that for the night fighters themselves. At least in the air the Beaufighter crews had a better than sporting chance of seeing the blips as real aeroplanes and of pumping lead into them.

The newspapers wrote about the crews, and they were the ones who were decorated, whilst the poor men and women actually behind the scenes, the ones who made it all happen, received little or no recognition.

It was so bloody unfair.

Terribly unfair, just as it was for the ground crews and all the other essential associated personnel who kept them fed, watered and flying.

It was exactly as Granny had drummed into him, each member of the team was an integral part of a complex machine. Without one of those parts, the machine could not function.

The credit of a successful interception belonged to them all.

Eyes glazing, Rose forced himself to concentrate on Morrow, as he continued to explain in some detail how the system worked. The two dusk patrol Beaufighters from A-Flight had presented themselves for duty, and now Morrow was conducting a practice interception with them, just as the crews of B-Flight practised against each other whenever the opportunity presented itself.

It was fascinating to see what was involved as Morrow smoothly brought the two fighters together on the screen.

And then, it was time to go. Any minute now the first of the enemy raiders would appear on the screen, and Morrow and his team would need to be able to concentrate on the task of interception without a lot of useless bodies gawping gormlessly at them.

Morrow smiled warmly at each of them, and then he clasped Rose's hand sincerely, promising to meet up for a drink and a chat whenever time permitted, and assuring Rose he would definitely take up the offer for a ride in D-Dog.

Wistfully he asked, "Perhaps I could cadge a lift on one of your patrols? We never did get a chance of bagging one of the blighters together, did we?"

"I'll run it by the Wingco, sir," Rose replied earnestly, "I'm sure he'll OK it. We owe you so much. It's the least we can do. Why did they put you in a caravan, though? Wouldn't a brick building be better? Even a Nissen hut?"

Morrow shook his head. "It's to allow the unit to keep a mobile facility, in case we need to move position. Unlikely, really, because security is really tight, we've got a good cover story, but you never know, old man. There're so many fifth columnists, you can't be too careful. That's why we have the trucks. Besides, we may have to relocate to cover one of the other GCI stations."

"And anyway," he added haughtily, "It's not a caravan, it's a Brockhouse 4 wheeled utility trailer."

As they left, Rose turned one last time and raised a hand in silent farewell.

Morrow solemnly inclined his head slightly and mouthed, "Say hello to Molly from me, Flash. Good luck and God bless you both. Take care." The cold light from the rotating trace lit his face fiendishly.

A light rain was falling, and they slowly and carefully picked their way back to their vehicles through the mud. More than once their feet slipped and slid, but they managed to reach the cars and begin the long drive home without a dunking in the icy sludge.

As they quietly drove away, deep in thought, ignoring Barr's grousing about ruined shoes and desperate for a drink, they left behind them the architects of their success, leaving those patient warriors to another night of hard work in a cold, dank and mouldy old caravan (sorry, Brockhouse 4 wheeled utility trailer), draped over in a dirty old tarpaulin for camouflage, and planted unceremoniously in the middle of a muddy, furrowed field.

Without glory or praise, indeed with very little recognition at all, they would continue to work diligently for freedom and for victory in their own uneven little corner of Britain.

Chapter 25

It was darkest night when the tired, muddy and rumpled crews of B-Flight returned home, the sliver scrape of moon weakly lighting their way to blacked-out Dimple Heath. More than once they got lost, but finally, thankfully, they arrived at the village of Dimple again.

Glad to be back after the journey, Barr suggested a quick pint in Dimple's public house, The Black Bull, but Chalky and the other sergeants decided to return to the airfield, and Rose wanted to get back to Molly.

Doubtless Mandy would be waiting for White, and his impatience was clear. Rose smiled at him and winked, "Behave yourself and keep your hands to yourself, you cheeky blighter!"

White blushed bright.

"You're no fun at all, Flash. I ain't playing with you no more," griped Barr sorrowfully, "Come on chaps, let's have a quick jug at The Bull, and then we'll see what's on the menu in the Mess tonight. Hope they have some of that Lamb Hotpot. I quite fancy a bite. Perhaps I'll be able to get Mabel to clean my poor shoes, too?"

Barlow grunted morosely, for both his shoes were still in Morrow's muddy field, sucked off his now very grimy stockinged feet.

"Crumbs!" Dear shook his head in disgust, "That Hotpot's oily

277

muck! And the meat! You'll eat anything, you will, Billy! I worry about you, I do, honestly!"

Rose watched fondly as, still bickering, his friends wandered away, then turned and walked the remaining distance to their little home, enjoying the scent of the clean night air and the asphalt beneath his muddied shoes. What a pleasure it is to return home to the one you love, he thought, heart full with gladness.

As soon as she saw him, Molly jumped from their threadbare settee, and he gasped as she threw her arms around him and hugged him tightly, soft and warm and immensely arousing. "Harry! There you are at last!"

Savouring the lithe, firm body of the girl in his arms, he closed his eyes and buried his face in her loose mane of midnight hair, inhaling the scent of fresh flowers, cotton and her warm sweet womanhood.

"Ah," he sighed, "that's wonderful. You smell magnificent, my sweetheart!" He held her close for a long moment, then he opened his eyes and noticed the needlework on the settee, and her spectacles balanced on the low table.

She released him and frowned, "You smell a bit muddy and ever so slightly of cow dung, young man; so, tell me, how was it?"

"Amazing. It's quite something to see how an interception's handled from the ground. And Molly, guess what? You won't believe it! I met David!"

Her brow furrowed, "David? Not David Morrow, surely? Good God! How was he? And how's Millie?"

"He was the same, but the absent-mindedness has gone! He was so sharp and focussed! He's the GCI Senior Controller for our sector, you know. I never realised that I was often talking to him over the last few weeks! And I forgot to ask him about Millie!"

"I thought he would have been in some pokey little office at the

Air Ministry performing an obscure but vital task, to be honest. He was quite brilliant."

"No, love. He was sitting in a rather tatty caravan in the middle of some forsaken muddy field, but his is the most vital of tasks, Molly! You know that without him we wouldn't have an earthly of catching the Huns at night. The technology was unbelievable!"

"Come and sit down, Harry. You must be tired. Shall we have a cup of tea, or would you like something to eat? Do you want to go to the pub?"

"Lord, no! Billy and some of the others are having a pint. I'd much rather be here with you. Chalky was pretty keen to get back to the airfield, though. I think he's got an assignation with the lovely Mandy."

"Talking of lovelies, I've heard that you were being chatted up by a pilot?"

Rose's brow crinkled, "Who? Billy?" *Oh Lord!*

Molly sighed in exasperation, "Not Billy, you silly sausage. That ATA girl."

He grinned in discomfort. "Oh, her. No, my little frilly flower, the poor dear had only just landed and she asked me if I could direct her to the Mess, that's all."

She gave him a knowing look. "Hmm. Mandy said that Chalky thought she was quite keen on you."

I'll bloody kill him! The little…

He laughed light-heartedly, "Chalky's such a sweet lad. He thinks I'm some kind of superman. He thinks quite highly of me. By virtue of being married to me, I expect you can completely understand that!"

Molly narrowed her eyes and elbowed him in the ribs, ignoring his groan of protest. "Superman? Hah! Just you remember, you cheeky man, that I'll rip out the eyes of any bloody floozie that so much as looks at you!"

279

"My sweet little rice pudding, you can't do that! The girls on the base have to look at me," he wheedled, "You'd have to rip out the eyes of half of Dimple Heath's WAAFs! That really wouldn't do. You might be the senior WAAF, with a GC and legs that go all the way up to your armpits an' all that, but that doesn't give you the right to rip out their eyeballs. Whatever did they teach you at WAAF totty officer school?"

The girl raised her eyes to the heavens despairingly, "Oh my God! Where on earth did I find a creature like you?" she elbowed him again, none too gently, and he beat a hasty retreat away from her along the settee.

Suddenly, Rose felt a sharp, lancing pain in his buttock, and he leapt up with a yelp.

Molly jumped too, face filled with concern, "Oh Harry, what's wrong?"

Clutching his backside, he looked down into her concerned eyes, "I think I just sat down on your bloody needlework, I've just been poked in the bum! The damned thing's shredded the seat of my pants!"

She tried keep a straight face, but a giggle escaped her and she collapsed.

"Good thing you weren't at Thermopylae, Harry. You would've given poor Leonidas grey hair!"

Rose scowled, still rubbing his stinging backside, "I've just been foully wounded and you're laughing! I think you just broke one of my ribs with all that vicious elbowing an' all, you coarse, brutish girl, and now your damned needlework's just ripped a ragged hole in my poor arse! I feel faint, quick, quickly, check it, am I bleeding?"

He lifted his tunic and presented his backside to her, which Molly promptly slapped, hard, and he jumped.

"Aargh! Ow! What kind of girl are you? I thought you cared! It's quite clear to me now that you are a monster."

Still giggling helplessly, Molly wiped her eyes, "My hero! I'm sorry, Harry, you just looked so comical standing there clutching your poor bum like that!" she collapsed into a fresh fit of giggling.

"Ow! It hurts! I think I'm bleeding like a drain! D'you think I should go to the sick quarters at Dimple Heath?"

She took his hand and pulled him down to sit beside her again. "I'm sorry, darling. Shall I kiss it better?" her eyes sparkled mischievously, and her hand slipped onto his thigh.

Rose perked up, his wounded bottom forgotten, "Oh, I say, that would be lovely, would you mind?"

Later, lying beside her, he sighed contentedly.

"Enjoyed yourself, did you?" She asked, and he raised himself up onto his elbows. In the dim light he stared at her nakedness in frank appreciation.

"I suppose you could say so." Rose reached out and gently stroked her smooth leg, and, as his hand reached the top of her thigh, his forefinger reaching out to gently slip sideways along the wetness between her labia.

"Oh dear, I seem to have married a dirty old man. You, Harry Rose, are a very bad man!" she shivered as the gently questing finger slid inside her.

"I know, my darling." Rose brought the finger up to his mouth and sucked it with enjoyment. "That's why you can't resist me, my sweetest, because I'm such a bad man. You're helpless against my limitless and amazing charms. You are like a lump of clay in my masterful hands."

Molly looked unconvinced. "If you say so, dear."

"I do say so, and may I also take the opportunity to say that you taste absolutely wonderful?"

She smiled dazzlingly, "Why thank you, kind sir! And, yes, I do seem to remember you saying something of the sort earlier."

He sighed. "I must say, my alluring sugared honey, that I still wish my tongue were a lot bigger."

"I think it's absolutely perfect, my darling, and I ought to know, believe me."

Rose smacked his lips enthusiastically, "I wouldn't mind another tasting, would you care for another kiss and a cuddle, you exceptionally gorgeous creature?"

One hand reached for his, "Mm, I think I could perhaps manage it."

Their lips met, tenderly at first, gently, rising passion turning it ever more hungry, and his hand reached up to cup one lovely breast, squeezing and gripping it, the nipple hard against his palm as Molly turned to face him.

And then he stopped, his eyes unfocussed, listening.

"Harry?"

"I thought I heard something, my love, um…yes…there. Can you hear it, Moll?"

There was nothing but the distant scream of a fox out hunting, and of course the distant, almost inaudible, murmur of aircraft engines at the airfield, but it was something one got used to when working on and living close to a day and night-flying aerodrome.

"Those engines…," whispered Rose, almost to himself.

Molly listened carefully, trying to understand his disquiet. She tried to focus on the distant murmur in the night sky.

And then she could hear it too. "Is it a German? Von Plop, maybe?"

No fear in *his* girl's voice, brave and strong, sweetest Molly. Quite unlike his own quavering tones.

The hateful desynchronised drone of Jumo engines whispered discordantly in the faraway distance.

Smoothly, Rose rolled out of bed and padded to the window, ignoring the sudden, sharp ache in his leg, carefully pulling back the curtains, goose bumps prickling as the tendrils of cold prickled his bare skin.

"You better put something on, Harry, if the ARP Warden catches sight of you in the altogether he might have a seizure," she giggled behind him, and he heard the click of the lamp switch as the girl turned it off.

The bed creaked behind him.

In an instant she was beside him, pulling on her robe, "He can't aim for toffee, Harry. I bet he can't even find the 'drome half the time."

The fragrance and heat of her body comforted him, and she handed him his trousers.

Rose nodded, but his face showed his anxiety. "I know, my gorgeous flower. I just worry that one of the squadron might be vulnerable when the bugger turns up. He is a bit useless, but a Beau on landing approach or taking off is a target that would be a Godsend for even old Plop."

He reached out to open the little taped window.

All flippancy aside, a well-placed bomb load could have a disastrous effect on any airfield.

At RAF Ternhill the previous year, a solitary daring Junkers 88 had destroyed 13 Avro Anson training aircraft, and damaged 20 more in a single raid. Almost three squadrons of aircraft destroyed or damaged by a single enemy raider.

As if to justify his feeling of utter trepidation there was the distant sound of another set of engines, separate from the first, and Rose could have kicked himself; wishing he hadn't given voice to his concerns, as if by saying what he feared, he had made it happen.

"Oh my God." Molly's voice was taut with tension, and she looked at him, "Those are Bristol Pegasus engines, aren't they?"

A little part of him proudly admired the fact that she could identify the muted sound of the distant engines.

What a girl!

But a far greater part feared for the vulnerable crew of the approaching RAF aircraft.

Rose nodded, "Yes, Moll, it's a Wellington. Hopefully control will warn him off." Condensation dripped from the fogged glass onto the sill.

His expert eyes carefully searched the darkness, and then he groaned in despair.

Apprehension rushed dread cold through her veins, and she shivered, "What? Oh Harry, what is it?"

He pointed, "Look!"

She followed his finger and saw what he could see. Flying in from the east was the shape an aircraft with its landing lights on and wheels down. It was the Wellington they had heard, on landing approach. The aeroplane was a sitting duck as it slowly approached the runway.

"Oh Harry!" the fingernails on his wrist cut into him.

He opened the window wide, oblivious to the blast of cold air as it rushed in, staring in despair, "Dear God! Why don't they warn him?"

Suddenly the Wellington pilot pushed forward the throttles and they saw it begin to claw for height, desperately, wheels slowly retracting, turning south-westwards.

But he had forgotten to switch off his lights, and the Wellington, engines screaming, remained brightly lit.

To their horror, and accustomed to regularly picking out aircraft flying close above the aerodrome at night, Molly and Rose saw an obscure shape, as if by magic, suddenly materialise out of the dark but clear night sky.

To Molly it looked like a harbinger of death, and her hand slipped into his, gripping him tightly. He could feel her trembling (or was it him?)

For Molly, the evilly sinuous shape was vague and unfamiliar, but to Rose's experienced eye it was very clearly a Junkers 88, and he cringed as the enemy nightfighter's nose glowed silent bright as tracer and cannon shells chased after the desperately climbing Wellington bomber, the belated chatter and sporadic thumping finally crossing the distance to their ears.

The first burst fell just short, but the second, following close behind, connected, and fire flared and coruscated awfully from one wing as the fuel tanks were hit. It shuddered under the terrible onslaught as if in pain.

More firing, more streaks of flame, and the bomber's nose came down for the last time.

Already the crew were bailing out, one, two, three and four parachutes burgeoning like strange airborne mushrooms.

Two more left on board, and Rose found he was willing them on. Jump, damn you, jump.

Come on, oh, quick! Quick! Get out! Jump!

Burning fiercely, the Wellington was now a flaming and uncontrollable torch that finally tumbled to earth, disappearing behind a low hill, an intense flash starkly outlining the ground between them, marking its final destructive embrace with mother earth, and lighting the night sky for an instant.

There was a faraway *thump*! A sullen thunderclap that they felt viscerally radiate up through the soles of their feet, and the bottles and jars on Molly's dresser jumped and rattled in sympathy with the distant explosion, the tinkling a delicate echo of the distant awfulness.

There were no more parachutes, no more survivors. The remaining crew members had still been aboard for the crash.

They had been too low to escape.

Just the terrible glow and the flares that streamed bright into the sky like gruesome fireworks, the occasional sizzle and crack and rattle and clamour of ammunition being set off by the raging fire.

Two precious lives, extinguished like a candle flame.

Silently they stood, horrified and helpless, unwilling witnesses to the sudden end; and as the wrecked aircraft burned, ammunition and flares popping and cracking distantly, intermittently lighting the night sky for a few moments with fresh eruptions and explosions, the sound of the Jumo engines now just a memory as the enemy nightfighter fled triumphantly for home and safety.

Nothing could be scrambled in time to catch him, and at such low level, the Beaus that were already airborne had little chance of finding him, his radar image on any airborne scope close enough being masked by the overwhelming ground returns.

At least the bastard hadn't dropped any bombs this time, or tried strafing the aerodrome.

Rose could feel her fingernails deeply puncturing his skin, and gently he eased her hand from its tight grip on his arm.

She was trembling terribly, and he closed the window carefully, and embraced her.

She was crying silently, now, and he cursed the enemy pilot for re-awakening the old and bitter memories in his beloved.

She was so very strong, his fearless Molly, but her heart bled liquid pain for the men killed now before their very eyes, their deaths reminding her of the Section of young WAAFs, her girls, killed the previous year at RAF Foxton.

Could she ever forgive herself for not dying with them?

He found to his surprise that he too was weeping, bitter tears falling as a tightly compressed and dark ball of anguish crushed him

286

from within, and in those tears he gave vent to the frustration and helplessness of his position and of his inability to protect those men, and for his Molly from what they had just been spectators to.

Rose thought of Morrow, mind and body exhausted as he strove with his people to catch the bombers that glowed on his screens, able to handle only one fighter at a time as the enemy waves came in, casting a net that had great holes in it through which the bombers slipped.

It could be likened to a game of football where the poor Goalie could be in only one place at a time, whilst the opposing team were each attacking his goal simultaneously.

It was impossible to save them all. But they would continue to try. They had to.

For what other choice was there?

What demons tortured poor David as he fell exhausted into bed each morning? Was his slumber dreamless, or was his sleep haunted by the dead, the murdered men, women and children, that despite his very best efforts he had been unable to save? Were his dreams filled with their screams and anger and pain and blood?

He pulled the curtain roughly across the window, so hard that the rail creaked complainingly, and then gently led the weeping girl back to their bed.

He could no longer look at the faraway glare, angrily lighting up the undersides of the clouds, and know that men who wore the same uniform as he lay killed within the scorching heart of that terrible glow.

Holding her close, Rose pulled the covers over the both of them, over their heads, trying to warm and comfort her at the same time. He held her tightly to him.

Her trembling soft lips found his and the tender, comforting embrace gradually became something more, a great lot more, as his clasp turned to gentle caresses.

Molly's quivering gradually lessened and stilled, and she moaned quietly as they found solace in one another. Her legs parted and he slipped between them eagerly.

Sudden, violent death was a grim daily reminder of the fragility and uncertainty of life in wartime, a reality that was as unavoidable as dusk and dawn.

Brutalised by the shock of the sudden and violent death of the Wellington bomber crewmen, they mutually sought the solace of their love as an affirmation of life.

Rhythmically and powerfully, Rose thrust himself deep into her, and she grasped his body hungrily, opening herself as wide as possible in response to his plunging, desperately pushing herself firmly against him and onto his hardness, joyously receiving him like a flower eagerly opening for the comforting warmth of precious sunlight.

Hungrily he nuzzled the sweet softness of her slim neck with gentle lips, firm hands holding her body against his whilst remorselessly thrusting himself into her stretched and flowing warmth.

The distant red flicker and the rattle of bursting ammunition beyond the sanctuary of their bedroom became as nothing, the only sound in their ears the echo of their breathing and the frantic and urgent slap of his body against and into hers, working together in union.

She gasped and whimpered quietly as the gathering waves of ecstasy broke over her faster, ever faster, and then Rose exploded within her, his body jerking, a constellation of lights bursting and dancing before his eyes as he emptied himself copiously into her.

Juddering together in their intertwined embrace, Molly and Rose clutched one another tightly, lost together in the rapture of their shared expression of adulation, shutting out the horror of what they had witnessed as best they could.

It was a long time before Rose finally fell asleep, holding and in turn being held by his precious Molly, still gripped firmly between her smooth thighs, their limbs entangled and bodies warmed intimately by one another, seeking and in turn receiving peace and comfort and purest love.

Life may be delicate and ephemeral and fleeting, yet true love is infinitely strong, serene and deep, and lasts forever.

Chapter 26

Molly was on duty early the following day, and she was long gone when he awoke in the mid-morning, just her lingering scent, the stained and rumpled sheets and a note on her pillow:

> *Ma chérie Harry,*
> *Je t'aime, mon homme le plus aimé.*
> *Meet me for lunch, in the Mess,, 1230 hours.*
> *I can't wait to kiss you again.*
> *Until then, my dearest, dearest love…*
> *Always and forever, yours alone.*
> *Molly xxx*

He folded the paper carefully. *Dearest Molly, wonderful girl, how I love you. You are everything to me.*

Rose buried his face into her pillow, inhaling her fragrance. Downstairs she would have prepared him breakfast before leaving, and he would get ready slowly, dawdling peaceably to the airfield for the briefing.

He turned over again and stared at the smooth ceiling above, remembering again the awful sight of the burning Wellington as it fell.

Unconsciously he reached out, fingers resting on the almost dried patch of dampness on the sheets where she had lain beneath him.

Death was no stranger in the RAF, but it was something else to helplessly watch from the ground a man you might have drunk tea with plunging to their death in a fiery ball.

He sat up, saw her clothing neatly folded on the chair beside the bad, reached out and pulled a pair of her 'blackout' knickers out to hold up against his mouth and nose, but they were freshly washed and there was nothing on them but the smell of soap.

Rose threw them back onto the pile of clothing in regret and went for a wash in the bathroom.

After leisurely eating his powdered egg omelette (Molly, bless her, could make even powdered egg taste delicious with herbs and spices) between a couple of fresh slices of bread, Rose locked the front door and made his way to RAF Dimple Heath on the creaky bicycle borrowed from the station.

This evening they would be flying again.

Despite the lively freshness of the morning, it was just possible to catch the hateful smell of the burnt out Wellington on the breeze, and Rose covered his mouth as he wound Molly's college scarf around his neck.

He didn't look in the direction of the crash. There was nothing there that he wanted to see. The crash site was not visible from where he was, but he knew a thin, dirty trail of smoke would still mark it. To look at it would be acknowledge the death of friends.

The long faces of the villagers he met showed that there had been other witnesses to last night's attack by the enemy intruder.

Mrs Humphreys from the Post Office had tears in her eyes and she hugged him tightly for a moment.

"Be careful up there, Harry," she whispered to him, placing a paper bag heavy with fresh macaroons surreptitiously in his hand. Her son was with the Royal Artillery in the North African desert and she had 'adopted' the young couple.

Rose smiled at her reassuringly and patted her hand kindly.

"Don't you worry, Mrs Humphrey. They won't know what hit 'em, I'll repay them in kind." It felt as if his face would crack with the effort.

He and his bicycle were lucky enough to get a lift in the late milk lorry, and were dropped off at the gates in a manner more sedate than his usual journey with Molly.

The scheduled meeting was for eleven, and he arrived just in time, a little out of breath.

Barr grinned smugly at him from an easy chair, and Rose was surprised to see Wing Commander James facing them all.

"Good God, Flash, where've you been? Thought you weren't coming. I was going to send a couple of SPs to fetch you." he grumbled.

"Sorry, sir, I hadn't realised what time it was."

"Yes, well, not to worry, you're here now, old man, don't dawdle, take a pew, there's a good fellow."

Rose slipped gratefully onto the seat next to White, who smiled blissfully at him.

Hm, looks as if someone had a good night. Hope the cheeky bugger got enough sleep.

James sat back against the table, checking first that the battered edge wasn't sticky or splintered or otherwise hazardous to his backside, flipped open a packet of Players and separated a cigarette from its fellows.

His face was tired and grim "You all know about the attack last night. It's the first time Jerry caught one of us at our most vulnerable."

He tapped the cigarette on the table top, lit it, and stuck it in his mouth.

"The IO doesn't believe it was Von Plop, the MO was completely different this time. No ineffectual bombs just a fast and accurate interception and then scarper sharpish. 'Course, ol' Plop may just have got lucky, but I don't think that was the case."

He blew out a cloud of smoke, and Rose fondly remembered for a moment his Polish friend and those bloody awful cheroots which he insisted on smoking endlessly. At least James' smoke was more fragrant.

"The Air Ministry are discussing options for improved defence, and the Adj and I had a talk. We're going to place trained observers at a perimeter five miles from Dimple Heath, and arm 'em with flare guns. If they see a raider they're to fire off red flares and phone the aerodrome. That way we should have some warning. I've submitted the idea for consideration. God knows how well it'll work, if at all."

Barr coughed, "It was Jonty Craig's crew, last night, in the Wellington."

James nodded. "Yes, poor old Jonty. And Sergeant Brennan was still in the rear turret. Extraordinary man. He could drink a yard of ale in about six seconds or something, bloody incredible. Saw it once, made me feel quite ill."

He shook his head at the memory, "Anyway, the station WO will be arranging training and a roster. Should be better prepared this evening. The Control Tower will also make sure to remind the landing aircraft to switch off their landing lights until the last minute. Furthermore, we're setting up a light from one of the Turbinlites to use as a searchlight. Hopefully, if Johnny Hun comes back, we might be able to use the light to put him off at least. Point it into the bastard's eyes. Problem is, the light may attract other Boche, and that wouldn't do."

James stubbed out the cigarette on a stale half-eaten sandwich, sitting forlorn and curled in a saucer. "If you have any ideas, please come and see me or the Adj. These intruder raiders are a damned nuisance," James sighed sadly, "and a damned costly one, too."

He looked at the sombre faces before him. "Any questions, chaps?"

White held up a hand, "Sir? Perhaps when we're taking off and landing the operators could keep a bit of a lookout whenever it's possible? Still belted in, though, of course."

James nodded approvingly, "Good idea, Chalky. I'll have a word with the other aircrews as well. Every little helps as the old woman said when she widdled in the sea."

White blushed and looked down.

James clapped his hands together and rubbed them. "Now, a spot of good news. I've been informed that His Majesty has most graciously approved the award of a Bar to your Distinguished Flying Cross, Flash, old chap."

Rose sat up in surprise and shock, "Who, me?" In his astonishment, he didn't see the blaze of fierce joy and pride wash over White's face.

"Yes, you, my dear fellow, congratulations, totally undeserved, of course. Can't understand it. They must be all bloody barking at Group. Definitely don't approve, not at all, and I've written to Winston to complain about it."

Amidst the catcalls and back slapping, James called out. "Shush, you rowdy shower! The glory doesn't all belong to Flash. There's worse to come, I'm afraid, far worse, it seems this young blighter here," and he pointed at White, "has been awarded a DFM at the same time. Very well done, Chalky!"

He had to shout amidst the fresh eruption of cheers, "Bloody disgrace, if you ask me, don't know what the RAF is coming to!"

Dear God! White gaped wide in stunned and overwhelmed disbelief, hardly aware of the shouts and the congratulatory claps on his back.

The Distinguished Flying Medal? *For me?* The room seemed to whirl dizzily around him as he took it in.

James was still talking, something about a Bar for Barr (!) and Dear's DFCs as well, amidst fresh bouts of shouting, but White hardly heard him.

Scant weeks ago he'd been cleaning latrines and oil trays, and now he'd been awarded the DFM. His world had turned on its head! He felt faint with amazement.

White had promised himself that he would ensure his saviour from the latrines received a Bar to his DFC, and he'd succeeded!

But in the process of doing so, he had somehow earned a medal himself!

He thought of the fair haired girl with the throaty laugh, kind eyes and those lovely, soft lips.

Oh My God! I've got to tell Mandy!

And then Rose was before him, the smile bright and filled with pleasure, his voice low and sincere, "Well done, Chalky!" he clasped White's hand warmly. "You more than earned your DFM, chum, and I owe the Bar to my DFC to you, too. Thank you."

White tried to speak but found that he couldn't, his throat clogged with emotion. Rose was thanking him, yet it was to Rose that White owed a massive debt of gratitude. He'd tried to repay Rose for his kindness, and his efforts had resulted in accolades for them both.

Smiling slightly, James indicated to Rose to join him with a subtle movement of one hand, and leaving his shell-shocked Operator to the ministrations of the others, Rose made his way to the Wing-Commander.

They shook hands, and James congratulated him again.

"I must admit, sir, I'm really shocked, it's come as a real surprise!"

James shook his hand. "The powers that be may be a pain in the bum most of the time, Flash, but despite all their faults, they do appreciate the difficulties, dangers and stresses that are involved in nightfighting. Your four confirmed were gained through a lot of effort, and the awards you've both received are very well-earned."

James looked at him for a moment, gauging his mood. "I'll be honest with you, Flash. I have a confession to make. Nobody else knows this, and I'm not proud to admit it, but I actually kept Chalky off the operational list of observer operators."

Rose's smile disappeared. "I beg your pardon, sir?"

His face grim, James nodded. "Chalky's promotion wasn't lost really. I kept it back."

"What d'you mean sir? Rose's lips thinned, angry by the admission, although he carefully kept his face as expressionless as possible.

And then another thought occurred to him, what about the girl? "Sir, did Mandy know?" was the girl's interest in White genuine, or born from guilt at involvement in the deception?

"I kept poor Chalky as an airman because he had no pilot and somehow he'd got a reputation as a jinx, unfairly I know, but what else could I do?"

James sighed, "And no, Mandy knew nothing about it. And she mustn't ever find out. She's rather attached to the young devil, and she'd never forgive me for the pretence. She wouldn't understand."

"I'm sorry sir, you're telling me that poor Chalky was emptying oil trays and cleaning latrines because you felt it was prejudicial to good order to make him a sergeant? I'm not quite sure that I quite understand either."

Despite his best attempts, Rose felt himself muscles stiffening and a frown slowly settling over his face. *Careful now, be careful, just watch what you say; you're talking to your CO.*

James sighed again and raised a hand in supplication to stop Rose. "Hang on, Flash, I'll explain. I know it was a mistake, but no-one would fly with him, and the last thing I needed was for my crews to be forced to fly with someone they didn't want to. It's not the easiest thing to do to place yourself in someone else's hands for an interception, you ought to know that by now."

He shook his head, "But if your crews think he might be a jinx? Well. You appreciate how superstitious aircrews are. I made the decision, right or wrong, and I'll stand by it. The crews come first, always will for me. You're all precious, each and every one of you. Alright, so perhaps it was a mistake, a terrible, grossly unfair mistake, but I'm going to make it up to him, I promise you."

James stared at him shrewdly, "I've put him up for a commission. It's all arranged, he's got an interview on Friday at Group. Just a formality, really, but I want you to take him for it, give him a bit of support. Alright? He can sew on his braid, now, though. I've asked Mandy to take him to Stores to get his rank issued. She's over the moon about it, bless her. Don't know how she kept it quiet."

Chalky, a Pilot-Officer? Rose's frown immediately evaporated to be replaced with a smile of glee. The lad had only just got used to being a Sergeant, and now he was going into the Officer's Mess, with a DFM to boot!

James noted his reaction, and nodded in satisfaction. "You can tell him, old chap. He's earned it and proved the rest of us wrong. Apart from you, of course. You believed in him and gave him the chance he needed, and he took full advantage of it. I can't tell you how relieved and happy I was when you agreed to fly with him. You two are one of my better crews, notwithstanding that you've been on ops for such a short time as a crew."

James looked at the small circle of happy pilots chatting animatedly, "I was able to turn a blind eye about Chalky and Mandy before, because they were both sergeants, but now that he's an officer, I think it might be an idea to remind him to walk out with her in civvies.

We don't want the SPs or the WO getting excitable, do we? They're usually OK about these things, but you always get one who's a bit over zealous, don't you?"

Of course. It would be frowned upon for an officer to have a personal relationship with an 'other rank', so poor Mandy would have to wear civilian clothes whenever she and Chalky went out together. It was ludicrous, as their relationship did not affect the service in any way, but those were the regulations, and they would need to follow them. There was no choice in the matter.

"Yes sir, them's the rules," he agreed, "I'll tell Chalky. Thank you." he smiled, "I appreciate you telling me."

James coughed, "The least I could do, Flash. I'm just glad it's all come right in the end. Get the lad to put up his rank up. I'd better have a chat with Williams, Heather and Trent, later; they're to be made acting pilot officers as well. Well, I'll be off then, get the wheels rolling. Good luck tonight, old boy."

James made to walk out, but at the doorway he turned to look severely at the group of pilots, "Carry on, then."

A frosty eye singled White out, "Oh, and Chalky, keep your mangy paws to yourself. You better watch it, because I've got my eye on you. Touch her and I'll transfer you to Army Liaison."

I rather suspect Chalky has done a lot more than just touching her, thought Rose gleefully to himself.

White grinned back at the Wing Commander, "Yes, sir. Of course, sir."

James' expression was stern, but one eyelid flickered as he winked covertly at Rose, "Right then."

298

Chapter 27

A week later, they were first on the patrol roster that evening, and the light was fading fast as they took up position just off the coast of Norfolk. Trade had been poor of late, but Rose was hopeful that they might catch an early raider.

"Right then, Chalky, you cheeky tart, you awake there in the back? I expect you to call me Flash now that we share the same Mess."

The interview at Group last Friday had been a mere formality after all, just as James had promised, and White's promotion to Pilot Officer was confirmed.

It had been a huge delight to see a diffident White enter the same Mess they first met in not so long ago, but this time as an officer, the thin stripe on his sleeve and the diagonally-striped purple and white ribbon of the DFM proud and vivid beneath his flying brevet.

What a change a few months could make!

"Oh, sir, I couldn't possibly." White replied, still sounded a bit dazed and slightly disbelieving by the fact he was an Officer.

"If you insist on calling me 'sir' in front of the others they're going to take the piss, and everybody's going to think I'm forcing you to do it. The other operators will think that I'm some kind of

299

tyrant. Do it, that's an order. OK? If you don't, I'll swap operators with the Norwegians. They like a bit of formality. How's that
grab you?"

"Oh God. I'll try, sir, er, Flash." White said uncertainly.

"That's more like it, you cheeky sod. While we've still got a spot
of light, have a shufti below us; see if you can catch sight of anyone
sneaking in low."

Rose's eyes watched the tiny shard of fading silver that was the
other patrol Beaufighter as it headed for its position to the south of
D-Dog, and thought back to earlier that day.

White and Rose had journeyed together that morning into London,
ostensibly to kit out White with his officer's uniform, but there had
been a second, hidden, agenda for the trip.

Rather than take the risk of denting Molly's beloved sports car in
the London traffic (God forbid!), the pair chose to sign out a service
Hillman from the MT pool instead.

The trip had been a pleasant one, more leisurely than the usual
hair-raising, insect-swallowing, wind-whipped and fume-filled dash
that he was accustomed to with his gorgeous Molly.

Certainly White wasn't as pretty, but the journey was far kinder
to Rose's blood pressure.

An Air Ministry allocation of just over twenty pounds had been
issued to White for his officer's uniform and gear, and Rose drove
straight to the little shop of the uniform outfitters that he himself
used in Sackville Street.

The tailor, Hobbs, bobbed his head when he saw Rose, then diffidently and quietly, professionally eyeing him up and down, asked if
White was wearing any underclothes.

"Erm, yes." White muttered in surprise. Rose grinned.

The tailor beamed. "I apologise for the impertinence, sir, but you'd be surprised how many people turn up for a measurement without anything on underneath."

He leaned forward conspiratorially, "Even some of the young gentry!" he'd looked mildly outraged.

"It's the war," Rose murmured drily, thinking, *you poor devil, sounds like a perfectly horrid job to me, give me a Beaufighter any day.* But, there were also female uniforms on the hangers. *Mm, a lack of underclothes might not always be that bad.*

Reassured that all was as it should be, Hobbs fussed and fumbled around a bemused White for over an hour, mumbling unintelligibly to himself and scribbling in the little notebook into which he recorded all the vital information for each new outfit or uniform.

Normally after receiving his commission, White ought to have received a week's leave in order to obtain his outfit and articles of rank, but knowing that Rose would remain on operations during that time, and fearing his pilot flying with another operator, White elected to postpone the leave to a more appropriate time.

After paying the necessary fee, and promising to return in just under a week for the finished garments, they left the shop and made their way to the second and (to White at least) more important part of their mission.

An hour later they emerged once more, this time from a shop in Bond Street. White was well pleased with his purchase, even though it had cost him an inordinately large sum of money.

As they got back into the car, gaily slinging their caps and gas mask cases onto the backseat, Rose cast a sheepish glance back at the shop from which they'd emerged.

Molly would love the gift he had chosen for her, as she loved everything he gave her, no matter how small or silly, but adoration had once again overwhelmed sense and he, like White, left the shop a lot lighter in funds than when he had entered it. But the moment he'd seen the bracelet, he knew he had to get it for the girl he loved so very much.

Already, in his mind's eye, he could see himself putting it on Molly's slim wrist. He sighed happily.

White shifted in his seat. "Thank you, sir, for bringing me and for all your help. I'd have been lost without you."

"It was my pleasure, Chalky. Nice choice by the way."

"I just hope she likes it, that's all."

"Oh she'll love it chum, trust me." Rose reassured him, and started the engine, "Well, that's us done. Let's go home. Do you fancy a bite to eat or a cuppa on the way back?"

"No thank you, sir. I promised to have a late lunch with Mandy. I think she's a bit concerned that I might elope with a showgirl while I'm down here. But she's the only one for me. I can't understand what a smasher like her sees in me! I'm still half-expecting to wake up and find out it was all a dream!"

Stopped at the traffic lights, Rose checked his mirror, and twisted around in the seat to check the red double-decker as it lumbered up the road towards them.

Molly, unflinching daredevil of the roads that she was, would have thought nothing of racing the bus, but Rose waited patiently for it to pass them, then inched the Hillman carefully out into the cloud of fumes behind it.

He wasn't as confident or skilful as his wife, and stayed well within the speed limit.

The driving lessons with Molly had been hell, and the memories still made him sweat, but the road was not as dangerous a place as he had feared.

Most of the other drivers he met seemed to drive with far less joyous abandon and a touch more responsibility than his dark-haired beauty.

It continued to be a great source of amusement and fondness to Molly that the man she loved, a man who deftly flew high performance fighters in deadly air combat, actually drove so diffidently on the ground, quite unlike most of his friends and contemporaries.

As they made their way along the North Circular, White turned to him. "How did you do it, sir?" he asked shyly.

"Hmm? What's that, Chalky, old chap? Do what?" The bus turned off the main road and disappeared, and he wound down the window.

"You know, sir, pop the question to Mrs Rose. How did you do it?"

"Oh. Well, I asked Molly in the garden of a pub. Not the most salubrious of places, but it was a summer's day, and the surroundings were quite spectacular."

It had been a wonderfully warm day, with Molly looking exquisite in the light cotton dress, smooth skin pale gold in the bright sunlight, the soft breeze playing tantalisingly with her hair and the hem of her skirt.

Molly hadn't said yes then, but at least she'd agreed to hold on to the ring he had bought in London with Granny. He smiled tenderly at the memory. He owed so much to that grubby, wonderful man.

"I suppose I could ask her in The Black Bull," White said doubtfully.

Rose thought that was a dreadful idea. The Horse and Groom's garden had been a great deal prettier than the Black Bull's. Prettier by far.

A convoy of three 15cwt army trucks passed them, going the other way, their exhausts leaving a dirty and malodourous cloud in their wake, "When are you going to ask, Chalky?" he wound up his window again.

"I was thinking of when we come back off duty, in a couple of days, sir."

Rose checked his mirrors and then pulled out, heart racing, to overtake a slow-moving lorry dawdling in the lane in front of them.

"Well then, why don't you take Mandy to the seaside, ask her somewhere memorable and picturesque?"

He watched the lorry carefully as he surged past, then settled back into place as it slid behind them and swiftly shrank into the distance.

White nodded thoughtfully, "Mm, I thought so too. It's a little bit dull around Dimple Heath."

"Scared?"

"Stiff, sir. What if she says no?"

Rose had snorted scornfully. "She won't, you daft pudding! She thinks you're wonderful, poor girl, bless her."

White shifted fretfully in his seat. "But just suppose?"

"Well, you'll still have me. What more could you ask for?" Rose simpered hideously at his crew mate.

"No offence, sir, but that's not much comfort. I'd much rather have Mandy." White settled into silence, staring morosely through the windscreen, one hand over the pocket holding the precious engagement ring.

"Charmed, I'm sure." Rose smiled ruefully to himself and wound down his window again slightly and settling comfortably back.

Should be back in Dimple Heath in a little while. An air test after lunch and then final preparations for the approaching night, perhaps another spot of practice.

He'd give Molly the bracelet after their two days of duty were over.

If you survive, the treacherous little voice whispered in his mind.

Shut up, he responded sternly.

"Can't see a thing down there, erm, Flash."

Over the intercom, White's voice broke through his musings, bringing him back into the cockpit of D-Dog.

304

"Shame. I was hoping we'd catch one of their pathfinders, Chalky."

The sun was just a memory now, as night rushed in and banished the light to a fast receding pink-purple line on the horizon.

"No such luck, I'm afraid."

"So, tell me, my old china, where is it?"

"Where's what?"

"Mandy's present, you thick plum, what do you think?"

"Oh, that. I've got it on me. I'm keeping it with me until I put it on her."

"You're sure you want to do this, chum? I don't mean to sound condescending, but you're both young, no need to rush, you know."
God, I hope there's no need to rush…

"Why? How old were you when you asked the Flight Officer, Flash?"

"Um, well…twenty, actually." Rose's eyes settled on a star, twinkling above them, was it moving?

He peered closely at it for a moment, and then relaxed. It was only a star after all, not some enemy bomber sneaking through the darkness.

"But that's only a year and a bit older than I am now! How long did you know Mrs Rose before you asked, Flash?"

Rose's proposal had come within two months of their first meeting. He heaved a sigh; White had him by the balls.

"Alright, alright, you damn rogue. I'm sorry I spoke, you do as you see fit, don't mind me. I'm only your experienced fucking senior. You youngsters are all the same, no interest in advice from your elders and betters."

White was behind him, a closed pair of armoured doors between them, but even then, he could feel his operators merriment.

His eyes were drawn to the star above once more. He could swear it was moving, but he knew he was imagining it. He'd heard the tales of the confused Beaufighter pilot who'd chased after a star for over half an hour.

Stop looking at it.

"Dagger 3, we may have some trade for you, what are your angels and heading?"

"Dagger 3 to Lamplight, Angels Twelve, one-eight-zero."

"Hullo, Harry, nice to hear your dulcet tones," Rose's eyebrows shot up, David! "Seems there's a bandit about, Dagger 3. Steer one-one-zero, please."

Best to remain professional, "Thank you Lamplight, understood, one-one-zero." Then, "Good to hear you."

"Thank you, Dagger 3. Remain on heading, range twenty five miles, angels ten, flash your weapon, please." A moment, "Thank you, steer one-two-five, angels fourteen."

"Angels fourteen, one-two-five confirmed." Rose switched to the intercom, "Hear that, Chalky? Watch out for the bandit."

"OK, Flash."

"Dagger 3, be advised that bandit has turned away, range twenty miles. Maintain angels and steer zero-nine-five."

"Thank you, Lamplight, heading zero-nine-five, current angels."

They flew along in silence for some minutes, Morrow occasionally correcting their course and altitude, and then, "Dagger 3, range is now five miles; bandit is at your twelve o'clock and still at your angels. Flash your weapon. Do you have him?"

"Chalky, can you see anything?"

"No, sorry, nothing." White sounded disgusted.

"OK, keep looking, chum," Rose pushed the throttles forward a little more. The fuselage was vibrating and the engines were howling as they dragged the Beaufighter ever closer to its prey.

Rose could even just hear the thin whistling of the slipstream through the fuselage behind him. He shivered in sympathy for his young operator, and continued to stare fruitlessly through the large clear pane of strengthened glass, but still there was nothing to see, despite the brightness of the moon.

Rose could feel the frisson of anxiety curling and building at the base of his spine in an icy ball, and he licked his lips.

Where the hell are you?

"I've got it!" White suddenly crowed triumphantly, "Dead ahead, range four miles, slightly above."

Thank God! "Thank you, Lamplight, we have contact. Stand by."

"Good luck, Dagger 3. Give him a round or two up the arse from me. Three would be even better!"

Safety off, throttles as far as they'll go, airframe shaking like a mad thing, howling through the emptiness, his mouth suddenly even dryer than before.

Keep looking…

A minute or two later, "Range three miles, maintain our current heading, still a little above, wait, he's turning! Cripes!"

Damn it! He's seen us! We're still too far away!

"Keep on to him, Chalky!" turn the grip…

"Turn to starboard by ten degrees, no, no, hang on on a minute, he's turning to port! Please return to original heading. No, sorry, continue turning to port. He's losing height."

He can't have seen us, despite the moon, surely? "Chalky what's the range?" Rose leaned forward as if that would help him to see the invisible enemy.

"Just under two miles and closing, we're turning inside him, oh, he's stopped turning, still losing height, though, now at angels ten. Course zero-nine-zero."

"Get me just below and behind him, please, chum."

Must have been a precautionary turn or jink to shake any possible pursuers.

But it hadn't worked, thank goodness.

And then he could see it, firstly the two pairs of faint blue exhaust, flaring occasionally, with a shadowy outline slowly formed between and around them.

Keeping formation with the bomber carefully, Rose peered upwards into the darkness. Now he could actually see it, it seemed so much clearer.

Moonlight caught smooth edges, a ghostly outline in the darkness.

Nervously he watched for movement from the gunner, but the almost-invisible thin black tube that was the enemy gunner's machine gun remained still.

"OK, Chalky, I've got him, take a quick peep." Already he was pulling up the nose to allow for deflection.

Quick, quick, get him before he wakes up…

"Ooh! A lovely fat Heinkel!"

"Stand by, chum." Rose's thumb caressed the gun button eagerly, "Firing."

The monstrous staccato thunder of the cannon reverberated and clattered through the Beaufighter as he gave the enemy bomber a two second burst, the disjointed reverberation echoing through their bones, deafening them, yet the Heinkel continued to cruise serenely through the air before them as if nothing had happened.

One (very) anxious eye still watching for the gunners to respond, Rose pushed down on the gun button again, the harsh clamouring overwhelming his, "Firing."

The quivering Beaufighter shook even harder than before, the imprisoned image of the dark shape blurring and dancing in his gunsight, a pattern of flashes splattering across the bomber once again, flaring and dying rapidly, and they felt the noisy yet harmless drumming of small torn metal fragments against the aircraft, but luckily nothing large enough to cause them more than a couple of missed heartbeats.

The banging roar ceased as his drums emptied, the mechanism clattering uselessly, and he lifted his finger.

Still the Heinkel continued to float peacefully along as if nothing had happened.

"Damn it!" he fell back a safe distance, even though there was no return fire, yet close enough to keep it in sight. "Chalky old lad, drums are empty, could you change 'em please?"

Still the hateful enemy continued peacefully along ahead of them, "No rush, I'll rock my wings if I need you, OK?"

And suddenly a tiny light appeared, flaring star-bright in the blackness, beginning to spread and surge.

"Wait, wait. Chalky?" there was no reply; White must already have begun the tiresome task of changing the four sixty-round ammo drums.

Mindful of his friend clambering around in the darkened space behind him, Rose carefully rocked the wings; that should be enough to get White dashing back to his seat.

Sure enough, "I'm back, have you lost sight of him, Flash? D'you want me to find him on The Thing?" White sounded slightly breathless.

"No, mate, look at Jerry, he's on fire!" By now, the flames had spread along the whole of the starboard wing, silhouetting the Heinkel's fuselage like a fat, black slug.

The enemy bomber was sinking, the nose dropping tiredly.

A streaming pennant of flame lighting up the thin trail of smoke curving downwards behind it.

Suddenly, a single stream of tracer, burning red luminous beads of hatred that seemed to stretch up towards them, but the glowing line gradually falling away to one side, to disappear below into the thin cloud.

The Heinkel was diving now, port wing burning too, the light gleaming from the Perspex of the windows in the side of the fuselage near the wing root and the gunner's position, the angle of the dive steepening sickly as they watched.

The swastika on the tailplane stood out starkly against the bubbling bottle-green of the Heinkel's paintwork, but the ravenous flames soon scoured it away.

The conflagration spread further now, everything from the leading edges of the wings back were burning, the bomber sinking, deeper and deeper.

"Strapped in, Chalky? Good. Let's follow it down."

He pushed the nose of D-Dog forward. The Heinkel was diving faster and faster, pulling away from them, and he eased the throttle forward to follow it down. Even then, despite their acceleration, the bomber was pulling away from them.

But as the Beaufighter passed through the trail of smoke, Rose smelt the stench of its death, the choking stink of the smoke mingling with the awful, nauseating smell of burning German metal.

The bomber was doomed, no chance of escape from the all-consuming fires that now enveloped it.

"Sir, Flash, best not get too close, he probably still has his bombs on-board. Best keep a respectable distance. He's done for, anyway."

As soon as the words had left White's mouth, the falling bomber suddenly ballooned explosively, the eye-searing flash blinding, seeming to fill the sky before them.

Fragments of the Heinkel spun out and back, and Rose flinched, resisting the urge to duck, as the Beaufighter, bucking and swinging, passed through the expanding hellish-bright cloud of flame and fury and sundered pieces of bomber, but providence was still with them and nothing large enough to cause them a serious problem came close.

Heart thumping, mouth wide in effort, Rose hauled at the controls desperately, pulling the fighter upwards through the boiling tumult of fiery air.

The hail of fragments pattered against the fighter, and White's screen flared bright and then died as the aerials on the port wing were shorn off completely by a twisted fragment of the Heinkel's port engine.

"Blimey!" the expletive was ripped from White's mouth (and he *did* duck) as part of the breech-block from the wretched rear gunner's ineffective machine gun smashed against the Beaufighter's Perspex dome, the impact cracking it, but their continued good fortune somehow prevented it from shattering as the spinning block whirled away and disappeared behind the Beaufighter.

Unable to say anything for a moment, Rose shakily turned D-Dog in a gentle circle, watching in awe through his oil and smoke-stained canopy the broken pieces of the bomber cascade down, the detached and burning wings slowly twirling downwards, like bent and battered sycamore leaves amidst the falling, slow spreading blossom of fire and metal and human beings.

A pair of parachute flares, part of the Heinkel's load, floated serenely down, following the tumbling wreckage, and lighting up the rapidly dissolving cloud of dirty smoke.

White found his voice first, and he quivered, "Oh my God. *Oh my God!* Dear God, Flash, how come we didn't go for a burton just now? How did we come through *that?*"

"Damned if I know," croaked Rose, licking dry, metallic tasting lips. "I thought we were done for when the bloody thing exploded. We flew through the fireball."

"Fuck me. I almost pissed myself, Flash. Is she OK?"

Below, the fragments of what was left of the Heinkel spattered for the last time across an empty field.

Rose carefully checked the controls, but the Beaufighter, at least as far as he could tell, was as right as rain. The engines were running smoothly and she was handling nicely, but his canopy was dirty, oil-hazy and smoke smeared, and he felt suddenly exhausted, the energy and tension draining quickly from him.

"Yeah, Chalky. She feels fine. Sweet as a nut."

Thank you, Lord. Shocked but grateful by their good fortune, Rose grasped the little bear for comfort.

"Flash, my set's sulking, it's gone u/s. I think something took a wallop when Jerry blew up."

He wiped his forehead. "What? Nothing at all?"

"Not a peep. Dead as a Dodo."

Or as dead as the Heinkel crew, Rose thought, and frowned at his poor humour.

"OK, chum, I think we'll head back. I was an idiot to follow the bloody thing down. Next time we'll observe from a safe distance. Without your set we're about as useful as a chocolate teapot. And, anyway, I'd be a lot happier if the boys gave her a quick once over."

"Sounds good to me." White replied, "I need to pee and I could do with a nice hot, sweet cuppa. I'm parched. Maybe a bite to eat?"

Oh, the resilience of youth, thought Rose, holding up one tremulous gauntleted hand, conveniently forgetting the fact that both he and the youth trembling in the back of the Beaufighter were not all that far apart in years.

He looked at Molly's picture, dimly lit by the cockpit instrumentation.

Thank God. I survived the odds again tonight, my darling, and I'll be

312

able to hold you in my arms once more, all being well. If our set's damaged,
then perhaps they'll stand us down for tonight.

Rose looked out, but they were alone in the night sky, survivors.
Thank you, God.

Chapter 28

Immediately after lunch (finished off delightfully by a hurried but extremely enjoyable and very passionate kiss with Molly in a hasty rendezvous behind the kitchens), Rose went to find White.

It was a kiss which left Elsie the Jankers Princess (an inadvertent witness) goggle-eyed and open mouthed as she sat disconsolately on a chipped wooden stool, peeling knife in one grubby hand, hidden away behind a huge pile of potatoes, a cold and muddy pail of water beside her.

As arranged earlier, Rose met White beside one of the B-Flight maintenance sheds.

The young AI operator still looked faintly bashful and uncomfortable whenever he received salutes from NCOs and airmen, but it made Rose glow with pride.

"So, Chalky, you cheeky blighter, what did you want to see me about?" he asked jovially, lips still tingling, *Mmm*.

"Got something to show you, Flash." Despite his initial reticence in using Rose's name, it now came a little more easily to White's lips. "There's someone I'd like you to meet."

Inside the twilight recesses of the shed were a number of offices, and a large workshop area. Rose's nostrils caught the odour of dope,

314

thinners, grease, oil and a multitude of other unidentifiable smells.

To his surprise White led him out through the other side back into the sunlight, towards a pair of Beaufighters.

To one side of the fighters was a little gaggle of WAAFs dressed in grimy overalls, gathered around a Hispano gun barrel on mounts, cleaning out its bore with a large, long-handled bottle-brush and chattering happily.

There was a piercing wolf whistle from one of the girls and White blushed bright scarlet and threw the WAAFs a half-hearted wave.

Rose looked at the girls with interest. "Friends of yours, old chap? Did we come here to see them?" he shook a finger reproachfully, "Mandy might not be very happy."

"Oh no, Flash, they're old friends. Of Mandy's, too. When I was still an aircraftman they used to look after me."

"Oh? Some boys have all the luck." Rose's lips quirked upwards suggestively.

White blushed again, "Oh no. No, not like that. The girls would share their tea and biscuits with me. Always saved me a couple of custard creams. That's all. Nothing else."

Rose looked at him doubtfully. "If you say so, old chum. I believe you, thousands wouldn't."

"No, I mean it, honest!"

Rose winked at his young friend. "Methinks the Operator doth protesteth too mucheth."

White rolled his eyes and shook his head, "You talk such nonsense sometimes, Flash. Utter bollocks. Behave yourself." He sighed, "Act your age, *sir*."

"Bet you can't even remember their names." Rose scoffed.

White sniffed scornfully, "'Course I do. Candy, Sandy, Pandy and Randy."

"Good Lord. Candy, Sandy, Pandy and, er, Randy? Are you pulling my leg? You're not making it up, are you?"

"Of course not! Their names are actually Candida, Alexandra, Pandora and Iris, but they prefer Candy, Sandy, Pandy and Randy."

"Iris? Then why on earth is she called Randy?"

White grinned, he had *very* fond memories, but damned if he'd tell Rose, though. "Don't ask."

Rose glanced at the girls. "Is she the brassy blonde?"

"Good grief, no. that's Sandy, er, Alexandra. Her father's the Earl of somewhere or other. Randy's the little brunette."

Rose looked back at the girls. 'Randy' noticed him looking and she blushed bright pink and looked down shyly.

"*That's* Randy?" he exclaimed in surprise, "But she looks sweet and as quiet as a mouse! Are you sure?"

"Am I sure, he says!" The young operator sneered.

They stopped beside the closer of the two Beaufighters, and White nodded amicably at the bored-looking sentry standing beside the operator's hatch. "Hello, Jim, I take it he's in there? OK to go in?"

The sentry saluted. "Yes, Chalky, er, sir, go right ahead. He's in there, doing his tinkering. He never lets me in, though, even though I'm his blinkin' security detail." the airman grumbled with exasperation.

Chuckling, White nimbly ducked under the fuselage and disappeared up the ladder. Nodding to the sentry, a curious Rose followed him inside, into the operator's compartment. At the top of the steps, he turned awkwardly to face the rear of the aircraft, taking care not to bang his head on the various boxes, panels and oil tank attached to the inside of the fuselage, crouching uncomfortably, despite his own slight stature, unable to stand up straight in the drab green-painted compartment.

A figure dressed in a set of blue RAF overalls was bent down in front of the AI set, squeezed in to one side of the four keel-mounted legs of the swivel seat. Despite the hinged Perspex dome being in the open position in addition to the lower escape hatch, it seemed stuffy and cramped in the confined space.

"Come on, Stan, show us what you're working on."

"Wotcher, Chalky! Come to see how the other half lives? How've you been? I hear you've been giving Jerry a bloody nose or two?"

The specialist AI technician, three stripes on his sleeves, looked around with a huge smile, eyes bright. Straightening as much as was possible in the limited space, he held out an oil-stained hand and White grasped it and pumped it warmly.

"Busy as always, eh, Stan?"

"As always, chum. You know how it is. So, to what do I owe the pleasure?"

The electronics specialist Sergeant noticed the young Flying Officer standing behind White and tried to straighten to attention, but Rose stopped him with one raised hand. "At ease, Sergeant, don't mind me. Carry on, please."

He shifted his position slightly, one of the bolts securing the flare gun pressing uncomfortably into his shoulder.

What an awfully poky little place this is, he thought to himself.

A sturdy work light hung from a stanchion, its thick black cable snaking down and out through the hatch, brightly lighting the interior of the space.

"I bought someone to meet you. Stan, this is Flying Officer Rose, my pilot. Sir, Flash, this is Sergeant Stanley Hale. He knows absolutely everything there is to know about these electronics, and more. He was in France last year with a British Expeditionary Force radar unit. Stan's the one who makes 'em tick!"

"Really?" Rose regarded the dark-haired young man with the friendly face and the ready smile with interest.

Here was one of the most essential components of without which B-Flight's operations were impossible.

If it weren't for the AI sets, there would be far fewer enemy bombers being brought down. Luck was an essential factor, of course, but with the help of science, defence in depth was both possible and a reality.

This electronics specialist and others like him were the one who made Britain's protection and the night fighting war a real and functional possibility.

Hale nodded, "Yes, sir. You flyers do treat my lovely bits of kit quite roughly, but, all in a good cause. It's a bit delicate, needs a lot of love. Very easy to get it damaged, you know. The equipment gets jarred during flight, shaken in the landings, mis-aligned, burnt-out by power surges, it's a wonder the thing works at all, and don't even get me started about damp on my aerials!"

He scratched his chin reflectively, "I've just been to sort out your kite, D-Dog, isn't it? Pretty straightforward, really." Hale beckoned them forward. "Here. Let me show you, Mr Rose."

White and Rose peered into open topped metal box. The young sergeant indicated a nondescript grey cylinder, about the size of a tin of peaches, with a variety of wires sprouting circumferentially from it.

"There was a power surge in the R3102A when the aerials sheared, um, that's the receiver unit, sir, and the thing is, it provides the power supply to the Type 48 indicator unit. That's why the whole thing died on you. Just one of those things, really. I changed the variable inductor, burned out I'm afraid, and a few other little bits and bobs. It's as good as new, now."

Rose tried to remove the glazed look from his face. Technical matters always confounded him. "Oh, yes…er, I see."

But he didn't. It was about as clear as a rusty bucket of dirty ditch water in a coal cellar at midnight.

White pointed at something in the box, "Did the four-way switch trip, Stan?"

Rose looked his operator in surprise. Airborne Intercept operators were not usually trained in the maintenance and repair of their sets, so to hear White casually asking Hale about the intricate workings of this incredibly complex piece of equipment was quite a revelation.

"No, actually it didn't at any point before the thing went pop, chum." Hale noticed Rose's face, "Chalky, er, Pilot Officer White here is a good student, sir," he explained.

White rapped his knuckles on the side of the indicator unit's casing, "Whenever I was free, Stan was kind enough to spend time showing me how it all worked."

Hale nodded. "Mr White, do me a favour? Would you ask the girls outside to disconnect my lamp? I'm all done in here for now."

"Yes, Stan, of course. Excuse me for a moment." White squeezed past Rose and clambered down the ladder and disappeared.

Hale watched him go affectionately, "May I speak frankly, sir?"

Rose adjusted his position again, *what a horrid little hole, give me a nice roomy cockpit any day.* "Please do."

Hale scratched one ear, "Pilot Officer White is highly gifted, technically, and he was being wasted as a general dogsbody. It was a downright liberty to treat him that way, if you'll pardon my saying so, sir. I was going to ask for him to become my assistant; and after a couple of weeks I would put in a request to the CO for a transfer for him to undergo training as a specialist."

He patted the swivel seat gently, "but then you came and took him away from all this, and up into the clouds and the moonlight instead. Where he really belongs."

Looking back at Rose, Hale added earnestly, "You saved him before I could, sir. Thank you."

Rose didn't know what to say. It seemed that there were others who cared for White's wellbeing just as much as he did, and at least one of them had been working on a plan to save the young operator from the purgatory he had found himself in.

He swallowed the lump that had somehow appeared in his throat. "Sergeant Hale, I want to thank you for what you do for us every day and night, but I'd also like to thank you for what you did, and also for what you were intending to do, for Chalky. You're a good man."

The lamp suddenly went out with a soft 'tick.'

Hale looked embarrassed in the sudden darkness of the shadowed interior, "it's no more than the lad deserved. He thinks very highly of you, sir. Looks like the dice fell right for him this time. I'm glad."

"Yes," behind him, Rose could hear the scrape of White's footstep on the ladder. Reaching out, he shook hands with Hale, "Thank you, Stan. God bless."

White puffed his way back up into the compartment. "Crikey!" he chortled, "What are you two doing here standing around in the dark? Waiting for a bus? Come on out, the NAAFI van just drew up outside."

Hale began throwing tools into his case, the clattering and clanging reverberating deafeningly in the enclosed space. "I'll be along in just a moment. I'll clean up after. Thirsty work this, could do with a nice steaming brew and an iced bun."

Rose stopped halfway down the ladder, grateful to escape the operator's section of the fuselage.

"Sergeant Hale, can I help take anything out?"

The young specialist shook his head, "That's kind of you, sir, but I can handle this. Leave these to me, but please, do me a favour? Well, two favours actually. Take good care of the lad, and keep shooting those Nazis down?"

Rose nodded firmly, "I will, Stan, gladly, and again, thank you. Thank you for everything."

Chapter 29

"A nun gave me a black eye once."

"What?" mumbled Rose, still staring blearily into the black and empty recess of his mug.

They were sitting on a pair of gaily striped deckchairs outside the crew room. Grey streaks of light warned of a sullen dawn that was approaching fast, the sky through which they'd flown scant hours before now lightening in preparation for the new day, the fresh fragrance of dew and earth blending with the sharp airfield odour of thinners, dope, glycol and fuel.

"A nun gave me a black eye once," White repeated patiently, tossing the cold dregs of his cocoa onto the pale frosted stalks of grass.

Rose stifled a yawn, and squinted at his friend in befuddlement.

"Cripes, I must be dozier than I thought, Chalky. I could have sworn you said that a nun knocked you out?"

Involuntarily, White yawned in sympathetic response. It had been a protracted and lacklustre night, and the thought of his bed was more attractive even than the flying supper which awaited them.

There had been just the one interception, and that had been a shabby Wellington bomber returning from the continent, sedately bumbling its way to its home airfield, the tired and strained crew unaware of the Beaufighter keeping station behind and below as they carefully identified it.

"Oh, for goodness sake! No, Flash. She didn't knock me down; she gave me a black eye. Stop being such a clot. Are you listening or what?" Irritability heightened the soft burr of the young operator's Highlands accent, and he put down his empty mug onto the paved slab beneath him with a dull *'Clunk!'*

Interest piqued, Rose straightened with an effort, his muscles, spine and the chair creaking disturbingly. It was the first time White had spoken about his past.

"I'm sorry, mate. What do you mean, though? Did I hear that correctly? A nun gave you a black eye? Strewth! What on earth did you do? You didn't try it on, did you? Bloody hell! You cheeky randy rascal!"

"Listen for a moment, Flash, will you?" White tucked his chin down and pushed his hands deep into his pockets. "It happened when I was a child. I was fourteen years old at the time."

Chastened, intrigued, and curious to know more about White's mysterious past, Rose was silent.

"Nobody here knows, excepting Mandy of course, but the truth is, I was raised in a children's home. My Mum died when I was six, and I don't think my Dad was able to look after me. He was in freight, see? " White's voice was low, carefully neutral, his face hidden in shadow.

"He came to visit me once, about six months later, bought me a big red enamelled bus. It was fantastic. He cried the whole time, kept asking me to forgive him. He'd married again, you see. And that was the last time I ever saw him. I always wondered why he never came back to get me. I suppose he just didn't love me enough to be my father anymore."

White sighed desolately, a long, low lament that spoke of pain and loss in the grey half-light.

Something hollow and metallic clattered suddenly in the distance, in the general direction of where the young Norwegians were mushroom prospecting near the edge of the runway.

One of them must have dropped the mushroom bucket.

The thought of those fresh mushrooms, sliced thin and fried in hot fat, and then served with their flying supper would normally have made him dribble, but White's revelations had driven away all other thoughts.

"As soon as he'd gone, Sister Katherine took my toy bus away, and said it wouldn't be fair for me to have a toy when all the other children had nothing. I never saw it again, either." The depth of his pain was all too evident, and Rose shivered involuntarily.

"God! It sounds bloody awful, Chalky." *Oh, how trite and inadequate those words sound!*

"Worse than that, chum. It was a living hell. They'd beat us for the slightest reason. There was no laughter within those walls, just pain and tears. Lots and lots of tears." He wiped his dry cheeks as if to wipe the memory of them away.

"Any display of affection, like hugs or kissing were disallowed. They forbade any kind of physical contact, so if you tried to comfort one of the smaller ones when they were upset, which was pretty much every day, you'd get a beating. You learnt pretty darn quick to hold in the tears, because if they saw even one, it was enough to earn another beating for being weak. But it was hard not to cry living within those walls. In the end, it taught me to be tough and not to cry, never, ever, no matter what."

Somewhere in the distance, an aircraft towing tractor coughed into guttural life, and White looked for a long moment, but there was nothing to see. Rose said nothing. What was there he could say?

324

They sat in silence together, Rose shocked and saddened and wide awake, all weariness gone.

What are you looking at? What can you see in your mind's eye, Chalky? What memories lurk there?

"I left that awful realm of torment at sixteen, when I joined up. Despite everything, it was the best experience I'd had for years. I'd just had the other kids, see, and then suddenly I had a family of hundreds that looked after me, kept me warm, and fed me 'til my stomach was bursting. All the other boys with me were missing their homes, crying in the night, but not me. For the first time since my dad left me in that shithole, I *was* home. We had a laugh. Even the old Warrant Officer seemed kind and gentle. He was strict and harsh, but never unfair. And he was a good man, just tried not to let it show. He must have been a good Dad, I reckon." White sniffed and then wiped his nose. "It's a bit chilly, isn't it?"

He nodded, "Yes, Chalky, it is a bit. And the black eye?"

"Sister Anna. She caught me sitting under a tree."

Rose shook his head in disbelief. "She hit you because you were sitting under a tree? Bloody hell!"

"No, not quite. The thing is, one of the older girls was standing on a branch above me."

Rose could hear White's smile, "Lily Evans, almost eighteen, long smooth legs and no knickers. Couldn't take my eyes off her fanny, even when the old dragon came up to me. Lily knew I was looking, knew I was there below her, pretended she didn't, but she did, and let me enjoy the view." He sighed. "Cor. What a view…"

His eyes were distant, remembering the sight, and the corners of his mouth turning up.

Rose waited quietly, scared to break the thread.

"Sister Anna would have skinned us both alive if she'd known

Lily had it all out on display, luckily she ranted and raved about eyes that were where they shouldn't be, and she had the right thing for them in her hand, and then *wallop!* Apparently, I was using them to do the devil's work."

White sighed again, but the sigh this time was in happy remembrance.

"It was worth two black eyes, Flash, and I got a real eyeful, believe me! Lily legged it, sharpish like, 'cause if Sister Anna had known she'd had no drawers on…!"

Rose chuckled, even though his heart weighed heavy for the tortured little boy that had grown into the slight young man now sitting beside him.

"Did you go to the Police, old mate?" he asked gently.

"Nobody cared a damn, Flash. We were problems no-one wanted to be responsible for. For instance, one of the girls got into trouble, in the family way, so to speak, and they labelled her as a brazen whore and pushed her down the stairs to avoid a scandal."

White shook his head with frustration, anger tainting his words. "Broken pelvis and neck, a verdict of accidental death and no further action from the authorities. The kindest girl you'd ever meet. On the way to Dimple Heath after training, I bought a pistol from a spiv at Glasgow railway station, and I went to the Home. I thought that I'd never let those nasty bitches hurt another child. I'd dreamed so many times of putting a bullet between Sister Patricia's beady little eyes."

A moth fluttered silently before them, a tiny wraith in the gloom. The taste of the cocoa was gone, only an acid bitterness pooling in his throat, "Chalky…you didn't…?"

White turned to face him. "No, Flash, when push came to shove, I didn't have the courage. I stood outside in the rain for over an hour, but I couldn't take those last steps to the front door. I let the children down, but I just couldn't do it. When my pilot was killed and I got ground duties, I guessed this was my punishment. Either I was being punished for contemplating murder, or because I let the kids down. I accepted it and got on with it. Whatever they gave me, I did. It was my penance for being weak. I deserved it. Do you believe in God, Flash?"

"Good Lord, if you'll pardon the expression, yes, of course I do. He kept me safe even when we were going up there piecemeal umpteen times a day in scrappy little formations against great clouds of Germans, he let me live when so many others, better men than me, didn't. And of course, he gave me a girl like Molly. I don't need any more proof than that."

White nodded in satisfaction. "Good, because so do I. I don't know why some things happen, but I know there must be a reason for everything that does."

Rose patted White's shoulder. "You weren't being punished, old son. I think you suffered more than enough in that bloody Home. I think everything happens for a reason, we just don't always know why."

"If I were being punished, I wouldn't have been crewed up with you, Flash. Where I am now is because of the path I've trodden. He sent you to take me up into the clouds. As they say, God moves in mysterious ways." Wearily, White rubbed his eyes.

"Exactly, my old son. Now you're here, you're not just looking out for the kids at the Home, but you're actually looking out for everybody who lives on these islands. That's a lot of people, a lot of lives, chum."

White nodded gratefully, "Thanks, Flash. Look, please don't mention it to anyone. I've never told a soul before, and I didn't tell you because I wanted pity, or anything. I told you because I want you to know who I am, where I've been, and what flying with you really means to me. You and Mrs Rose are my dearest friends."

"Does Mandy…?"

"She does. She's wonderful," then, almost defiantly, "and she's seen the scars. All of them."

Rose surprised himself by blushing like a schoolboy, momentarily lost for witty repartee. "Ah."

White smiled. "I must have done something right to be loved by someone like her. Her old man's a High Court judge, a KC, you know. God only knows what he'll make of me."

"Talking of black eyes, tell me about that one you were sporting just before the first time we flew together?"

White winked at him. "Settling old scores, Flash. I'm glad you saw fit to let me keep the stripes, though, or else I'd have been right up shit creek, without the proverbial! I'll tell you about it one day, I promise."

They sat quietly now, comfortable in each other's presence like an old married couple, enjoying the burgeoning bloom of light glazing the undersides of the clouds and the straight edges of the wet grass, yet another night of operations survived, and another day of life to be savoured and celebrated.

Another dawn witnessed, a success in itself, and another morning to experience, to live and rest, and to love.

Rose closed his eyes, and thought of Molly, his special girl.

I love you, Moll, and thanks be to God, I get to share yet another day with you…

The telephone shrilled behind them, and they tensed but remained seated, unable to turn their heads in dread, nerves jangling and skin prickling, hearts thumping, trying to make sense of the muted murmuring inside the hut.

Rose felt like crying at the unfairness of it. *Damn it! The night's over! Dear God, Please let it not be a scramble…*

The murmuring inside stopped, and then a moment later they

heard the swish of the blackout curtain behind them, footsteps, and then Barr was standing behind them both.

"If you two poor, romantic fools can stop holding hands and canoodling in the moonlight, would you mind coming back in?" he asked conversationally, conveniently ignoring the fact that the dawn was breaking and that the moon was nowhere to be seen.

Oh God, don't choose us, it's not fair…

"Sector have kindly told us to call it a night," Barr looked up at the brightening sky ironically, "and some of us would like to nip along for a spot of breakfast. Would you care to join us? Flash, your missus should be waiting for you, come on. You too, Chalky, I daresay there might be a glamorous young blonde WAAF around here somewhere waiting for you, too. Hard to believe, of course, but there you are…"

Like arthritic old men, the two young men stood and stretched, dry-eyed, stiff and slow and aching, before gratefully following their flight commander to a well-earned flying supper/breakfast.

Another long, dark night survived, another cold but infinitely beautiful dawn savoured, and yet another personal victory against both the Germans and Sir Isaac.

Thank God.

Chapter 30

With a final wave goodbye, the airman turned and disappeared into the swirling eddies of fog, leaving them alone.

After the endless din of the Hercules motors, the sudden silence was deafening, broken only by the occasional *tink-tink* of the engines as they cooled and the creaking of the airframe.

"There was a moment there when I was starting to get a bit worried, Flash." White's voice was shaky.

Rose licked dry lips. "I know, mate. The fog was already rolling in when we made our approach. Another thirty seconds and Sir Isaac would have had us. The lights wouldn't have been visible anymore. We were lucky."

Rose looked out past the starboard engine to the indistinct, almost indiscernible shape of a Hawker Hurricane fighter parked nearby, then down at his hands, clasping them together to still the faint tremor.

Lady Luck had remained on their side once more.

The erks would be along soon, and Rose unstrapped himself. "Come on, Chalky, let's get out, our truck should be along shortly. I need a sweet cup of char."

"Me too, sir, I'm gasping, and I could do with a pee."

Rose pulled the lever to lower the back of his chair, and using the bars, tiredly lifted himself with weary arms over the well in front of the armoured doors and, unlatching the hatch, he climbed down the little ladder and onto the tarmac.

Despite the dampening effect of the sluggishly swirling fog, he could just make out the muted grumble of a truck in low gear as it made its way to them. White joined him, and together they peered out into the murky darkness.

"I'll put in the locking pins, Flash, make sure the dear old bus doesn't roll off while we're away."

"OK, chum." Rose closed his eyes for a moment. He'd completely forgotten about inserting the locking pins. *I must be even more exhausted than I thought.*

After a few minutes, the dimmed headlight, and then the boxy shape of the crew truck slowly emerged and disgorged a glum knot of duty groundcrew.

Rose felt like laughing at the bewildered expressions of doubt on their faces when they caught sight of the huge engines on the Beaufighter. This was a single-engine fighter base, and these massive power units were not at all what they must be used to.

So where on earth is the security detail? He wondered. It wasn't unknown for Luftwaffe aeroplanes to land at an RAF airfield, so a standing security unit was supposed to be on standby at all bases.

The crew chief shone his torch apprehensively onto the Beaufighter. "Would you gentlemen please get into the transport, sir? The driver will take you to the Officer's Mess." He sniffed as his eyes roved professionally over the heavy fighter.

Serving as groundcrew on a Hurricane squadron, the solid, pugnacious shape of the crouching Beaufighter looked to him as big as a small battleship.

"Well, my beauty," he murmured, "What're we going to do with you?"

Rose looked back at D-Dog, mindful of 'The Thing.' The AI equipment was top secret.

"Corporal, please ensure that no-one enters my kite. I want a sentry posted PDQ. Are you armed?"

The crew chief looked at him in surprise.

"Understood, sir. I think there's a rifle in the back of the truck. We'll stand guard on it while we take a look at her. In the meantime, I'll get my lads to have a look at your Bristols."

Realising what he'd just said, he grimaced with embarrassment, "Sorry, sir, I didn't mean that, what I meant to say was -"

Masking a grin despite his weariness, Rose shook his head impatiently. "That's quite alright, um, Corporal-?"

"Masters, sir."

Rose clutched his maps and parachute pack closely to his chest. "Corporal Masters, it's imperative that none of your lads enter the machine. I'm going to ask for a guard as soon as I get to the Mess. In the meantime, you're it. Guard it with your life, that's an order. Nobody gets in the rear compartment of the machine, OK?"

Disconcerted by the mystery, the chief nodded dubiously, eyes stealing back to the squat twin-engined fighter. "Sir."

A few quiet words of instruction and reassurance, and then into the transport for the slow, careful drive to the Mess.

"Why not to Dispersals? We aren't really dressed appropriately for the Officer's Mess." asked Rose.

The driver shrugged. "Dunno, sir. The Hurricane CO just said I was to take you gentlemen directly to the Mess."

Fair enough.

Rose settled back into the seat and closed his eyes. Strange that the fighter CO was still around at this hour of night, usually the whole aircrew complement of a day-fighter squadron were off duty, generally following the nightly pursuits of fighter pilots everywhere, namely guzzling prodigious amounts of beer and/or chasing girls.

Talking of girls…*I must call Molly first thing*, he thought wearily, trying to keep his eyes open, *tell her we're OK. She'll be worried sick.*

And Operations at Dimple Heath, of course, they must be concerned that we got down alright.

The fog-dampened sound of the engine in low gear, and the swish of tyres on the tarmac was a powerful soporific. It was an effort to keep his eyes open, and he stifled a yawn.

A few short minutes later they arrived at their destination. The Officers Mess was a large building close to the Operations Block, and from it they watched the tail light of their ride disappear into the gloom.

Suddenly a door was jerked open, the light making them blink with discomfort, and from the brightly lit interior, a huge and hairy shape appeared and flung itself at Rose. He was lifted bodily into the air and the breath was squeezed out of his lungs before he could scream.

Dear Lord! I'm being attacked by a bloody grizzly bear! In England! A shocked Rose thought in stupefied astonishment, and heard White cry out sharply in fear.

Suddenly an asphyxiating cloud of beer, cigar smoke and horrendously familiar-smelling Cologne washed over him.

The 'Bear', still roaring raucously, spun him round joyously and then set him carefully back onto the ground.

"Flash! You ugly, miserable toad! Fuck me! I can't believe it! What're you doing here? Was it you just landed? Who's this? Where's Molly? Did you swap her for this little one? Not a good decision, my friend." He looked searchingly at his friend for a moment, "Bugger me! You don't get any better looking. What is with you British? At least the girls are pretty."

His eyes found White, "at least most of them are."

Rose looked up with a mixture of irritation and sheer pleasure at the towering figure before him, struggling to breathe with a bruised chest.

"You mad bastard, begging your pardon, sir," He wheezed, "I think you've crushed my bloody chest!"

"Bah! Ugly as sin and such weaklings!" The man before him was outsized to begin with, but the great fur coat and woollen balaclava he was wearing made him appear even larger.

He was smiling, a slightly disconcerting expanse of natural teeth and metal crowns, not in a snarl as he had initially thought, but in an achingly wide Cheshire Cat-like grin of pleasure.

Before he could say anything more, the other man picked him up and kissed him wetly on both cheeks, before setting him down again.

Stunned, Rose wiped his cheeks, but found that he, too, was smiling with delight; but he was also secretly very pleased that he hadn't wet himself.

White watched them both, his jaw hanging open and eyes wide and round and shining like dinner plates in the light cast by the open door.

Still unable to believe his eyes in the semi-darkness, and desperately trying to regain his shattered composure, Rose turned to White. His heart was racing ten to the dozen.

"Chalky, meet a very, very dear friend of mine. This is Squadron-Leader Cynk. We fought together last year. Sir, this is my, um, navigator, Pilot Officer Chalky White."

He smiled slightly at his young friend, And added, as if in explanation, "You'll have to excuse him, Chalky. He's Polish. Begging your pardon, sir."

Cynk stuck out his hand to White, who gingerly took it. "Pleased to meet you, sir."

"Likewise, Chalky," the huge bulk of Cynk dwarfed the slight figure of White.

"Flying Officer Rose speaks very highly of you, sir."

Cynk roared with laughter, "Of course he does, I taught him everything he knows!"

Wonder where Stan got that fur coat? I suppose they aren't that particular about Mess Regulations here, if they let him wander around dressed like that.

Rose looked at the big Pole. "Is this where you're based now, Stan, uh, sir?"

"Yes, Flash, but forget the 'sir', we're old friends, in case you'd forgotten. Now, stop jabbering bollocks and come in. we'll organise a bite to eat and somewhere you can sleep tonight. How's that lovely WAAF beauty of yours?" Asked Cynk solicitously, "Has she had enough of the scrawny little runt she married, yet? What? Not left you yet? What's wrong with her? She's too beautiful to be that desperate."

"You do say the nicest things, Stan."

"'Course I do, pal, you're my friend. Blood brothers, we are, you and I. Now get your fucking tiny arse inside before we all drop down dead of hypothermia."

Not sure if he should grin or feel outraged for his pilot by Cynk's comments, a bemused White followed the two old friends as they made their way inside.

335

Chapter 31

Half an hour later the three of them were sitting down comfortably in the deserted Mess, having arranged a suitable guard for D-Dog, and then polishing off a platter that had been groaning beneath a mountain of corned beef and pickle sandwiches.

They had talked of their experiences since their last meeting. It turned out that Cynk and his squadron were engaged in offensive intruder missions over Europe.

It was now the job of the day fighter squadrons of RAF Fighter Command to wrest control of the skies of France, and they were doing it in various ways.

Termed 'Rhubarbs' and 'Circuses', small units of fighters were ranging on free hunting missions whilst in other missions larger 'wing' formations covering bomber formations were sent to tempt the enemy into interception.

To Rose's despair, Cynk pulled one of his cheroots from out of the coat and lit it. The air began to fill with that peculiar smelling smoke he remembered so well. Despite the venomous effect of it on his nasal passages, the odorous cloud brought back fond memories.

Inwardly he smiled, and took a sip of sweet tea, watching White surreptitiously wiping his reddening eyes, tears spilling down his cheeks.

All we need now is for one of those interminable dirges about his homeland.

A tiny WAAF Warrant Officer of mature years and very determined in visage came into the room. "Squadron Leader Cynk, sir, how many times do I have to repeat myself? We've spoken about this before, haven't we?"

To Rose's surprise, Cynk jumped to his feet, looking sheepish. "Oh, Mrs Dalton! I wasn't expecting you."

The WAAF crossed her arms and a thunderous look settled on her resolute face. "I can see that! Really, sir, you can't come in wearing that filthy thing! And those cheroots – dear heavens!" she made a disgusted face.

And then she saw White wiping his face. "Sir, you really must put out that smelly thing out. I insist! Look at this young man here, you're poisoning him!" she shook her head despairingly, "And that awful coat. I won't have it in here, really I won't. Please take it off, sir."

Cynk looked at her for a long moment, opened and closed his mouth, then sheepishly turned and walked out past her silently, trailing a vile, perfumed aroma.

Having dealt with the immediate problem, the WAAF turned her attention to Rose and White, her stern expression softening, magically transforming her face from that of a severe and daunting woman to that of a loving mother. She leaned towards them solicitously.

"Gentlemen, can I get you anything more? Some more tea, perhaps?"

Rose patted his stomach tenderly, "Thank you, no. I couldn't eat another crumb. That was a lovely."

Cynk came back in minus coat and cheroot. "There, better?"

Warrant Officer Dalton nodded approvingly, "Much better, sir, thank you."

The big Pole lightly kissed the top of the WAAF's head. "You're just like my mother, always nagging. Nag, nag, nag," he scolded her gently.

Her face softened further, "No one could ever take her place, sir, but I thank you for the compliment. It's an honour and a great pleasure to do what we can to look after you and your naughty boys. You take care of us, and so many of them have already given their all for us; we'll take care of you the best we can."

Incredibly, the tough little WAAF Warrant Officer had tears in her eyes as she fussed over the crockery.

Rose understood it then, that Dalton must have somehow discovered that Cynk's mother and young wife were killed by the Luftwaffe in the merciless bombing of Warsaw during the invasion of Poland in 1939, and seen fit to reward him with her affection.

Did she see in him someone that was, or perhaps had been, close to her? Or did she just see the little lost and bereft orphan, hiding inside the big, brash exterior of the tough Polish Squadron Leader?

Whatever the truth, Rose was glad that his friend had somehow inherited a fairy godmother. His eyes followed the WAAF as she exited.

"So where did you get that bloody awful coat, Stan?"

"It's an old family heirloom, Flash, my fragrant old fart. My Grandfather wore that coat at Kiev in 1920. They say Red Ivan still talks of the Berserker Bear seen fighting at the front for the Polish forces."

He scratched an ear and smiled smugly, "Must've given them the shits to see their national emblem fighting against them. Wish I'd been there."

"I'm glad you weren't, otherwise you wouldn't be here now, although I must say that when you burst out through the door yelling like a lunatic, I thought you were a bloody great brown bear myself. I know it sounds crazy, but I was so surprised, I forgot to wet myself!"

"You scared me sodding shitless, sir," said White simply, and blushed a bright pink.

Cynk grinned broadly, "Glad to hear it, dear chap, good to get the old blood pumping hard! Keeps your brain working and your cock stiff!" he smiled kindly, "though I suspect with faces like yours you don't get much chance to use your cocks!"

Rose set down his mug of tea. "Most kind. However, I want to know what you were doing skulking around the operations block at this time of night? I can't believe that you were here waiting for us! What a turn up for the books!"

"Fortuitous circumstance, Flash. The thing is, I had no idea at all it was you. I didn't want any crew landing here at night shivering in the dispersals when there's loads of space here, and nice soft beds."

He sniffed disparagingly, "Of course, if I'd known it was you, I'd have left you out there."

"Ah, there's the hard-nosed warrior we all know and love."

"Actually, the reason I'm here is I was just returning a lady to her quarters when you two turned up and started buzzing around."

Rose sat up, interest piqued despite his tiredness. He was terribly exhausted but it wasn't every day one met on old friend. And Molly would kill him if he didn't get all the gen.

"Ooh, I say! The plot thickens! A lady? Do tell, Stan, Molly will be fascinated." Beside him, White's eyes closed and he began to snore softly.

"Her name's Anna, and she's an Assistant Section Officer here. Blonde, curvy, legs right up to her arse and tits like watermelons." He coughed awkwardly, "Um, Flash, if I let you meet her, don't let her know I said that. She's wonderful." He sighed, "I think I'm in love."

Stan was in love? Dear Lord!

339

"She thinks I'm wonderful, bless her, but then, how could she not? Tall, handsome, intelligent, in fact everything you're not, Flash my dear boy."

"Enchanted, I'm sure. Much as I admire you, O tall, handsome and intelligent warrior, those extra stripes won't stop me from punching you on that big lumpy nose of yours, Squadron-Leader, sir."

Cynk flicked a cigarette stub at him. "You're lucky I like you, otherwise you'd be on a charge, you cheeky bugger."

"Lucky me." Rose leaned back comfortably. "So tell me about Anna. Molly will chuck me out if I don't gather as much information as I can."

"She's sweet and kind and gentle and clever. Very like my sweet Helena, may God bless her."

His wife's loss still cut brutally deep into Cynk's heart, and he had to stop for a moment, working to keep the emotion from his face.

Rose looked away, unwilling to see his friend's moment of weakness, but reached over and laid a hand on his friend's wrist. He felt tears prick the corners of his eyes.

Dear, sweet God, thank you for saving my Molly. If I had lost her, I would have surely gone mad. How can anyone bear the loss of the one they love more than life itself?

Cynk patted his hand and smiled gently. "Sorry, Flash, I'm getting a bit soppy, aren't I? Becoming British, God forbid. But, you know, I do still miss her terribly."

He cleared his throat noisily. "I feel perhaps I would never love another girl the way I loved my sweet Helena. I worry that I ought not to love another the way I loved her."

Words could not help heal his pain, and Rose returned the smile sympathetically.

"Helena loved you as much as you did her, didn't she? Would it make her happy to see you miserable for the rest of your life? She would want you to be happy, wouldn't she? She'd be happy if you were, wouldn't she? You'll never forget her, I know that. But you must go on. Life is so precious, and so is happiness. Appreciate every moment, live each second, for Helena. Now come on. Be Mum and make me a nice cup of tea."

Cynk sighed, "Fuck me, I despair! If you drank more coffee rather than that bland piss you wouldn't be so damned feeble. I don't know how you haul your kite around with puny muscles like that!"

The old bugger was back. "Yes, I thank you for your soft, kind words. You were telling me about Anna?"

"Yes, such a lovely girl. I can't believe my luck! Don't know what she sees in me, chum. She even looks a lot like Helena, isn't that strange? Two wonderful, beautiful girls, so very alike, and somehow both of them seem to think I'm special. How unbelievable is that?"

"Not all that unbelievable, you know, mate. There're a few of us who like you, though the Good Lord alone only knows why. We think you're special, Stan, even though you're such an ugly, smelly bugger!" He hid a stifled yawn.

Cynk grinned at him, all maudlin feelings dismissed, and he bounced onto his feet, joints popping, the cracking sounds making Rose wince.

White stirred but didn't wake.

"Well come on, then, you twitchy little sod, let's get you a bed for the night. But don't get any ideas, you're not getting into mine. You're not my type. Far too ugly. That particular honour's reserved for Anna." He smiled dreamily, "What tits! What a woman!"

The big Squadron-Leader looked at the slumbering White. "You'd best wake up Sleeping Beauty, too. You do know how the prince woke her up in the fairy-tale?"

Cynk smirked, puckering his lips and pouting them at Rose with a hideous leer, "But I'm not kissing him, you'd best do it. Seems like a nice lad, and I like him, but not that much. He belongs to you, after all. He seems a decent boy, bit shy, though. Looks a bit weedy and feeble, too, just like all the rest of you British blokes. I look at you sometimes and wonder how you managed to find such a sweet flower as you have." He reflected, metal teeth flashing, "I suppose even the most undeserving are allowed a little luck in life."

"It's so good to be loved," replied Rose drily.

Cynk's eyebrows knitted together as he stared at White, "And, talking of flowers, does he have a girl?"

His body aching painfully, Rose slowly got to his feet. It felt as if every part of his body was tender.

"Yes, there's a little WAAF Sergeant, back at Dimple Heath, quite a looker, actually, and a very, very sweet girl. Thinks the absolute world of him, too, I'm pleased to say."

He smiled fondly and looked down at the sleeping boy.

As do I.

"It's a good match, Stan, they're well suited. They're a really nice pair of kids."

The Pole scratched his cheek. "Fuck me, she must be daft, blind or desperate, but I'm glad. There's too much sadness in this bloody world. We should grab every chance of happiness that we can. As you said."

Cynk leaned towards him and put a huge, muscled arm around Rose's shoulders, "It's really good to see you, Flash, really good. It's a shame Granny and Dingo aren't here, though, hope they're doing OK."

Rose tried not to gag or faint as a particularly powerful fragrant wave of tobacco and cologne swept over him. He hadn't missed *that*.

"I do hope so, chum. Granny's still up north, moaning about a lack of women."

Cynk grinned, then sighed and stared pensively at the floor. "Do you remember Foxton, Flash?"

The long lines of dead girls in RAF blue layed out as if in some grim parade, torn stockings and shoeless, lipstick and mascara replaced by blood, dirt, and smoke stains, shrouded and anonymous beneath a dirty tarpaulin.

The stink of fire and death, the sour taste of hopeless despair, and hanging over everything, a spreading mantle-like cloud of filthy smoke, blocking out the light, hiding beneath it their sea of tears from the sun.

The sound of Molly's guilty sobs and the sight of her cruelly torn back, her blood warm and scarlet and unspeakably terrible on his fingers.

Anguish and bitter acid in his throat and heart, the despair black and hollow and hideously vengeful.

How could he ever forget?

On that awful day the Luftwaffe had stolen the fruit of their future, the depth of happiness they might have shared.

The doctors were certain that Molly would never conceive after the terrible injuries she had experienced, and even to this day, even when she smiled, Rose could still see the faint resonance of wistful sadness in her eyes.

Oh, how badly he wished he could chase away the sadness.

What was it mother used to say? Where there's life there's hope? He would hope for as long as he lived. Who knew what the future might one day bring, if they were fortunate enough to see it.

Forget Foxton? Never in a month of Sundays.

His reply was quiet, "Some things you can never forget, Stan."

"Yes." Cynk nodded at his friend's grim face, and exhaled heavily. They were silent for a moment, caught in recollection, and then his mood brightened.

"I know! Shall we sing a song, Flash? How about '*Kocham Polskę?'* or perhaps even *'Mój Najukochańszy Narodów?*"

Rose felt faint. *Oh God, no. I heard enough of those mournful dirges last year. More than enough of them. I must know all the blinkin' words by now. Wonder if they've actually got any happy songs?*

If they do, dear old Stan doesn't know any of them.

Cynk was looking at him expectantly. "Well? Fancy a sing-song? Shall I get my violin? Mm? Flash?"

Fucking hell. I'll be bloody deaf by dawn.

Rose swallowed and summoned a sickly smile. "Oh, I would, Stan, I'd love to, honestly," he lied smoothly, "but it's been a long night, and I'm bushed."

And then Rose cocked his head to one side, lips quirking, "So, tell me Stan, will Molly need to buy a hat?"

Chapter 32

Molly cupped her face in her hands and sighed in exasperation, with more than a little irritation mixed in for good measure.

The object of her ire stood before her desk, looking shamefaced, and unable to meet Molly's eyes, whilst the SP Warrant Officer, ramrod straight, stood balefully behind the girl, his leathery face wearing a typically neutral senior NCO expression.

It was nothing new for him, and if truth be told, he just wanted to dump his problem on the Flight Officer and go back to his normal airfield policing.

Molly sighed once more and looked back up. "Alright, Mr Edwards, thank you. I'd be grateful if you left the matter with me now."

"YES, MA'AM!" Screeched the grizzled senior NCO ear-piercingly, conveying a world's worth of disapproval in those two shrill words, but said no more and turned away, shiny shoes creaking, and stamped smartly out of the room.

Molly drummed her fingers on the blotter and looked down again. On one margin of the blotter she'd written in blue ink 'I love Harry' and enclosed the words within a frilly heart-shape.

She picked up a sheaf of papers from one side of the desk and nonchalantly covered the little doodle.

The girl shifted restlessly, in her own special version of standing at attention, and the young WAAF officer's eyes shot back up to scrutinise her. "Do you hate me?"

Elsie, standing before her, shifted again, this time in discomfort, and looked confused. "Um...?"

"What kind of answer is that?" Molly's eyes were like flint. "I asked if you hated me, did you not understand? Are you even more stupid than I thought you were?"

The girl looked startled. "No, no, I don't hate you!"

"Say Ma'am when you address me!"

Jankarella blushed. "Ma'am."

"And for goodness sake, stand to attention! Don't slouch like that. You're not in the pub." Her eyes narrowed as she stared coldly at the young airwoman. "I do believe you hate me. In fact, I'm sure of it."

"No, Ma'am, I don't. Honestly!"

"I don't believe you. The only reason you're here must be because you hate me. Can't be any other reason. Why else would you continue to be on my defaulter's list?"

Molly did not wait for a reply but tapped the charge sheet on the blotter before her.

"What on earth were you thinking, you stupid girl?"

Tap, tap, tap.

"Er, I –"

"This says that you were out cavorting in the village with an officer pilot."

Tap, tap.

"I wasn't –"

"You weren't? Then the SPs are lying? Hm. How very interesting." Molly peered down at the sheet. "Perhaps I should call Mr Edwards back?"

"No, Ma'am, they weren't lying, but what they say isn't quite true."

"Oh? You mean you weren't with this pilot?"

"Well, I was, but we weren't cavorting. We were having a cup of tea." Elsie smiled bashfully. "We were holding hands."

"Dear God." Molly leaned forwards and steepled her fingers thoughtfuly. "Elsie, you must know as well as I do about the Women's Forces Defence Regulations they've recently passed in Parliament? We're all of us subject to RAF Rules now, and that includes discipline. For heaven's sake, why were you in uniform, why didn't you wear a dress? You'd have got away with it. Why don't you even try? Do you like peeling potatoes? Is that why you joined the air force? We're fighting the Germans, you know, not the Air Ministry. Didn't someone tell you?"

"Ma'am, I sort of forget, and when I remember, it's sort of a bit too late."

"You're a good worker, you're drill's not the best and you are a bit of a scruff, but your Sergeant speaks well of you. You're letting her down as well you know. The rest of us follow the Regs, why on earth can't you?"

Elsie looked miserable. "I don't mean to, Ma'am. I just can't help it."

Molly shook her head sadly and stood up. "The Wing Commander has asked to see you, Elsie."

Jankarella's eyes widened and the colour drained sickly from her face. "But-"

"I've tried to help, Elsie, God knows I've tried, but you seem to spend half your life on punishment duties. Aren't you tired of peeling vegetables? This really can't go on."

"But Ma'am, the Wing Commander…?"

Molly carefully checked her hat was on correctly, straightened her tunic and then opened the door. "Step out, airwoman, we have an appointment."

Eyes downcast and silent, Jankarella followed her out.

"And for goodness sake, straighten your shoulders and keep in step. Try and look like what you are. And when you're in front of the CO, for goodness sake keep your mouth shut, stand up straight, and only speak when you're spoken too." She shook her head severely, "And whatever you do, when you answer him, don't *mumble*!"

Two young aircrew were sitting on the grass outside, and they scrambled up and saluted as Molly and Elsie came towards them. Molly recognised them as a crew in B-Flight, two young Norwegians, fleeing from the Nazi occupation of their homeland.

The blonde youngster wearing the 'AG' wings held out his hands questioningly, "Elsie! *Hvor skal du?*"

Elsie scowled at him, "*Jeg må gå og se den kommanderende offiser. Det er din feil!*"

Molly stopped dead in her tracks in surprise, and Elsie, still looking at the Norwegian youth, walked straight into her, almost knocking Molly over.

"Oh, Ma'am, I'm sorry!" Elsie turned furiously on him. "*Nå se hva du fikk meg til å gjøre!* Idiot!"

Molly looked questioningly at the younger woman.

"Ma'am, this Olaf Axelsen. He's the young man I was with."

Hmm. Molly looked with renewed interest at the young man. Behind him, his pilot stood uncomfortably at attention, eyes looking at something in the near distance. What was his name, Harry had mentioned it…?

Ah yes. Alstad, Petter Alstad.

The young man was wearing RAF uniform, but with a 'Norway' flash on his shoulders, the Norwegian golden 'wings' flying badge on his right breast and a single gold star of his rank on each collar lapel.

Axelsen was equivalent to an RAF Pilot Officer. What was the rank? Sounded similar to a herb, erm, which one? Ah, it sounded a bit like like fenugreek, didn't it? Mm. Oh yes, it was *Fenrik*.

Molly returned her gaze to Elsie. "What were you saying? Was that…?"

Elsie nodded grudgingly. "Norwegian. My mum was a lassie from Bergen, so I learnt to speak it on her knee. Olaf was asking me where I was going, so I told him, and how it was his fault."

"Yes, I got the gist of it."

Elsie brightened, "Do you understand Norwegian as well, Ma'am?"

"No, not at all," Molly said drily, "I just caught the 'idiot' part, though. What was he doing here? Waiting for you?"

"Yes, Ma'am, we were going to go into town for lunch."

Molly rolled her eyes and groaned. "Dear Lord. You're in uniform, for heaven's sake! Listen to yourself. If you have to go out with an officer, put a dress on."

She turned to Axelsen, wondering how he'd escaped any form of penalty.

"*Fenrik* Axelsen, Elsie has been put on a disciplinary charge because she was with you in uniform. I would be grateful if you ensured that when one of you is in uniform that the other is in civilian clothes whenever you meet. Otherwise it just means that both you and Elsie will get into trouble."

She shook her head in exasperation (*youngsters nowadays!*), forgetting that she herself was only a few years older than the 'youngsters' herself.

The young man nodded anxiously, "I understand, Ma'am. I am very sorry for the trouble." He looked apologetically at Elsie, "*Jeg er virkelig lei meg, kan jeg møte deg senere?*"

The girl smiled slightly, "OK, Olaf, I'll come and find you, after I see the CO, that is, and if I haven't been thrown into the guardhouse."

She turned her gaze to Molly, "And I'll change into civvies, next time. I promise."

"Right, come along then, young lady, best not to dawdle."

As they walked Molly asked the girl about her past. It had been quite peculiar to hear the Norwegian spoken in the girl's soft Scottish burr.

"How did your parents meet?"

"My dad was on a fishing trawler that ran into shelter in Bergen during a storm, and my mum was working in a drinking house, Ma'am. Dad got a run ashore, they met over a mug of beer, he gave her a prime codfish for her pa, she gave him a kiss, one thing turned into another, and here I am!"

"Came as quite a surprise to me, I must say."

"I know, Ma'am. When I joined up, they took me from my batch and asked me a lot of questions. I think they were scared that I might be a Quisling spy or something."

Soon after the invasion of Norway, Vidkun Quisling had taken power in a coup d'etat, and the allied security forces feared that many pro-Nazi Norwegians may have entered the UK under the pretence of wanting to continue the fight against the Nazis.

Each potential spy had to be checked, even those who were British citizens with family connections.

I'd better check the girl's papers, thought Molly in alarm, making a mental note. One can't be too careful, although a spy would have made efforts to remain hidden, and Elsie had already been vetted.

Elsie's behaviour constantly brought her to the eyes of her superiors, not what you'd expect from a spy. And to be fair, the SPs must be quite familiar with Elsie's file.

But nowadays, with all this talk of Fifth Columnists and spies, it wouldn't hurt to check, although when Molly looked at Elsie, it wasn't a German spy she saw but a rebellious young girl.

And then they had arrived, and a smiling Mandy took them into James' office.

Molly stood with Elsie before James' big desk, but with an impatient gesture he waved her to a chair beside the stove. He ignored the airwoman completely and continued to pore over the papers before him.

Time seemed to stretch interminably and Molly began to worry. Any moment now Elsie might say something.

Suddenly James stood up, the screech of the chair legs setting their teeth on edge, and leaning forward he roared, "What the devil are you doing here in my bloody office, airwoman?"

Later, Molly would swear blind to Rose that she had jumped a foot into the air as the CO squawked ear-splittingly at Elsie.

"Sir-", began the girl sickly.

"Don't you *sir* me, Dyer!" the young airwoman flinched as if the Wing Commander had struck her full on the face.

"D'you know how many complaints I've had to field regarding your behaviour?" he raved, "You're a damned disgrace to the service! They must have been bloody mad to let you into my RAF!"

Molly watched in fascination as a glistening blob of saliva from James' mouth shot out to land on Elsie's hair.

"But sir-"

"Did I give you permission to speak?" James eyes were glittering wickedly like a madman's, "No? So shut your damned insubordinate mouth!"

Amazingly, the tough young woman, once responsible for dislocating a drunken soldier's jaw with a single punch was trembling, yet she stood her ground defiantly.

Good for you, Elsie! Molly could feel herself trembling.

"So, what shall I do with you, Dyer? Shall I have you thrown out of the WAAF? Fancy being a Land girl? They're bit relaxed about their uniform code. How does that sound? Shall I have a word with the Land Girl Supreme Leader? Hm? Fancy pottering around in the mud? I daresay a layer of mud would suit your manner of dress. Does wonders for the complexion, I'm told."

"I'm sorry sir, please don't-" Jankarella quavered.

"What?" He shrieked hoarsely, eyes rolling wildly, "Don't? DON'T?" he raged, "Why not? You don't seem to be able to fit in here at Dimple Heath, and you're driving an excellent Station Warrant Officer to an early grave."

Flecks of James' spit shone on her face. "Please-"

James' was frothing at the mouth as he bawled. "SHUT UP!" his voice dropped bur Molly was sure he was still probably audible in the Outer Hebrides.

"You know, Dyer, I'm tired of listening to you. I'm sick to death of your whining, moany voice. I've had quite enough, so I'm promoting you to Corporal and transferring you with immediate effect to the Catering section."

The girl stared at him in astonishment and shock. James' shook his head in disgust, "God knows you spend long enough in the cookhouse. Let's see if you can manage cooking and serving the spuds rather than just peeling the little blighters."

His jaw jutted obstinately, "I've spoken to your Sergeant, and it's all squared with the Catering Officer. I couldn't find you before, Flight Officer, that's why you knew nothing about it."

Elsie's jaw dropped, and Molly stood up in surprise.

"Please sit down, Flight Officer. Dyer's conduct reflects poorly on you, but we'll overlook it because you're a fine young officer. A credit to my station." James's voice was cool, and his eyes slipped back to the stunned Jankarella.

"I expect great things from the kitchen, Dyer, I have always received the best in the past, but if I hear of even the smallest indiscretion, if I find a cockroach in my Spotted Dick, if you poison my people, I'm going to drum you off the station and straight into the Tower of London. I'll not hesitate in calling a Court Martial. Understood? Now get out of my office and put up your stripes. And remember, I like my chips a little overdone, and I want to see more stews, preferably mutton." He glared reprovingly at her, "And a lot more suet pudding and custard on the menu! Dismissed."

He fell back onto the chair, which protested with a monstrous creak like a tree branch splitting, and resumed perusing his papers as if nothing had happened, dismissing them completely.

Elsie appeared frozen in place, her mouth open and a look of shocked wonder on her pale face. The glistening blob of saliva began slowly to slide down a tress of her hair, leaving a shining trail behind it.

He looked back up, face thunderous. "What the hell are you doing still here? Are you bloody deaf? Dismissed! DISMISSED! GET OUT!" he bawled.

Quickly taking the dazed girl's elbow, Molly guided her swiftly from the room. At the door she risked a quick glance back, and caught a broad wink and a cheery thumbs-up from a smirking and very smug looking James.

What the...? The wily old rascal! What a performance! Absolutely brilliant.

Outside, Elsie took a deep breath, and then another. Turning to Molly, stunned blue eyes wide, she opened her mouth, but nothing came out and she closed it again with a *plopping* sound.

Molly stared at her sternly. "Well, there you go, Elsie. The CO's given you one last chance for redemption. It's much more than I would have given you, and far more than you deserve. Are you up to it? Or ought I to go back in and ask the CO for your discharge papers instead?"

With an effort, Elsie squared her shoulders and breathed out hard. Her world had changed, turned upside down in just the matter of a few seconds.

"No, Ma'am, I can't let the CO down. I'm going to do my best for him. He's relying on me, and I'll not let him down."

She was still trembling, and took another breath, "Corporal Dyer! My Mam won't believe it!" Tears glittered bright but she beamed at Molly, "Bloody Hell! *I* still can't believe it!" Elsie looked contrite, "Ooh. Pardon me, Ma'am."

Don't worry, I can't bloody believe it either....

"When you get back, Elsie, come and see me and we'll get your stripes sorted out."

"Back, Ma'am, get back from where?" Elsie's smile slipped and she looked at Molly uncertainly. The blob of saliva, having gracefully slid down one strand of hair, now dropped to gently settle onto the girl's shoulder, and the fabric of her tunic slowly began to absorb it.

"Why, when you return from the trip with your young man, of course. Olaf, wasn't it?"

The new young Corporal made a rude noise, and wiped her eyes roughly. "He'll have to wait! I can't go out now! I've got to sort out my new duties, report to the Catering Officer. No time like the present! We'll have chips tonight! A little bit overdone!"

Elsie wiped her face absent-mindedly, smearing his saliva around her face, then looked down at her open palms, "Corporal. Corporal Elsie Dyer." She said it to herself in wonder, still not quite trusting it was true. "Ma'am, please excuse me, I'd best get started."

Elsie smiled hesitantly, shyly, "And thank you, Ma'am. For your support and your patience. For everything. I'll make you proud, honest."

354

"Go on, then." Molly nodded curtly, and watched the girl bustle smartly away, and smiled secretly to herself.

Perhaps James had found the answer after all.

Might it work? Could the inveterate offender Jankarella be transformed into an efficient young NCO? Was it even possible?

Only time would tell, but so far, it was looking good.

Chapter 33

Keeping one eye on the sleeping girl, Bruno surreptitiously picked up the medal from the dresser, and placed it onto his palm, enjoying the weight of it, the lines and points of its shape, the coolness of the metal.

He held his dream lovingly.

The Knight's Cross of the Iron Cross. The thing he had coveted and yearned for so very long. His at long last.

The black, white and red ribbon hanging down, a black cross metal pattee with silvered edges and a swastika in the centre.

A medal he'd dreamed of for endless months, and which had finally been placed around his neck by the *Fuhrer* himself in Berlin, that very morning.

Anja had been overwhelmed by the experience, and she'd hung from his arm, mute and awed by their company, yet shyly basking in his reflected glory.

The day had been a dizzying whirlwind of meetings and parties, a day of unimaginable delights, but he'd sighed with gladness and more than a little relief when the *kubelwagen* had finally stopped outside the hotel arranged and paid for by the *Wehrmacht*.

And oh, how he'd enjoyed the sight reflected in the great mirror on the ground floor of their hotel!

The image was still in his mind's eye, the handsome young Luftwaffe pilot in his perfectly-tailored blue uniform, chest bedecked with decorations, the prized *Ritterkreuz* at his neck; and on his arm the beautiful dark-haired girl, trim and shapely in her uniform.

A photographer had taken their picture (just one of many) and one of *Der Fuhrer's* aides promised that their picture would be in all the newspapers and on the cover of *Signal*.

The brave and honourable Warrior Knight of the Luftwaffe bedecked in his medals, and his beautiful Lady, delectable and brave in her uniform. It was the sort of story that the masses lapped up.

Personally he thought he'd looked a little dull in the picture, but Anja had loved it.

The girl now lay sleeping, her back towards him, exhausted by the excitement of their day as new members of the elite of Berlin, and by the frenzied lovemaking that had followed their arrival at the hotel.

The thin sheet had slipped down to expose her smooth back, slim waist, and the rounded curve of her firm buttocks, a sheen of sweat making her skin glow golden and glisten delightfully in the soft light.

His gaze lingered pleasurably for a moment over the cleft between her magnificent buttocks, knowing that after such a hectic day he should be trying to sleep too.

But the adrenaline still coursing powerfully through him meant that he just couldn't sleep.

The sweet scented fragrance of her body seemed to blend perfectly with the new fresh fabric smell of the medal ribbon, and he breathed in appreciatively. They were both all he could ever want, and he was content.

I am complete. I thought it was all that I wanted, yet now that I actually have The Medal, I finally realise that it isn't enough. I need my Anja, too. Even more than my Knight's Cross. So much more. I know that now. She's the future, my true happiness.

It is the medal that will make me known amongst my friends and enemies alike, it will allow me a kind of immortality, and yet it is the girl nestling in my heart that is my life's fulfilment.

Bruno leaned over to the ice bucket, carefully removing the bottle of champagne (from a case courtesy of Fat Hermann) as quietly as possible and poured himself a measure, ice water dripping onto his toes.

It was for Rudi and Mouse as much as it was for himself. He wondered what they were doing at this moment.

Like Bruno, they too had been recognised for their part, each receiving a promotion and a week's leave. Rudi looking relieved when he heard, but Mouse's face had cracked into a huge grin as he thought of a week in the fleshpots of his hometown.

Bruno took an appreciative sip of the chilled champagne, icy bubbles fizzing merrily in his mouth and up his nose, and then carefully placed his prized decoration back onto the dresser.

He could not remember a time in which he'd felt happier.

"I've got something equally shiny to show you, *Herr Leutnant.*"

Startled, Bruno turned to face Anja, her hair mussed and beautiful eyes bright with mischief.

Had she seen him fondling his medal? She must think him terribly conceited.

Bruno realised that he didn't much care for the fact that she might think him vain. Feeling rather annoyed with himself and very self-conscious, he saluted her gallantly with his glass of champagne.

"I thought you wouldn't wake until morning, my dearest. You were dead to the world."

He grimaced inwardly at the poor choice of words. What an awful expression! *Idiot!*

"I was completely exhausted, and just needed a little sleep, that's all, my darling."

358

The girl pushed back her hair and sat up, full breasts dancing delightfully. His heart tripped dizzily at the sight. "It's been the most amazing day of my life, and after your performance in bed, I think I just passed out."

The warmth in Anja's eyes matched her gentle smile, "Thank you, dearest Bruno, for sharing such a wonderful experience with me. It's been a wonderful day, but being with you is what made it so special."

Who else could have been with him on this wonderful day? Father was in North Africa with his beloved Panzers. And, being the dutiful wife that she was, *Mutti* was languishing in the senior officer's quarters in Sousse so that she could be close to her beloved husband.

How lucky I am, to have such a beautiful girl with me. Today he'd been swamped in clamouring crowds of *Blitzmadel*, but there was only one girl he looked to, the one who really mattered.

He smiled back at her easily, and thought of the little box tucked carefully into his tunic breast pocket. Seeing the simple happiness on her face now made him want to get it and ask her, but he stopped himself. It could wait until tomorrow.

They were planning to have a peaceful day visiting the museums on the Museum Island in the River Spree, and he would ask her by the riverbank, or some other suitably romantic spot. It would have to be special, because the girl herself was, immeasurably so.

Perhaps he ought to take her to the *Tiergarten*?

I really ought to show her Berlin by night. "Would you like to go out for dinner, my darling?"

Anja shook her head. "No, Bruno. I was talking to a lady at the presentation, the wife of some Party official. I think she thought she was more powerful than he was, quite awed by herself. Awful old hag. Had breath like a rotten egg. Made me feel like throwing up. Anyway, she said to me that there's been a series of murders in Berlin. Women going home from work on their own in the evenings on the S-Bahn. I wouldn't like to go out tonight." She shivered and hugged herself tightly.

"Besides the RAF might raid. We're near the centre of the city so we should be safe. They'll find it hard to get anywhere near us."

Bruno had seen the day's headlines earlier, screaming about the latest victim of the mysterious killer stalking his solitary female prey on the rail system that served the capital.

He sat down next to her on the soft mattress, feeling the heat of her body, and passed the icy flute of champagne to her.

"Oh, but that's horrible, *liebling*! I hope they catch the swine. Not to worry, my love, we'll ask for room service. Stay in here with me, nice and warm. Best place to be, actually, I don't believe there's a more handsome man in the whole of Berlin than the one you're with."

She laughed and put one arm around his waist. The scent of her body filled his nostrils and he felt a fierce surge of lust flare through the tip of his penis, up through his testicles, along his spine and explode into his brain. He yearned for her hand to hold him there again.

"Well, I must be really fortunate to be here with you, then. Room service would be perfect. I don't feel all that hungry at the moment, though, my darling. Perhaps a little later?"

Bruno slid one hand along her inner thigh, caressing her velvety skin with pleasure, and then bent forward to kiss her lightly on the nose, "Really? Is that so, young lady? Then why don't I do you a kindness and help you to work up an appetite?"

They had almost a week to spend together. A week in which he could enjoy a time without war and killing and danger.

No more talking.

Bruno's lips found hers; Anja hungrily drawing him down onto

360

and into her, and everything else was forgotten as they fell back onto the bed, the last droplets of chilled champagne spilling from the overturned crystal flute onto the splendid carpet.

The war could wait.

She was now.

Chapter 34

At that very same moment, five hundred and eighty miles to the west, a bored Rose looked out to starboard at the distant darkened sprawl of London on the horizon.

Unlike earlier evenings that week, the Luftwaffe were mounting a more concerted effort, the GCI control had their hands full, and, being unable to match up all the available fighters with hostile contacts, now allowed a few of the waiting Beaufighters to go off hunting within certain safety guidelines of their own.

Gnashing impatiently at the bit, and without a contact of their own, D-Dog had been provided with a patrol area, and the southern end of their search area brought them close to the furthest outskirts of northeast London.

The entire city would have appeared dead, were it not for the distant prickling sparks of AA, fires burning and explosions, an endless desolation of unlit concrete and brick stretching for miles into the distance, myriad barrage balloons and dim clouds of smoke floating high above the metropolis, and Rose shivered involuntarily at the apparent emptiness of the great city in which he had married and first made love to the girl he adored.

The deceptive desolation was heightened because the night was not momentarily split by occasional errant bright actinic flashes from the Underground tube train electrical system, now switched off and the stations awash with those sheltering in the Undergound, whilst here and there, in the distance a searchlight or two would probe the sky with its attendant flurry of sparkling points of ack-ack ground fire hunting an elusive prey.

The fire from AA Command was light tonight, not the usual blanketing storm the enemy bombers had to brave as they sought their targets.

He knew that the city far beneath was heavily-populated, and that hidden behind blackout curtains and moving around in the darkness below, working and living and loving, were millions of people. *His* people.

Months earlier, he and Molly had both been down there too, enjoying each precious, memorable moment together.

Might this war go on until we're all dead? He wondered. Might the city below them truly be empty of life one unimaginable and awful day? Might the buildings and spaces be all that is left of us? Is it possible that man's inhumanity to man could finally result in their extinction? Could this be the war to truly end all wars?

Eyes tracing the distant outline of the River Thames as it gracefully wound around the Isle of Dogs like a strand of silver thread, Rose recalled the first time he'd spoken with his beautiful girl, of his musings of life from beyond this planet, and his fears that the hesitant gibberish might destroy completely any tenuous interest that the lovely WAAF had in him.

He smiled to himself; Luck had been on his side then, too. He looked down at the city again.

At some time in the future, would visitors from another world arrive to find a dead one, and wonder at the decaying empty cities spreading across the land? Would they search the deserted schools and libraries and offices for signs of what humanity had been, and how it all gone so wrong?

Or perhaps the cities would not be empty, but rather, would be filled with acres upon acres of desiccated bones, or even the feather-light husks of what had once been their inhabitants?

He shivered at the terrible (if unlikely) possibility, eyes flicking automatically to the controls.

Good, no change.

They were almost at the end of this leg and it would be time to turn back in a few minutes.

His earphones crackled. "God, this is so boring, Flash, I'm starving, and I think my feet have fallen off."

The grim mood in the cockpit broken, Rose grinned at the plaintive voice from the rear compartment, "What d'you mean, you think? Don'cha know?"

"I can't tell, Flash. I've been sitting on this hard seat for so flipping long my bum and legs have gone to sleep, and my stomach thinks my throat's been cut."

"Well, get off your blinkin' arse and run on the spot or something, then, you lazy sod."

"Charming. It's nice to know you care…oh, hullo, what's that?" White's voice trailed off uncertainly.

"What? What's what? What can you see?" Rose's heart lurched and a thrill of fear coursed through him. The thoughts of dead worlds were forgotten at the prospect of facing a very alive and highly dangerous enemy.

"Sorry boss, a searchlight just lit up to the west, our two o'clock, oh! There's another one!"

Rose looked, and sure enough, long thin whiskers of white light were reaching out and criss-crossing over the city, occasionally coning together, as if duelling with one another in order to rivet an invisible enemy aircraft against the sky.

As they watched, there were a series of searing, twinkling pinpoints of pulsing light, followed by a linear eruption of bright flames on the ground in the middle of the city, made small by distance.

"Damn it! The bastards dropped their load. Strapped in, chum?"

"Yes, *mon capitaine*." The prospect of action seemed to have dampened White's cheer.

"Let's go and have a shufti. With a bit of luck we can catch the bastard as he heads for home."

"If we do go in, boss, we'll be entering the city's AA gun zone. You know what the ack-ack boys are like, terribly keen. And the thing is, he has already dropped his bomb load, so we can wait for him to come to us?" The young Pilot Officer behind him sighed, "Sorry, Flash, didn't mean to tell you how to suck eggs."

White looked across the city again to where the tiny fire was burning, a growing pillar of grey smoke angrily lit beneath by the furious blaze, now reaching past the height of the barrage balloons, and he could feel the flames curling around his heart at the thought of the men, women and children dying horribly in the embattled city.

"I'm game if you are, though." Another thing occurred to him, "You'd best watch out for the barrage balloons, too, stay high."

Rose bit his lip as he considered. In the distance it was just possible to make out the discrete red glitter-flash sparkling of heavy and light AA.

White was right, the AA gunners defending the cities of the nation were notoriously indiscriminate, and often night fighters foolhardy enough to brave the storm of ground defence in the gun zone had limped home with damage.

Those that were lucky, that is.

There was a rumour going around that the senior officer of AA Command, General Pyle, had ordered his gunners to fire at everything and anything that might be hostile; or, in other words, they were to throw everything but the kitchen sink every night at the enemy.

If it flew over London, friend or foe, the anti-aircraft boys would shoot at it. But Rose could sympathise. When the safety of the city was under threat, it was better to shoot first. But it didn't make life any easier for the nightfighters.

"OK, Chalky, you're right, the searchlight beams are getting closer, it's coming our way, best keep an eye on your set, chum. We're quite far out, I'll throttle back and we'll make a wide circle away. Let's see if we can intercept them once they're clear of the AA limit. We'll approach again from the north, so, with a bit of luck, the bastard will cross in front of us from right to left."

After informing sector control, Rose and White circled around once, the thin weaving fingers of light dancing ever closer as they waited.

For a moment as they turned, Rose fancied that he saw the momentary gleam of metal in one of the beams of white, but it disappeared instantly, leaving him wondering if he'd seen it all.

"Lining up on the approach, Chalky."

"Standby, nothing yet…"

The last of the beams wavered aimlessly, and then went out, and the sparkling of anti-aircraft fire also ended, leaving only the distant fires burning on the ground and the remote glitter of AA to break the veil of darkness.

Come on, come on. "Chalky?"

"*Got him*! Crossing directly in front of us, descend to angels ten, turn onto one-two-zero, range five miles."

Throttles hard forward and with his heart banging and pumping painfully within his quickly tightening chest cavity, Rose pulled D-Dog after her prey. *Check the guns are ready to fire? Yes, all set, good.*

"We're closing fast, Flash, range just under four miles, directly ahead of us now, still descending…"

Rose crinkled his nose, for he could smell the bitter stink of smoke, and something else. Burning metal.

Granny once mentioned of how the odour could be bad enough to make one physically vomit. It was something he himself had experienced since. The smell was sickly, a disgusting stench. "Chalky, old son, I think he's damaged, I can smell smoke. He's burning. Range?"

"Just under three miles, maintain heading, still closing pretty rapidly, throttle back, port five degrees. Bandit still going down."

And then he could just see the thin trail of smoke, a pale finger faintly visible against the darker sky just to starboard of the Beaufighter's line of flight, and looking forward along it he could make out a faint glimmer, which began to resolve into a murky glow as the distance lessened.

"OK, I can see something ahead, but keep giving me directions." The Beaufighter was fighting him a little, engines grumbling as she floundered uncomfortably at the slower speed. The glow had resolved into a small spill of flame that was maundering back from one wing of an aircraft that now appeared before D-Dog.

Rose assumed position just below and a thousand feet behind the enemy bomber. He checked the altimeter. They were at seven and a half thousand feet now, and still descending.

They didn't have a lot of time for the intercept, soon the enemy aeroplane would be swallowed up by ground returns.

"Chalky, take a squint, what do you see?"

"Crumbs! Looks like a Heinkel, I think. And it looks like it's been chewed up a bit by AA."

It was true; the Heinkel was not looking its best.

367

The enemy aeroplane was still flying in a straight line, gradually losing height, with the port Daimler Benz sporadically leaking incandescent droplets of burning metal, and the propeller was windmilling. Great rents, tears and punctures dotted both wings and the fuselage, with the upper rear gunner's machine gun pointing impotently upwards.

Was it plunging for sanctuary, or were they all dead abroad, and the aircraft was in a shallow dive to oblivion?

White's voice, anxious and raised, urgently reminded him that time was of the essence. "Finish it off, Flash, before Fritz wakes up and give us a nasty dose of hate."

The range was now closed to a range of two hundred feet. The pungent smell of burning metal, rubber and acrid smoke filling his nostrils like acid, choking and bitter.

One last check for deflection. The jumping, vibrating airframe wasn't making it easier.

No more time. Kill it. Kill *them*. "OK, Firing."

Rose punched and held the button, and the machine and cannons thundered deafeningly for a full two seconds until he lifted his thumb, still feeling the harsh vibration resonate through his bones.

The Heinkel wobbled, and then began to slide gently into a turn to starboard, shedding pieces of itself as it went.

Maintaining a safe distance, Rose emptied another burst into the enemy bomber.

Hits sparkled bright along the fuselage and wings as the Heinkel's turn steepened, and there were one, two, and then a third, larger explosion, the final dazzling detonation ripping the port wing completely off just inboard of the port engine.

The boiling fireball expanded hugely, dissipating almost immediately, but the sudden flash momentarily stole his night vision away.

Rose quickly pulled the fighter away into a climbing turn to port as the Heinkel's separated wing and engine, vomiting a wildly twisting shimmering spinnaker trail of burning fuel droplets, whipped back towards them.

It passed behind and below D-Dog in a terrifying blur, missing the Beaufighter by a generous distance, although to Rose it seemed to twirl past by a far smaller margin.

Another, much smaller piece of metal hit them with a *bang!* just missing the propeller blades and glancing off against the underside of D-Dog's fuselage, but causing no damage to the Beaufighter whatsoever, just to their nerves.

"Bloody hell! Are you, OK, Chalky?" Rose called, blinking his eyes rapidly to regain his night vision. The image of the wing, lit from behind by the flaring explosion, blown off and twirling towards them still embedded on his retina.

"Crikey, luvaduck! That was a bit close!"

Rose craned his head around to look back, but his eyes hadn't fully yet recovered, and he could see nothing. "Did we get him, then, Chalky?" immediately cringing inwardly at the absurdity of the words, even as he spoke them.

"Dunno, can't see him, I can't see anything yet." White began to giggle hysterically at his pilot's ludicrous question, partially in nervous reaction, and Rose joined him.

There was no way that the enemy bomber could have continued to fly minus its port wing. Success, again.

Thank you, dear God.

Rose lifted his goggles for a moment to wipe his tears, then reached out his gauntleted hand to lightly touch Molly's photograph.

Just then, a smear of flame flared harsh on the ground far below.

"Oh my God!" breathed White, "he just splattered into the ground! We got him!"

369

"Well, he was a bit dented beforehand, Chalky, we'll have to give the AA boys a half-credit, at least. At least Sir Isaac will be happy."

The fire was still burning on the horizon, and if anything, seemed larger than before, dampening Rose's sense of relief and the feeling of success. "I wish we'd managed to get him before he'd dropped his bloody load, though, Chalky."

"Me too. But at least he'll never do it again, Flash. And your Lady Luck was on our side tonight."

"Yours too, my old chum. Make a note of the time and place, would you, then just check on the ammo drums, and in the meantime I'll get on to control. Maybe we ought to give the credit to the gunners? He did look a bit beat-up when we found him. I think they were all dead inside, y'know."

"Not on your Nelly! You know how happy the boys are when we've had a spot of luck! Every time we get one it's their reward for all the hours of hard work we, I mean they, put in! They'll be so happy and proud they helped to crack another nut! Even if we only get a half-credit, it belongs to them!"

Rose nodded, slightly ashamed, it was true, "OK, Chalky, fair point, mate. Thank you for reminding me, it's not something I should have to be reminded about."

He thought back to one of the first flying and fighting training sessions Granny had given him on arrival at Excalibur Squadron the year before, and how heavily his dear friend emphasised that it was the groundcrews that shared the responsibility for success.

And dear Granny should know, for he had been one of them, a Halton brat, before the war.

Hundreds of hours of toil went into getting the aeroplanes up and in keeping them flying.

An aerial victory was one of the few rewards for a very hard, barely recognised and thankless job performed regardless of conditions by a highly dedicated band of men and women, often in the open air, unsung heroes each and every one.

The proud ribbons on his chest were there in large part due to the taken-for-granted grind of those who kept them flying.

With one last look at the red-hot flaming remnants below them, Rose levelled out the Beaufighter and turned his eyes up to the Heavens for a moment.

Thankyou.

Chapter 35

Bruno circled the Ju88C carefully as the last of the daylight drained away into the encroaching darkness. Further up it would be so much brighter, but at the lower height that they were at the Junkers would be concealed by the dusk against the sea.

Rudi and Mouse kept up a vigilant scrutiny of the sky around them, the distant east coast of England just visible as a shadowy grey line on the horizon.

Beneath them the darkening sea roiled and lurched sickeningly, and Bruno's stomach churned with it, reminding him why he usually ate little before an operational mission. That would teach him to be such a greedy pig.

"How much longer, Herr Leutnant?" moaned Rudi beside him. "I don't like the look of that sea down there." Hs friend was peering nervously through the Perspex.

Neither do I, my friend, neither do I. Even the Junkers was harder to control this low down, brisk and rough, as if complaining about their altitude.

"Soon, Rudi, very soon, don't fret. It's almost time. Are you ready with the course?" It still felt wonderful to feel the *Ritterkreuz* hanging gloriously from his neck. It was difficult not to reach up every other minute and touch it, caress it.

A fresh young aircrew had arrived on the base whilst he'd been in Berlin with Anja, and the way in which the newcomers stared at him had been both embarrassing as well as extremely gratifying. Mouse had winked at Rudi and begun the first of many tall tales of their operations.

The base was quieter now, with fewer groundstaff and aircrews, and many of their friends had mysteriously disappeared whilst they'd been away. The *staffel* was greatly depleted, and the *Herr Oberst* grimly tight-lipped.

It was obvious that his crews were being transferred for the coming offensive in the east. Security was poor, and the imminence of the attack was common knowledge.

Upset that his fellow gunners would be fighting without him, Mouse demanded a meeting with the *Herr Oberst*, demanding to know when they, too, would be transferred to the new front.

For Bruno the allure of combat was not now as golden as it once was, and he was appalled by the possibility of being separated from his beautiful young fiancée, whilst Rudi, nerves slowly fraying, quailed at the idea of flying over vast empty plains in sub-zero temperatures.

The far-reaching frozen steppes weren't his idea of a desirable battleground.

Luckily, the *Herr Oberst* wouldn't even entertain the suggestion of a transfer to the big build up on the borders of the USSR.

"You're my best crew," He'd bellowed in red-faced outrage at the gunner, "I'm not losing you bastards as well! Piss off out of my office, Mouse, you bloodthirsty little fucker, and get me a Tommy tonight!"

Mouse sulked for the entire afternoon in his room, but his good humour returned when they were kitting up in the crew room.

Bruno's own mood improved immensely when he noticed the slight figure waving from near the base hospital, and he'd patted his breast pocket, knowing her photograph was there, capturing the wistful look in her eyes, the ways her lips always seemed to be smiling.

Dear God, I love her. I love her so much it bloody hurts. The depth of his feelings still surprised him.

Bruno shook his head to clear it; this close to the enemy coast, less than one hundred percent concentration on the job before them was unacceptable.

"Course, Rudi." Spoken harsher than he'd intended.

Uh-oh, thought Rudi, someone's got a wire brush up his arse, better be on my best cockpit behaviour. Before he could speak however, Mouse urgently shouted out from behind them, "*Achtung, achtung!* Aircraft! A thousand feet above and behind."

Bruno and Rudi both turned as one to gaze frantically through the canopy at the shadowy cruciform shape just visible above them.

"Is it an enemy nightfighter?" asked Bruno, muscles tensed painfully, and ready to turn into the other aircraft.

"No, Herr Leutnant, sorry, it's one of ours. Looks like one of the smelly Heinie one-eleven mob."

A flash of inspiration struck Bruno, "Forget the course, let's follow the Heinkel, and see where it's going."

Rudi was hesitant, "Are you sure, Herr Leutnant?" he had visions of being dragged along into the gun zone of a large city.

"Yes! Let's see where they go! If it's an attack on an airfield or military installation we could mount a follow up attack after he's dropped his bombs. They wouldn't expect us to strafe them so soon after the bombs hit!"

Rudi bit his lip, turned to look at Bruno, "But what if he's going to bomb a city?"

Mouse laughed, but not unkindly, "Don't worry, Rudi, Mouse is here to protect your tender little pink bollocks. I won't let them hurt you!"

Rudi glowered, but said nothing, peering at the chart in his hands. *Big stupid turd.*

Just as Bruno began to pull back the control column to climb the Junkers, Mouse called out again, "*Achtung, Herr Leutnant!* Another aircraft behind, twin engine, another Heinkel, I think. Same course and height as the first."

Unusually, this time the burly gunner didn't sound too sure of himself.

This now left Bruno with a dilemma. Follow the first one or the second? They were both on the same heading, might be the same target, a big city after all? The idea of flying through the hellfire of the AA-blasted airspace above cities like London did not appeal to him in the slightest. Should he go back to his original plan?

"Herr Leutnant, the second one-eleven, I'm not sure about it, it looks a bit strange…"

Bruno looked back at the second shape, dimmer now that dusk had changed to night. "What do you mean, Mouse?"

"It just looks…wrong. I don't know what it is. Can we get a bit closer, sir?"

The enemy bomber continued to sail blissfully through the night sky before them, unaware of the Beaufighter closing the distance between them.

The RAF fighter pilot excitedly keyed his intercom; "I can see it now, Icy; you can leave the set now, have a wee peep, my old fruit, and confirm. I'd say it's a Heinkel 111. I'll hold position at five hundred, just under the tail." Barlow checked quickly to make sure for the hundredth time that the guns were set to 'fire.'

"Oh, golly gosh! I agree! It's a one-eleven! Quick, give it a squirt!" Cole's enthusiasm was understandable, the last month having been frustrating and unproductive for them.

Four times in that period, they'd lost a hostile contact, and on the one occasion, even though they had managed to get an enemy bomber in sight, it had dived away at a speed they were unable to match. Each time had been like a kick in the teeth, leaving each of them acutely depressed.

Unbelievably, this time their luck had held.

Eagerly, unaware of the Ju88 slowly rising close behind the tail of their Beaufighter, C-Cindy, Barlow fired, and a cluster of vividly glowing fireballs ripped out to pass painfully close to one side of the enemy bomber.

Cursing foully but holding his thumb on the button and still keeping it depressed, Barlow adjusted his aim to play the stream of fire across the Heinkel's dim shape, hits on the enemy registering brightly, and brief rents of fierce flame suddenly streaming back brightly before going out.

Pieces of aeroplane continued to fly off as the RAF fighter smashed at it with its storm of metal, and then suddenly the Heinkel drunkenly tipped over onto one wing and the tilt turned into a sideways slide, Barlow turning after it as his drums of ammunition finally ran dry.

A piece of flap and the rudder twisted messily off the Heinkel, and it began to tumble as the desperate pilot lost control.

Both propellers had stopped turning under power now, windmilling, and there was no chance of salvation available anymore to the terrified young German aviators.

But the Junkers 88C had finally closed to less than two hundred feet behind the victorious Beaufighter, and now it was Bruno's turn.

He and his crew were sickened by the sudden destruction of the bomber as they frantically moved into position.

Jaw clenched in fury and eyes burning with liquid fervour, Bruno opened fire on the shadowy shape of the fighter before him, but it was just too late to save the lives of their bomber brothers-in-arms.

The yells of triumph in the Beaufighter were abruptly cut short as glowing German cannon shells suddenly ripped a fiery path into the RAF aircraft, shredding the Beaufighter's tail plane into tattered, flapping ruin.

Barlow fought desperately with the yawing aircraft as a second burst of fire splattered against the British fighter. The starboard engine began to vibrate, sparking, the glowing innards clearly visible as covers ripped away.

Cole's AI set suddenly blew up with a flat *Bang!* Whilst he was still recoiling in shock from what had happened to cause the aircraft's loss of control, the shattered set now peppered him with piercing shards of metal and glass, and he cried out in shock and fright and pain.

The sharp, whirling smithereens that hit him were closely followed by more cannon shells from the pursuing Junkers, one of which caught him high in the chest, exploding catastrophically outwards against his sternum, the racing hot fragments ripping through him and propelling torn slivers of his internal organs and spinal column out forwards towards the cockpit, the impact spraying the inside of the compartment with blood and ricocheting bits of metal, wire, glass and 'Icy' Cole.

Those deep lungs with which he had lustily belted out songs at any and all possible opportunities were torn out like so much offal from within him, but it no longer mattered to him, because by that time he was very dead.

With a visceral *'CRAAACK!'* the rear third of the battered Beaufighter flexed, twisted and suddenly broke off, taking with it the eviscerated corpse of Cole, and Barlow was alone, fighting to keep a very badly vibrating and juddering C-Cindy in the air, desperately trying to feather the starboard engine, and finding the remnants of the aircraft he was trying to fly were completely uncontrollable.

C-Cindy was finished.

It was time to go, but he was pinned back by the centrifugal forces, and couldn't reach the release lever of the upper hatch.

"Icy, get out! *GET OUT!* We're finished!"

Unseen and unknown to him, the torn rear third of the fighter and his operator spun lazily away earthwards.

"BALE OUT!" Desperation fought bubbling panic and Barlow let go of the control column and undid the safety harness clumsily, before pushing down the seat's backrest and turning with difficulty onto his stomach so that he could push open the doors and lift himself into the exit well.

"Bale out, Icy," he coughed to clear a tightening throat, "FUCKING BALE OUT! BALE OUT!" his muscles were straining, trembling with effort, and his mouth gaped wide with the sheer effort.

The doors were so heavy that Barlow was still trying to keep them apart to climb through when C-Cindy slammed into the ground, disintegrating devastatingly into a thousand flaming pieces, the larger parts of her wreckage being pushed deep into the soft, rich soil, the massively expanding fireball incinerating what torn fragments remained of Barlow, and lighting the night sky and everything all around for an instant, like some great photoflash.

Rudi crowed with delight at the sudden flare of light on the ground below, and Mouse hooted, "Got you, you fucker!"

Less than three miles from where the main part of C-Cindy had fallen, the embers of her fifth and final victory fizzled and glowed cherry-red in the middle of a field, the Heinkel bomber pulverised first by the crash and then almost instantaneously shattered by the devastating explosion of the bombs she had carried.

Mouse grunted with satisfaction as he surveyed the Beaufighter's crash site, "Well done, Herr Leutnant. That's one bastard who'll not shoot anymore of our boys down ever again. Nobody got out, we killed them."

"Watch out for more of them, boys. I don't want a surprise. Did either of you see where the Heinie went?" Bruno's voice was bitter with the acid of self-loathing.

If only I'd acted faster…

"They hit the ground behind us, Herr Leutnant," said Rudi miserably, the sight of the falling Heinkel still fresh in his mind's eye. "I can see the point they hit."

"My fault, Rudi," Bruno shook his head, and thought of Anja. Was there anyone waiting for the crews of either of the two aeroplanes that had just been destroyed?

"We know the swine are hunting our bombers, I should have realised it might have been an enemy night fighter. Do either of you know what it was?"

"I thought it was a Heinkel when I first saw it, too, but it looked a bit more like a Blenheim when we were behind it, I think, sir. Definitely radial engines. Did you see a turret on top of the fuselage?"

"Rudi may be right, Herr Leutnant, I need to check with the Intelligence Officer when we get back."

"Orders, sir?" Rudi looked expectantly at Bruno. He could feel that treacherous twitch just starting in the toes of his left foot. *Stop that.*

"There may be more of those *schweinhund* around, or on the way."

Anja's sweet face surfaced again in his minds-eye, "I think it would not be very sensible to continue. We've accounted for one of their fighters and we might have useful intelligence. We're going back."

"But I haven't fired my guns yet, Herr Leutnant," griped Mouse.

Shut up, you miserable devil, Rudi glanced outside, eyes searching for more of the enemy, wiping his face with shaky hands, and flexing his twitching toes nervously.

Bruno's voice was grim, "Next time, Mouse; patience, have patience. I've had quite enough for tonight. We allowed Tommy to shoot down one of our bombers right under our fucking noses."

He clenched his teeth and took a deep breath, breathing in the bitterness of failure, despite their success, "In the end, the responsibility for their deaths is mine. I'm not very happy at all, and I've had more than enough. We're going home, and I want you to continue to keep a sharp lookout."

Thank God, thought Rudi gratefully, looking back at the fading glow of the destroyed Heinkel below as they turned onto a heading for home.

That could have been us. A few more seconds and it would have been. He breathed out slowly.

But, in the end, it wasn't. And that's what matters.

The silent enemy coastline, dark and hateful, passed beneath and then behind them, and the Junkers dropped down low over the water once again, Mouse staring at the receding coastline with sullen eyes.

But as England disappeared behind them, Rudi breathed easier. They had scored and survived. And, even better, were now on their way home again.

It was a good night.

Thank God.

Chapter 36

June came, and the weather remained unsettled, one night clear and bright, but dirty, wet and windy the next.

A grim and deeply saddened B-Flight operated under-strength for a week, only five crews covering their area until the replacements for Barlow and Cole arrived, but it was enough, because enemy activity had tailed off.

The Luftwaffe was girding their loins for a prolonged campaign fighting in the second front to the east, and many more squadrons and units were being transferred, leaving fewer to continue the campaign against Britain. It was a quiet period, with fewer intruders.

The new members of the flight finally arrived, another Norwegian crew, a pair of RNAAF *Loytnants* by the names of Caspersen and Fosse.

Unlike the crew of Alstad and Axelsen, the newcomers were serious, asking questions about equipment and operational tactics with a quiet intensity.

And they didn't take part at all in the high-jinks of the mess. Rose and the others left them to it. Their land was occupied, after all.

Some of the Poles and Czechs he'd met were pretty intense too. Fun probably took a far lower priority to revenge.

On more than one occasion, B-Flight spent a lot of time on the ground for the whole period of duty as no major attacks developed, the only flying being training flights when conditions permitted.

Even the patrol aircraft waiting at immediate readiness remained impotently on the ground, buffeted by rain and wind and useless.

On such nights, even the Luftwaffe would not fly, and only the occasional raider slipped across the water to raid coastal targets or mine the approaches.

The braver ones tried further inland, knowing the aerial defence was severely compromised by the weather, but even then, the same dangerous conditions affected them as well, and Sir Isaac continued to claim a handful of them.

The brilliant crew of John Cunningham and his trusty operator Jimmy Rawnsley of 604 Squadron would risk it all and test conditions in the air in almost all weathers.

Only when he felt it safe would Cunningham call his colleagues into the air.

For that incredible man, they were his valued and precious crews, the men he protected so zealously. He would not risk them unnecessarily.

The indomitable 604 pair had little interception luck with the few raiders that there actually were, but they managed to demonstrate that the Beaufighter, in well-trained and expert hands, was a real (almost!) all-weather interceptor fighter aircraft that could be used in conditions that were less than amenable.

On the better nights the enemy bombers continued to come over, but the numbers were fewer than earlier, far less than in late 1940 and early 1941.

The Luftwaffe crews were growing a bit cannier, too. Gone were the nights when some enemy bombers flew over Britain with their navigation lights showing; and more of the pilots flew lower than before, the unwary ones finding high ground or electricity lines and becoming Sir Isaacs's grim trophies.

Enemy gunners, too, seemed to become even twitchier, and more of the defending fighter crews found themselves facing streams of what Rawnsley would later describe as disconcerting torrents of what looked like 'flaming tomatoes.'

The darker the night and the poorer the visibility, the higher Rose flew. More than one British Beaufighter crew found themselves terminally meeting with the earth when caught by high ground in a low-level pursuit.

Such 'packed' clouds were a regular danger for the crews of both sides in this nocturnal war.

By mutual agreement, White and Rose decided that they would not descend below two thousand five hundred feet in a chase.

At least it was warmer now, the freezing conditions having lasted through much of April and almost into May, and the piles of snow which had interfered with flying were now only a less-than-fond memory, and, as enemy incursions lessened, there was even more time to practice, and more time to spend together with loved ones.

June when it came was more wet than not, the spring flowers and grass in their little cottage garden growing defiantly in the soft drizzle; and it gave Molly an excuse to cuddle up to Rose whenever the chance arose, though none was needed by either of them.

The happily newly-engaged young couple of Mandy and Chalky White occasionally dined with Rose and Molly at their cottage, and they enjoyed a night out at the 'Black Bull' together, but the difference in their ranks left Mandy shy, tongue-tied and overwhelmed in Molly's rather senior presence.

Besides, the two young lovers craved each other's time more than anything else in the world, for each second together was the most precious thing in the whole world.

This suited Rose and Molly perfectly, allowing the pair to enjoy as much of their available time together, too.

To Rose's dismay, Molly's half stripe arrived at the beginning of the month, and she was now a Squadron Officer.

The dark-haired girl smirked smugly whilst waving her newly augmented fabric bracelets of rank beneath his nose, and Rose groaned in frustration and disgust.

His own single rank ring of a Flying Officer seeming terribly insignificant by comparison.

"I'll never catch up," he grumbled gloomily, but with more than a little grudging pride as well.

With her increased rank, Molly's responsibilities increased, and she became even busier than before. The opportunity came for WAAFs to learn to fly, but seeing the stricken expression on Rose's face when she mentioned it, the naked fear for her in his eyes, Molly said no more, kissed him gently, and quietly tore up the application form in her office with a sigh for what might have been.

Their love for one another continued to deepen, the tenderness and love soothing the stresses that came as part and parcel with both operational flying in wartime and with being in love with an operational wartime flyer.

With the warmer days and when it was dry, they would lunch and, when chance permitted, love in a discrete and beautiful meadow, and Rose revelled in the wonderful sight and smell of his beautiful wife in the midst of nature in bloom.

Concerned about the effect of Rose's amorous intentions on her uniform, Molly would undress completely first, and for a moment he would savour the beauty of her body, for even the cruel scars of Foxton could not mar her perfection.

In his mind's eye was a library of images, Molly lying on her back on the striped rug, sun-dappled beneath the great oak tree, the sun catching the golden glow of her curves, her darkly erect nipples, the light softened by her thick waves of midnight hair and the vivacity of her smile, the bright glisten of the hot sunlight on the perspiration of her upper lip and chest, long-limbed and elegant as a gazelle, the joyful radiance in her eyes.

And those breath-taking images were multi-dimensional, for the taste and smell and sound of her were caught up within them.

It was a time he would remember for many years, a time of serenity and simple happiness encapsulated within him and undisturbed by the dangers and stress he experienced every day.

It was his inner Place Of Peace.

Being with Molly was the best treatment, the way in which he healed inside, her mere presence beside him calming and serene.

What a wonderful thing love is, he would reflect again and again, as the annals in his head continued to grow wonderfully in size.

The loss of Barlow and Cole hit B- Flight and RAF Dimple Heath hard, not least because of their popularity but also as Barr's command was reduced to five crews and aircraft until the new Norwegians arrived.

Despite the reduction in enemy sorties, however, the flight was still regularly in demand, and the pace seemed almost unchanged.

In early June, Squadron-Leader David Morrow MBE RAF, senior GCI controller and ex-operator, on an invitation from James, visited RAF Dimple Heath for an afternoon party.

It was a very pleasant affair for everyone, and as Millie came with him, their two wives had a very enjoyable time catching up.

After a quick word with James, Morrow managed to wangle a

ride with Rose on the first patrol that evening, leaving an extremely anxious and irate young operator behind on the ground, his only contribution to the flight being one to quickly re-familiarise Morrow with the AI set and 'cockpit' procedure, and to ensure he was properly attached to everything he was supposed to be properly attached to.

Rose refused his request to stay aboard for the trip as there would be no seat and safety harness. He wouldn't allow White to stand precariously behind his seat. He was far too important to risk.

"You're far too valuable to me, Chalky. I daren't risk you," was all he'd said firmly to prevent further discussion.

It had been difficult to see the small slim figure, made even smaller by distance, standing disconsolately at the door to their dispersals hut, but Morrow was a dear friend to all of them, and if it weren't for him, the odds would be stacked so much more heavily against them. The least that they owed him was to practise the art for which he had been initially trained.

Morrow's eyes betrayed his excitement despite his attempt to remain phlegmatic, and Rose could hear his breathing quicken as they lifted into the early evening sky from RAF Dimple Heath.

At eight thousand feet, ten miles out from the east coast, the sky was still clear, even though it was already dusk below.

They themselves would enjoy light for a few moments more before the low red sun dipped below the horizon of their viewpoint.

"I must say Flash, I'd forgotten how grand it is to be flying so high above the earth."

Rose smiled at Morrow's ebullience. "Yes, David. If you weren't so important on the ground, this is where you should be."

As he spoke, Rose expertly quartered the sky as Granny had once taught him. It wasn't often he needed to check the airspace around his aircraft so minutely (and to be honest the only enemy fighters at this late hour of the day would most likely be the larger Junkers 88s or Dorniers).

The night sky was a big place, so much more so when you couldn't see very much.

Already the light was fading, and he looked hopefully for the moving dot of an enemy bandit with his peripheral vision, but there was nothing.

"See anything?"

"'Fraid not, Flash, just lots of empty sky."

"I'm going to call home, David." Rose switched from intercom to radio, "Dagger 3 to Lamplight, got anyone for me to play with?"

A woman's voice, "Hello Dagger 3, standby, nothing at present, please orbit Beacon at angels twelve."

"Understood, Lamplight."

The voice was pleasant, "We'll try and find something for you, Dagger 3. Standby, please."

"We'll have to wait, David."

"Flash! I just saw something glint off to starboard, two o'clock, above. D'you see it?"

Rose looked, watching for a moment as the small shape gradually move to port. It was two thousand feet above them.

"It's OK, David, it's another Beau. He's orbiting the Beacon just like us. I think it's the Norwegian boys. I'm going to have to talk to them about that. You picked him up quite easily. It's really not good enough. They ought to know better."

Inside he marvelled at his words. Who was this stern RAF officer? Where was the anxious young boy who alighted from the train at Foxton less than a year ago?

"Is the line private, Flash?"

"Oh yes, we're on intercom only, old son. Why?"

"I wanted to tell you about the girl. Ask your advice."

"Girl? What girl?" *Oh Lord, what on earth was David wittering on about?*

"You were talking to her just now, Flash. You know, Lamplight. She's a young Assistant Section Officer, one of my young understudies, used to be one of my students. I enrolled her to work on the GCI unit. Very nice girl, incredibly clever, blonde."

The saucy old dog. "David! I can't believe it! What about Millie?"

"What? What about Millie? What's she got to do with this? Oh! Dear Heaven! No, it's not like that! You cheeky devil! D'you think I'm some dirty old man? She's only twenty, for pity's sake! I love Millie." Morrow declared reproachfully, "I'd never be unfaithful to her, and I'm surprised at you for asking!"

"Well, why on earth are you jabbering on like some lovelorn youth about a blonde girl, then?"

"I don't know why I mentioned the blonde bit, honestly, but her name's Helen, and she's brilliant, despite her age. She's learnt a lot and I've asked for her to be promoted immediately to Flight Officer. I want her to take over a new GCI site, she's really awfully good, but every time I make a request, the twerps at the Air Ministry ignore it."

"What do you expect, David? They're still getting used to the idea of the fairer sex actually wearing the uniform; the thought of a woman in charge of a station would likely give the old duffers a seizure."

Rose gazed longingly at the photograph in front of him. "Just look at my Molly, she's intelligent, brave and capable. Far more than I'll ever be, but the daft old brass'll never ever allow her to command an RAF station. It's not the safest job, but I'm not complaining. She's not one to shy from danger or shirk responsibility. I think they should give her an airfield to command of her own, but of course they won't."

Rose sniffed, readjusted his face mask. "Nevertheless, you should keep trying, David. Things will change one day, but it'll take time. Don't expect miracles, but don't give up."

"It's a waste, Flash, if we're to win this bloody war, we need the right people in the right places." sighed Morrow. "But I'll keep trying."

Rose laughed, "Please do, just don't hold your breath, chum!"

A quarter of an hour later, Morrow's young blonde, Helen, in her official guise of Lamplight, directed them onto an approaching contact.

Over the next few minutes she deftly brought the two blips on her PPI screen closer together, all whilst the two aircraft were still out over the sea.

"Dagger 3, I have you four miles behind the bogey, angels one below. He's quite fast, Please flash your weapon."

"David?"

"No joy, Flash, not a bean." Morrow sounded annoyed and frustrated.

"OK, not to worry, we'll soon remedy that, hold onto your hat!"

Rose pushed the throttles as far as they could go, the airframe quivering and bucking as he tried to follow the enemy raider, the engines shrieking thunderously.

The once glittering sheet of water below was now a flat black expanse, the horizon a faint, blurred line.

Every time the Beaufighter juddered so, Rose half-feared that she would fly apart, despite knowing how sturdily the aircraft was made.

His eyes flicked across the controls nervously. "Dagger 3 to Lamplight, more help, please."

"Range is less than three miles now, still one angels below, maintain your current heading."

"Thank you, Lamplight."

Suddenly, "Flash, I think I've got him! Stay at this angels, but turn five degrees starboard. I have the range as three miles. We'll approach him just below." And then, "See? Told you she was good."

"Hmm. Turning five degrees starboard, arming guns." Fruitlessly for a moment, Rose scrutinised the darkness ahead, but then, almost immediately he could make out a just-discernible hazily glowing point of light, no, two sets of glowing points higher up.

His heart reeled with excitement and he took a deep lungful of oxygen, easing back the stick to reduce the difference in altitude.

"I think I can see him, David, but keep following him on the set, call out any changes."

Each of the pair of sparks gradually further resolved as they drew closer into twinned glimmers of yellow-blue flame, and he reduced throttle automatically without realising it, until the Beaufighter was holding station five hundred feet behind the other aircraft, and just below.

Hopefully they should blend into the black expanse below.

"OK, David, have a look and tell me what you can see." A Heinkel 111 bomber by the looks of it, but it would be interesting to see if Morrow could identify it.

The guns were armed and waiting as he watched tensely for a response from the enemy bomber.

Warily, he eased the fighter closer, ready to twist them away at the first sign of trouble; and still no response from the bomber.

His fingers twitched.

Quickly now, David! Quick!

"Oh my! A Heinkel One-Eleven, I'd say. My God, I can't believe we're so close to it!" Morrow's voice shook with excitement, and he was whispering, as if the enemy would hear him.

Remembering his own reaction on seeing an enemy bomber at night for the first time, Rose smiled, but his eyes were hard, voice carefully controlled, "Let's wake him up, then, shall we? Mind your eyes. Firing."

A gentle pressure on the firing button and a tight burst of bullets and cannon shells spat out into the night and connected with the Heinkel, but without appreciable effect.

Rose cursed and fired again, but the Heinkel was already sliding to starboard, and a burst of return fire lanced out from the bomber towards them, surprisingly well aimed, and passing terrifyingly close beneath them.

Fuck!

"Bloody hell!" cried out Morrow in shock, even as Rose turned the controls.

His heart was hammering so hard that it felt as if it would bash its way out of his chest, and his vision blurred as he threw the Beaufighter into a sharp turn to port, hearing Morrow grunt behind him, and then back to starboard, before levelling off behind the diving Heinkel, which itself was now turning to starboard.

Again the enemy rear gunner fired a burst at them, but the range was too great and it rose towards them, but then fell uselessly away as Rose opened the range whilst trying to keep the enemy in sight.

"Flash! Flash, are you OK?"

"Fine, David." Rose was gasping with the effort, chest hurting and throat raw, and he lined up for another shot at the enemy bomber, automatically calculating the deflection even as he curved in smoothly behind the jinking Heinkel 111.

Once more he pressed the firing button, and again the fighter bucked and swayed, and a swathe of death swept across and onto the fleeing bomber.

This time their efforts were rewarded with a sparkling shimmer of hits and a small explosion on the starboard wing of the Heinkel, followed by a streamer of white flame that flared and then disappeared within seconds.

"Oh, good shooting! Well done! Oh, I say! You hit him, Flash!"

"Yeah," Rose rasped drily, "but he's still running, and it doesn't look like he's hurt all that much."

The twin engine bomber was diving desperately away from them now, the angle steepening further, and angrily Rose pushed D-Dog's nose down and chased after it.

Another line of flaming traced reached out for them, but the range was still too far, and although it did them no harm, the sweat stood out on his forehead.

Again Rose slammed forward the throttles, throwing the fighter into an ever deepening dive after the enemy, the engines screaming as he fought to catch the bomber as it sought sanctuary below.

The bandit passed through seven thousand feet, the dive even steeper than before. It was pulling away from them, even though the Beaufighter was diving after it at full speed, shaking wildly now, and despairingly, Rose pushed the firing button down for a fourth time.

The cannon banged again deafeningly, and then ran silent. Once more the target sparkled, and a few more pieces flew off, but it continued to dive, the altitude falling away at an alarming rate.

"David, I'm out of ammo, have you still got him on the set?"

We're too low! Damn it, these controls are stiff! Got to pull out…

Morrow was panting, and he was breathless over the intercom. "I'm sorry, Flash, the ground return's just swallowed him up. I've nothing on the set."

Pull back! "Nothing at all, chum?" he gasped.

Rose heaved back even harder on the stick, and the Beaufighters' nose began to come up, *if we can regain contact, I'll hold him while David reloads.*

But he knew there was little chance of seeing it again (unless of course Sir Isaac, the Black Knight, claimed the Heinkel in a final fiery blast on the ground).

"I don't have him. I think you got him, though, he was going down quite steeply."

Rose was not so sure. "Maybe, old chap. Keep a look out below, we might see him hit the ground."

They circled the area for a while, but there was no death flash on the ground. Finally, Rose spoke. "Could you reload, please, David?"

Morrow was deflated, "Yes, of course, Flash. Sorry."

What for? Forgetting to change the drums or for losing the bandit in the ground clutter? Nothing to be sorry for.

"Don't worry, chum, he probably went straight in, I don't think there was any chance of him pulling out. We almost went in ourselves. His angle was far too steep for his velocity." He shuddered involuntarily. "There's little chance he recovered. But we didn't see him crash, we'll likely only get awarded a probable."

"Wish we could be sure."

Rose's heart was slowing to a more reasonable pace, and he wiped his face. He was slippery with sweat.

"At least we hit him a couple of times, David. His gunner came close, but no coconut. Best change the drums, I'll give you a shout if I need you. If it's a bit hard to change 'em while your leads are connected, so leave your flying helmet on the seat. I know we're fairly low, but just make sure you keep taking gulps of oxygen, and keep on checking in with me. If you can leave your flying helmet on though, leave it on. I'll rock my wings if I need you back in place, OK?"

"Fair enough."

"Meantime, I'll call your little blonde and tell her what happened."

"Don't joke about it, you cheeky blighter. And if you call her 'my little blonde' in front of Millie I'm going to punch you right on the nose. Squadron Leaders are allowed to do that with snotty juniors. And don't forget, wherever you hide, I'll find you. They don't call me the King of the Intercept for nothing, y'know."

Rose chuckled and squeezed the little pink bear in his pocket. It had been a bit close that time, but in the end, not quite close enough to really make a difference.

And hopefully, with a bit of luck, the Heinkel hadn't pulled out of that dive.

If he'd bought it tonight, Chalky would have never forgiven Flash or himself for not being there.

And Molly? Dear God. Rose shuddered at the awful nearness of death and of what might have been. He could almost feel the beat of Sir Isaac's scaly wings.

He could still see the flaming red rounds streak past in his mind, and he closed his eyes for a moment. They hadn't got the bomber for sure, but they had survived.

It was enough.

Thank God.

In any event, there were no more contacts for them that evening, although there was some enemy activity in neighbouring sectors.

After a couple of hours in the air, Morrow's little blonde understudy finally gave them permission to return to Dimple Heath.

The Flight would be on Readiness of thirty minutes, and there would be the chance of a cup of tea, a bite to eat, and a little kip.

"It was good to fly with you again, Flash. I wish we'd been able to get that one for sure, though. You'll have to give me a ride again. Let me have another go. You've given me a taste for it, now."

Rose stifled a tired yawn and nodded, "I'd like that, David, very much. Anytime you'd like."

Morrow chuckled, "Not too soon, though. I think young Chalky would have a fit if I took his seat again. He looked positively murderous just before we took off."

The night duty finished without further incident, and at the end of it, Morrow got to enjoy his first operational fried egg.

"I've never tasted an egg as delicious as this one," he smiled beatifically as he forked the last of it into his mouth.

White watched him darkly, before directing his attention back to carefully mopping up the last of his own yolk with a buttered crust.

Enjoy it, chum, Squadron-Leader or not, it'll be a long time before I let you fly with Flash again!

Chapter 37

The following night, Chalky was back where he belonged, in his own seat, the old pretender banished back to his cold utility trailer in the muddy field. White surveyed the darkened sky carefully, seeing nothing untoward but grateful that life had returned to its normal routine.

They had been in the air for over two hours now, with not a single contact to show for the boredom.

He stifled a yawn and tapped his fingers on the coaming of the perspex dome.

Ho-hum.

A quick all-around check through his dome again, nothing to see out there, no German bomber trying to stick a bullet or two up their collective arse, just miles and miles of emptiness around them.

Bored, bored, bored.

Even the throb of the powerful Hercules engines sounded petulant and fed up, *Bor-rring-bor-rring-bor-rring-bor-rring-bor-rring…*

Removing one glove, he rummaged around in his pocket until he found the crumpled little paper bag, picking out one of the boiled sweets Mandy had given him earlier.

Unwrapping it carefully, and tucking the wrapper tidily away into a pocket, he lifted the oxygen mask from his face for a moment and popped the sweet into his mouth.

Ooh, a lemon sherbet!

Yummy.

Mandy knew exactly what he liked, he thought blissfully, slobbering on the sweet, trying not to crunch.

In fact Mandy knew everything there was to know about him, everything, and yet she loved him still. Absent-mindedly he held his hand before the air vent to warm it in the weakly warm waft coming from it, before putting the glove back on.

Dearest Mandy, the girl was an angel, and more important than anything else in this world, she was *his* angel.

Beautiful and strong and gentle and kind and compassionate.

And such sweet, soft lovely lips.

White still found it hard to believe that she had actually said 'yes' to him and that she was now his fiancée, and he wondered for the thousandth time what it was she could see in him.

Scant months earlier he had been a part of the dregs of Dimple Heath, and somehow his luck had changed.

Neither Rose nor Mandy cared what he had been, or from where he came.

They only saw *him*, and wonder of wonders, they'd both liked what they'd seen.

He closed his eyes again and thought of those soft lips, sighing again, but this time not in boredom but contentment.

White resisted the urge to bite down as sherbet powder leaked onto his tingling tongue. He peered quickly but carefully out at the sky again.

The sweet felt nice, but when she kissed him, it was *her* tongue which made his entire body tingle. He wriggled his fingers inside the glove and flexed it into a comfortable position.

Over the intercom, White heard the voice of Morrow calling out to Rose, the Squadron Leader now back on his own seat, once more in his usual guise of Lamplight, and the young operator stopped sucking the sweet for a moment to listen better.

"Dagger 3, thank you for waiting so patiently, we might have some custom for you. Please confirm angels and heading."

"Lamplight, good to hear your voice. Angels ten, heading zero-four-zero. What's the gen?"

"We have an empty for you, please adopt heading zero-zero-five, maintain angels, he is one above but currently descending, range fifteen miles."

An 'empty' was the term used for a bomber which had already dropped its bomb load and was heading for home, lighter and faster. The window of opportunity for the attack would be small.

Before very long, they had been brought to within three miles of the bandit and Morrow asked them to flash their weapon.

White was ready and waiting, but he was still surprised to see the blip of the bandit bright on his scope, five thousand feet and below. He juggled the remnants of the hollowed sweet hurriedly around as he tried to speak, pushed it into one cheek.

"Got him! Bandit is closing, slightly to port and below five hundred feet, closing fast, looks like a head-on, turn to starboard immediately onto one-nine-zero!" the words literally fell out of his mouth as he gabbled the instructions out quickly. The sweet shifted in position and almost lodged itself in his throat.

White braced himself, his head painfully catching the side of the Perspex dome as the Beaufighter tilted over, Rose dragging D-Dog around into a turn even before his operator had finished speaking.

The engines were howling now, and White crunched down on the lemon sherbet, wincing as a shard scratched the side of his tongue, but his eyes remained resolutely on his scopes.

The blip had disappeared from the set, but any moment Rose would pull out of the turn and he would need to pick up the trace again to continue the interception. His cut tongue stung as the last sherbet crystals found it, lemon with the metallic taste of blood.

OK, where are you?

Crunch, crunch. Quick, quick! Finish the bloody sweet, you've got to give directions…

There! Sliding in from the right side of the scope. "OK, Flash, regained contact, level out, where do you want him?"

"A little to starboard and above, please Chalky."

Crunch, crunch, ouch! Those pieces are sharp! He tasted more blood.

White licked his lips, "OK, er, steer five degrees port, lose five hundred feet, range less than four thousand."

Rose pushed the throttles forward, edged the fighter to port, settled on course, "Range?"

"Just over three thousand, still closing."

"Tell me when we get to a thousand feet, Chalky, how's his height?"

"You're just below, Flash, about a hundred feet below now. Range three thousand, steer five degrees to starboard."

The ear-splitting racket of the screaming, howling engines increased, and the tiny howling draughts of freezing air continued to whistle in to torment him through the interior of the fuselage.

They flew in silence for a minute or two, and Rose began to fear something would fall off the madly vibrating Bristol fighter if this continued for any longer, "She's getting difficult to control, how're we doing, Chalky?"

"We're closing the range, still behind. Range two thousand; he's still above, flying straight and level."

Rose relaxed his eyes, trying to defocus them, and almost straight away he fancied that a there appeared to be *something* moving ahead of them, although with the vibration it was actually difficult to make out anything clearly.

No wonder the Air Ministry kept trying the Turbinlite idea, this night hunting really was bloody hard work. At least during the day you could see the enemy from miles away.

Was it his imagination, or…?

"Chalky, how close are we now?"

White's voice was strained, "Fifteen hundred, a little under, perhaps. Can you not see anything yet, Flash?"

"Maybe," he replied uncertainly, "Hmm. There is something…," he squinted, straining his eyes.

Yes, there. A patch of something that almost, but not quite, disappeared when he looked directly at it.

Certainly, ahead of the Beaufighter, an obscure patch seemingly somehow different from the surrounding darkness.

It *had* to be the bandit.

Rose carefully eased slightly back on the throttles, and stared hard at the vague shape of the aeroplane flying before them as the vibration of the airframe slackened somewhat.

The shape was far more distinct now, and he could just make out the faint flicker of a twinned pair of pale blue exhaust flames.

"I've got it, Chalky! You can have a look, old chap, but make sure you keep us in contact."

"Where is it? Oh…crumbs, it's hard to see, isn't it? I can't make it out, it's pretty big, two engines, um…"

"I'm going to get closer, chum, keep your eye on the 'scope, don't lose him."

"OK, Flash."

"If he's a Hun, Chalky, I'm going to give him a burst straight away."

"Sounds like a good idea…but I still can't tell what it is yet."

A terrifying line of hot red tracer suddenly lanced out towards them, but then fell away below.

"Cripes!" gasped White.

Instinctively, Rose punched the firing button, and his cannon and machine guns roared in reply, the harsh hammering surging over them in a deafening wave.

Neither the enemy rounds nor his own connected.

He released the button. "Chalky! Did you see any hits?"

White was still peering through his dome, "I don't think so, Flash." A last piece of the sweet was stuck beneath his tongue and he worked to dislodge it.

Suddenly the other aircraft tipped over to one side and dived straight down, and Rose immediately saw the classic plan view of a Heinkel 111.

"It's a Heinkel, Flash," White called out instantly.

Tell me something I don't know. He pushed down after it, "OK, chum, we're going after it, keep 'em peeled."

And then they were hurtling straight down after the enemy, one eye on the altimeter as it spun crazily down.

The controls fought him as the heavy fighter gained speed in the descent, buffeted viciously by the other aeroplane's slipstream.

Rose's heart lurched with fear as his sight began to grey and fade and the controls began to stiffen.

He could feel the blood vessels in is head bulging painfully huge, and he wondered what it felt like when one's eyeballs popped. He grunted under the strain.

This is madness, we're going to lose control any moment, can't even see the Hun, what if he's pulled out of the dive, we'll shoot straight past.

Oh my God. What if we hit him? I'm pulling out of it...

Hunched forwards, gasp by painful gasp and inch by painful inch, Rose pulled D-Dog out of the screaming plunge downwards, expecting to see the ground loom terrifyingly before him at any moment.

And then they were climbing again, and he almost collapsed backwards with relief, numbed fingers stuck to the control column.

He looked down but saw with both irritation and gratitude that the ground was still quite far below. His heart was booming heavily, and he feared that it would suddenly cease beating.

Fuck it, I'm losing my nerve...

"Chalky, you still back there, old bean? Haven't baled out have you?"

White's voice, weak and shaky on the intercom, "Jesus! I think I've wet myself!"

Rose smiled hollowly with little mirth, "You won't be the only one if you have, old son. D'you have him for me, chum?"

"Sorry, Flash, the screen's just full of clutter, nothing."

Far below, a flaming white flower suddenly bloomed silently, large and incandescent. It subsided to form a short stripe of vivid fire on the ground.

"Did you see that?" His voice was a whisper, "Might it be Jerry?"

White's voice was stronger now, but shrill. "He must have gone straight in!"

"Yeah, mate, he must have. I'm sure we didn't hit him, he must have been unable to pull out, poor bastard."

White was silent, then, quietly, "Could have been us..."

Rose tried to sound strong and confident, but it didn't work, "But it wasn't, old man. Ol' Sir Isaac will have to do with the Jerry crew, he's not getting us as well."

"I s'pose one out of two isn't bad."

There but for the grace of God…

Chapter 38

James looked at the fuming Rose, and smiled brightly. White stood in the corner, looking uncomfortable and dishevelled and vaguely lost.

"Flash, my dear boy. How perfectly awful. I appreciate how you must feel. And I agree with you, it really is not good enough. Not good enough at all." James nodded sympathetically, but the smile remained.

Uh-oh. Rose's tight scowl slipped a little, and he stared at his CO suspiciously. That look was awfully familiar. The old dog was up to something, but what was it?

The Wing Commander's smile stretched even wider. He picked up a piece of paper from his desk, looked at it and put it back down.

Oh God. He's looking happy for some reason. There's something coming. Something rather scary. And I just hope that it's something I can stomach.

The commanding officer solicitously waved the two young men towards the chairs arranged in front of his desk. White took his gratefully, his eyes drooping with exhaustion.

James leaned back. Since Cousin Charles' telephone call earlier that night, he had been deliberating on who to send when the angry young pilot stormed in his office, frothing and raving about 'bloody searchlights.'

Problem solved.

"Yes, I'm very pleased you came to see me about your experience. The thing is, I received a call from AA Command, and it seems they would very much like some crews to visit one of their sites. They would like to do a co-operation thingy, and they asked for one of the best, so you popping in to see me now is an absolute blessing. My best crew. You two can tell those army wallahs what's what, eh?"

Oh, my giddy aunt. "Um, what exactly do you mean by what's what, sir?"

"Tell the silly buggers what it's like to fly up there when you can't see a bloody thing, the wind's throwing you all over the place, your kite's icing up, bits of equipment fall off or break down, and all the while Sir Isaac is flitting around like a tart trying to make you prang the kite. And that being blasted away at by AA while you're up there chasing Jerry is the last thing you need."

He sniffed. "I think I'm coming down with something. I could do with a hot drink."

Rose looked glumly across at White, but his young operator had fallen fast asleep, and there was no support from that quarter.

"I'm sure one of the others…" he began.

"No, no, Flash my dear fellow, I've made up my mind. It'll do you good to spend a night with one of their metropolitan ack-ack positions. Wish I were going with you, too. See it as a little holiday, what? I'll draw up the appropriate travel orders for you."

He picked up the telephone, "Fancy a cup of tea, old man?"

Game, Set and Match. Bollocks.

Rose sighed sadly. Beside him, White slumped further and began to snore softly.

I've been had. Good Lord.

An army 15cwt truck bearing the arrow-pierced target badge of the

6th Anti-Aircraft Division was waiting for them, parked to the side of the station, just off Station Road.

Rose turned to look back at the LNER railway station, one he'd visited as a child with his parents. A little boy clutching his teddy bear and awed by the bustling activity.

The red-brick Victorian building was substantially the same as he remembered, except for the sandbags, missing signs, and the partially-boarded and taped up windows.

The same, and yet so different.

A Corporal doubled up to them and saluted, "Flying Officer Rose, Sir?"

"Yes, Corporal?"

"Corporals are called Bombardiers in the Royal Artillery, sir. I'm Bombardier McManus, and I've been detailed to take you both to your destination, sir."

"Right, I stand corrected, thank you, Bombardier. Come along, Chalky, don't dawdle, man." Rose waved an arm imperiously.

White shook his head and grinned as he followed them to the truck.

They watched with interest as the truck passed through this extended eastern part of the Metropolitan sprawl, comfortably ensconced in the cab beside the Bombardier, as he skilfully guided the vehicle north along Whalebone Lane on the way to the Eastern Avenue.

All too soon the journey was over as they quickly reached their destination, a Royal Artillery Heavy AA gun site in a hilltop position on Boyn Hill, situated close to the boundary of Hainault Forest, almost a kilometre to the north of the Eastern Avenue. The truck turned onto a smaller access slip road that led via a guarded gate into a neatly arranged small army camp.

McManus nodded to the sentry as they were waved through, "Here we are gents, the ZE1 gunsite. You'll find the CO in the office."

The neat arrangement of concrete and brick structures included an administrative block, shelters, stores, ordnance stocks and barracks.

Beyond the camp buildings were the 4.5 inch guns, two sets of four guns in pits with holdfasts, each set in a semi-circular open fan-shaped eastward inclined ground formation. Each set of four guns incorporated a partially-sunken command post.

The seven acutely angled barrels reached up like a deadly forest of huge metallic thorns, patiently awaiting the chance to sting their enemy.

An eighth gun was being worked on by its crew, the barrel depressed downwards. Rose shivered involuntarily at the sight.

It was just one of the twenty-three batteries that formed the north-east sector of London's Inner Artillery Zone.

The Royal Artillery had ensured that there would a warm welcome waiting for the Luftwaffe.

As the two young flyers stepped down from the truck, McManus pointed towards what Rose imagined to be the Headquarters building, "If you could just see the Sarn't Major, sir? He'll get you to the OC."

"Hulloo there! Gentlemen! I say, hullo there!"

They turned towards the shouted hail as behind them the truck eased its way away to the motor transport pool. A painfully-thin army officer was striding towards them from outside the building McManus had directed them towards, beckoning them over.

"How d'you do? I'm Martin, the Battery CO. welcome to ZE1. You must be Rose and White? Or is it White and Rose?" he smiled disarmingly and stuck out his hand. The youngsters stared at the middle-aged officer with interest.

Martin wore the three pips of an Army Captain on his shoulders, and on his chest were the faded ribbons of the Military Medal with a bar rosette, War Medal, Victory Medal, Efficiency Decoration and a *Croix de Guerre avec palme*.

In contrast to the tarnished bronze oak leaf spray of his Mention in Despatches, a second, much shinier, bronze oak leaf was sewn onto his battledress beneath the ribbons.

This officer had been decorated again since the Great War.

Martin noticed their interest. He smiled grimly, "We had a little bit of excitement last year, quite rousing, even had a Messerschmitt fighter crash here last year. A 109. The RSM was quite outraged, made him spill his tea!"

White cleared his throat, "You've seen quite a bit of action before, then, sir?"

The captain nodded, "I was in the last spot of nastiness as a Linseed Lancer."

White looked mystified but Rose had heard the term before, "A stretcher bearer. My father said they were the bravest men on the battlefield. The truest of heroes." The MM and bar on Martin's chest revealed his courage.

"I'm not sure about that, but we might have been the ones with the brownest trousers!"

Martin's eyes twinkled merrily. "It was one of the roles available to Conscientious Objectors, and it was either that or the Mines. But, as you can see, I'm a bit happier to take up arms this time around. Besides, I hear you two have seen a bit of excitement as well. I'm glad to have you both here. Let me show you around, introduce you to my chaps, and then we'll nip along to my office to have a hot cup of char. Have you ever tried a nice mug of real gunner's char? No? You're in for a treat then!"

It was with more than a little relief the following morning that Rose gently closed the railway carriage door and settled back into his seat with a grateful sigh. He looked across at White, who stared back at him through exhausted, shadowed eyes.

He knew his own face mirrored that haggardness of White's.

The huge breakfast they had eaten earlier, golden scrambled eggs, fried mushrooms and thickly buttered fresh bread, washed down with more of that appalling hot sweet tea, felt like a solid weight wrapped around his middle, and he adjusted his position.

"Crikey, Flash, I'm pooped. If that's a normal night in AA Command, they can bloody keep it. And I can still hear those bloody guns in my head."

White groaned, looking as pale as his name. "I think I might be a bit concussed from all those bloody explosions!"

Rose rubbed his face with both hands, bristles rough against his palms, desperately wishing for a hot bath and clean bedsheets. His head, too, was pounding.

"Me too, chum. I've got a cracking headache, and those mugs of gunner's char have made my blinking teeth ache, too. Wish I'd brought my toothbrush. Never drunk anything so sweet in my life. I'm surprised my teeth haven't dissolved."

"Mine feel like they're covered in tar or pitch or something 'orrible. I'm not quite sure that they're all still there!"

They cringed together as the guard's whistle lanced painfully through tender ears into their dazed minds, and the final banging of doors resounded achingly through their concussed skulls.

Martin had been the most considerate of hosts, his men friendly and considerate, and the two young Flyers first received a VIP tour of the site after arriving, sat at the guns and peered gormlessly through the gun sights, after which they'd enjoyed a deliciously rich chicken stew dinner and fresh baked bread ("One of the perks of being so close to Warren's Farm!" Martin had smiled), before settling down for the evening's show.

There had been no invitation, though, to look at the mysterious

409

circular arrangement of wires that was the site's GL Mat. With sentries posted, it was off limits.

There had been little activity until just after dusk, when the first of the night's raiders approached from the north east.

The guns had cracked and boomed and bellowed ceaselessly throughout the endless night, the relentless clamour battering and pounding constantly at the two young airmen as they squirmed in a trench outside the Command Post.

One particular gun, nicknamed 'Whalebone Annie' by the soldiers, was particularly ear-splitting in its reports. Rose would have sworn the damned thing was twice as noisy as its brethren.

Despite the awesome quantity of high explosives and metal being hurled upwards, they were lucky and less of it found its way back down onto them.

They were lucky, for it was widely known that the shrapnel was a greater risk to civilians than to German aircrews.

Martin appeared a few times, invited them for tea and buns in his command post, but they could see his mind was on his duty, and so they left him to concentrate on directing his guns, cowering instead in a trench for an extremely stressful hour.

Their only company during this time were a small team of anxious looking young ATS girls, one with a twitching eye, dwarfed inside their greatcoats and faces hidden beneath steel helmets, shouting instructions above the firing of the guns into microphones, ably working together to operate one of the gunsite's Kerry Predictors.

Martin had explained its use, but it had all gone over Rose's head, though White seemed to have grasped the basic concepts and procedures.

The guns fired non-stop, huge flames shooting from their muzzles as they fired, the stench of burnt cordite and smoke, choking and thick, dust and dirt swirling around them. Small pieces of shrapnel rained down incessantly all the while.

Finally unable to withstand the relentless and endlessly deafening *CRUMP! CRUMP! CRUMP!* of the guns battering at them, the two of them left the girls to their dangerous task and retreated to an empty office in the semi-subterranean southern Command Post.

Despite the reassuring thickness of the brick gun base which formed the wall of the office, they each found a table to crawl beneath.

In the early hours, as the first pink blush of dawn lightened the eastern horizon, the all clear could be heard sounding out over the city, and the smoke stained and weary men and women of the unit were stood down for breakfast.

Like Rose and White their eyes were red rimmed, lined faces greasy and slack, totally exhausted, both mentally and physically.

Breakfast had been welcome, the milk, eggs and butter a pleasure (and wholly earned by the gunners, felt Rose fervently), marred only by a single distant explosion that seemed to mock them.

Martin flinched only slightly, a spoonful of stodgy porridge halfway to his mouth, tired eyes distant.

"That's the UXB boys," he explained, and wiped his chin, "Poor, brave bastards. They work all day and all night. Hope they were clear when it exploded."

They bade farewell to the gun site, borne home (or at least to the Railway Station, if it hadn't been bombed) by the same young driver they were picked up by, and grateful to be returning to their own world, wiser to the realities of another aspect of the defence of which they were a part.

The train chugged its way out of London, the fragrance of blooming countryside spoiled by the reek of smoke and brick dust and cordite, whilst behind them the great city burned, the stink of burning and despair and pain hanging low like some awful cloud over it.

Memories of Foxton, never far, crowded in on him.

A lesson had been learned, life on the AA guns was certainly no cushy number. A memorable night not easily forgotten.

James would not hear them moan about the men and women of the AA Command again.

Chapter 39

Corporal Elsie Dyer cursed long and hard as cold water sprayed across her, spotting her tunic further and splashing her already very wet face. If she didn't sort out the matter in hand soon, she was going to be very late for sorting out her dinner preparations.

No matter what she did, no matter how hard she toiled and scrubbed, even using her button brush and the hard bar of Coal Tar soap, Elise could not get the stain's outline out of her regulation blue bloomers.

Standing at the sink in the 'Ladies' in Dimple village's public house, washing her drawers feverishly in the big deep sink, her hands glowing an angry red from the icy water, Elsie fumed.

Olaf was a sweet man and a very considerate lover, and, although she had not meant to, Elise had fallen in love with him. She loved everything about him, the way he deferred to her, the way his lips curled over his crooked incisor, the way in which he hugged her close wherever they were and whatever the company.

But what she definitely did not love was the way he withdrew just before he ejaculated.

Actually, that wasn't quite true. Olaf insisted in lovemaking without protection, because she was his beloved *'Kusymre'* (which he assured her was a delicate yellow Norwegian flower), and he needed to feel her directly, without there being anything in between their organs.

"I cannot bear anything between us, my darling flower," He would say, with that curiously vulnerable look on his face. "I must be inside you fully. I must have the feel of your skin and body against mine. Completely."

Hardly poetry, but sincerely spoken.

In itself, it was not really a concern for Elsie, because Olaf was reliable and thoughtful and always withdrew before he climaxed, and to be honest he felt rather wonderful just as he was.

It did feel much nicer without one of those awful french letters on his todger.

What really irritated her, however, the thing that drove her bloody barking mad, was the fact that Olaf *always* ejaculated onto her bloomers, without fail.

And whilst he would be cringingly apologetic afterwards, he could not stop himself in the heat of the moment.

And that left poor Elsie with a warm and relaxed feeling and very sticky drawers that needed immediate washing to prevent them staining.

It was as Mum always used to say, men were good at making a mess, but it was always the women who had to clear it up.

But the sex *was* fun, lots of fun.

She stopped for a moment, and blew a loose strand of hair away from her face.

Flipping Heck, what a life.

In the momentary calm from her frenzied cleaning, she held up the offending garment and examined it closely.

Just outside, in the garden, audible beyond the joyous singing birds, Elsie heard harsh voices in the garden outside, and she leaned closer to the lowered upper sash to hear better.

It might provide a welcome distraction from this bloody awful task.

It was a man, voice lowered, but not lowered enough for her not to be able to make out his words.

She frowned. It sounded like that new Norwegian pilot, Loytnant Fosse, and he was speaking in Norwegian.

"Vi må ta flyet i kveld, vil vi å få det til Gilze-Rijen. Du trenger for å fyre av nødbluss som vi lærte, og vi vil være trygge."

Elsie frowned in confusion at the window. What on earth? What did he mean by saying, *'We must take the aeroplane tonight, and we'll be able to get it to Gilze-Rijen. You'll need to fire the flares as we were taught, and we'll be safe.'*

There was something fishy going on. But what? And what was Gilze-Rijen? Fire flares? What on earth could it mean? Dodgy, and no mistake.

Elsie reached for the sash window to ease it further down to listen better, but as she pushed it, it dropped with a crash that reverberated in the sudden silence.

Elsie stared at it for an instant, aghast, frozen in shock. *Oh no, they'll have heard me!*

Dropping her sodden knickers into the sink, grimacing at the wet *'thwop'* sound they made, she scampered hurriedly into the toilet cubicle, being careful to leave the door open.

Even if someone were to hoist themselves up, and peered into the ladies, they ought not to be able to see her.

But, nonetheless, she clambered onto the toilet seat and crouched down on it, taking care not to touch the chain hanging from the cistern.

Any movement might betray her.

There was a rustle in the shrubbery outside, and she heard something

415

scrape against the brickwork of the wall. There was a grunt, and then the sound of heavy breathing as a heavy object was lifted up. Elsie closed her eyes, and held her breath.

"Det er ingen der. Vinduet må ha glidd." (*'There's no one there. The window must have slipped'*).

Then there was a different voice, strained, *"Takk faen, kom ned før du bryte ryggen min!"* (*'Thank fuck, come on down before you break my spine!'*).

There was more rustling and grunting and a *'Thunk!'*, as if a sack of coal had suddenly been dropped onto the ground outside the window.

Then the rustling sound of footsteps as they walked away.

She began to lift her head, and then stopped. What if they had not gone? What if they were waiting?

Her ankles and thighs were beginning to ache, and her wet clothes were horribly uncomfortable, but she remained still, crouching precariously on the toilet bowl, wondering how she could explain what she was doing if anyone were to come in. That would be awfully difficult.

She was aware that her stockings were sagging, her uniform soaked, and she must look a dreadful mess. She would need to make herself presentable before getting back to the airfield.

But what had it all meant? What did they mean about taking the aeroplane tonight? Were they on the duty roster tonight?

After five minutes Elsie had had enough. Just as she were about to move, there was a rustling outside and then the sound of a second set of footsteps as someone else walked away.

A cold shiver rattled its way down her spine.

There had been someone waiting outside, after all!

For a long moment after the sound of the footsteps had faded, Elsie remained where she was. She began to tremble, why had there been someone waiting?

Although she had continued to hide, she had not really believed that there might actually be someone remaining outside to catch her out.

There was something really wrong about all of this, and suddenly she longed to be in Olaf's arms. She felt safe with him, even if he always came messily in her pants.

Carefully she stepped down, wary not to slip in her wet shoes.

She needed to speak someone, Squadron Officer Rose lived nearby, just further up the Lane, and perhaps she was home?

Elsie peeked around the side of the cubicle wall, but the window was empty, showing only the bright green of the shrubbery outside.

Her shoulders sagged, and she pondered for a moment about slipping into her soggy knickers, but decided against it.

No matter how much they were wrung out, there was no way she could walk back to the airfield in them.

No, she would leave them where they were, wretched and wrinkled in the sink, try and tidy herself up and get Olaf to run her back.

Perhaps the journey on the back of his rattling deathtrap of a motorbike would help to dry out her damp uniform.

Elsie turned to the door that led into the narrow dark wood lined passageway. Hopefully, he would be waiting for her in the Snug, the big stupid loving smile on his face, monstrously pleased with himself, a pint of beer untouched before him.

But when she opened the door, there was someone else waiting for her in the darkened passage, and she recoiled in shock.

Elsie felt the wave of fear wash over her, like an icy tide that coursed through her from her toes upwards, and leaving her hair feeling as if it were standing on end beneath her cap.

The big man dressed in the Norwegian air force uniform sneered at her, a twisted, spiteful smile filled with cruelty.

417

"Ah, Elsie! Onsker du en tur tilbake til flyplassen?" he said, asking her if she would a lift back to the airfield.

Elsie scowled at him, "What?" she tried to brush back the rebellious strands of damp hair escaping from beneath her hat.

"Why do you pretend not to understand me?" RNAAF Loytnant Fosse raised his bushy blond eyebrows in puzzlement, "Olaf told us that your mother was from Bergen."

"She was," replied Elsie defiantly, inching slowly along the wall towards the Snug. "And Olaf talks too much. I'm going to have a word with him about that now."

"Very well, then we speak in English. He sent me. Olaf is outside. He asked me to bring you to him."

Why would he do that? They had earlier agreed to meet in the pub for a drink, not outside.

Sensing her confusion, Fosse indicated the open door to her right, "Come, come. Please."

Elsie looked longingly to the left and the sanctuary of the Snug, and then to the right and the open doorway that led out into the garden.

This felt so wrong. She tensed, ready to race to the left, and without a change in expression, still smiling, Fosse lunged forward, one hand slapping hard against her mouth, the other clamping around her neck.

"Now we go. Come, Elsie, be good. It will be better for you, you know. "

Her throat and lungs were hurting, burning, and she couldn't see straight, but still her knee shot out,straight and true yet somehow missing her intended target and instead slamming painfully against his inner thigh.

The smile on his face disappeared, disappearing into a injured grimace, and he grunted in pain.

Elsie could feel the pressure against her neck increase, even as she gloried in delivering the blow, and as her world dimmed, he took his hand from her mouth and punched her straight in the face.

And the world exploded into black.

A cool breeze washed over her, and she smiled as the boat rocked gently on the river, Olaf looking down at her, the sun a blinding white circle behind him, his features obscured by the light.

The smile made her mouth hurt, and Elsie tried to touch her aching face (why was her face hurting so?), her tongue licking dry, crusted lips and meeting with a sharp surface that shocked her back into full consciousness.

Her questing tongue found the cracked tooth again, and she tried to sit up.

What...?

She couldn't move! Someone was holding her arms tightly, and squinting into the eye-watering glare, she saw that it was not dear Olaf's face looking down at her after all, but rather that of Fosse.

And she wasn't in a boat, but in a speeding car, the cool breeze really the flow of air as they raced between high hedgerows,

With a thundering and juddering rush recent events flooded back into her mind, and she began to struggle against his grip.

"Oh, you're awake! Had you been listening to us? Tell me what you heard!"

She tried to speak, but her throat hurt and all that came out was a croak. The pain reminded her of the hard hands at her throat.

"What's that? I can't hear you." He smiled, but unsurprisingly there was no warmth in it, and the speculative malice in his eyes made her shiver with fear.

He was disappointed. She had awoken earlier than he had hoped.

Lifting her into the car, Fosse had enjoyed the feel of her breasts and buttocks.

He leaned close, "You are nice-looking girl, even if so messy. Perhaps I might take a parting present with me."

One hand slid down from her shoulder, heavily brushing against the side of her breast, to come to rest on her left hip.

"You like Norwegian boys, yes?" he asked diffidently.

Elsie's mouth felt stiff and bruised, and she felt beaten and battered all over. Anger quickened through her, burning through her confusion and fear.

Like Norwegian boys? Goodness only knows where Olaf is right now when I need him most, and you've just punched me in the face, you bastard. I'm not so sure. You Norwegian boys aren't doing me any favours.

But conscious of his hands on her, and the fact that she had no knickers on, her modesty only protected by a pair of sagging and semi-soaked stockings, she nodded carefully, working an expression of fright and trepidation onto her face. *Look scared. If he thinks you're scared, he'll underestimate you, he won't be ready when the time to act comes.*

She tried to sit up and nodded hesitantly, but her seemingly-anxious eyes looked ahead through the windscreen for an instant, seeing the rippling sparkle of the river to the left catching the lowering sun through the thinning undergrowth.

Elsie knew the area well and recognised instantly that the car was less than a mile upriver of the village of Dimple.

I need to get away.

"If you give me a kiss and hug, we let you go, OK?" his grip enfolded the curved ridge of her hip, and she knew there would be no choice, the look in his eyes those of one enjoying their thrall over another.

"Alright", she slurred, "just a kiss? You promise?"

He nodded; licking his lips eagerly, "Just a kiss. I promise." But the hand slipped downwards.

"You promise?" she asked again, and her voice was a whisper.

"I promise." His hand reached the hem of her skirt and slipped beneath it. In the front, his pilot laughed, but did not look back.

With one trembling hand she reached out and hesitantly stroked his cheek, "Nothing more?"

"Of course", he agreed, but the hard fingers creeping up her inner thigh revealed the lie.

Her hand still on his face, he leaned over and touched his lips with hers.

In exactly the same instant as their lips touched, Elsie's hand flew back to her hair and in a single motion pulled out the long hairpin that had been a present from her grandmother, reversed it and rammed it hard into the side his face, aiming for his eye, but instead it pierced his cheek, just beneath his left eyeball, scraping against the lower border of the orbit and tearing ruinously through the Orbicularis Oculi muscle.

Fosse shrieked shrilly in pain, jumping backwards away from her and disappearing over the side of the car.

As he fell, Fosse's foot caught the back of Caspersen's head a glancing blow, and the car screeched to a halt.

Elsie was thrown forwards and found herself lying with her head and shoulders in the front passenger footwell, her exposed legs sticking out over the seat.

Stunned for a moment by the sudden braking, she soon regained her senses, and urgently struggled out, seeing as she did that Caspersen had caught his head against the windscreen. He looked over at her blearily, bleeding from a cut on his forehead. There was no sign of Fosse.

I hope that fall cracked your head open, you fucking pervert.

Caspersen reached for her but already she was out of the car and running for the river. It was hard going, for the sudden stop, its consequences and Fosse's blow had skewed her sense of balance, her stockings were sagging badly, and she ached horribly all over, but her parents had not raised a weakling and she struggled grimly onward. Hot Viking blood rushed through her veins.

She had lost her hat and both her shoes somewhere, and she felt the unevenness of the ground against the soles of her feet as she drew ever closer to the riverbank.

With a bit of luck, she could swim downriver, back to Dimple village and get some help.

There was a sharp *crack!* and a bullet whistled past, well over to the right, almost immediately another *crack!* Still to the right, but much closer this time.

Time slowed and she could feel the stones and grass beneath her feet, almost stumbling as she caught the toes on her left foot against a sharp rock.

Tears wet her eyes with the pain, but she didn't stop, her muscles pumping as she drove herself onwards. She didn't flinch as a third bullet whistled an inch to the left of her head like a huge, angry wasp.

Her heart was thumping and the river was swimming in her vision, but she was scrambling down now, and she leapt for the surging water as she reached the edge of the bank. The daughter of a sailor, she was a strong swimmer and was confident that she could handle the river.

The fourth bullet smacked into the ground at her feet, but the fifth caught her just before she hit the water.

Caspersen puffed his way to the river edge, but was just too late, catching sight of the girl's tunic disappearing beneath the heaving surface for only a second or two.

Lining up his pistol, he waited for her to resurface, but she did not.

Wiping away the blood as it dripped from his forehead into his eyes, he emptied the remaining bullets in his clip into the water where she had disappeared.

"Faen! Faen! Jævla kjerring! " he shouted in anger. The bitch had almost destroyed their plans.

The bitch *must* be dead, he thought, for he had seen the pink spray of blood when his shot had hit the girl in the back. They should have killed her at the beginning and dumped her body in the river. They would have been well away and safe before she would have been found.

Fucking Fosse! How could he think of a quick fuck when the mission should come first?

With one last look at the frothing, seething river hiding their secret, he turned back for the car.

There was no time to spare. There was no more time, they would have to leave soon, now if at all possible, at the very latest tonight, come what may.

There was no more time for further preparations thanks to that damned woman, he thought darkly.

"FAEN!" he swore again.

Fosse was sitting in the road, uniform ripped and bloody and holding his face. Caspersen could hear his pitiful groaning even from the river bank.

At least the blundering idiot was still alive. His knowledge and experience of AI was central to the success of their mission.

There was still a very good chance that despite the complications of that bloody girl's involvement, they might yet succeed in their mission in bringing back to their Nazi overlords a fully functional example of a Beaufighter (with its immensely precious collection of electronics) by flying it to a *Luftwaffe* airbase.

With a bit of luck she ought to be dead by gunshot or drowned.
Bitch.

Chapter 40

Molly took off her shoes and sat down with a sigh, her heart still beating wildly.

What had that madman been thinking? The near collision with the onrushing car had been so close, it seemed that there was no way that they would not run into one another.

The whole thing had happened so fast, but Molly was certain it was one of B-Flight's Norwegians staring back at her through the windscreen, a maddened, bloodied stare that still sent terror skittering down her spine. It had been the look of a desperate animal, and she could have sworn that staring face was covered with blood.

She really ought to get up, make herself a cup of tea and change out of her uniform, but she remained where she was. How quickly death could come, lightning fast and without any warning.

Harry would have been preparing himself for the night's work, whilst she could have been lying dead on the road in the middle of a pile of twisted metal.

First thing in the morning she would report the incident to James. Let the CO sort things out. They were his damned crew after all.

Her heartbeat gradually slowed to a calmer pace, and with it her anger cooled.

Best have that cup of tea.

There was light tap on the kitchen window, quickly repeated.

Tink; tink.

Suddenly alert, her brow creasing, Molly leant forward to look into the kitchen.

Tink, tink, tink, tink, tink.

What on earth?

Padding lightly and slowly into the kitchen, her eyes fixed on the window, Molly reached down into the umbrella stand to carefully pick up Rose's old school cricket bat, scarred and dented from past heroics in his early teens.

If there was someone out there who should not be out there, Harry's bat would gain another battle honour and a very unlucky someone would collect a dent in their luckless skull.

Tink, tink, tink, tink.

A cold shiver spiked through her. What if it was a German soldier? What if there had been a paratrooper landing? What if it was a shot down enemy flyer, on the run?

But of course, if it were a German soldier lurking out there in the shadows, he wouldn't be knocking, but would instead have kicked in the door. She giggled to herself, and she fancied she could hear a touch of hysteria in it.

Only someone up to no good would knock so timidly, and remain hidden as they did so.

An enemy flyer then? Hunted and on the run? Desperate and dangerous?

Tink, tink, tink, tink.

Molly's slippery grip firmed on the handle. If it were an enemy on the run, she would knock his bloody block right off. She owed the Germans for killing her girls at RAF Foxton last year.

Owed it to them with interest.

She took a deep breath, realising that she had been holding it. If it *was* an enemy flyer they were in a for a very nasty surprise.

Come on, then, you bloody Nazi, I'm going to make sure you regret ever attacking us...

Her fingers tightened around the handle of the bat.

To her surprise, she found that she rather hoped that it *was* a German trying to get in.

Molly sensed movement and suddenly noticed that there were three fingers resting against the lowest pane of the window, a quivering forefinger raised against the glass, whilst the rest of whoever was out there remained hidden below the level of the sill.

Molly reached down for the key in the door, tensing to jump out and deliver a first blow, the bat held low to swing up into any attacker's unprotected crotch or, better still, catch their face if they were still crouched down, when a dark shape suddenly rose up to the window in the ebbing light outside.

Stifling a scream from bubbling up, Molly half-raised the bat before recognising that there was something familiar about the bedraggled figure outside.

"Elsie? *Elsie!* Oh my God!"

Dropping her wooden weapon, Molly hastily fumbled the key and opened the door, stepping back as the girl outside stumbled into the kitchen.

The girl was soaked through and shivering, her tunic, skirt and shoes gone, wet hair hanging down lank, dirty shirt clinging to her body, whilst sagging and sopping stockings drooped to reveal the exposed cleft of her pale bottom. A dead leaf clung forlornly to a patch of dirt on one buttock.

Conscious of a sudden feeling of the immediacy of danger, Molly

427

banged shut the door and locked it, eyes anxiously scanning for a second to see if there were anyone outside, but there was no one else, either in the garden or beyond.

"Oh Elsie!" the girl looked exhausted, and fell to her knees on the floor, eyes haunted and terrified in a pale and dirty face, her lips swollen and torn.

"Ma'am…," the girl gasped for breath and closed her eyes, one dirty hand clasped hard against her chest, the other raised palm outwards.

Molly stared aghast, the girl was a mess, and she was bleeding, and not just from the scratches and contusions on her face and arms, but from a weeping angry red wound with torn and filthy edges on her arm.

She had seen enough already in this awful war to know that it was a bullet wound.

And, merciful goodness, where on earth had her knickers gone? She felt her eyes drawn again to Elsie's semi-exposed buttocks.

An icy dread stabbed her heart.

No.

Oh, please, no.

Dear Lord, had Elsie been…? Her mind skittered away from the horrible possibility.

"Fosse," Elsie muttered, and gasped another breath, "Fosse, Ma'am…"

The unwelcome memory of a line of dead girls in bloodied and torn RAF blue pushed into her mind, but this time instead of just the heart breaking sorrow, there was also a burgeoning flare of burning anger.

Who had done this?

Who had *dared* to injure one of her girls so cruelly?

Molly felt like screaming in incandescent rage, but her voice was gentle, if a little tremulous, "Fosse?" a flash in her memory of a tall unsmiling Norwegian, one of B-Flight's Beaufighter AI operators.

The revelation shocked her, for she and Rose greatly admired the gallant Norwegians, fighting courageously alongside them against a shared enemy.

One of the men in Harry's flight, for heaven's sake!

She ran back to the couch and pulled off the throw.

"Oh Elsie, who did this to you? Did that man...um, touch you?"

Elsie's chest was still rising and falling rapidly, but this time she was able to speak, as Molly arranged the throw over her.

"He did, and he would have done a lot more than that, Ma'am, a lot more, but I stuck my hat pin into his fucking eye before he could," she gasped another ragged breath, "That cooled his ardour a bit, he fell out of the car. Should have cracked his bloody skull open if there's any justice."

She grimaced gingerly and touched her lacerated arm. "I think he shot me, but I think it's only a flesh wound, stings like a bastard." She blinked, "Him or that other fucker." Fresh blood dripped from her torn and bruised lips.

The girl's eyes were brimming wet with unshed tears, but her jaw was firm even as she continued to tremble. "I managed to get to the river, and I swam with the current."

Molly stood and stared out of the window into the gathering gloom, across the meadow behind their cottage, even though the river wasn't visible.

"Good God! You swam in the river after being shot?" before this she would never have thought it possible.

Through bleary and reddened eyes Elsie regarded Molly as if she were a stupid child, "I told you before, Ma'am, my old man was a fisherman. He taught me to swim before I even learned to walk. He took me fishing on his trawler the first time when I was ten."

She coughed and grimaced, her voice still ragged but tinged with pride, "He'd kill me if I ever dared to drown."

Molly's voice was gentle, "I need to get you dry, Elsie." She hesitated, nails cutting into her palms. "Elsie. What happened to your clothes...?"

"I shrugged 'em off in the water, they'd have weighed me down, and I was scared I might not make it." The girl smiled shakily, "My old man would've killed me! I kept my shirt and stockings, though. I'm a good girl, not a tart."

The girl's words were defiant, remembering those eager fingers sliding beneath her skirt, and she shuddered again. Angry tears spilled down her already damp cheeks.

"Where're your knickers, though, Elsie?"

The girl sighed and rolled her eyes, "Don't ask, Ma'am, it's a long story."

Molly sighed and stood up, "Right, well, let me get some towels and clothes for you. Then I'll get the stove going and dry you out, you poor thing, and make us both a nice cup of tea."

"NO!"

Molly started in shock at Elsie's sudden cry, and the girl smiled weakly in apology, but her words were urgent, "No, Ma'am, sorry. There's not a moment to lose. We need to get back to the airfield, Ma'am. I'm not sure, but I think it's important."

"What on earth? Why?"

"I overheard Fosse and Caspersen talking, Ma'am, at the Inn, and they said something about taking a plane and firing flares to be safe. It sounded a bit fishy to me. They mentioned a name, but I can't remember it properly now. It was important to them."

Elsie's brow furrowed and her eyes narrowed as she struggled to remember the unfamiliar words. They'd sounded foreign…

"I can't rightly remember, Ma'am. It sounded a bit like 'Hillsy-aryan.' D'you know what that is, Ma'am?"

It sounded familiar, but Molly shook her head, "Oh, goodness me! Don't worry about that, Elsie; we'll talk about it once you've warmed up a bit."

She touched Elsie's face gently, "Oh, my dear! You're like a block of ice! It's amazing you haven't frozen to death already! And that wound! We must dress it properly, at least for the moment."

Molly smiled at the girl reassuringly, "We'll drive down to the airfield straight after, get you to the MO, and I'll have a word with the CO."

The girl bit her lip, just shivering occasionally now, and shook her head.

"No, Ma'am, please. It won't wait. I think it's really important about them taking a plane. Caspersen seemed a bit put out that I might have heard."

Elsie's breathing had settled, her chest no longer heaving, but there was a strange brightness in her eyes. *I'll get that dirty pervert!*

Molly frowned, "Surely they can't do much in the next hour or so? You're as cold as ice, girl! I'll not let you catch your death. Let's get you out of those wet clothes and into something dry."

Grabbing the towel they used to dry the dishes, Molly made to dry Elsie's hair.

"Come along, dear, then I'll make you a nice hot toddy." She patted Elsie kindly on the shoulder.

The girl's eyes flashed, "The cold can't hurt me, Ma'am, there's Viking blood running hot through these veins. That bastard touched my boob and then he was about to finger me. He would have forced me to be with him, you know, lay with him…"

She shuddered, a spasm that shook her entire body as she remembered his breath hot against her skin, body hard against her, the eager hand sliding up her thigh to her crotch, what might have been had she not fought, "First he tried to get into my drawers, and then the other one shot me!"

Elsie struggled to her feet, the trembling now muted, but her eyes burned with anger and humiliation.

"He would have forced me," she repeated, and then she smiled, a tooth-filled grimace that resonated thickly of blood and pain, "But I cooled his ardour for him. He had his hand right up my skirt when I stuck my hatpin in his fucking eye! You should have heard him scream! Like a pig!"

Molly felt like weeping at this new and awful revelation, even as anger flared afresh, "Oh, Elsie, my poor, dear, dear girl."

She blinked her misting, stinging eyes, nose heavy with liquid sorrow, "Come on, then. Let's get you dry and dressed, we'll bind your injury and get you to the airfield, I promise. Just get you dry first, though. Then you can have a word with the Wingco and we'll get your wounds dressed properly by the MO at the same time."

Chapter 41

Corporal Frank Suggs, veteran of the North West Frontier province, stared with more than a little concern as the little red sports car screeched an erratic path towards his guardhouse.

Dear God. That bloody woman again. Couldn't she just let him have a peaceful night for once? Better to get a bullet in the gut from a bloody Jerry paratrooper than die crushed beneath the wheels of that ridiculous little car.

The long-healed scar on his neck, legacy of a bullet fired from a long barrelled *Jezail* in a high mountain pass with a name he could not pronounce, prickled as the little car skidded to a halt scant inches from knees that yearned to knock, stilled into immobility by years of will power and stern training.

He noticed there were two people in the car, and he moved to the driver's side.

The figure in the passenger's seat stood up unsteadily, drunkenly, he fancied almost in indignation.

"Frankie! Let us through!"

Surprised, all pretence of military bearing and decorum forgotten, Suggs gaped and peered uncertainly at the figure, noticing it was a WAAF officer, but it wasn't the Squadron Officer, the Flight Officer's uniform tunic she wore open and ill-fitting over a pair of dungarees.

The woman wore a wide-brimmed summer hat, tied down by a scarf over a grimy balaclava, but the face beneath the cap was one he knew well.

"Elsie!" He roared in outrage. "What on earth are you doing? That's no' your uniform! For Christ's sake, scarper before the Warrant rolls up. He's doing the rounds!" he looked around anxiously but there was no sign of the Station Warrant Officer.

The girl leaned forward, clutching the windscreen precariously. "Don't play silly beggars, Frankie, let us through!" her voice was thin in the darkness.

Oh, Elsie, you're slurring, you've been on the drink, I should report you, but I can't. You silly girl! And why on earth is the Squadron Officer with you. It'll reflect badly on her if this gets out. He felt a strange sense of disappointment. What was the service coming to?

"Me? Play silly beggars?" he roared indignantly, "You're the one masquerading as an officer? What's going on? Are you trying to get court-martialled?"

"Corporal Suggs!" the woman behind the wheel half stood, "Sit down, Elsie, for goodness sake! You'll fall over!" she turned to address Suggs once more.

"Corporal, get your bloody finger out and let us through. I've no time for this nonsense! Get that fucking barrier up! Now! That's an order!"

Suggs gaped anew, his rifle bayonet drooped, and even Elsie looked stunned. She subsided slowly back into her seat.

Molly looked across to the private peering nervously out of the guardhouse.

"You there! Don't just stand there like a blithering idiot, move your bloody backside, get the barrier up! Then call the HQ building and tell them that I'm on my way and to get the doctor out of bed for a bullet injury. Tell him to meet us there. Oh, and get hold of the CO, tell him to meet us there too, alright? Got that?"

The sentry nodded jerkily and disappeared into the hut as the Corporal slowly raised the barrier.

Bullet injury? Aiding and abetting. Oh my Gawd…

She was talking to him again, "Suggs, get in, man! Hop in, I need you to arrest someone. Come on then, sharpish, don't hang about!"

As if in a dream, Suggs thought for a moment, then shouldered his rifle, and climbed onto the running board next to Elsie, and was shocked by how pale and tired the girl looked. She looked all in.

"Elsie?"

Her face was bruised and creased with pain, and her voice was a whisper now. "I'll tell you later, Frankie. Just hold on tight!"

Her breathing was shallow and laboured, and Suggs, gripping the side of the car as hard as he could, gazed helplessly down at her.

Next to her, Molly frowned grimly, and pushed down hard on the accelerator.

The lonely figure of the Wing Commander was standing outside the Headquarters building as Molly slewed to a stop beside it, Suggs hanging on for dear life.

"Will someone tell what on earth is going on?" he barked, "Molly, what the devil…?"

The petite WAAF officer who stepped from the car was not the one he was accustomed to.

It *was* his Molly, but there was a brittle hardness in her manner, a frozen darkness in her eyes that made a tiny part of him shiver.

"Sir, the doctor?"

"On his way, Molly. Why…?" He caught sight of Elsie as she struggled from the car with Suggs help, and his eyes widened with shock.

435

Her endless source of energy was visibly depleted, and Molly put an arm around her.

On Elsie's other side Suggs tried to hold her up, surreptitiously slipping a supporting arm around the girl's waist, whilst also trying to adopt a semblance of standing to attention.

James was aghast, staring in disbelief for a moment at the sight, his excellent catering NCO clad in the most outrageous ensemble, being held upright by his superb senior WAAF on one side and one of his most trusted and reliable security people on the other.

"Dear God, quickly, bring her in, bring her in."

Inside, James pulled out a chair and Elsie's erstwhile assistants helped her into it. Molly helped her remove the ridiculous headgear and wiped her strained face.

James felt an icy hand settle over his heart, the girl looked so vulnerable as Molly fussed with her hair.

As they settled her in the chair, James strode to the telephone, snatched up the receiver, and bellowed into it at the sleepy WAAF on the switchboard, "Where's that bloody doctor! Get him here NOW!" he banged down the telephone so hard Molly feared it would break.

Molly took his elbow. "Sir, there's something fishy going on, Elsie's been shot, but she insisted on talking to you before getting medical attention."

James knelt before Elsie, "Elsie? You wanted to tell me something?" his voice was soft, little more than a whisper. "What was it?"

A single tear tracked down one filthy and already tear-stained cheek.

"Sir, I heard either Caspersen or Fosse say something about taking a plane to some place called Hillsy-something. When they thought I'd heard something, they kidnapped me and they would have hurt me but for the fact that I stuck a hair pin into Fosse."

"Take a plane to Hillsy something?" James' face was thoughtful. "Suggs?"

"The Norwegian gentlemen," Suggs began, but then he grimaced, Fosse and Caspersen were *not* gentlemen in any shape or form, and he'd not address them as such.

"I mean those officers, arrived at the front gate about an hour ago, sir, and they said that they'd been in an accident, there was blood all over their uniforms, so I asked them to go directly to the sick quarters."

Suggs swallowed, "Sir, I'm sorry if I've done wrong, but, they might still be there? Do you want me to get an escort and get them? The both looked to be in a bit of a bad way…"

James face was wooden, and he nodded, "Yes, go and get them, in shackles if you must."

Suggs reached for the telephone on the desk.

Just then the door crashed open and the duty doctor, a fleshy, amiable and highly capable Flight Lieutenant by the name of Andrew 'Bruiser' Brown, lumbered into the room.

"Bruiser! Thank goodness you're here! You need you to look at Elsie, as quick as you like. Are Fosse and Caspersen still in the sick quarters or have they been discharged?"

Brown was already kneeling before Elsie, gentle fingers pulling back the shoulder strap of the dungarees, exposing the torn flesh.

"Hm, nasty. I need to get you back to the sick quarters, Elsie, no peeling potatoes for a little while, I fear. I'll miss your chips. Fosse and Caspersen you say, sir?"

"The new crew on B-Flight, the Norwegians?"

Brown raised his eyebrows and puffed out his cheeks as he unclipped his bag and pulled out a dressing. Outside, the sound of engines grumbled as the crews continued their preparations for the night's preparations.

"Still bleeding, let's dress it before moving you, Elsie, don't want to lose any more of the red sauce than you have already, my dear. Not to worry, have you right as rain in a tick." He nodded at the uniform jacket she still wore, "I see you've been promoted again."

Brown deftly unrolled a bandage with one hand, "Norwegians, sir? The only Norwegian I've seen today was the other lad from B-Flight, that young Olaf. Had a nasty crack on the ol' noggin, I've given him a sedative. Should be fine, no flying for a while, though. I say, Elsie! Isn't he your young man?"

Worry flooded across the girl's face. "Olaf? Oh no! He was supposed to meet me after I came out of the lavatory."

James looked bewildered for an instant, before his face cleared, "They never went to the sick quarters! So where...?"

And then he smacked the wall in anger. Suggs flinched, "Of course, I've been an idiot! They came back here for their Beaufighter! They must be Nazi sympathisers! Hillsy-something you said, Elsie? Oh my God! I know what they intend to do now. They're going to steal their kite and fly it to Gilze-Rijen in Holland. The Luftwaffe has a major night-fighter base over there!"

He strode back to the telephone, "Get me the control tower." He waited for a moment, and then, "Johnny? This is James. Hm? Yes, yes, thank you. Johnny, now, have you given flying clearance for any members of B-Flight? Rose and Barr? What's that? Caspersen's just asked for it? Last minute air test?" he looked at the others, his face drawn with tension. "We're too late, they're already taxiing!"

He turned to the duty officer sitting aghast in the corner. "Sutton, alert the defences, target the Beaufighter."

"Uh, which one, sir?" she asked.

James looked crestfallen, "Mm, see your point. Can't have the AA bods shooting at Beaufighters willy nilly, could cause a lot of confusion. Don't want the silly buggers shooting down our own ones."

Molly jumped up, "Corporal, come with me, and bring that rifle of yours." She patted Brown's shoulder, "Look after her, Bruiser, she's been through a lot."

He didn't look up, "I will, Ma'am. She'll be fine, she's a fighter."

James stood, "I'll drive, Molly, you stay here."

Molly shook her head, "No, sir, you need to alert the authorities. We need to stop them getting away. Can't let the Nazis get their hands on that Beaufighter."

James nodded regretfully, not liking it but there was no time to argue, and Molly's words made sense. "You're right, of course. I'll contact Group, get fighters in the air. Good luck to you, then, Molly."

"And to you, sir."

Chapter 42

The little red sports car careered wildly towards the main runway as the Beaufighter turned onto it from Dimple Heath's southern ancillary runway.

Suggs gritted his teeth, checked the rifle clip and made sure for the umpteenth time that the safety was off.

He was always telling her to go slow, but now he wished she'd go faster!

What a crazy fucking world it was!

Come on, woman, floor that bloody accelerator! Go faster!

"Get ready, Suggs!" she shouted. Her hat was gone, and her hair streamed back like a banner in the half-light.

What a woman. Like Boudicca racing into battle!

That Flying Officer Rose was one lucky bastard.

"Ma'am. "He half-stood, bracing himself with his right thigh and knee against the backrest and the seat, left leg ramrod straight holding him in position, boots firm in place, and hoping she wouldn't make him pay to clean it.

They were closer, now, and Caspersen opened the throttles.

As the Beaufighter jumped forwards, Molly brought the car alongside, but they would not be able to match the aeroplane's speed for

440

long. She struggled with the wheel, trying to keep the car level with the aeroplane's wingtip.

If they were to get caught in the slipstream, the car would be tossed around or flipped over like a desiccated autumnal leaf.

The car sprung and bounced and Suggs hung on for grim life, his backside slipping and sliding dangerously against the seat back, but his braced legs kept him in.

He brought the rifle up to his shoulder, sighting carefully along the iron sight.

Don't shoot her, for fucks sake…

She could hear them now, inside her mind. Her girls were calling out to her, *avenge us.*

It was a struggle for him to aim the rifle as they bounded around, but he'd fought on the Northwestern Frontier, where the unwary died a horrible death.

He'd learnt to shoot on the limits of the empire, and he'd make each of the bullets in his 10-round magazine count.

Suggs sighted carefully on the Perspex bubble of the Beaufighter, and there was the pale blob of a staring face looking back at him.

Elsie's poor tortured and dirt-stained face came into his mind's eye and he pulled the trigger just as Molly screamed out:

"NOW SUGGS! NOW!"

CRACK! The rifle shot snapped out, and Suggs kept pulling the trigger, sending one .303 round after another into the shape of the speeding Beaufighter.

CRACK!

The Perspex bubble crazed as the round smacked into it. Thank God the Beaufighter wasn't fitted with a rear-facing gun!

CRACK!

Molly saw the Perspex bubble crack and splinter, the cacophany from the shots, the screaming Bristol engines and her car's wildly racing engine deafening her.

CRACK!

Suggs legs strained to keep him braced as the car jounced along, the recoil from his rifle threatening to knock him off his feet.

CRACK!

She would have grabbed his greatcoat to help keep him stable, but she daren't let go of the wheel.

CRACK!

Please God, don't let a tyre puncture, she prayed silently. At this speed they'd have no chance.

The aeroplane was pulling away now, holes appearing as if by magic in its fuselage as the bullets ripped into it.

CRACK! There were three holes now against the AI operator's position. Suggs must be aiming to damage the box of tricks.

I hope that hit you too, you damned pervert, she thought vengefully. In her ears, blending into the harsh dissonance of the screaming engines, screeching tyres and rifle shots, she could hear the merciless cries of her dead girls for revenge. If Suggs fell she would drive into the tailplane and destabilise the aeroplane's takeoff.

CRACK! Another shot spat out at the squat shape alongside. The Beaufighter was ahead now, and she could feel the effect of the propeller wash and its slipstream.

She fought with the wheel to keep it steady. Her arms and legs aching brutally as the aircraft gradually began to open the distance between them.

Don't waste your shots, she ached to cry out but she couldn't utter a sound, *fire at the fucking engines!*

How Suggs had managed to stay inside the car and shoot so well was anybody's guess.

CRACK!

She didn't see the penultimate .303 round bury itself in the starboard engine. Her eyes felt as if they'd been immersed in a bucket of sand, her tongue stuck against the roof of her mouth and she could feel the car slipping, whipping wildly, any second now she'd have to finish this.

For an instant she lost control but regained it almost instantaneously before they slipped off the runway. Her heart was banging wickedly inside her, and her hands were slipping on the wheel now.

Oh God, we're too close, can't hold her steady...open the distance between us before we get flipped over...

Is this what it was like for Harry? The excitement and the numbing fear of impending death?

She could feel the satisfaction of her dead girls as the rifle thumped out again so close above her head.

CRACK! Another round, last one, again into the engine, but it continued to roar smoothly.

The big fighter's wheels lifted from the runway.

Time to go! Gratefully Molly eased off the accelerator, let the car slow and skirt the edge of the runway as the Beaufighter, carrying all ten of Sugg's .303 rounds with it, thundered off into the approaching darkness.

James must have told Dimple Heath's defences not to engage the Beaufighter, for it disappeared without a single AA shell being fired at it.

Too close to the edge, the car bumped and lurched as the rear tyre caught the rougher earth.

Molly's right nearside tyre slipped onto soft grass and the car slewed around, flinging Suggs from the car, his rifle pirouetting to smash against the side of the car.

The soldier was there one moment, and gone the next, disappearing without a sound. Amazingly, he did not catch her with his boots on his way out.

Something smacked and ripped at the car's underside.

A cry was torn from her lips as Molly felt herself losing control, see-sawing as a tyre blew against a stone, and, just as she expected the car to flip completely, it suddenly bedded down into the soft earth and stopped dead.

She sat motionless in the car for a moment, unable to believe that she was still alive. The engine was still running, and she reached forward and switched off.

After the deafening noise, the sudden hush was thunderous.

Dearest Harry was always groaning and moaning about her seat-belt, so much so that putting it on had become automatic, and now she thanked God for it. The little leather strap had held her in safely in her seat.

The car hissed and sighed and ticked, and she patted it affectionately. She felt a sudden urge to burst into tears and with an effort she controlled herself.

They had done all they could, and with a bit of luck, they'd inflicted enough damage to spoil Fosse and Caspersen's day, although if truth be told, Elsie had been responsible in large part for doing that already.

She closed her eyes, breathed out and took another long, deep breath in.

Her nostrils were filled with the dizzying blend of fresh earth, dope, oil, acrid smoke from the Beaufighter's exhausts, hot metal, and petrol.

Petrol? Oh no…!

Desperately, Molly ripped off her seat belt and knocked open the door, it caught on the earth, and she kicked it hard, stubbing her toes and jarring her leg, but it opened further and she launched herself out of her seat, fighting her way out of the car.

One of her shoes had come off but she left it where it was, she was scrabbling on her hands and knees on the grass and she fought her way onto her feet and ran as fast as she could away from the car, her injured leg aching.

She could see Suggs lying motionless on the darkened edge of the runway, and she ran unsteadily to him, limping, expecting any moment to hear the fuel tank in her little car blow.

"Corporal Suggs!"

He was lying on his back, eyes wide, and at first she feared the worst, but as she came up to him, he sat up with a groan, face heavily lined with pain.

"Blinkin' heck, that was a ride and a half!" he turned his head one way then the other, testing his neck. "I think I understand now why Mr Rose always looks a bit pale, Ma'am, poor blighter."

Molly giggled with relief. "Don't be cheeky, Corporal!"

He turned to look at her. "I've lost my bloody rifle!" he peered up at her, made as if to get to his feet, swayed, thought better of it and stayed where he was.

"Well done, Ma'am. You were amazing. How you kept the car under control in that slipstream beats the hell out of me!" he groaned, looked at her feet, "you've lost a shoe."

Suggs shook his head and looked at her dazedly. "Fuck me, what a night. Pardon the French. Are you OK, Ma'am?"

She smiled shakily back at him, "Quite well, thank you, Suggs. That was very good shooting. I'm sure you did some damage. Hopefully at least one of them collected a bullet in the guts!"

"I shot at both crew positions and the engine, Ma'am." He shifted his position, and she saw the agony on his face. He hadn't escaped scot-free. "I've guarded the kites during maintenance. The lads told me where the box of tricks was. I had an idea where to shoot," he gasped.

She looked towards the eastern night sky, but the Beaufighter had disappeared. "Did we do enough…?"

Behind her the flames reached the torn fuel tank at last, but it was nearly empty, and there was a little, almost apologetic *Whump!* That they felt more than heard, but it ensured that Molly would never drive her car ever again.

Molly didn't turn to look. She didn't want to see her little red car, such an important piece of her life, die. It was like the death of the dearest of friends.

The damned Luftwaffe (curse them!) had been unable to destroy her dear little car even when they had destroyed the rest of RAF Foxton. And killed her girls.

But their cries for retribution, cries that never fully left her mind for so long, were silent now.

At her feet Suggs lay back down, trying to clear his befuddled mind as waves of pain deluged his senses.

Tears welled in her eyes, but she smiled through them as James pulled up in his car.

His face was appalled as he stepped onto the runway, "Molly?" his eyes took in the montage of his people and the flames bright behind them.

"We did our best, Sir. I just hope it was enough."

She nodded at him calmly, dark liquid eyes serene, despite the trembling of her hands, a girl with one shoe, dishevelled uniform and torn stockings, tear stains down her cheeks, cut and bruised and with her open hair a dark halo catching the breeze. She looked magnificent, a warrior. Bloodied but unbowed.

At her feet lay the winded, injured soldier, knocked about and dazed, gasping in pain, looking about him as if he wasn't quite sure where he was, whilst some distance behind her the little red car she adored so much burned quietly in its last resting place, a worthy combatant in its own personal Viking funeral.

It was unutterably splendid and a sight he would never, ever, forget.

"Your best was truly amazing. *Amazing.* Truly. I can see why the powers-that-be saw fit to award you a George Cross." He shook his head in wonder.

Molly smiled tremulously at him, trying to calm the quivering, but her ears were still ringing, almost deafened by the rifle firing so close above her head, and the thunderous sound of the screaming Hercules.

"Every day I find out how incredible my people are," he spoke softly, almost to himself. "I can't find words to describe what I've just witnessed. All I can say is that the spirit of British heroism lives on. Come on, let's get you back. Get a nice hot cup of sweet tea into you."

James looked uncertainly at the soldier sprawled on the runway." Both of you." He added, "Are you alright, Suggs, old chap? Can you get up, at all?"

The soldier tried stiffly to get to his feet, and promptly fell back onto his backside with a low moan as his leg gave way.

"I've lost my rifle, sir." His face was drawn.

Suggs sounded distraught at the loss. Luckily, he hadn't yet realised that his helmet had disappeared somewhere, too. The bloody man would be suicidal if he knew that was missing as well.

"Don't worry about that now, for goodness sake! The ambulance and fire truck are on their way…"

James heaved a sigh, he could feel the treacherous prickling of tears behind his eyes, and there was curious thickness developing in his throat and nose.

Don't cry…

In the distance behind he could hear shouts and the tinkle of the ambulance and fire tender, and a proud tear ran down his cheek.

His voice was gruff, stiff with emotion. "Forget about the bloody rifle, *Sergeant* Suggs, I'm going to make sure you get a third stripe and a decoration for your actions this evening, same for our Elsie."

He coughed to clear his throat and smiled again at the tired and stained girl, "You and Elsie and our unbelievably extraordinary Squadron Officer here. I could not have asked for more. Courage, quick thinking and action. Amazing. Bloody amazing."

Molly closed her eyes for a moment, and he steadied her gently as she swayed. Suggs groaned quietly and passed out.

James had to pause for a moment, lest the depth of his pride betray him, "I'm so very proud of you both, of all three of you. You acted in the very finest traditions of the service." He looked away so that she would not see the brimming glisten of his eyes.

"All I can say is thank you. It seems a bit inadequate, but it's all I have to give you for the moment. Your deeds were mighty, yours and Elsie's. I'll see that your actions are recognised."

His voice caught in his throat, "Thank you."

Chapter 43

Bruno was panting with exertion as he hauled the Junkers from the runway, the screaming Jumo 211 engines pushing them dangerously close to the emergency speed at low-level.

There had been no warning of the scrambling series of urgent take-offs. Already two Junkers 88s of his *staffel* had disappeared into the darkness, and his was the third of the four crews available being sent out.

It had been less than fifteen minutes since the crews had been roused by the shrilly squawking tannoy from a late snack of *knockwurst, brötchen* and hot black coffee.

"Alarm, Notruf-Alarm!"

As Gilze-Rijen vanished into the murk behind them, Rudi diffidently turned to his pilot.

"Herr Leutnant, care to tell us what's going on?"

"You won't believe it; I don't believe it, it's like something out of a film!"

"What is?"

Bruno hesitated, but how much could he divulge to his lads? Oh sod it! Telling wouldn't make any difference now. If the German crew got away they'd got away, talking about it wouldn't make a difference now.

"We're on a special mission. It looks as if the Abwehr managed to get a couple of our aircrew boys past British Intelligence, and it seems they've managed to steal one of their night fighters. We're not sure where, if, they're coming in so we're to form a welcoming cordon, and if necessary, provide protective cover. Hope they make it."

Rudi looked confused, but Mouse crowed, "Whoo-hoo! If that's so it'll make our job so much easier!" *It'll become so much easier for us to fight if we get the same tools*! "I hope it's true, *Herr Leutnant*!"

Sitting behind them, Mouse pulled out a *knockwurst* wrapped in a thick slice of black bread and bit into it contentedly. The fragrance of his snack filled the interior of the cockpit, and Rudi shook his head in disgust.

Mouse was happy. It didn't matter to him why they were flying, all that it meant was that, with a bit of luck, he might get the chance of firing his beloved guns at some damned Tommies.

Herbert banged the side of B-Baker's cockpit with one hand, "C'mon Trolley, can you see them?"

'Trolley' Trent's voice sounded apologetically over the intercom. "Sorry, boss, nothing doing."

Herbert cursed foully, then, "Dagger 5 to Lamplight, still no joy. Can you help?"

"Lamplight to Dagger 5, the bandit is one mile ahead and below you one angel. Intercept and destroy, immediate. Bandit is confirmed as hostile."

Herbert's forehead creased in bafflement. Bandit is confirmed as hostile? What on earth did they mean? Must be hostile, wouldn't be a bandit otherwise. Would it?

"Something a bit queer's going on, Trolley, any luck?"

"Nothing." Trent's voice was heavy with disgust. "Can't pick up a blessed thing"

"Well give the fucking thing a kick, then!" Herbert pushed the Beaufighter into a sharper descent, they were so damned low, ground-return was interfering badly with the interception.

He sighed and relented, "Trolley, sorry for being snappy, just keep trying to pick it up, OK?"

"That's OK, guv, I understand how you feel. I got crabs from a bint in Southend once. I know what's its like having itchy balls."

Herbert grinned despite himself, "Just keep searching, you cheeky wanker…"

The *knockwurst* was long gone, and Mouse belched reflectively, brushed crumbs from his lap. "*Herr Leutnant,* I'm getting really bored. When're you going to give me something to shoot at and kill?"

"Patience, Mouse, patience." Bruno could feel that prickling in his fingers, they were close, he was sure of it.

But was his Junkers close enough?

The Brass had told Bruno and his fellow *Staffel*-mates in that rushed briefing to get as close to the English coast as possible. The chance of stealing enemy technology did not come every day.

With the enemy's magic, *Luftwaffe* crews would turn the airspace of Britain into a happy hunting ground.

They were to get close and fly offshore, but Bruno decided to go one better.

His Junkers was drawing closer to the coast, and he intended to fly along the coastline, just inland, in a pattern that covered the sector assigned to his crew. But he would stay low, really low.

And if they managed to bag a bomber or two while they were there, then all the better.

He explained the plan to them, but Rudi was doubtful of Bruno's wisdom. What if they'd missed the rogue RAF aeroplane? They'd be wandering around up there waiting for someone to notice and shoot them down.

The British night fighters were uncannily good in their interceptions.

Hell, they might even be shot down by their eager *Staffel*-mates in a case of mistaken identity.

"*Herr Leutnant*, perhaps we're a bit closer than we ought to be?" Rudi tried to keep his voice level.

"No, we'll stay here for a little while. If they're out over the water, we'll cover their arses, close the door on any pursuit." He was less certain than he sounded, and there was quite a bit of area to cover.

"Don't worry, Rudi," rumbled Mouse, "Don't piss yourself, we aren't close enough yet. I can't smell the haggis yet."

Rudi turned to give Mouse a withering look. "You damned moron, haggis is Scottish, not English. You are so dumb, I can't believe it, how did an idiot like you manage to get into the Luftwaffe?"

Ignoring the banter, Bruno muttered a prayer beneath his breath. The Knight's Cross made a man a champion, but it also meant that he was the one expected to succeed.

The one who *had* to succeed. Time after time.

A blessing and a curse, all rolled into one, which was the lot of the champion.

But it was not something he would change. Ever.

The medal felt good at his throat. It was a symbol that showed he was the one the others would look to, the one that others would follow.

And come what may, he *would* be successful.

"Contact! Dead ahead and a little below, range half a mile. See anything, boss?"

At the same moment as Trent called out the contact, Herbert noticed a thin line of smoke tenuously stretching out ahead of the Beaufighter.

"OK, I can see something, but don't lose touch with what you have, I may still need you to guide me in, Trolley. There's some kind of smoke trail in front of us, I'll follow it, hopefully should lead us to the target. Are we drawing closer, pal?"

"We're closing fast, Boss, down to a quarter of a mile, ease off the throttles, we're still a little above. Yuck, I can smell that smoke, bit grim, isn't it?"

Even as Herbert eased the snarl of the engines back into a grumbling roar, and the vibration in the airframe lessened, the opacity of the banner of smoke deepened, and suddenly the target aircraft appeared, a vague outline towing the streamer of stinking smoke behind it.

The bitter odour of scorched metal and burnt oil filled their nostrils, but amazingly there were still no visible flames from that injured port engine on the other aircraft, and it continued on its way.

"I can see it, Trolley! Bandit dead ahead, we're catching up fast, I think he's a Junkers, twin engine job, take a look. See what I see?"

"Gotcha, boss. Definitely a twin, um, could be a Junkers 88. Wait…stop! It looks like a Beau!"

Herbert stared in disbelief at the dim shape. Despite the poor light, Trent was right.

With every passing second, they were drawing closer to an aircraft identical in shape to their own and bearing the same markings but one from which smoke belched.

But despite the smoke, there were no flames, and the prop was still turning normally. Its nose was pointed unerringly into the North Sea, not for home.

"What the hell? It's one of ours! Fuck, it's those Froggies!"

453

It was surreal, the Beaufighter before them flying steadily as if they were not there, no acknowledgement to their presence.

"They're Norwegians, you bloody plank, not blinking Frenchmen!" Something was really wrong here, Herbert wondered, why, with a damaged motor, was it heading away from Dimple Heath?

"Dagger 5 to Lamplight, bogey is friendly. Repeat, bogey is friendly, bogey is Dagger 6."

The coast was close, would pass beneath the nose of their fighter in a few seconds.

"Dagger 5, bogey is not friendly, bogey is a hostile, engage immediately!"

What was this madness? *Dagger 6 was a hostile?* There had to be some kind of mistake, surely?

"Dagger 5 to lamplight, please repeat? Dagger 6 is hostile? Confirm, please?" *Hostile? What the hell?*

"Lamplight to Dagger 5, engage, Dagger 5, engage immediately! Destroy your target! Confirmed hostile!"

Fucking hell! "Hang on to your bollocks, Trolley, we're attacking."

Bruno felt like shouting with joy when he saw the Beaufighter, drawing a line a thin trail of smoke behind it as it sped over the coast and headed eastwards in the general direction of Holland.

It was them! Their timing could not have been more perfect. He had been right!

"My God!" breathed Rudi in awe, staring up as the shadow passed above them, "How did you manage to do that?"

And then he started in shock, for above them a second shape had joined the first, slipping into formation behind and to one side of the smoking fighter.

"Nobody said anything about two enemy aeroplanes! Can you

454

see what's he doing?" Bruno eased back and pulled up his big night fighter, turning gently to cautiously bring the Junkers upwards, but remaining below and behind the two British night fighters.

"Might the agents have pinched two Beaufighters, *Herr Leutnant*?"

"I don't believe so, Rudi, I think our boys are in the wounded one. They didn't get away easily, by the looks of it. Looks as if the second one intercepted them but he doesn't know what to do next, he's either confused or having second thoughts, he's not sure about killing them. They can't have been told yet the target is one of their own."

Bruno shifted in his seat, "Stand by, boys, I'm going to sit back behind and below the second one. If he moves into firing position, on the first one, I'm going to blast him from the sky. If he stays in formation, we'll just keep an eye on him. He's so busy gawping at the first one, he hasn't seen us yet."

But, as soon as their Junkers was positioned comfortably behind and below the second, undamaged Beaufighter, it shifted hesitantly and began to fall back, throttling back to slide behind the damaged aircraft.

"He's decided." Bruno glanced quickly at his controls to ensure everything was in order, "Alright. Here goes…"

Chapter 44

Rose yawned, blinked to clear his tired, dry eyes, and yawned again. Trade was quiet so far, but it was early yet. "Are you eating sweets back there, you cheeky bugger?"

White sounded hurt. "No, Flash, I only had a couple of humbugs left and I've eaten them both. I think we need to go back for supplies."

"Anymore of those sweets and we won't be able to get you through the hatch."

"What are you trying to say? Are you telling me you think I'm getting fat?"

"Oh, I wouldn't quite say that, old son," Rose said dryly, "it's just that whenever I look at you from behind, the words 'ugly', 'barrage' and 'balloon' come to mind. Dunno why."

White sniffed disdainfully, "You know, sometimes you can go right off someone. I'd be grateful if you didn't disturb me for a while. Much as I love the sound of your voice I've far better things to do than chat sweet nothings to you. I'm just going to do an inventory check. I might have a toffee or a pear drop stashed away in one of my pockets. I'm afraid there probably won't be any for you." White didn't sound at all sorry.

Rose smiled to himself, looked down to where Molly's picture graced his control panel. He idly wondered what she was doing.

He scanned his instruments again and began to hum quietly.

"Lamplight to Dagger 3, vector three-two-zero degrees, angels two. Immediate, acknowledge, please."

Immediate? What on earth? What was the range?

"Dagger 3 to Lamplight, vector three-two-zero, angels two, acknowledged."

"Dagger 3 to Lamplight. Received." So, how far to the bandit? Stern chase or an interception? He waited.

But Lamplight remained silent.

Strange. What was going on? "Dagger 3 to Lamplight, any further gen?" *Are we close or not? Do I need to lose height fast?*

"Lamplight to Dagger 3, please follow instructions faithfully, you will be fully debriefed on your return."

Hm, OK. If that was the way they wanted to play it, "Dagger 3 to Lamplight, understood." Keep it succinct.

"Grab yer gnashers, Chalky old chap, we're on."

"I heard Flash, Just when I was hoping they'd call us back for tea and buns and sweeties."

Rose gently pushed forward the throttles and the control column, and the Beaufighter began to descend, the tempo of the engines sending sparks of excitement and apprehension through him.

They were at twelve thousand feet already, so it would take some time to get to two thousand at the current rate of descent.

D-Dog was at six thousand feet and still descending leisurely.

When they'd first crewed together, Rose impressed on White the importance of a good awareness of what was happening around their aircraft.

After flying Hurricanes in daylight, initially Rose found it a significant challenge to adapt to the position of being unable to keep an eye on what was happening to his rear.

Granny had hammered into his head the importance of keeping one eye on his rear-view mirrors, a lesson which greatly helped him in surviving the savagery of last year's desperate fighting when others had not, but such visibility in the Beaufighter was relatively hampered.

With White aboard, and flying by night in limited visibility when enemy interception was a lot less likely, Rose relaxed a little, even though he still found his eyes anxiously straying to the side mirrors he insisted on installing, despite the grinding of Chiefy's teeth, and the (very) slight degradation in aircraft performance.

True, White's dome and the large tailplane limited visibility considerably, and of course in the darkness there was very little visible at all in the mirrors, and certainly the mirrors kept breaking off in the air when Rose heaved the big fighter around in combat, yet Rose continued to insisted new ones be fitted. Their presence made him feel secure, although they were doing the Chief's teeth no favours at all.

The recent shoot down of the Wellington, the deaths of Barlow and Cole and the wreckage of the enemy night fighter found nearby made all of them brutally aware that the hunter so easily turned into the hunted, and that the Luftwaffe was sending marauders ever more frequently into British skies.

When not actively engaged with his AI set, White now spent a lot more time watching the airspace behind and around them.

Even now, as he wistfully rooted through his pockets for a sweet, his eyes were searching the darkened firmament through the Perspex of his dome.

"Lamplight to Dagger 3, please make your angels two, range closing."

"Dagger 3 to Lamplight, am increasing rate of descent to angels two."

Rose pushed the fighter into a steeper downward slope.

They were passing over the coast now, and Rose watched it pass beneath them regretfully.

The previous year, many RAF aircrew shot down over The Channel were found dead of hypothermia when help finally reached them, and Rose hated being over water. The thought of being shot down into 'the drink' scared him more than he would care to admit.

Like many of his anxieties, Rose's fear of open water was something he chose not to share with Molly, preferring instead to be the kind of man he thought he ought to be for her, the kind of man such an extraordinary woman deserved..

"Lamplight to Dagger 3, range four miles, flash your weapon, please."

Almost immediately White piped up, "Contact! I have contact, no, wait, two, no, multiple contacts! Bloody hell, Flash! I have more than one!"

Rose's heart slammed uncontrollably hard against his sternum.

Fuck!

What now?

The Beaufighter was speeding after the contacts, trembling and eager like a thoroughbred and the control column stiff in his grip, the enemy was less than a few miles away, and Rose found himself rocking nervously in his harness as they strove to catch up.

"Stand by, Trolley, firing…" the message from Lamplight was clear, the Beaufighter in front of them had to be destroyed.

The other aircraft wasn't making any attempt to evade, making his job a great deal easier.

Herbert mashed down hard on the firing button and their guns coughed out a clipped burst that sprayed the other aircraft, the fire focussing on the undamaged Hercules engine.

The target aircraft before them sparkled and flashed in the darkness, and as fragments flew around and past B-Baker, Herbert ducked involuntarily, but nothing substantial hit them.

He thought nothing of it as the airframe juddered harder around him, but then the starboard engine flared bright and his Beaufighter began to skid out of control as Bruno's cannon shells and bullets smacked into B-Baker.

"*What the fuck?* Trolley, quick, check behind us!"

"Junkers 88 on our tail boss! Jesus! I'm bleeding!" the pain in Trent's voice terrified him.

Herbert fought with the controls, juggling with the throttles as he strove to keep the failing Beaufighter flying. "Trolley, we're proper fucked, pal, bail out, get out! Get out now!" he gasped a breath, *"GET OUT!"*

Trent sounded scared and confused, "I've lost my pinky, boss! Bullet took the top right off it! I saw it happen! I can see the bone! I'm bleeding!"

"Bail out! Get out, you daft bastard! Now! I won't be able to hold it for long! We're near the coast! Try and get as close to it as possible!" Herbert roared, and the gauges shattered before him as a cannon shell ripped into his console, covering him with wickedly sharp slivers of metal, glass and plastic.

Something awful smacked against his goggles, but only cracked one lens. A second wickedly sharp splinter tore open one cheek, but he didn't feel it. "Christ! Get out, get out, oh fuck, get out! GET OUT! *GET OUT!*"

The starboard engine exploded, the flames casting a searingly harsh light onto his ruined instruments, and he knew there was no time.

A shattered length of propeller blade thumping jarringly into the fuselage behind him.

Remarkably, the Beaufighter was still flying, but it would not continue to do so for very long.

Herbert released himself feverishly, reaching for the handholds and yanking himself backwards to the escape hatch, hoping desperately, oh so desperately, that behind him, his wounded friend was doing the same.

Fierce elation snapped through Bruno as his fire ripped through the Beaufighter before him, the bullets and cannon shells shredding the big British night fighter into a tattered and sparking wreck.

Bruno fired his guns the same instant as the pilot of the enemy aircraft, but whilst his gunfire inflicted mortal damage on his unsuspecting victim, the Beaufighter he had been sent to protect, although hit, continued to fly eastwards.

The stricken Beaufighter before him was falling away now, streaming droplets of liquid fire and an object rolled away from it.

Rudi was bouncing in his seat with excitement, "Another one! Well done, *Herr Leutnant*, ooh, that's one of them managed to escape! His parachute's opened nicely."

As Trent's parachute deployed fully, Mouse glanced at it for a second, and he contemplated putting a few rounds from his MG 131 into the delicate fabric dome.

They passed through the thickening and billowing smoke cloud, and the parachute rapidly shrank behind them too fast for him to draw a bead on it.

Damn. That crewman may have been responsible for the death of good bomber crews. Killing him would surely have saved others.

And it would have felt good.

Suddenly a second parachute appeared alongside, billowing like a blossoming flower in the darkness, rapidly following the first.

Mouse smiled grimly, and tilted the machine gun at the helpless pilot of the enemy night fighter beneath the second parachute, finger eagerly tightening on the trigger.

Just a quick burst…

Which was why, most unusually for him, Mouse was completely unprepared for what happened next, when a *third* Beaufighter emerged from the stained darkness of the night.

And, unlike the first two, this one was *behind* Bruno's victorious Junkers.

Chapter 45

The elation Rose felt as he caught sight of the bandit withered almost as soon as it flowered, and he flinched in horror as the Junkers spat out a hail of hot lead and B-Baker flared and died, twitching in agony and dying beneath the storm of withering fire from the German night fighter's guns.

Too late, oh God, too late! Why didn't I dive faster, steeper?

As he willed his aircraft onwards, the other British fighter shook and shivered under the merciless guns of the big German fighter.

Oh God, no!

B-Baker was losing height now, the battered shape now falling rather than flying, and the port wing outboard of the Bristol engine suddenly broke off and whirled away, and the stricken Beaufighter lurched horribly.

No!

Worse still, yet another aeroplane with a very familiar shape (*Another Beaufighter? What's going on?*) was, even now, fleeing from the pursuing Junkers.

Anger pulsed liquid hot through his body, and he closed the distance even as the burning and broken remnants of B-Baker spun away out of control down towards the cold waters below, wreathing the victorious Junkers for an instant in acrid smoke.

Relief spilled through the molten fury like iced water as a parachute emerged from the smoke, luckily well clear of his line of flight.

At least one of the RAF crew had managed to get out of their doomed fighter.

And then, another parachute materialised as if by magic and whipped past to one side of the Junkers.

Two parachutes! That was both of the RAF flyers, and they had survived the destruction of their Beaufighter.

Thank God.

And Rose could wait no longer. He caressed the button hungrily, raging with an incandescent flame from within after seeing the death of the other British fighter, but striving to control his fury and despair.

He considered the angles, shoot before and a little to one side to allow for deflection, play the stream of cannon shells, armour piercing incendiary rounds and high explosive incendiaries over that shadowed shape.

They were just over four hundred yards behind the Junkers now.

At last, they were close enough to destroy the enemy; they *must* be close enough, "Chalky, keep an eye on him in case I lose him in the smoke and darkness, stand by, firing…" and at last he pressed the firing button.

D-Dog shuddered and shook as the cannon and machine guns within her hammered out a powerful two second stream of devastation at the German night fighter, the image of the Junkers shuddering in his windscreen.

Just as he was about to fire his machine gun at the second parachute, Mouse's instincts sensed the presence of death, and his eyes opened wide in shock and his blood turned to ice as the avenging shape of the third Beaufighter soared out at them like some predatory beast of the night.

In that awful moment the veteran German gunner felt an awful helplessness wash over him, and he knew his war was about to end.

Time slowed and dragged as Mouse desperately dragged his gun away from the parachutist and onto the bearing of the RAF night fighter.

But in his desperate haste, as he swung the machine gun onto the new bearing, the barrel hit the traverse check aerial post directly behind the glasshouse cockpit.

Desperately he tried again, wasting precious seconds as he fought to raise the barrel vertically over the post.

"Fucking hell, night fighter! Herr Leutnant...!"

And then the nose of the Beaufighter lit blindingly, and for a split second Mouse, wrestling with a gun that he once thought of as a dear friend, yet which now which fought him, saw bright silver skewers bursting out from it and lancing unerringly towards them.

D-Dog's first burst slammed blisteringly into the Junkers 88, tearing into the port wing and engine, and suddenly Bruno was fighting with the controls as devastation ripped into the port-side Jumo 211, stitching brutally through the crank case, destroying the crank shaft, pistons, con rods, bearings, cylinder liners and other delicate components, the beautifully crafted aero-engine instantly transformed into twisted, useless, ruined wreckage.

A choking cloud of pitch-black smoke billowed from beneath the cowling of the port radial engine, followed by a thin stream of light-coloured glycol, then replaced by blackest smoke once more, before a jet of searing white flame swept out and backwards towards D-Dog.

With the port motor junked and only his starboard engine now remaining functional, Bruno found the Junkers wanting to roll and

465

yaw to the right, and he frantically struggled with the rudder, trim and ailerons to find that magic balance that might yet save them and keep the battered Junkers in the air.

The next one-second burst from D-Dog's guns passed uselessly just inches over the Junkers' cockpit, but the third entered it.

Mouse was still trying to train his sights on the shape behind them, unable to see anything clearly yet, his night vision wrecked by the bright flare of Rose's first burst, and he jerked at the trigger, hoping for a lucky hit or at least to put the enemy pilot off his aim with return fire.

And even as his last despairing burst spat out, he knew that he was too late.

He'd fucked up, and now there would be a terrible reckoning.

Perspex, plastics and metal erupted in a whirling storm of terror, shocking in its suddenness, shattering as the cannon shells and bullets from Rose's guns smashed their way into the glasshouse cockpit and its delicate contents.

The bullet hit Mouse on the outer upper edge of his goggles, the impact with the edge of the eyepiece causing the course of the piece of speeding metal to turn inwards rather than outwards, such that it slammed (closely accompanied by fragments of glass, plastic and metal) into his left eye, ripping a ragged, pin-wheeling path through his eyeball, breaking the rear of the eye socket and cribriform plate in an expanding wave of shattering destruction that pulverised his brain, before blowing a very large hole out through the back of his head.

Mouse was dead before he even realised he'd been hit, and his corpse jerked fitfully, the triggers tightened by dead fingers sending a flailing stream of bullets arcing uselessly away into the dark emptiness.

Of his last burst, nothing came even remotely close to the pursuing

Beaufighter, spraying away harmlessly into the emptiness of the cold and uncaring night.

Bruno and Rudi were showered with a high velocity stream of fragmented blood, bone and brains, the wet, fast moving mess mixed with bullets and shards of the Junkers.

The slowing fragments of metal which had obliterated Mouse's brain now sliced past Rudi's neck and opened a shallow laceration which, together with the maelstorm of D-Dog's blasting broadside made his bladder loosen, and he wet himself as he ducked down in terror, cowering with his eyes tight shut behind the armoured seat back.

In the left hand seat, stunned into terrified immobility by the sudden onslaught, Bruno recoiled with shock and pain as a bullet sliced across the top of his left shoulder, whilst a second pierced his side, despite the armoured seat in which he sat. Brains and shrapnel spattered him.

Reeling in pain and sucking oxygen desperately through his mask, Bruno hauled back on the on the control yoke, the wounded Junkers reared up, and as the speed bled off, it hung suspended for a long moment, before falling away towards the freezing waters below.

Fierce elation coursed powerfully through him as his fire seemed to pin the Junkers against the backdrop of night like a bug on a piece of card, and the enemy fighter seemed to reel as if in pain, one engine torn and disintegrating, rear-facing machinegun flopping uselessly after that one useless, hopeless line of tracer.

As it pulled upwards, Rose smiled grimly as he lined up the enemy aircraft in his sight for a final devastating burst, and as he prepared his last blow, White suddenly cried out.

"Break! *Break! BREAK!*"

Trained to react instantly to such a cry, Rose pulled back on the control column instinctively, kicking the rudder and slewing the Beaufighter.

Meanwhile, Bruno's wounded Junkers 88 disappeared downwards into the darkness, losing height as Bruno fought to keep the mortally damaged fighter flying.

Just a year earlier, Granny Smith, that most magnificent and yet scruffiest of characters in the whole of the RAF, and also the finest fighter pilot Rose had ever met, taught the younger Rose how to *really* dogfight in a packed week culminating in live firing exercises.

Knowing now the shortcomings of manoeuvrability in his current mount after the superb Hurricane, and fearing the capabilities of an unknown foe behind them, Rose made his aeroplane 'crab' across the sky, turning and climbing, nose pointing one way, the direction of the Beaufighter's flight another.

With a bit of luck with D-Dog pointing one way but moving another they would confuse their attacker.

"Chalky?" He panted, muscles complaining at the effort, vision blurring and dimming, *bloody hell*, "Chalky?"

A lightning-fast stream of flaming red balls shot past beneath and to one side of their port wing, the balls seeming to coalesce to a point as they sped away from the D-Dog, growing smaller and arcing downwards towards the black water below.

His throat as dry as death, Rose dragged the Beaufighter quickly over to the left, and a second line of tracer flared past to starboard, closely followed by a dark shape, frantically climbing upwards as it tried desperately to avoid them, and D-Dog faltered as the turbulent disturbance of their attacker's slipstream caught at them.

He did not feel the burning in his muscles or the tightness in his throat as he hauled desperately on the controls.

Even as he fought to regain control in the madly turning, shaking fighter, that split second view of their pursuer was enough for Rose to recognise the lines of a second Junkers 88, the droning sound of its Jumos audible for a moment above the sound of their own Hercules.

As D-Dog settled, Rose breathed a sigh of relief, blinking his stinging eyes, already searching for the enemy aircraft in the empty darkness.

His entire body ached but there was no time to allow himself to feel it. "Thanks, Chalky, you just saved us. Are you OK, chum?"

"Fucking hell! Thought we were dead then for sure, Flash!" White's voice wheezed.

"You saved us with that call, Chalky." Rose repeated. Over the intercom there came something that sounded suspiciously like a sob.

Thank God Chalky was OK. He gripped the little bear in his pocket, the desire to weep overwhelming.

Lady Luck had not abandoned them yet.

He turned his head achingly, his neck muscles complaining. He couldn't see where the second Junkers had gone. Of the one they'd just blasted, there was no sign. "Chalky? Can you see where it went?"

"He's right ahead, can't you see him?" White exclaimed in surprise, voice still unsteady and laboured.

There was a pause, and then, again, "Can't you see him? I thought you were chasing him!"

Rose blinked rapidly and squinted, and immediately he could see it, twin blue exhausts there, flying straight and level, a hundred feet or so above them, the Junkers was weaving gently from side to side.

Relief washed through him like a cold tide rising. The damned thing was clearly visible, how could he have missed it?

"Thanks, Chalky, I've got him now, hold on to your hat, pal."

"Make 'em count, Flash, I haven't been able to rearm the cannon. You'll not have more than a couple of seconds worth, I reckon."

Sighting carefully, Rose remembered how close they'd come to getting shot down in flames, if it hadn't been for White…

Thank God.

"Watch our backside, matey, stand by, firing…"

One more time Rose pushed down hard on the worn button, and D-Dog barked a second's worth of cannon shells before the whirring magazines ran dry, and Rose sat in disbelief as their cannon fire ceased.

The machine guns in the wings, however, continued to chatter.

That handful of shells was enough. The crew of the second Junkers, squadron-mates of Bruno, were totally unprepared in the switch from hunter to hunted, and the shells penetrated the port inner fuel tank sited just behind the crew cabin, igniting just under eighty gallons of 87 octane gasoline in a catastrophic explosion that spread in a millisecond to the other fuselage fuel tanks.

One moment the Junkers was before him, wreathed in a sparkling cloud of impacts, and the next it disappeared in a blinding flash of searing light, exploding devastatingly and flinging fragments of itself outwards, leaving Rose so stunned by the abruptness that he flew through the billowing oily fireball.

Unknown things scraped and skittered alarmingly across the Beaufighter's skin, and the aircraft juddered and wallowed its way through the glowing and expanding field of what remained of the blasted Junkers.

A blob of oil *splotched* onto his windscreen, making him jump and streaking dirtily across an already smoke soiled surface.

But luckily for them, none of the pieces through which they flew were large enough to damage them, just big enough to scare them both.

A sickly burning odour of metals and plastics and of something else assailed his nostrils, and he choked involuntarily on the hot, cloying bitterness.

For what seemed like an endless moment, Rose could see nothing, and his heart clenched painfully.

It had taken his eyes weeks to recover from the bright flash of his Hurricane being blown apart the previous year.

How would he land the Beaufighter if he were unable to see?

Had he killed Chalky and himself in his eagerness to destroy the second Junkers?

Had he forgotten the hard-earned lessons of last year by being too close? He kicked himself mentally. *Idiot.*

Rose gripped the control column warily. What if his eyes never recovered? They filled with tears, and he lifted his goggles and cuffed away the wetness.

Oh God! What if he never saw Molly again? This time he was unable to stop them, and they spilled unchecked down his face and onto his oxygen mask.

He sniffed, and the intake of breath involuntarily hitched in his throat.

White had still been staring backwards into the darkness, who knew how many German fighters were out there. There was every chance that they could be jumped again. It was like friggin' Piccadilly Circus at rush hour out there tonight!

He'd jumped when the sudden flash lit up everything around, signifying the death of the second enemy fighter.

Resisting the urge to look forwards, he was treated to the sight of two separated and burning wings pirouetting downwards just before D-Dog passed through the fireball and night turned to day fleetingly. Instinctively his eyes closed against the harsh glare and sudden heat.

Something *whanged!* Off his Perspex dome and he ducked as fragments of the Junkers scratched and skittered against the Beaufighter.

471

And then they were through the maelstrom, the fireball behind them dissipating into a dimming and shrinking glow, pieces still falling from within it.

Of the Junker's fuselage itself, there was no sign.

There was a strange gurgling sound over the intercom. Fear swept through White. Oh God! What if Rose were injured? He groped anxiously for his good luck charm.

"Flash? Are you OK? Flash?"

"Mm." Rose grunted, knowing his voice would sound thick with emotion, and he cleared his throat noisily. Already, his sight was returning.

Thank God.

"Sorry, Chalky, caught a whiff of that Junkers, made my eyes water, I can tell you!" Rose cleared his throat again, and wiped his eyes carefully. His eyesight had returned almost to normal.

White chuckled. He sounded quite cheerful now. "Crikey! I know, stinks something chronic, doesn't it?"

"Not half! " His heart rate was settling and he felt ashamed at his unchecked emotions, but also incredibly grateful to have survived a combat involving not one but two Junker 88 fighters. *You bloody great baby...*

"Chalky, any sign of the first Junkers?"

"Can't see anything out there, chum. It's blacker than anything out there!"

"Right-oh, OK mate, have a quick shufti around, then change the ammo drums. Lord knows what's going on, but there may be more Jerries out there. I'll get on to Lamplight and ask 'em to search for our crew." He thought for a moment, "We'd better check on that other kite with the dodgy engine. I think it was one of ours."

"Gotcha, Flash. Just rock the wings if you need me."

472

Still ashamed of his moment of weakness, Rose searched the dark sky for other aircraft. Somehow, they'd survived.

One more time.

Thank God.

Junkers and.

Chapter 46

"Lamplight to Dagger 3. Are you receiving me?"

Whoever it was on the other end, they sounded incredibly relieved to hear Rose when he replied, "Dagger 3 to Lamplight, receiving."

"Lamplight to Dagger 3, please report. Did you destroy the bandit?"

"Dagger 3 to Lamplight, two Junker 88s engaged, got one for sure and are claiming the other as a probable. Regret to report the loss of Dagger 5, but crew managed to escape, could you please arrange ASR? We are in the vicinity."

"Lamplight to Dagger 3, two Junkers? Dagger 5? What about the bandit?"

What?

Rose's brow creased in bewilderment, his mind turning with confusion. Lamplight didn't sound at all interested in their combats and success.

Not even a word of congratulations. Miserable old beggers!

"Dagger 3 to Lamplight, I don't understand your last request... please clarify?"

"Lamplight to Dagger 3, the bandit has RAF markings." The voice sounded peevish.

A cold dread trickled down his spine.

Oh God, not the Beau with the dodgy engine? Was it the real bandit? Had some Nazi spies stolen it?

It didn't bear thinking about the secrets of AI being captured by the enemy. The thought of enemy bombers coming over with AI-equipped fighters was terrifying.

Before he could reply, "Lamplight to Dagger 3, the bandit is a Beau. Repeat, the bandit is a Beaufighter. Locate and destroy, repeat, locate and destroy. Confirm."

Shit. So that's why the damaged Beaufighter had been heading east. Why hadn't they said so before?

"Dagger 3 to Lamplight, confirmed, locate and destroy the, er, bandit…can you give me a vector?"

"Lamplight to Dagger 3, we do not have contact."

Damn and blast and bloody blue bollocks! Rose waggled his wings gently.

Because the hunt wasn't over yet. There would be more pain and killing this eventful night.

Come on, Chalky, chop, chop, get back into your seat. He waggled his wings again.

Breathlessly, "Flash, I've changed three drums, is that enough?" white sounded winded as well as exhausted.

"That'll do nicely, you rascal, now get back onto your seat and get belted up, we've not finished yet."

Exasperation peered through the exhaustion in his operator's voice. "Blimey! We've shot down two already! What more do they want? Capture ol' Goering and bring him back with us? Cor, luvaduck! We need to get back home. I've got no sweets left and I could do wiv a brew!"

"Forget your bloody sweeties, you 'orrible bloody tart," Rose scolded, "There're a lot of Jerry fighters around, Chalky, so I'll need you to keep an eye on the sky outside. Thing is, we've got to find that last kite with the dodgy Hercules. Seems the bandit is a Beau, and it's flying to Hunland with a serviceable AI set."

"No! The bandit's a Beaufighter? You're kidding me! Cripes!" the enormity of it sank in, "Oh, cripes!"

"Quite. We've got to find it and shoot it down, matey, and sharpish. It was heading east last time we saw it. It's probably on the same heading, and I need you to find it for me." Rose paused, "Lamplight can't see it, I've asked. It's just me and thee."

"So, what's new?" grumbled the youngster in the back.

Rose found he was clenching his jaw tightly again, and he forced himself to relax. His teeth were aching from the pressure, and Rose ran his tongue gingerly over them.

"Mmm." He could almost hear the gears in White's head whirring as he pondered. "We'll go east, then cut a north-south search line. Flash, take a heading of eighty degrees, full throttle for twenty miles. Then ten degrees for ten miles, and then one-seven-zero for twenty." White's voice still sounded unsteady.

Rose chewed his lip. "Er, what, um, what was that first heading again?"

"Gawd help us." White sighed theatrically, "Take a heading eight-five degrees, driver."

Rose grinned into his oxygen mask and mentally doffed a non-existent cap, "Yes, guv'nor."

So far so good. Lady Luck was still with them. We've not finished yet, Ma'am, stay with us, please...

He caught sight of the flames from afar, a fiery dot glowing like a flaming ember in the darkness, visible from many miles away, the intense glare twinned with the reflected yellow-white blotch on the surging waves close below.

The other Beaufighter was low, so low *(How on earth can he still be flying?)*, perhaps less than a couple of a hundred feet up, standing out clearly against the fretful waves and the dark sky, a silver speck lit up by the brightness of the fiery streamer and the thick, flame-lit smoke trail it towed grudgingly behind it.

And then he could smell its burning, sickly sweet, rank and horrid.

Although the rogue aircraft was still flying, it had lost a lot of height since they'd seen it last, and was gradually losing what little was left whilst still far from landfall.

The port wing was blanketed in flames, streaming back in a long yellow-white sheet, the plume of smoke blooming out in a thick cloak that reached almost down to the clutching, agitated sea.

"Contact!" yelled White triumphantly, "I've got him, Flash! He's close but awfully low, though. Ugh-phew! I think I can smell him. Whoa, what a stink! Hope that's not us! Can you see him?"

Rose shook himself guiltily from his musing. There was no need for the AI with their target lit up like a beacon. He really ought to have told White as soon as he'd caught sight of it.

"Yes, I can, thanks. It's alright, Chalky, he's not going to get away. Have a look, old chap, but keep 'em peeled on the sky. I'm feeling twitchy after seeing all these Junkers. If we can see him, so will others."

"Don't I know it! Just like buses, wait for weeks to catch one, then two come along at the same time!" White sounded thoroughly pleased with himself, the shakiness all but gone.

"There may be a third one out here, maybe more, and that Beau's a juicy looking target. He'll light us up a bit, too." Rose paused for a moment. "I suppose we'd better finish it."

"We better had, Flash." White's voice was quiet now, "If there are more Jerries about, we may not get another chance."

477

How the aircraft was still flying with his wing alight like that was anybody's guess. Throughout the air battle, it had not taken any avoiding action whatsoever.

"He *is* going down." Rose looked at the burning aircraft doubtfully. "He's done for, doesn't need our help." Somehow, the thought of firing on the stricken aircraft seemed horribly unfair.

"What if he ditches and the AI's recoverable? Better do it, Flash. Best kill 'em too, Jerry could pick their brains for information. I don't reckon they'd resist. And anyway, we need to get the kite home, soon as. Flying through the fireball of that Junkers might have damaged us."

They couldn't afford to lose the edge that AI gave them. The thought of similarly equipped Nazi night fighters ranging over Europe and Britain was terrifying.

Why the hell was he dithering around like an old fart? The target was a Beaufighter, certainly, and indeed the crewmen within wore the same uniform as he, but they were the enemy.

He was wasting time and placing both his and White's life at risk with each passing mile.

He sighed, feeling suddenly weary.

Time to get on with it.

He closed the distance on the other aircraft rapidly, agitatedly stroking the firing button as they drew closer to it.

"Firing pass from starboard to port, stand by, Chalky, and watch our arse, OK?"

"Gotcha, Flash. Do it."

Rose licked his cracked lips and eased back on the throttles now they were closer, just keeping enough power on to creep up slowly on the other aircraft, smoke continued to billow back thickly, and his nostrils were crammed full by the odour of the burning 'enemy' Beaufighter, dense and pungent and broiling hot.

478

The other pilot must be straining desperately at the controls, he thought, to hold the burning Beau in the air, and he pressed down firmly on the button.

The cannon thumped and the machine guns chattered once more, and their angry message burned across the distance between them to ply awful destruction.

Almost instantly one of the cannon suffered a stoppage, but although the steady thump of the cannon was weaker, there was still enough weight of cannon fire to ruin what remained of Caspersen's day.

Caspersen, hunched and sweating in his seat, never even knew D-Dog was there, and he only heard a fleeting whirlwind of sound like a sudden hailstorm, and his mind was just beginning to register and wonder what it was before the incoming fire instantly pounded him into a bag of torn flesh and shattered bone, spurting and leaking blood, smashed shapeless against the side of the cockpit.

Rose's torrent of fire tracked along to tear through the operator's compartment, wrecking its contents and tearing the AI equipment into useless, sparking shards.

It also tore a gaping hole straight through Fosse's chest as he lolled in his seat, but he felt nothing as his ribcage and innards were blown out, for one of the bullets from Suggs' rifle had already ripped out his throat, and he had been alone in the dark as his life bled out, dying and unable to respond to his pilot's desperate queries.

D-Dog's fearsome metal bite crunched down hard, Rose directing a constant stream of bullets with minimal deflection into an easy target that still took no avoiding action.

Like shooting fish in a barrel.

Caspersen's Beaufighter, after flying so far and holding together so well despite the mortal damage already done to it through Molly and Sugg's efforts, bloomed bright, exploding catastrophically in a

479

searing boil of angry light, and it came apart like wet tissue paper, showering the sea with flaming and guttering pieces.

Rose's eyes, already squinting against the glare from the target's fiery port wing, snapped shut in the sudden flaring of light.

His finger came off the firing button, the thunder of the guns fell silent, and he pushed upwards into a smooth climbing turn *into* the thick line of smoke, fearful that he would frame himself nicely against the flames to any lurking Junkers if he turned away.

For a moment the shadowed world outside disappeared into blackness, and for an instant the memory of a desperate scrambling take-off through a cloud of choking smoke over RAF Foxton came back hard, the fear stabbing at him, and he quashed the rising unbidden memory of that awful day of blood and pain and stolen dreams when Goering's best had killed so many of those who had become his family, wounding his beloved Molly so cruelly, and broken his heart.

And then D-Dog erupted back out into the lesser blackness of night over the North Sea, torn ribbons of black and grey smoke trailing back from its wingtips, and he hunched as he waited for German bullets to tear into him, but there were no enemy fighters waiting.

The sky was empty, and they soared away.

Rose glanced quickly at Molly's picture, tears coming from nowhere, *it's over, Moll, and we're coming home. I can't wait to see you. I love you.*

He thought of the sanctuary of her arms, as he pulled the Beaufighter up and around and pointed the nose back towards the English coast, checking his fuel levels and pushing the throttles forward. The sooner he was back over Britain and at Dimple Heath, the better.

He needed her, and a hot cup of tea to wash away the bitter taste of what they had had to do.

"Chalky, you still with me? Course for home, please."

"Still here, Flash, well done, they'll not find anything to recover.

All they'll find is little tiny pieces after that, no chance they'll learn anything, thank goodness."

White sounded deflated. "I feel knackered, and I could do with a drink. Head two-eight-zero."

Rose dashed the drying tears of the past from his eyes and glanced searchingly through the canopy. They had been successful, but the victory tasted of ashes.

"I know how you feel, mate, didn't feel good at all, did it? Two, maybe three kills, but I feel like crap."

"It felt so wrong Flash, really wrong," his young operator said disconsolately, "But we done what we had to. Could easily have been us."

Below and behind the last of the burning fragments were quenched by the icy spray and disappeared into the deep waters. The other crew could not have survived the livid fireball, of that he was certain.

"But it wasn't us, pal, it was them, thank God. We had no choice, remember that. And keep your eyes open. I'll be happier when we're back over friendly territory. There may still be more enemy fighters around."

But he need not have worried, the other fighters scrambled along-side Bruno were patrolling further north.

There but be for the grace of God…

Rose shuddered and one hand reached for the little bear in his pocket, giving it a squeeze to reassure and comfort himself.

Lady Luck…

The thick smoke, so dense and thick moments ago, dissipated and cleared quickly, leaving nothing behind within seconds to show for an ingenious but ultimately desperate attempt to steal knowledge which might have swung the course of the war in favour of the Axis forces by a pair of carefully chosen and well placed agents.

When Rose's confirmation of success reached James, he breathed a deep and truly heartfelt sigh of relief and offered up a prayer of thanks.

Admiral Canaris and the Abwehr would never know now of how close their agents came to pulling off an incredible coup, thwarted by the bravery and tenacity of a girl with Viking blood and an indomitable spirit, a young WAAF with the heart and courage of a warrior, and a grizzled soldier with a sure eye and a steady finger.

With men and women like that, they'll never beat us.

Meanwhile, out over the North Sea, the sound of D-Dog's Hercules faded until the only sound was the rushing lap of the waves and the moaning of the wind.

But there was no one left alive to hear it.

Epilogue (1)

The night had drawn in earlier than normal this mid-September evening, and Rose felt comfortable, nestled in the darkness at sixteen thousand feet, the stippled blackness of The Wash laying open below them as they orbited in a wide clockwise turning circle around the beacon.

High above, at twenty thousand, he could see the other Beaufighter in the 'cab rank' waiting for 'custom', but the last hour had been dead quiet.

The Germans were already getting bogged down in their Russian adventure, and resources which could have been used in the bombing campaign against Britain were now being funnelled off in even greater numbers to satisfy the needs of the units fighting on an Eastern Front, a campaign in which the advances were stalling.

The Citadel of Moscow would be seen, but not touched by the German armies of the East, the *Ostheer* slowed and finally halted by sheer bravery, sacrifice, and a reorganisation of the State into a mechanism single-mindedly focussed on the production and maintenance of war-fighting capability, bolstered very substantially by Lend-Lease help from Russia's new allies.

Barr and Dear had gone, Billy being promoted to command a night fighter unit in North Africa.

"Think of me, old chap, when the winter draws in, will you? I'll be sunbathing, taking a dip in the Med, and scouring the fleshpots of Cairo. When your balls finally do drop, if they ever do of course, and I have my doubts, you might get the chance to join the big boys." He leered and winked, "We'll make a man of you yet."

Herbert and Trent had survived, but it would be a long time before they would be ready to fight again.

This would their last trip, or so James had intimated. Rose and White would begin a well-earned rest touring factories and undertaking administrative duties, and there were whispers of a tour of the United States.

Rose was not sorry. He was ready for a break from operations. The erosive effect of the tension and stresses of the last months had had its effect on him, and while he did not feel now that he was a sufferer of what was popularly known amongst aircrew as 'The Twitch,' he certainly felt he needed a rest.

White, too, seemed a little on edge, despite his attempts to hide it, but the lessening in pace of Luftwaffe activities relative to the earlier months of their tour meant that he managed to behave as if all was well.

For Rose it had begun with D-Dog's return to Dimple Heath following their successful pursuit and destruction of Caspersen's rogue Beaufighter.

The instinctual seed of guilt and general 'wrongness' he felt with destroying the mortally damaged aeroplane, despite the clear and legitimate reasons for doing so left a bitter taste within him, and a part of him on the way back began to wonder fearfully if there had been a mistake.

That feeling of melancholy had blossomed explosively from

glumness into a soul-destroying terror as they came onto their final approach and the burnt-out shell Molly's car appeared to one side of the runway.

That landing was the worst of his career, and it was lucky that D-Dog was designed with such a solid and sturdy airframe and under-carriage as Rose tried to get down as fast as possible.

It was only because of the Beaufighter's robust design that they did not end up in a smoking heap of torn, charred metal at the far end of the runway.

White suffered the alarming experience of a sharp braking that, had he not been securely strapped into his seat, would surely have smashed his head severely against the metal coaming of his Perspex dome.

Yet even as a shocked Rose, clumsy and faint with emotion, was struggling with recalcitrant straps to untangle himself from his cockpit, James screeched to a halt beside D-Dog with Molly.

Rather than try and talk to him over the W/T, the CO decided Rose would be better served by the evidence of his own eyes.

The sight of the battered and red-eyed girl horrified him, but she was alive!

Rose, incredulous and distrustful of his senses, believing that only the worst could possibly be true for them, buried himself into her embrace and hugged her as tight as he could until she complained, her aching body screaming protestation at the rough and unseemly treatment.

James sat in the car and tried not to look, seemingly engrossed by and glowering at an innocuous dent on the dashboard.

Later, being driven back by James, Rose and White were fed (two eggs each!), debriefed and stood down, and all those involved were told in no uncertain terms by a nameless Air Commodore from RAF Intelligence that they were never, ever to mention the events of the night to another living soul.

There had been a week of blissful leave, most of which Rose spent in bed with a very willing Molly at a friend's Welsh cottage.

"I say there, are you awake up front?" White's voice interrupted his reminiscences.

Rose cleared his throat. "What do you want?"

"Oh that's nice, that is. Try to start up a conversation and get your head bitten off instead. Pardon me for trying to be friendly."

Rose grinned. "Sorry. I'm not used to being bothered when I'm having a kip."

"I'm sooo bored. Where're all the bombers? We haven't shot down anything for ages and ages."

Rose grinned at the childish whingeing from behind. "Dunno, pal. Be patient, perhaps Lamplight'll have something for us soon?"

White harrumphed. "Don't hold your breath. Jerry's too bloody scared of gambolling onto our patch. I fancy a cuppa and a fag. What say we head back?"

Later. "What was that you were saying, old chap?"

"I can't believe it. My throat's drier than Margate beach, I'm dying for a gasper, and bloody Jerry decides he wants to mount a raid. Got no blinking consideration, the selfish bastards."

"Stop being such a whinging old bag, you cheeky tart. How're we doing? What's the range?"

"Range 3,000, turn port five degrees."

"Port five degrees." Rose gently adjusted, carefully trying not to over-correct. The bellow of the Hercules subsided to a throaty cough as he eased back on the throttles.

"Range now 2,000, throttle back, chum, we're catching up a bit fast. You're right behind him, 10 degrees above, easy...easy, throttle back a touch more, easy, range now 1,200. See anything yet?"

"No, count me down, Chalky." One hand slipped down, almost without thought, to quickly squeeze the bear. He blinked his eyes to clear them of sweat, and peered forwards again.

"OK, range now 900, 850, 800. Ease back a bit more, chum. 700." White's voice had lowered to a whisper, as if the enemy might hear them.

Rose reduced the throttles further, and D-Dog began to swing, the engines seeming to wheeze in discomfort as the speed rapidly bled off.

"500, 450, 450, OK, increase by a smidge, we're not closing anymore."

Rose pushed the throttle forward slowly, and the swing lessened. They continued to close, but slower now. "Thank goodness, Doggie wasn't enjoying that."

"Range 500, closing, 20 degrees above, can you see him yet, Flash?"

"Erm, um, hang on…" yes, high up, a squat shape hanging in the sky. Four flickers of blue, almost invisible but definitely there.

Rose grunted with satisfaction. "I can see it, Chalky. Don't lose contact with it, I'm going to close the distance, see if I can identify it."

"I won't even blink, Flash."

"Good man." Rose closed the distance carefully, but remained below the flight level of their prey. He was relying on the deep grey murk into which the sky and land merged behind them to keep D-Dog hidden from the enemy gunner.

Finally they were close enough, and his eyes urgently passed over the shape of the enemy outline.

A thin fuselage tapering aft, broad wings, twin engines and twin rudders.

Not a Whitley nor a Hampden, but something else. Definitely not friendly. His heart punched the inside of his chest with excitement.

"OK, Chalky, quick, take a gander. Tell me what you can see."

Almost immediately, "Blimey, he's right overhead, isn't he? Dornier. Pencil-thin fuselage and radial engines by the look of it. A Do 17? Mind out for the gondala, Flash, there might be a gunner. Nothing else in sight behind us. Clear to fire."

Rose reduced speed and the dim silhouette of the Dornier began to draw ahead.

And still no stream of tracer.

They were wasting time unnecessarily. They had been lucky so far, but any moment they might be seen. "Chalky, I'm going to fire, stand by. Keep us in contact."

"You're all set."

"OK, thanks. Here goes nothing…"

Rose pulled back the control column, pushed forward the throttles minutely, and the Beaufighter began to rise up into a position directly behind and slightly below the enemy bomber.

Allowing for deflection, Rose aimed just above the starboard wing, and let fly.

Thunder filled their ears as the guns snarled out their message of venomous hatred, and the Dornier seemed to quiver in agony beneath the tearing onslaught.

Hits sparkled bright all along the wing and the wing root, and a searing yellow-white tongue of flame suddenly licked out from the engine.

The Dornier swung desperately to one side, and Rose followed him, pulling the heavy fighter into a turn after the German bomber. More hits sparkled across the enemy's fuselage, and then the rear gunner finally responded, but the arc of incandescent rounds curved too far to pose a threat to the pursuing Beaufighter.

But it was close enough to make Rose sweat harder as he dragged the fighter after the fleeing Dornier.

As they dived, the enemy bomber began to pull ahead.

There was no flame, but he could smell burnt fuel as the Beaufighter shuddered after it, and he pressed the firing button again until the cannons ran dry.

As it pulled away further with its greater speed, he lost sight of it in the murk. "Chalky, can you see it? I've lost it." his muscles were throbbing and the controls were getting stiffer.

The Hercules were howling like banshees and the airframe juddered terrifyingly as they continued downwards.

"I can't see it, Flash,"

"OK, chum, the controls're getting locked up, I'm pulling up whilst we still can."

It took some effort, but finally he managed to bring D-Dog back into level flight, and they began a wide orbit.

Rose regarded the ground below doubtfully. "See anything, mate?" at exactly the same instant an intensely bright line of fire spread brilliantly on the ground below.

"I'll say! Did you see that, Flash? I think they were incendiaries! They must have been dropped low down to be spread out like that!"

His hand clenched for a moment around the little bump in his flying suit. Luck had not yet deserted them. They had delivered enough of a blow to cause the ditching of incendiaries that would burn no British cities tonight.

A second, larger streak of flame suddenly bloomed on the ground, punctuated by a series of pulsing explosions as the enemy bomber ploughed at full throttle into the ground and was blown apart by its own bombload.

White whooped with excitement, and Rose felt a fiercely primal thrill.

The attack had not been his smoothest, and the damage had

appeared minimal, but they'd inflicted enough of a blow to bring down the enemy after all.

Over the last few months , on more occasions than he could count on the fingers of both hands, an apparently undamaged (despite a hammering from their guns) and diving enemy bomber (more often than not a Heinkel 111), would disappear into the murk of darkness never to be seen again.

Rose was sure that at least one of those *must* have crashed, but there had been no sign of destruction, so without proof these bombers could only be officially classified as 'damaged' or 'probable.'

However, this time there was no ambiguity, and their success was proven by the shattered mess the Dornier made as it smeared itself across the land below them.

"Can you see any parachutes, Chalky? Did anyone get out?" his hand was trembling, and he clenched it into a fist.

They'd got one more, one less to bomb the innocent.

Thank you, Lord.

"I hope not, Flash. Can't see any. I think we got 'em all. This Nazi-bashing is hard work, really satisfying though. I'll reload if you wouldn't mind flying straight and level for a few minutes."

"That gunner was a rotten shot." White sniffed, but Rose could hear the strain in the youngster's voice, "Got any sweets, chum?"

Epilogue (2)

The crystal clear water gurgled quietly beneath them, and the girl kissed him on the cheek and snuggled closer.

In the far distance, the snow-mottled slopes of the Bavarian Alps reared majestically up into the sky, their white peaks glittering pale against the sky.

"Are you feeling well, my love?" she asked him diffidently.

Her husband shifted slightly where he leant against the wooden rail, his eyes watching the busily racing water beneath the bridge they stood on, the fresh air cool and beautifully fragrant from the forests.

"You needn't keep asking, you know. I'm perfectly fine."

His voice was still weak, as his body gradually recovered from the terrible wounds he had suffered in that last awful duel in the dark.

Bruno was thinner now, still gaunt weeks later, the proud uniform hanging off him, although he had a better colour on him now, and he hardly needed to use both the crutches anymore.

"I know, but I can't bear the thought that you almost died." She sniffed.

"Don't cry, sweetheart. I made it back."

"I'm not crying, there's still a bit of a chill in the air. I think I may be getting a bit of a cold."

His arm tightened around her, despite the stinging pain from his back and legs. He tried hard not to wince as his injured body protested.

"Mm. If you say so. I do love you, little snowdrop."

In answer she made as if to kiss him once more on his cheek, but he turned and his lips met her for a prolonged moment.

When they parted his eyes came to rest on the white church of St. Sebastian in Ramsau, and he wondered if Anja had been christened in there.

Bavaria was his most favourite place in the world, even more so because his Anja was born here.

His flying career was over, at least for the immediate future, perhaps forever.

Anja commiserated with him when he shared the news with her, of course, but he saw the heartfelt relief naked in her dark eyes.

The ensuing weeks had been a blur of treatment, operations, and pain, unrelenting pain, all made just bearable by the unadulterated joy that being with Anja brought him.

He thought back to his last meeting with Rudi.

Unbelievably, the two of them working together had somehow managed to successfully fly the savaged and dying Junkers back, by some miracle carrying out a successful wheels-up landing on the beach at Texel in the West Frisian Islands.

Rudi could remember very little of the return trip, the memories, such as they were, guiding Rudi through a fog of mind-befuddling pain.

Poor, terrified Rudi, now promoted to *Oberfähnrich* and himself wearing a Knights Cross around his neck in recognition of saving Bruno's life, looked like a hunted animal when they last met at dear Mouse's funeral, the gunner's flag-topped coffin forlornly followed by his medal-bearing and weeping cousins, their *Wehrmacht* husbands, and the rest of his family and friends.

Rudi was an instant propaganda hero, his startled face plastered across the newspapers and with a posting straight into pilots flying training. It was an opportunity many would have envied, but not Rudi.

The Eastern front was beckoning, and poor Rudi looked grey and haunted at the thought of further combat and danger.

At one time, Bruno would have been jealous of him.

But no longer.

Bruno closed his eyes and nuzzled Anja's hair. Perhaps later he would envy Rudi the chance to fight on the Russian Front, but at this moment in time, he felt nothing more than relief.

There may never be another opportunity for him to fly a fighter on combat operations, the wounds too severe to allow him back onto flying duties, yet it was only with mild surprise that he found he didn't really care.

He needed nothing more than what he already had, and although his body ached from his injuries, his mind was at peace.

He was happy to remain on extended leave in beautiful Bavaria, attended to by his very own loving nurse.

The damned war could wait. At least for now.

Rose pushed back the gate that led to their front door, and stopped for a moment, enjoying the sight of the autumnal flowers still scattered randomly between the paving slabs of the front path in glorious and lively abandon, the bright morning sunlight illuminating them so they glowed vivid as if lit from within.

It was a delight to see them at this time of the season, a delicate promise of the future as another year of war waned.

Rose inhaled their sweet fragrance with pleasure, and adjusted the heavy satchel on his shoulder.

Elsie had chased after him and quietly passed it to him as he left the Mess following breakfast, and it was bulging, heavy with fresh rolls, cheese, butter and eggs.

"For you and Mrs Rose, sir," she had breathed shyly, for the girl was completely different from the troublemaker who had endlesslly tortured Molly with her unfailingly regular infractions, now the (almost) fully-recovered and newly-promoted WAAF Sergeant was always smart and immaculate in her uniform, proudly bearing the vivid ribbon of her very well-deserved Military Medal.

The inveterate pest once notorious as 'Jankarella' was gone forever, and Elsie was now known by one and all as 'Dickie' (apparently shortened from 'Boudicca').

The station was immensely proud of their fighting Viking princess, and even the grizzled Station Warrant Officer treated her with something approaching respect.

Rose stopped and bent down suddenly on impulse and gently picked a delicate blue flower, holding it up carefully between forefinger and thumb.

He didn't know what it was (Molly would, because she knew everything), but its simple beauty caught his eyes and his joy at seeing yet another colourful dawn was enhanced by the knowledge that his tour was done.

For once he could afford to truly enjoy the simple pleasure of being alive, and there would be no more operational flying and fighting for White or himself.

James, now wearing the four rings of a Group Captain (great things were being planned for RAF Dimple Heath as part of a Bomber Command expansion programme in early 1942, the rumour mill heavy with suggestions of it becoming a heavy bomber squadron base for the newer four engine bombers coming out, with James the new Station

494

Commander), with the ribbon of an OBE now proudly alongside his DSO, had been there to congratulate them on their latest victory.

He was waiting for them, legs braced, as they taxied into dispersals, his new spaniel cowering behind his legs.

With a wide smile and a warm handshake, James proudly confirmed to Rose and White that their operational tour was finished, they were done, and that they were to get a month of leave, beginning immediately, before their new postings arrived.

There had even been mention of a possible tour of the United States.

Rose would keep his fingers crossed, but could not dream of going without Molly. Already his mind was busy pondering how to get Molly onto detached duty so that they could go away together if the opportunity did come.

For the immediate future at least, each day would be one of gentle administrative duties and peace, whilst each night would be filled with Molly's sweet embrace.

He stood there for a moment, eyes closed against the sun, the fragrance in his nostrils, revelling in the moment.

Was it his imagination that the air somehow smelt fresher this morning, the sunlight warmer?

But Molly was inside, and if he didn't get a move on he'd be meeting her on her way out to begin today's duty at Dimple Heath.

With one last glance around, and a very self-satisfied smirk at the rather less sporty 1928 Ford Model A Tudor car now parked sedately like a large shiny box on the kerb outside their cottage, he closed the gate behind him.

Molly appeared appreciative when he had presented it to her as a replacement for the little red car, but the rather slower pace (no matter what she did with the gears) was so much kinder to Rose's heartrate and that of everyone else they encountered on the roads.

Sometimes, when they were bumbling along the road at a leisurely snail's pace *(Thank the dear Lord!)*, he would gleefully wonder if the grating and grinding was from the recalcitrant gears or from her clenched teeth.

Suggs was still recovering from a broken leg and collarbone, but the news of his award of a Military Medal and promotion to Sergeant had cheered him up immensely.

The good sergeant would be very pleased on his return to see the new Ford chugging unhurriedly up to the gate when he returned to duty. It would be difficult to get squashed by Molly's new mount.

With a little smug nod to himself, Rose pulled out his keyring and pushed it into the lock in the front door and let himself in.

The back door was open, and Rose could hear the girl singing softly to herself in the back garden.

He smiled, closed his eyes and listened blissfully for a moment, revelling in the sweetness of the sound. But he could not remain inside for long when she was waiting for him, and Rose made his way outside, stopping only momentarily to place his tin hat, gas mask and the laden satchel carefully onto the kitchen table.

Molly heard his steps and turned to him, and the radiant smile on her beautiful face made his heart dance with pleasure.

As expected, she was in uniform, ready for her morning duty, and his eyes happily noted for a moment how pleasing the bright red and white ribbon with the crossed silver oak leaves of the MBE for Gallantry looked amongst her already rather impressive line of decorations.

Molly was *his* Boudicca, his courageous Warrior Queen, the proud ribbons on her uniform and the ragged striations of the scars on her back testimony to her courage and strength and resilience, and he found with wonder that he admired and loved her more and more with each passing day.

Gentle, beautiful and unflinchingly fearless, she was, quite simply, incredible.

For the umpteenth time since their wedding, he thanked God for the incredible gift of her love.

What was it that such an exceptional woman saw in someone as boringly normal like him? How on earth had he managed to excite and then maintain an interest from someone like her? Whatever it was, Thank God for it.

Her dark liquid eyes danced and sparkled in the brightness, and his grateful gaze relished the way in which the nimble breeze played with the strands of her hair and how the sunshine created flickering golden and scarlet highlights in her rich midnight tresses.

"Harry!" she called out, so much happiness and pleasure in that one word, and oh, how lovely his name sounded when she uttered it!

Her eyes glowed with heartfelt pleasure when she caught sight of Rose, and she came eagerly to him.

He took her into his arms and held her tightly, savouring the feel of her body against his as if it were for the first time. "Hello, my darling."

She smiled radiantly, eyes searching his face, "How was your night? Any luck?"

He raised his arms momentarily like a triumphant and strutting prize-fighter.

"Chalky and I got another last night. A Dornier."

Her teeth shone. "Good, I'm glad." She said simply, and took a step back to look at him, "And, even better, you've come back safe and sound."

"Nothing to it. Piece of cake," he told her casually, every bit the consummate and supremely nonchalant fighter pilot.

It was time to share the good news; he couldn't keep it inside any longer.

"It was our last trip, Molly! The CO's taken Chalky and I off operations. He's resting us. It's all over. The tour's over!"

Her fingers tightened around his, and her face shone. "I know. I'm so glad, Harry. He told me. I wasn't allowed to say anything."

"Who? James?" Why, she already knew!

She nodded. "He also told me to take the day off today. Poor old chap must be getting soft in his old age!"

His heart skipped with delight. "So I've got you all to myself! Today just gets better!" he pulled her gently into another embrace. He could feel her heart flickering as she enfolded herself against him.

"Oh Harry, I thought last night would never end. It seemed to go on and on forever. I couldn't wait for you to come home." One finger lightly stroked his cheek.

He kissed her forehead gently. "I missed you at breakfast, my love, had to eat the egg by myself."

That egg had tasted even better knowing his tour was over and that he had survived it. He could hope for a future with Molly once more…

"The boys gave Chalky and I a little send-off, but it just wasn't the same without you there."

He kissed her again, lingeringly, enjoying the warm softness of her lips. "Mmmm, lovely. You taste delicious. I love you, Squadron Officer, Ma'am."

"Mm. I think I'll keep you after all, then. I love you too, more than I could ever say, *Flight-Lieutenant*."

He smiled at her emphasis of his new rank. "*Acting* Flight-Lieutenant, Ma'am. You know I'm still only a war substantive Flying Officer."

She ran a forefinger lightly over his line of ribbons. "Hm, whatever you say. That DSO ribbon looks good on your chest, Harry."

He looked down at the ribbon. "I feel a bit of a fraud, really. You and Suggs were the ones who foiled the Nazis. Chalky and I just helped them on their way. They weren't going to make it."

She smiled. "You made sure of it, you daft man. And you both *did* account for a few others. You earned it."

For a moment, his eyes were far away. He had fought as part of a team, and he felt that any recognition should have been the same for both of them.

"I really think Chalky ought to have got one, too, but he seems happy enough with the DFC to add to his DFM, poor sod, bless him."

He made a disgruntled face. "I still think that they don't appreciate the boys in the back as much as they ought to. We run all the same risks, after all. Cunningham's always in the papers, and good for him, of course, but there's hardly ever anything about Jimmy Rawnsley. And the ground crews get sweet Fanny Adams, despite all their efforts."

But he was too happy to remain miserable for long. Rose cupped her left breast in one hand and squeezed it playfully, enjoying the firmness of it against his palm, his fingertips resting against her line of ribbons.

"However, that MBE ribbon looks *really* good on your chest, Ma'am, although I must say that, on balance, given the choice, I much prefer the look of your chest a great deal better without the uniform! You've got the most remarkably fabulous tits!"

She giggled, and made as if to smack him. "Why, what a terrible sort you are, Mr Rose!"

"Don't I know it! But that's why all the girls find me simply irresistible. All the girls love bad men, and of course, as you know, I'm a very bad man! Why d'you think you find me so desirable?"

She nodded thoughtfully. "Oh. Yes. I see. I had been wondering what it was that women saw in you. Thank you for explaining that to me, otherwise I might never have known!"

They laughed happily in unison, relishing their shared bliss. And he held out the (now slightly squashed) flower to her.

"I saw this and thought of you, honey. Beautiful, elegant, fragrant and lovely in blue."

Oh, you silver-tongued, smooth talking old rogue, you. What an irresistible charmer you are!

Molly stroked his cheek, her fingertips catching the stubble on his cheek, her thumb soft against his lips, "Harry, my beloved darling, I have something very important to tell you."

"Oh yes?" he sighed with pleasure, watching a Red Admiral butterfly fluttering brightly over Molly's shoulder, enjoying the warmth and scent of her body.

"After the incident at the airfield, the doctor has been keeping an eye on me. Just to make sure there were no delayed effects of the car crash, such as it was."

What? Warning bells began to ring in his head. What did she mean? Doctor? Delayed effects?

Oh God. What exactly was Molly trying to say?

"I've been feeling a little bit funny for the last month or so, so I went to see him. He did some tests, hummed and hawed, and then he sent me to a specialist. And *that* specialist did some more tests, and then *he* sent me to another specialist."

Feeling a bit funny? Specialist?

What?

Something stirred strangely, painfully, in his stomach.

Her moist eyes were wide and bright, the gloriously thick dark lashes suddenly wet.

"They said that sometimes a sudden shock or a powerful visceral experience can have unforeseen physical effects on a person. They can cause changes."

A single tear, a shimmering clear liquid crystal in the warm sunlight, spilled down onto her smooth cheek, and his breath hitched cruelly in his chest as it painted a glittering trail down one cheek.

Oh God!

A frozen barb of cruel ice pierced him with a painful jolt, lancing through his heart, and he began to tremble involuntarily as an overpowering surge of pure terror thumped uncontrollably through him.

Rose's limbs felt suddenly weak, the energy draining swiftly through the soles of his feet.

Even as he faltered, his mind inexplicably recalled the scene from the film *Rebecca*, in which a stiff, brittle and rather feeble-looking (to Rose, at least. Molly, however, had thought Laurence Olivier appeared terribly noble and rather tragic) DeWinter finally learns the truth from his first wife's physician that Rebecca had actually been terminally ill before her untimely demise. An awful secret she had kept from them all.

They had suffered so much already, oh, so much cruel hurt and loss. How much more awfulness must they face and endure?

She was so very wonderful, the sun in his sky, the air beneath his wings.

Oh, dear God! Oh sweet, merciful God, save my Molly, please let her be alright! Please. Please let her be alright. If I did something wrong, forgive me, forgive me if I have displeased you. Please just don't take my Molly from me, oh, please God…

She was everything, all that there could ever be for him.

The thought of losing her was unbearable. The garden seemed to spin overwhelmingly for an awful second, and he felt as if he might fall.

"Oh, Harry! Goodness me! You're trembling!" She said in surprise, "Come here, my silly, darling man."

She pulled him back into her warm and fragrant embrace, hugging him tightly to her and he desperately returned her hug as a drowning man would fight for the smallest shred of driftwood in a churning and hungry sea.

In truth, he felt he could no longer stand unsupported on his own two feet.

The tears were already forming heavy in his eyes, and the sticky lump in his throat ensured that he was unable to utter a word.

He knew that he would certainly fall without her arms to hold him.

She kissed him gently then, and sighed contentedly against him, the softly soothing zephyr of her breath playfully dancing lightly over the surface of his crumpling face.

"I love you, my dearest, sweetest man, my beloved darling," she breathed, "and I have something wonderful to tell you, a wonderful, incredible present for you."

Wonderful? Incredible? What…?

A Wellington bomber mumbled its way distantly across the light blue sky, out for an air-test for tonight's operations perhaps, and all around them, the birds were twittering.

But he did not, could not, hear anything else but the sound of her voice.

There could be no one else ever for him in this life but Molly, and she was all that really, truly mattered in the world.

She was the light, the brilliant radiance that illuminated his heart and soul.

The centre of Everything That There Could Ever Be in his life.

Her cheek was soft against his, their warm tears mingling, her lips oh-so gentle against his ear, hair warm and fragrant against his face,

502

the harmony of her voice sweet music, bursting uncontrollably with infinite happiness, and now she softly whispered to him:

"The doctors have confirmed it," her voice caught raggedly for a moment, with raw, joyous emotion, and she took a deep breath, "Harry; you're going to be a father!"

Afterword

As a schoolboy in the 1970s, I discovered a copy of Rawnsley and Wright's superlative '*Nightfighter*' in the local library, and their incredible story immediately captured my imagination.

Rawnsley's account describes his war-time career as an RAF AI operator, and tells us of the incredible men and women who made the night time defence of our country possible using (at the time) cutting edge technology, and their incredible deeds enthralled and inspired me.

In 1940, successfully intercepting enemy bombers (let alone shooting them down) in the night skies was an almost impossible task, but the introduction of AI changed everything, allowing the RAF to give the *Luftwaffe* a bloody nose at night, just as they had done during the great aerial battles in the Battle of Britain.

Of course, the RAF's night fighters were just one part of many in the defences of Great Britain, whilst a well-organised and extensive anti-aircraft system was another.

Despite the best efforts of the defences, however, the *Luftwaffe* still inflicted a great deal of damage and devastation during 'The Blitz', but was ultimately unable to deliver the knockout blow promised to Hitler.

After reading *Nightfighter*, I searched for more books of aerial night fighting, but whilst there were numerous accounts from the *Nachtjager* of the *Luftwaffe*, there was almost nothing written by RAF Flyers (Lewis Brandon's account in *Night Flyer* being one of a few exceptions).

Yet these outstanding people were the ones who pioneered, improvised and adapted this kind of combat, fine-tuning and developing a system that was to make the skies over Britain very hazardous to health for the bomber crews of the *Luftwaffe*.

These experiences and their subsequent developments also made it possible to devise and conduct successful night intruder and bomber support operations using AI over the continent later in the war, and helped to create the all-weather combat aircraft.

Rawnsley's *Nightfighter* is an excellent source of information and references, illustrating how the night fighter war evolved and developed during the course of the war, whilst also suggesting storyline scenarios, and it was invaluable in the writing of Harry Rose's night time adventures with Chalky White.

Other excellent accounts describing the work of RAF night fighter crews and their operations during this period are the aforementioned *Night Flyer* by Lewis Brandon, and Richard Pike's moving and exceptional *Beaufighter Ace*.

I would highly recommend reading these books to find out more about the cold, lonely and perilous defensive war fought in the dark heights of the night skies of Britain during the Second World War.

We owe these incomparable men and women an immense debt of gratitude, and in tribute to them, I placed Harry Rose amongst their ranks to continue his war against the airmen of Nazi Germany.

I hope I will be forgiven by the gallant Norwegians who resisted the Nazis whenever and wherever possible for including two Quislings in this story. The truly incredible contribution provided to Britain's war effort by servicemen and women from abroad is incalculable.

To my amazing wife and children, Thank You Lots for your endless love and support, which remains a shining constant in my life, and of course, thanks to my friend John Humphreys, London Underground Maestro, who told me of the story of the Tube's runaway monkeys.

The *Luftwaffe* planned The Blitz as an overwhelming night aerial offensive to defeat the UK following their failure during the Battle of Britain.

But once again they were beaten, and many bomber crews, expecting minimal opposition by night, experienced instead their own destructive blitz of death and destruction at the hands of RAF night fighters.

Beaufighter Blitz.